MARKED

ALYSSA HUCKLEBERRY

First edition 2025

Cover, Map, and Interior design by Natalia Junqueira

For Jenny,
living proof of the depth of a sister's love.

SOULBOURNE

CALLINGS

LAND

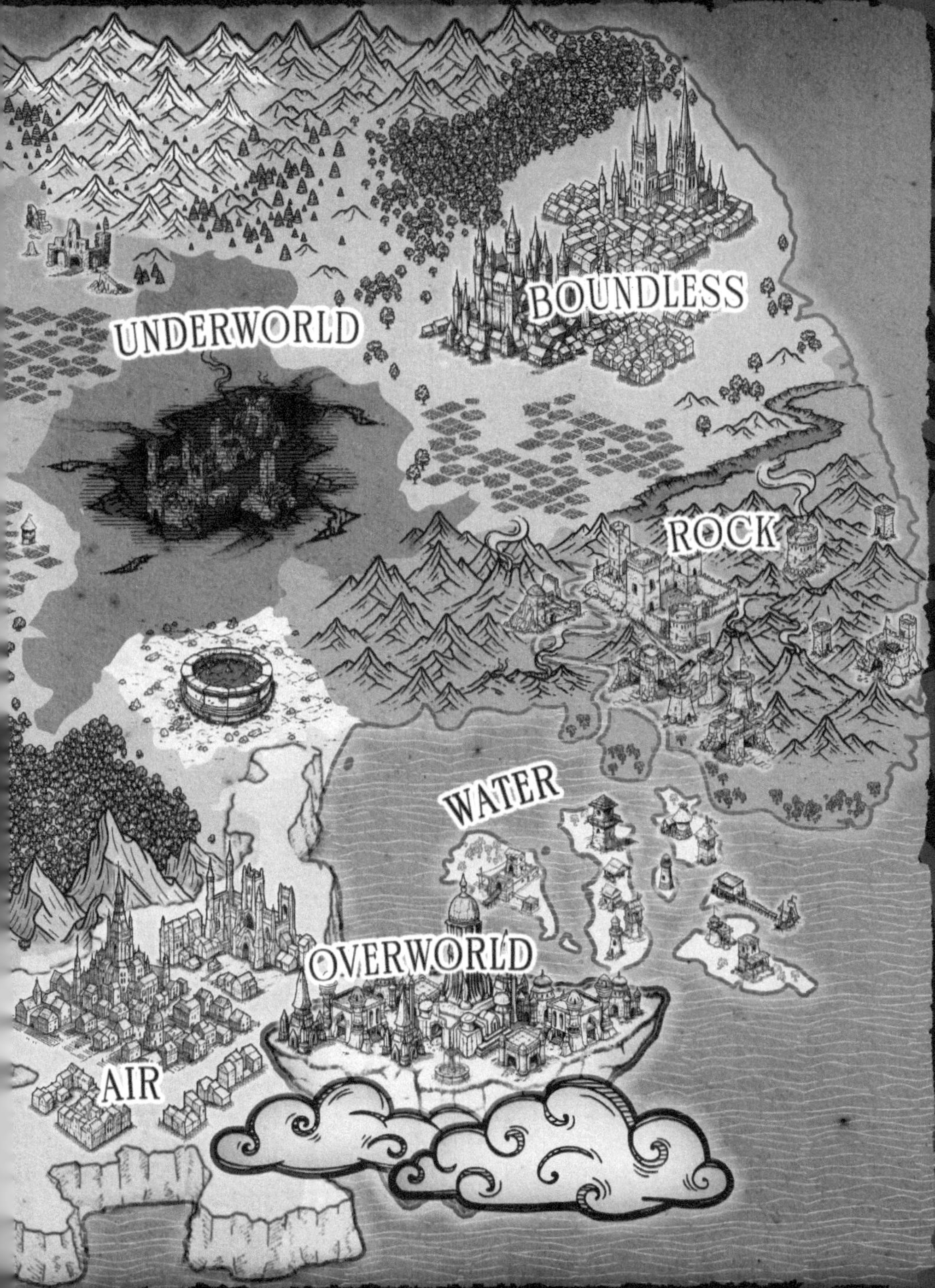
BOUNDLESS
UNDERWORLD
ROCK
WATER
OVERWORLD
AIR

ONE

There are fates worse than death.

This is the first lesson a child of Holostown learns. No regard is given for the child's maturity or threshold for fear—these are luxuries in a realm that cannot afford them. Parents don't hold back: wide-eyed children are made to listen to horrific tales of magnificent beasts with jaws as large as barns and curved claws thicker than steel. *The beasts are the safe ones*, they say. *It's worse to encounter a spirit.*

Like every other child of Holostown, my early years are spent in abject terror that I might encounter a beast or spirit. My younger sister Elara and I obey every rule, and there are quite a few.

In particular:

Don't venture into the woods.

Don't speak to strangers.

Don't play games of make believe.

Don't ask questions.

Don't stray from marked paths.

Most important of all: *don't go out at night.*

Our parents are strict but not cruel; my formative childhood years boring but not traumatic. We never go hungry; we always have a bed to sleep in and clothes to wear. When we're of age, we attend school.

Here, our parents' rules are reinforced. There are three subjects taught: math, reading, and civics. No tolerance is given for creative diversions or conjecture: students who attempt to entertain or hypothesize are reprimanded and sent home. We are taught to stand on the wisdom of previous generations—to question that which has already been proven is foolish; *disrespectful*.

A second offense brings the punishment of public humiliation and scorn. The aberrant child is struck on the knuckles and afterward made to stand on a box in the middle of the town square. Only when the sun has dipped low in the sky are they allowed to return home, often at a breakneck sprint to avoid that which comes out at night.

In my lifetime, there's only been a single third offense. I don't know what happened to the girl—she disappeared from Holostown and I never saw her again.

It's rare to see someone break the rules.

Elara and I struggle with different rules. I enjoy the thrall of a good story; Elara is full of curiosity: it takes effort for her to keep her questions and wonderings to herself. We learn early on that while these pastimes are dangerous at school, violations are much harder to regulate at home.

Our parents try, in the beginning. My storytelling earns me soap in the mouth and stern admonition; Elara's incessant questions earn her rebukes and raps on the knuckles. When these efforts do little to stop us, our parents' irritation turns to frustration and then into fear. Our punishments become harsher.

Without acknowledging it, I know the moment our parents see that Elara and I are innately wired to create and to question. They change tactics altogether.

Instead of banning behaviors, our parents preach the importance of *secrecy*. No one must ever see us engage in these activities—the consequences will be dire.

The arrangement suits us fine: we're the only ones we know of who hold such interests, and we're perfectly content to indulge these tendencies with each other.

When I am seven years old, signs start to come.

A long, blue feather laid out across my pillow when I wake. Soft as silk and deep cobalt in color, it's unlike anything I've ever seen. The pillow presents continue for a week: I receive a pearlescent-colored shell, a gold charm, a music box, a peppermint stick, a book, and my favorite gift, a tiny black kitten.

Elara and I marvel at each. At seven and five, we already know not to show these articles to our parents.

The feather, shell, and charm are tucked neatly inside a pair of folded socks, the music box and book are hidden in the bottom drawer of our clothing chest, and the peppermint stick is made to last two weeks—Elara and I each pick an end and allow ourselves ten licks each night before slipping into bed.

The kitten is the hardest to hide, though she seems to intuitively understand the necessity for secrecy. We name her Boo and hide bowls of water and saucers of bread and cheese under our bed. At night, we trade off snuggling with her under the covers.

The eighth morning, I wake with disappointment. There's nothing on my pillow.

At first, I imagine I must be mistaken. I flip my pillow and search under the covers and bed, certain my present has fallen. When Elara wakes, she helps me search—but after ten minutes, we concede that nothing has been left.

We walk the path to school in silence.

My thoughts drift to the reason and origin of the gifts in the first place before a glimmer in the woods catches my eye. It's gone a second later. I glance to Elara to see if she noticed, too.

"What?" my sister asks, frowning.

I look back to the woods—there's nothing amiss. "Noth—"

I stop when the glimmer materializes again, an opulent sheet of rainbow light that ripples through the trees. Without finishing my thought, I take a step off the path and into the forest.

The act alone is a major transgression—one I should not take lightly. But curiosity trumps pragmatism, and my boots crunch leaves as I tramp directly to the glimmer. I hear a second set of boots crunch sticks and leaves, and I know Elara follows. There's no hesitation as she sidles up on my right, squinting into the forest.

"What is it?"

I point. "A glimmer."

Elara is silent.

I step closer, stretching my hand out tentatively. When my fingers touch the glimmer, it materializes into something tangible; a gap appears.

Elara's gasp stops me in my tracks. But my sister's face isn't marked by fear, but awe. Her cheeks are pink and her eyebrows arch and her mouth is parted in a perfect "o."

"I hear it," she whispers reverently.

"Hear what?" The words come out like a complaint. I didn't hear a thing. When I reach my arm farther through the glimmer, Elara's eyes sparkle and her mouth widens to grin. She hops up and down in delight.

At five years old, she lacks the words to describe the sound, just as I lack the words to describe the glimmer. But we're both sure of the magic and *otherness* of the place.

Over the years, we discover other glimmers. Always on the periphery of town, in places we're not supposed to explore.

At school, and in the presence of our parents, we are Andra and Elara Bretton, model students and children. We fulfill the perfunctory roles expected of us, withholding the best and truest parts of ourselves for each other.

And when we're alone, we indulge every creative whim and investigate every idle wondering. We write stories and perform plays and dissect tulips and read books. Boo is there for it all, though she slips through the window and down the tree during the day while we are at school.

A proper Holostown citizen, even Boo knows not to be out after dark—she is safely tucked in the confines of our shared room by the time the sun sets.

We grow up polite but guarded. Our peers grow dull from unimaginative repetition, but Elara and I rely on one another for growth and stimulation. We know we are disparate—we must be, to be hardwired so much differently than everyone around us. But in Holostown, a place that prizes conformity and obedience, we never voice such thoughts. Even when we are alone.

In those first years of life, we do not encounter a beast or creature. The warnings are proliferate—the one time embellishment is accepted—and no one questions whether the stories are true. Elara and I rarely discuss the beasts and creatures, though the lofty trepidation we harbor as children begins to fade to a general sense of caution.

That is, until the spirits visit.

TWO

Technically speaking, it is the creatures who come first.

The beasts come on a Wednesday of no particular repute, when Elara and I are helping to clear the dinner table.

A high-pitched shriek of terror and an otherworldly growl slice through the dark, raising hairs on the back of my neck. The initial scream is followed by others before the night grows deathly still and preternaturally silent.

"Upstairs. Now." My parents' orders are stern. I note the loaded look they exchange as I reach for Elara's hand and make for the loft.

"What about you?" Elara asks, resisting my pull.

"We'll be down here," my father announces definitively.

"We'll be fine. They don't want—" My mother doesn't finish her sentence. Her hand covers her mouth, as though to physically bar words from leaving. My father waves us upstairs, and this time, we obey.

Huddled under the bed, Boo at our side, Elara and I don't make a sound. My heart thunders in my chest and the blood pumping in my ears roars, making it difficult to notice anything beyond my own physiology. Elara's eyes are wide and I hear her sharp inhalations, discordant and fragmented.

There are more screams; a myriad of sounds that are difficult to place. My ears strain to detect and place each noise, but without context or vision, my efforts are in vain.

"Do you think they're close?" Elara's breath is warm on my cheek. We never lie to each other.

"I don't know."

I think again about my mother's truncated statement. *They don't want*—before she cut herself off. Her words suggest that she knows what they *do* want.

At some point, we fall asleep.

I wake the next morning, neck stiff and back tight from an uncomfortable night's slumber. Our parents never climbed into the loft, and they never called up that it was safe to come out.

Elara and I descend the ladder steps with apprehension, wary of what we might find below. But my parents receive us in the kitchen as though the day were like any other—my mother hands us breakfast and my father smiles in greeting, albeit with dark circles under their eyes.

"Do not go off the path," my father orders sternly as we pack our bags for school. He says it like the rule is new and not something we've been told to do every day of our lives.

The static electricity in the air is enough to warn me that something in Holostown is still not right. The sun shines too bright, the birds warble traitorously. The trail is clear and silent—the morning commute starts off familiar enough.

Half of a mile in, the nutmeg-colored dirt takes on a rust-colored hue, and the grass lining the trail is flattened as though something has been dragged over it. Flies congregate in black clouds some feet in the distance, and my eyes squint in the harsh daylight to spot a carcass.

"Is that—"

I nod my head and squeeze Elara's hand, grateful I'm not walking the path alone.

The farther we go, the more carcasses we spot—mangled piles of flesh and muscle and bone that I don't care to investigate. I can't tell if I'm looking at dead animals or people. I don't want to know.

Nearer the school, there are further signs of struggle.

A house has been burned to the ground. Windows are broken; shards of glass litter the earth below. Evidence of struggle exists in the mess of debris that border either side of the path and the blood-red splotches of grass and dirt. Elara and I don't say a word.

"The creatures came."

Our teacher's explanation for the past night's events is bald and disappointing. "This is why it's important to follow the rules." She does not mention *what* creatures came or *where* they came from or *why* they decided to lay waste to Holostown. The rules dictate that we keep our musings and questions to ourselves.

The day passes in a blur.

Three of my classmates are missing, though I have no way of knowing whether it's because they were mauled to death in the night or kept home by frightened, protective parents. The mundaneness of the day, the false pretenses of *normalcy*, make my skin crawl.

At the end of the school day, Elara and I make a beeline for home. We've made it halfway when I track movement in the woods. My entire body goes stiff as a tree trunk.

"We're not alone," I tell Elara when she looks over in concern. My gaze combs the forest; I glare out at the woods until my eyes burn and yellow dots form in my periphery, but to no avail. I can't pinpoint the threat. Elara and I walk the rest of the way home on feet that are light and ready to run at a moment's notice.

"The threat has passed," my father announces at dinner. It's the closest he'll come to addressing what happened. Elara and I know better than to ask questions.

No one ever speaks about what took place that night, though Elara and I engage in plenty of speculation.

Six years later, a shrill cry and a chorus of wails wake me. Our parents call up for us to hide, and foreboding bubbles inside of me. I know better than to stay in the loft.

"The forest," I tell Elara.

She nods her agreement, as though she's also come to the conclusion that the sanest thing we can do is defy our parents' order and leave the warmth and safety of our home for the dark obscurity of the woods. We leave through the window, crawling along Boo's preferred branch to scale down the tree trunk and disappear into the woods.

I stumble through the darkness with Elara, allowing intuition to lead the way. Without realizing it, I guide us to a glimmer. In the pale light of the moon, it looks similar to the pearlescent shell I once found on my pillow.

"It's not time yet."

The voice catches me off guard—this, and not the cries in the night, causes me to jump.

"Who's there?" Elara asks, but the layers of darkness are resolute—there isn't a whisper of movement that suggests another's presence in the woods.

"You'll know when it's time," the voice continues. "We'll make sure they don't get you."

A chill that has nothing to do with the temperature races up my spine. "Are they here for *us*?" I croak. For all our speculation on the beasts, I never dared to consider that they might be after Elara and me.

The voice doesn't answer, but the wind seems to. An arctic breeze takes my breath away and sets my teeth to chattering. *You'll know when it's time*, the wind wails through the trees.

Neither Elara nor I see a thing, but we will later agree that it was a spirit that addressed us in the woods. A rather vague spirit, we complain. We huddle in the woods for the better part of the night, unsure if the "protection" we are promised applies to our specific spot in the woods or if it is a general avowal of security.

For seven years, Holostown is quiet.

There are no beasts, and there are no signs of spirits. Elara and I spot glimmers, but these become motifs of our daily existence and not marvels to regard. The past becomes a muted memory. And then one morning there is a 7 carved into the trunk of a spruce tree.

There's nothing inherently special about the marking, though it's neatly outlined in black and it sparkles in the sunlight. I can't think of a blade that would procure such a lovely mark. I puzzle over the meaning for the better part of my morning, then promptly forget about the unusual etch in the tree.

The next morning, I spot a 6. The marking is in a different tree—a small birch sapling that can barely accommodate the wide loop of the 6—but the style is the same.

I'm wise to the game on the third morning, and I feel a rush of delight and premonition when I spot a 5 etched into a chestnut tree. I investigate, careful to check if there are any accompanying artifacts or subsequent messages, but I can't find anything.

"I found something interesting in the woods," I tell Elara later that day, sure she will be miffed that I didn't alert her to the tree marks sooner.

Elara's eyes flash to meet mine, her sky-blue irises sparkling with curiosity. I describe my findings as neutrally as possible, but Elara sees the excitement I work hard to suppress.

"I'm going with you tomorrow," Elara declares matter-of-factly. "You can show me."

The next day, the 4 is carved into an elm—but when I point it out to Elara, her brow furrows in agitation.

"I don't see anything."

"Here," I say, moving closer to the trunk to finger the edges of the mark. Elara's lips form a tight line; her eyes go cold. She shakes her head *no*.

Confusion buzzes through me.

Elara and I are a partnership, our strengths and proclivities so complementary that it's hard to know where one starts and the other ends. But in this moment, I feel Elara's ostracization and the weight of her disappointment. Anticipation rides my nerves—what does it mean? It is almost certainly the work of spirits, and it appears to be a countdown.

You'll know when it's time.

The words bloom in my chest like a promise, then wither at the understanding that this countdown is for *me*—not for Elara.

I don't talk about the *3* in the maple tree or the *2* in the cedar. I start to feel a little nervous when I find the *1* in a willow: I have no idea what to expect.

On day *0*, anticipation shadows me like a loyal mutt.

By the end of the day, my body hums with energy. I don't overthink my urge to go for a late afternoon walk...and though I would usually invite Elara, today I know to walk alone.

My feet move with intentionality, crunching dirt and rock and branches like the steps have been ordained. I forge through dense brush until I find myself before an outcropping of rocks I've never seen before. Muted yellow light warms the limestone under the palms of my hands as I push over sizeable boulders.

Go farther.

The frenetic thrum in my veins and quickening pulse draw me on in silent obedience. Like a moth to a flame, I am pulled in.

My breath is steady, if shallow, when I summit. The limestone beneath me glitters, the sunlight cuts at a deep angle through the surrounding trees. The sun begins to wink its goodbye; in the residual glow of dusk, my heartbeat quickens. Wherever I am going, I haven't made it there yet.

I'm close, though. I can feel it.

The next morning, the sky is cast in muted grays and browns. Mist and fog clog the forest, wisps of cloud settle low to the ground. My footsteps are swift and light. A sheen of sweat covers my brow by the time I make it to the outcropping. I pause at the base and wait.

A low, insistent beat begins in my toes and pulses through my body. With each tremor, a piece of the puzzle falls into place.

Come. Closer. Enter.

I climb.

When my boots slide against slippery limestone, my arms flail and my left knee rams into a rocky ledge. My right hand claws unsuccessfully at loose stone before I tumble down a landslide of debris that spits me unceremoniously on the dirt below.

I stand up and brush myself off. Blood trickles down my elbow; the skin around my left knee looks mottled and pasty. The heels of my hands are scraped raw and I taste blood where I bit the inside of my cheek.

What are you doing, Andra?

I'm out in the middle of the forest standing atop a pile of rubble. What *am* I doing? What did I expect to find? The thrall of the moment is gone, the beat and the inspiration have gone quiet.

But then—ten feet above me, silent and black as the night sky, is a gaping hole in the rock. A cavern.

The invisible pull is absent, the air around me still. I am careful as I climb—the shifting rock makes a precarious path.

When I draw near, I can tell the cavern is manmade. The entrance is six feet tall and four feet wide—just large enough for a human. The dank, musty smell of stale air plies my nostrils.

I walk forward, uncertain what to expect but certain that I must do so. There's a ringing in my ears and an otherworldly stillness of my nerves that suggests I'm on the precipice of something substantial.

A passageway illuminates.

Lanterns on either side of the hall suddenly flicker to glow warm light on the cavern floor. A glint of a shadow and a cool breeze suggest someone is near.

"Hello?"

No answer.

I take a deep breath, then step inside.

BOOM!

A low, thunderous echo sends vibrations through the cave walls. Icy tentacles of consternation curl up my spine and summon goosebumps to my flesh. The air around me is impossibly still as I slink further inside. My arms cross my chest to staunch the cold that slithers off the cave walls to cling to my bones.

Ten feet.

Twenty feet.

Fifty feet.

The passage twists and curls like a grapevine; I can't see more than fifteen feet ahead. At no point does it cross my mind that I should stop, that I should go get Elara.

The next curve brings me to an expansive chamber so tall the light doesn't reach the ceiling. I feel the change immediately.

The air is different—it smells different; it settles in my lungs different. With increased caution, I continue forward. I can't tell if I'm being watched, but I feel like I am.

"Are you sure you want to cross the threshold?"

The words are smooth as butter and cold as ice. My spine stiffens at the first syllable. I turn slowly.

A man stands before me: a man with pale blonde hair, slate-gray eyes, and a sharp nose. The fabric of his plum-colored clothes is rich: it hangs heavy and folds neatly to his body. He is handsome, in the textbook kind of way, but there is nothing that attracts me. His eyes are calculated and discerning, his lips thin.

"I said, are you sure you want to cross the threshold?"

My mind spins. I don't see a "threshold." I don't know what the consequences of crossing might be.

"Where am I?"

A predatory spark lights the man's eyes and his stingy lips part to reveal two perfect rows of teeth. He moves forward to circle me like prey. I'm conscious of my bloody elbow and bruised knee, the dirt on my clothes. I am resolute on one point: I won't abide a tepid first impression.

I stand my ground, chin held high, and wait for the man to complete his assessment. By the time his gaze returns to mine, his grin is wide. "What's your name?" he asks, leaning close enough that I can see his pupils dilate with excitement.

"Where am I?" I repeat.

The man tents his fingers, tapping the tips together. "That's not how this works. *You* came *here—you* answer the questions. You don't get to ask them."

"I can't answer your question if I don't know where I am."

"You found your way here, didn't you?" the man asks, eyes narrowed. "The path wasn't even marked. You forged a way."

"I didn't *forge* a way," I correct. "Rocks fell."

"You forged the way," the man counters with an unnerving jack-o-lantern smile.

I frown. "Who are you?"

"Syphus. And you are?"

"Andra."

"Nice to meet you, And-*ra*," Syphus intones, mocking me with a slight bow. "Back to the original question—will you cross the threshold?"

My head spins. I have no idea where I am and this looks like a bad idea. "Where is the threshold?"

Syphus jerks his head to the side. "You can't see it from here."

I crane my neck and try to peek anyway. Nothing.

Syphus smirks. The appraising look he gives me inspires a jolt of anger. He thinks he knows me; he thinks he has me figured out after a whole two minutes.

Ignoring the danger emitted from his very pores, I pin Syphus with a withering gaze. It's a *threshold*—how bad can it be? "I'll cross the threshold," I growl.

Syphus' smile shines brighter than the sun. "Of course you will."

Heat rises to my cheeks.

"I recommend you sit down, And-*ra*," Syphus sings my name. "It would appear you've accrued enough injuries for the day."

I take a step forward. My irritation masks most of my fear, but not all of it. *How could I get injured crossing a threshold?*

"You won't see it," Syphus repeats. "I recommend you sit down." He pauses, smiles in a serpentine way. "Or not. Your choice."

"Of course it's my choice," I bark, not bothering to hide the fact that he's ruffled my feathers. "I don't even—"

The words are cut off when I take my next step—a step that doesn't end with rock flooring, but with air.

THREE

A sharp intake of air is all I can manage. My butt hits the ground with a thump and I hurtle down a steep ravine, but I'm not in free fall. It's dark enough that I can't see a thing.

My knees take the brunt of the impact as I collide with rock. The wind is knocked out of me and I feel a stinging pain in both legs, but there aren't any crunched bones or twisted joints.

I'm assessing my limbs for damage when low lighting flickers on; a dim, honeyed glaze that grows brighter. Another path snakes up through the cavern before twisting out of sight. I move under a high ceiling that slopes dramatically: I have to duck at times, but the path is smooth and well-lit. I feel the end before I see it.

The lighting takes on a whiter hue and there's a hum of energy as I emerge. I blink several times, eyes working to adjust to the bright light. The tunnel led me to a circular room—an arena—with seats built into every inch of space. Most are full.

I'm not an imposing figure, but my arrival hushes the crowd as though a spell has been cast. Then, a moment of prolonged silence.

"You didn't kill her."

The back of my neck heats and my heart races, but I keep my

composure. The air crackles with tension, but I stand still; wait. The voice is a deep, velvet baritone...but the reply comes from Syphus.

"You can't smell her?"

Syphus' voice is haughty and elite. From beneath the fringe of my lashes, I watch him emerge from the tunnel and prowl about the arena. *I* might be nervous to face the scrutiny of the crowd, but Syphus preens and struts like a peacock.

My smell?

I grow smaller with each second that passes, my fear giving space for mortification.

"Get within ten feet of her and you'll note it." Syphus looks my way, his upper lip curling. "She reeks."

No one answers.

The arena is split into sections. Six groups are made up of humans; the other two include a mix of what appear to be spirits and creatures. All of them stare; unmoving except for their vigilant, assessing eyes.

I take a half-step forward into the arena and there's an audible gasp quickly followed by murmurs, wide eyes, and meaningful glances. My blood runs cold; my gaze jerks sharply behind. Nothing.

Syphus smirks, his gaze slipping to the ground below me while he knows I'm watching. His eyebrows rise with smug arrogance. "Well, at least you can *see* it," Syphus muses loud enough for the entire arena to hear. "Trust me, the scent is there, too."

"Where am I?" I ask Syphus in a low voice.

"She'd like to know where she is," Syphus announces to the crowd. Turning to me, he offers a wolfish grin. "Careful, And-ra." His murmur tickles my ear. "They haven't yet decided what to make of you."

"She's interrupting the Prosphora. She shouldn't be here."

The voice belongs to a woman, her squat frame adorned with armor that makes her look like an armadillo. Her attire is bland and militaristic, save for the rings that cover her fat fingers—brilliant, gaudy gemstones that broadcast prominence and power.

"Of course she shouldn't be here."

Another woman, this one adorned in a lavender gown of gossamer silk and velvet trim. Her hair is so blonde it looks white and her almond eyes are an incredible shade of violet.

"Who marked her?"

It seems that the only people bold enough to voice their thoughts are those seated at the front—this voice belongs to a broad-shouldered man with a brown beard. His question lingers, eliciting murmurs from the crowd.

"Who marked her?" the man tries again, this time louder. His eyes rove the crowd as though the answer may be buried in someone's eyes.

"That seems to be the question of the hour," Syphus sneers.

"She's interrupting the Prosphora," the squat woman repeats indignantly.

There's a protracted silence, during which glances are exchanged amongst the prominent figures. In this space of quiet, my wits return. I have no idea what a *Prosphora* is or where I've entered, but it's time to leave.

"I'm sorry for interrupting. I'll go home." I walk past Syphus, intentionally bumping him with my shoulder as I pass.

"You may not leave."

This voice—it sounds like gravel and smoke and chains. It's deep and low and full of authority. Four words, and they're uttered in such baritone that the ground rattles with waves of vibration.

I stop in my tracks.

I turn slowly to regard the man who spoke, a muscled figure with jet-black hair and inky-black eyes. A serpent rests lazily across his shoulders; an assortment of hair-raising creatures lurk just behind. My stomach roils.

I wait for the man to elaborate. He doesn't. His cold gaze is enough to freeze my innards—I will not attempt to go anywhere whilst that man's eyes—and the eyes of his cadre—are upon me.

"What of the Prosphora?" the armadillo woman tries once more.

The man with the gravel voice slides his eyes to the other section of the arena chock full of spirits and creatures. He meets the gaze of the prominent figure in front before lifting his chin with authority. It's clear that these sections carry the most clout—no one dares to speak in the expanse of the man's silent consideration.

"The terms of the Prosphora have changed." The gravel voice is slow and deliberate, taking up space and demanding attention. "Give us time to confer. We will meet again tomorrow. Until then, we need a domain to host the girl."

"We'll host her," the man with the beard offers.

The arena is silent.

After a moment, the bearded man waves his hand in unspoken command and a guard appears at my side.

"Follow me," the guard prompts.

It's not as though I have a choice. I allow myself to be ushered away, aware of every pair of eyes that monitor our progress. I keep my head down.

I crossed the threshold.

I had no idea what that meant. Now, I'm getting the strong impression that it means I'm in really deep shit.

"You're in Soulbourne," the guard says as we leave the arena. "We're taking you to Perrin's domain."

My spiraling thoughts prevent me from responding; my mind a veritable tornado of doomsday scenarios and pessimistic cogitations. I follow in silence.

We exit the tunnel and turn left, then climb a staircase to emerge in a rainforest of balmy air and floral fragrances. Gigantic ferns and leafy trees line the mulch pathway, rainbow-colored birds perch atop nectar feeders.

"This is Land," the guard grunts.

My brows knit in confusion. "Isn't it all land?"

A derisive chuckle. "Well, yes. *Technically* it's all land. But I'm talking about the domains. We're in the Land domain—Perrin's territory. There's Air, Water, Rock, Overworld, Underworld, Callings, and Boundless."

I consider the groups from the arena and the domain names—

some are easy to match, others are less obvious.

We walk for another ten minutes before we approach a large cabin that stands alone at the end of the mulch path.

The guard nods in invitation. "This is where you'll stay."

"It looks...nice."

"It *is* nice." The guard steps up onto the porch.

Every inch of the cabin is crafted from elegant planks of wood—variant shades of tan and brown and red meet in thick veins that run in striking patterns.

Inside, a long dining table sits beneath a chandelier winking with tea lights. There's an oversized fireplace with cozy chairs and sheepskin rugs and a birdcage-style chair hangs from the rafters of the ceiling. Cashmere blankets and plush pillows adorn a settee. An expansive washroom draped in ferns and flowers stands to one side and a bed shrouded in sheer silk panels is tucked in the back corner. But the showstopper is the view from the back deck, the miles of green rainforest that stretch for as far as the eye can see.

The guard clears his throat. "Settle in. I'll get you when you're needed," he grunts, taking up watch at the front of the cabin. He hesitates before adding, "Good luck."

These two simple words spark a flicker of emotion—one I am quick to tamp down. "I think I'll wash first—get rid of that smell," I jest.

When the guard meets my gaze, there is pity in his eyes. "You can wash, but that's not going to get rid of the mark." He offers a sympathetic smile before closing the door to the cabin.

Afternoon fades into evening. The worry buried inside of me bubbles, looking for a way out.

I don't know how I'm going to get myself out of this. I don't know if I *can*. Is it worse to stay put or to try to escape? I wrack my brain for an elegant solution, but there's no way to strategize with the little information I have—there are too many unknowns.

When panic darkens my door, I decide to shower.

The hot water stings at first impact, but soon enough my body relaxes into the heat and the feeling of *clean*. I take longer than necessary, losing myself in the luxury of the moment.

When I step out, there is a woman sitting at my dining room table. She's dressed in an eclectic ensemble featuring every shade of purple. When she blinks, sparkly mauve eyeshadow flickers.

"Sorry to startle you. I was told you needed clothes. I thought you might want help getting ready." She tucks a strand of brown hair behind her ear.

My pulse quickens. "Get ready? Where am I going?"

"Oh, sorry. You're not going anywhere. I don't think you're allowed to," she adds, cheeks flushing. "My name is Lenna. I'm from Boundless." She looks at me shyly, her large brown eyes hopeful.

I smile cautiously, unnerved that the guard let Lenna inside the cabin without asking my permission. "I could use clothes."

Lenna smiles back, oblivious to my discomfort. "You have a few choices," she says, gesturing to garments that rest on the bench.

I point to a set of mahogany-brown pajamas. "If I'm not going anywhere, I may as well get comfy."

Lenna bites back a smile and hands me the set. After I don the silky pajamas, we settle into the oversized chairs by the fireplace.

"You came from another realm," Lenna narrates. She says it as fact, but her eyes are wide with question.

"I guess so."

"How did you do it? Is it true you were summoned?"

My heart skips a beat; I work hard to keep the surprise from my face. I need to play this carefully—I want to glean information from Lenna without compromising my own situation.

"I felt a pull," I answer carefully.

"And you answered. The path opened for you."

Another chill.

I *did* feel a pull. But the path itself isn't sentient...my pull was planned by some*one*. The idea sends shivers up my spine—who called for me?

I shift my legs and push my wet hair over a shoulder, feigning

21

nonchalance. "What have you heard?"

"Gossip," Lenna answers matter-of-factly. "There was a huge crowd in the arena that saw you enter—when word got out that a marked woman had crossed the threshold, everyone went berserk."

"People don't come here often?"

"Never."

I try not to let Lenna's words affect me. This doesn't feel like good news. "So someone planned for me to come?" My tone is casual but my mouth is dry.

"Someone did, but no one knows *who*. It's why Syphus didn't kill you," Lenna explains.

I flinch and Lenna's face shifts. "He *won't* kill you," she reassures me. "Not since you've been marked."

I look again at my arms and legs, clear except for the cuts and bruises I accrued during the fall. "I don't see a mark."

Lenna smiles. "For one thing, your smell. It's also the sparkle."

"Excuse me?"

"Look," Lenna commands, pointing to the floor between the fireplace and the shower.

I follow her gaze. "Wet footprints," I observe.

"No—the glitter dust." Lenna looks from the floor to me. Her mouth falls open in a small "*o*". "You don't see it," she whispers.

"I don't."

I'm suddenly weary, exhausted from playing a game I don't understand in a place I don't know. Tears creep to the edges of my eyes. I'm worried what Elara and my parents will think and I miss home and I don't understand who could have summoned me when I've never been here before. I don't know anyone in this place.

"Can I braid your hair?"

The question catches me by surprise—I look to Lenna and see that she is earnest, presumably both to braid my hair and to distract me from my present unhappiness.

When she points to the sheepskin rug, I slip from the chair to sit before her. Lenna wastes no time brushing my damp strands, her busy fingers gently untangling knots. "Back where you're from—

22

what do the spirits ask of you?"

A light shiver creeps up my spine. I wish I could see Lenna's face to know if there is more to the question. "I'm not sure what you mean."

Lenna stops brushing—she leans forward to look me in the face. "Don't spirits protect your realm?"

I shake my head—a subtle back and forth is all I can manage with Lenna's firm grasp of my hair.

"Who rules your realm?" Lenna asks softly. The brush is suspended in midair—progress interrupted until she gets an answer.

"People?" I recall my father's words after one of the raids on Holostown. *The threat has passed.* No details offered.

Lenna's mouth drops open. "Who protects you?"

"We protect ourselves?" The answer comes out like a question, a testament to the uncertainty that has overtaken me since entering Soulbourne. Lenna's questions are ones I've asked myself for years— I've just never had license to investigate.

"Hmm." I don't have to see Lenna's face to know her features are riddled with doubt.

After a moment, Lenna's fingers gently twine the strands of my hair again. "I can't imagine a realm without spirits. They keep Soulbourne safe—they're the reason for the Prosphora."

"Tell me about that." Learning the answer to this question feels significant: there was an intimidating crowd gathered in the arena… for what?

"The Prosphora is the annual gathering to identify the year's sacrifice," Lenna explains. "The spirit domains require tribute in exchange for protection."

"What kind of tribute?"

"It depends on the year." Lenna studies the progression of my braid, then pulls the strand on the left tighter. "And it depends on what the spirits need. The need drives the sacrifice—most years it's fairly modest, but other years it can be quite cruel. Domains gather to learn the requirements of the year's sacrifice."

My blood chills at the unspoken implication in Lenna's words. I think back to the sections I saw gathered in the arena and my brows furrow. I still don't understand the threat Soulbourne faces. "And every domain participates?"

"Usually, yes."

Lenna finishes the braid and pushes it over my shoulder for me to admire, but I'm too preoccupied with thoughts of iron-fisted leaders and human sacrifice.

"Who put the domain leaders in charge?" I ask. As horrible as the Prosphora sounds, I don't plan to stay in Soulbourne. I need to learn about the individuals who will determine my fate.

Lenna shifts. "It depends on the domain. The leaders of Air, Rock, Land and Water were all appointed...but I'm not sure when or how. Boundless and Callings elect a new leader every two years, and we're kind of penalized for it because our leaders don't have the same clout. Overworld and Underworld, the spirit domains, have the real power. Achlys and Justus have always been in power—no one contests their authority."

"Has it always been that way?"

Lenna shrugs. "Maybe?"

"It seems like—"

"The past doesn't matter," Lenna interrupts. "The Prosphora for this year has changed—which means the spirit domains are rattled by your arrival."

I don't know what to say. Lenna doesn't make the statement like an accusation, but it feels like one. To be the cause of such emotional turmoil doesn't feel good. The fact that my arrival has changed the terms of the Prosphora is unsettling, to say the least.

I'm poised to ask my next question when we're interrupted by a knock on the door.

FOUR

Lenna opens the door to welcome a woman with fair skin and freckles. The petite redhead can't be older than twenty-five, but she gives off the aura of a stern librarian.

"Hi." She waves from the porch. "My name is Emberlyn. I'm from Callings."

"My name is Andra." I pause. "Your domain name doesn't really mean anything to me."

Emberlyn regards me with open curiosity. "You really are an outsider, then. Why did you come here?"

In the absence of a reason, I am silent.

Emberlyn squints in confusion. "*How* did you come?"

"Through a cave." The truth sounds tired and flimsy.

Emberlyn and Lenna exchange an uneasy glance rife with subtext. "In Soulbourne, we're known by our domain," Emberlyn explains.

"Overworld, Underworld, Land, Air, Water, Rock, Callings, and Boundless." I visualize the groups as I tick them off. "I know the names, but not what they are."

Emberlyn studies me like a puzzle. "I'm a scholar. There are many vocations in Callings—emissary, prophet, scholar, seer, healer..." She looks to Lenna in silent invitation.

"I already told her I'm from Boundless. We have..." Lenna's gaze flits to Emberlyn in a way that strikes me as self-conscious, "...a mixed reputation."

Emberlyn doesn't bat an eyelash. "Boundless is mostly hired for dirty work." Somehow, she's able to make the assertion without sounding judgmental. "Spies, assassins, bodyguards—that type of thing."

"I'm not a spy or an assassin," Lenna is quick to clarify.

"I'm surprised they sent you," Emberlyn says.

"They *didn't* send me. I sent myself. I brought Andra clothes."

"Why did you come?" I ask.

Lenna blushes. "I love art. Dressing you is a chance to demonstrate my skill." She shrugs. "Maybe it will lead to something."

My smile is tepid. "I'm not concerned about my appearance." I don't begrudge Lenna an opportunity to showcase her talent, but I'm not the boon she thinks I am.

"You will if you're smart. The verdict is still out on you, Andra—your clothes send a message," Emberlyn corrects.

I roll my eyes.

"Someone *marked* you," Emberlyn reminds me.

"So people have said. I still don't see how it's possible. "

"The mark is obvious. Syphus didn't exaggerate."

"You see it, too?"

"The glitter dust? Yeah. It's everywhere. So is the smell. "

My stomach knots. It's hard to resist the urge to look over my shoulder for glitter or surreptitiously sniff my arm. "Why would someone mark me? What does it mean?"

"It means...someone wants you here," Emberlyn answers carefully.

I lift my eyebrows. "And their reason for that is..."

"That's what everyone wants to know."

"It's weird that no one has come forward," Lenna interrupts. "If it was so important to bring you here...why keep it a secret?"

I shake my head in dismay. "I can't imagine why anyone would bring me to Soulbourne. I don't know anyone here. It must be a mistake."

Lenna is silent, eyes wide and sympathetic.

Emberlyn is slow to respond. "I don't think it's a mistake, Andra."

My eyes meet hers—she has a thoughtful expression and an inscrutable sheen to her eyes. "The truth doesn't matter, anyway. *They* won't accept that it's a mistake."

"That man," I say, thinking of the leader who told me I couldn't leave. The one with the voice so deep I'd felt the earth vibrate when he spoke.

"The leader of Underworld? Achlys?" Emberlyn guesses.

Lenna shudders. "He's scary."

"All of the leaders are dangerous, for different reasons," Emberlyn warns. "But Achlys is the worst."

"He told me I couldn't leave," I say, unsure if this part of the story was passed along to them.

"You can't," Emberlyn says. "That's not because of Achlys, though."

I swallow and readjust my body, hoping to quell the panic that travels up the base of my spine. "Why, exactly?"

"Your mark identifies you as a threat," Emberlyn explains. "They're afraid of you."

"It's a big deal that they're changing the Prosphora," Lenna adds. "That's never been done before."

"You might not want to be here, Andra—but think of this: you've been here less than a day, and you've thrown Soulbourne into a tailspin. That's *power.*"

I stare down at my hands. "I don't understand this place," I say quietly. I certainly don't feel powerful.

"You just need an education on Soulbourne," Emberlyn declares. "That's why I'm here."

"Okay."

It's not an exuberant okay, or even a determined okay. If I'm honest, I sound like a petulant toddler who's realized they're out of alternative options. This doesn't faze Emberlyn.

"Great. Why don't we start by reviewing the Land domain—we can discuss it over dinner." My stomach growls in response, and Emberlyn looks to Lenna. "Can you ask the guard about food?"

Emberlyn gently grabs my arm and guides us to the table. I'm not yet seated when she begins. "We're in the Land domain—Perrin is the leader. He was married once, but his wife died years ago."

I recall the man with the beard who agreed to host me.

"He's really proud," Lenna calls on her way to the door. "In a bad way. He can be kind of petty."

Emberlyn nods in solemn agreement, then lectures on.

Over the next hour, I learn about the domains.

Air is led by Imara—the gorgeous woman with violet eyes I remember from the arena. Imara is single, never married. She has no desire for children; her greatest passion in life is collecting beautiful things.

Water is led by Elinarr. His domain is free-spirited, cunning, and athletic.

Rock is led by Tyra, the squat woman I likened to an armadillo. Tyra loves precious gems—her garments are bland, but she enjoys showing off the prized jewels of her domain in necklaces, bracelets, and rings.

When we finish the first four domains, Emberlyn and Lenna hesitate. "Callings is going to want to study you," Emberlyn says carefully.

"Boundless..." Lenna struggles to find the right words.

"You think they'll try to kill me."

"You're a threat," Emberlyn reminds me. "Boundless will likely be hired to kidnap you for ransom or they might be hired to kill you."

It's a terrifying revelation. But at the end of a long day, I can't muster additional anxiety. I can't hide my yawn, either.

It's dark outside; firefly lights twinkle on the patio and the hypnotic movement of the flames in the fireplace threatens to lull me to sleep.

Emberlyn frowns. "You should rest."

"I haven't heard about Overworld or Underworld," I protest. The spirit domains are the ones I'm most worried about.

Emberlyn looks around the room. "I don't mind staying the night. Want to cover the rest in the morning?"

"Really?" The idea brings immense relief.

"I don't mind. Let's finish in the morning."

"I'll stay, too," Lenna says.

Suddenly aware of how drained I am, I brush my teeth and fall into bed. As exhausted as I am, my brain won't stop. I worry about Elara and my parents and surviving and intruders and marks and spirits. At some point, my mind goes still.

A loud *snap* wakes me.

I bolt upright in bed, utterly silent as my heart pounds out of my chest. The noise came from outside—something is moving alongside the cabin.

My eyes adjust to the dark and I quickly take inventory of Emberlyn's figure tucked in one of the oversized chairs by the fireplace. Lenna's asleep at the dining table, hunched over a pile of fabric. Neither of them startled at the noise.

Carefully, quietly, I peel back the covers and slip my legs over the side of the bed. I glide across the room, footfalls light and intentional. For a moment I stand at the deck door, back pressed against the silky wood, and listen.

At first, my straining ears hear only the buzz of insects. Then, there's another rustling. Not as loud as the first one, but something is definitely moving outside the cabin.

I glance towards the front door. Through the window, I see the silhouette of the guard's frame hunched in his chair. *Is he even alive?* It's hard to tell. One thing is for certain: he won't neutralize the threat.

I slide to the dining table and grab a knife. My fingers curl around the stem; my breathing becomes arrhythmic. I've never stabbed anything before—I'm a little worried I won't be able to. I have no qualms about throwing a punch; it's a very different thing to plunge a knife into someone's flesh.

If it comes down to your life or theirs, you will do it, I tell myself. I ignore the critic in my mind that reminds me that I have saved bumblebees from puddles and earthworms from parched earth. *This is different. Your life is on the line.*

I hesitate at the deck door, listening intently for any sign of activity. The door glides open without a sound and I slowly lean forward to peer outside when hands come out of nowhere.

Fast as lightning, one covers my mouth. Another wraps around my middle to pull me in hard. Whoever has grabbed me is *strong*—I wriggle and squirm to get free, but it feels like I'm pushing against a brick wall. *At least it's a person,* I tell myself. It feels like a man—not a creature.

I still my movement. When the hand moves to tighten its grip, I stomp hard on the man's foot and plunge my elbow into his midsection. A muted *oomph* is all I'm awarded. If I want to break free, I'm going to have to come up with something far better.

Sheer panic lights my core. Lenna and Emberlyn's words flit to the forefront of my brain: *Boundless will probably be hired to kidnap or kill you.* I ram my head back and make connection. The hands stay in place, but the one over my mouth loosens enough that I'm able to bite down. I taste blood and bite harder.

I've surely made the man angry now—I don't dare back down. I look to the knife in my hand; a knife I can't wield because my arms are pinned to my sides.

Maybe I can move a little, though. I test it out and find that because I'm pinned around my elbow, I can raise my arm slightly. Enough to stab the man in the thigh or spear his foot.

I'm weighing my options when I hear the rustling again. My body tenses. If *this* man isn't responsible for the noise…who *else* is out there?

The man begins to move, whisking me along as though I'm no bigger than a paper clip. "If you value your life, stay silent."

The words are spoken in a low, warm voice that tickles the stray hairs by my ear. He doesn't say more as he pulls me away from the cabin and into the rainforest. Belatedly, I think of Emberlyn and Lenna and wonder if I've abandoned them to some monstrosity. Trapped in the ironclad grasp of the man, I can do nothing to warn them.

The man stops behind thick foliage. I watch with wide eyes as shadowed figures prowl the perimeter of the cabin. One moves close, venturing inside the deck door.

A moment later, the predators exit without a sound...and without Emberlyn or Lenna. The shadowed figures slink away.

Five minutes pass.

The man holding me doesn't move an inch. And then he suddenly releases me. "Stay put."

I don't have the opportunity to look at the man before he disappears into the rainforest.

Stay put?

I consider the command, the asinine order I won't follow. A group of would-be assassins just gathered outside my cabin to murder me in cold blood, and I'm supposed to *stay put*?

Home.

A firework of hope flares in my chest—this might be my best chance to escape. I'm dressed in silk pajamas; all I have is a knife. But—I remember the way I walked to get here. I can retrace my steps to the threshold. If I hurry, I can make it before the sun comes up, before anyone notices I've left. I've already escaped the notice of the guard positioned outside the cabin.

Hope trumpets through me; my mind is made up. With one breathless look over my shoulder, I'm off.

FIVE

The moon provides some light, but not a lot, as I pick my way through the rainforest. I move fast, but not so fast that I trip over a raised root or fail to notice someone tailing me. It's a tricky balance, but adrenaline courses through my body and propels me forward. I've nearly made it to the tunnel when I hear a branch snap.

I freeze. I can't see anyone, but I hear voices. I strain to hear what is said over my thundering heartbeat.

Instead, a hand clamps down over my mouth and I'm heaved into the air. I guess right away that it's the man from before: his manner and smell are both familiar.

I attempt to wriggle free, but without much effort. I don't want to attract the attention of whoever else prowls about…most notably, the people I heard conversing. That, and I have the growing suspicion that this man might *not* be my enemy. If he wanted to kill me, he would have already done so. I let him carry my dead weight through the forest.

Ten minutes pass.

When the man sets me down, it's in a clearing. He folds his arms over his chest. "I told you not to move."

I cross my own arms over my chest. "So you did."

The man mumbles a curse and shakes his head. Under the cloak of darkness, I am able to discern movement and shadows, but nothing more. I can't see the man's face.

"Who are you and what do you want?" I demand.

The man scoffs. "You were going to get yourself killed."

My nostrils flare—a warning that the man cannot see under the cloak of darkness. "That doesn't answer my question."

"I don't answer to you."

I glare through the darkness. "Consider my perspective: I'm plucked out of thin air and carried off into the night. What did you expect me to do?"

"Listen?"

"Who are you?" I seethe, inflamed by the presumptive arrogance that seems to beleaguer the citizens of Soulbourne. "I will—"

"What? Stomp on my foot and run?"

I hear the smile in the man's voice, and my body crackles with white-hot energy. But even my anger-fueled menace is not enough to physically harm him. I don't need proper lighting to know he's all muscle. I *felt* that muscle. I need a different strategy.

"What. Do. You. Want?" I bite out. "Why did you bring me here?"

"*Here* is the safest place to talk. Something it seems we need to do, since you don't listen to instructions."

"I require *explanations*, like a sane, rational person."

The man laughs with derision. Here, at least, is one person in Soulbourne who does not perceive me as a threat. "You're a pain in the ass."

"I'm a pain in *your* ass," I clarify. "And for the petty offense of sound judgment. You're just upset because I don't accept strangers' advice like an idiot."

"My name is Warrick." The name is offered as an olive branch after a moment of silence.

"I'm Andra," I huff. "But you probably already knew that."

Warrick snorts. "Yes. You've made quite an impression."

I ignore Warrick's bait. "Why were you outside my cabin?"

Warrick doesn't answer at first. A little intake of breath makes me hopeful, but the words aren't what I wanted to hear. "You're in danger. I was watching over the cabin."

"I *have* a guard." My retort is snappy, even if it lacks bite.

Warrick doesn't say what I'm sure we both think: the guard outside my cabin is a sham, for appearances' sake only.

"What is it to you, anyway? What domain are you from?"

"Boundless," Warrick answers levelly. "And right now, my job is to keep you alive."

I squint into the darkness. It'd make me feel better to see Warrick's eyes. "Seriously?"

"Seriously." He doesn't say more.

"Who...hired you?"

"That's enough questions. You're going to need to trust me, Andra. You don't have many friends in Soulbourne."

I bristle at the slight and Warrick's continued conceit (*what reason do I have to trust him?*) but fall short of a snide retort.

"Do you know who marked me?"

No response.

"Do you know who that was that came after me?"

No response.

"Can you get me out of Soulbourne?"

This elicits a response. "Is that what you were trying to do? Leave Soulbourne?" Warrick asks.

"You mean, why would I want to leave paradise?" I laugh drily. "Lush, tropical rainforest, lovely accommodations, attempts of *murder* in the night..."

"They might have planned to kidnap you," Warrick corrects.

"Like you."

"I kidnapped you for safety."

"And yet, you offer me no proof."

"You can't leave Soulbourne," Warrick says gruffly, ignoring my barb. "The spirits won't allow it."

My nails dig into the flesh of my palms. "I can't stay here—I don't *want* to stay here. I need to go home. My family—they'll be worried sick."

"I'm sorry." Warrick's voice sounds more matter-of-fact than sympathetic. "You crossed the threshold."

A cold chill settles in my bones, dampening the rage and giving birth to dread. "Please help me. Get out, I mean. Help me escape. *Please.*"

"I'm not here to help you escape. I'm here to keep you alive." This time, there's a note of sympathy to Warrick's tone.

"Why?" I throw my hands in the air in exasperation. "What is this about? Please—I need answers."

I'm again met with silence. Insufferable, suffocating, agonizing silence.

"I want to go home," I announce when it becomes clear I won't get any answers. "My *Soulbourne* home," I add distastefully before Warrick can protest. "I'm getting bitten by mosquitoes." I wave a hand in front of my face for emphasis and to distract from the fact that there are tears in my eyes.

"We can do that," Warrick agrees. "But tell me: why did you run when I told you to stay?"

I roll my eyes. "Maybe because the man who told me to stay was prowling around outside my cabin and then abducted me?"

Warrick sighs. In the dark shadows of the forest, he runs a hand through his hair and shakes his head. "Let's go."

Silently, begrudgingly, and a little bit gratefully, I follow. The moonlight casts a dim pearlescent glow over the lush foliage, but it's only enough to make out shadows.

Warrick curses under his breath.

"What?"

Warrick's answer comes in a grandiose sweep of his hand. I follow his gaze, and I'm not sure if it's because it's dark, but I don't see anything.

"You don't see it, do you?"

I shake my head.

"There's glitter everywhere." He sighs, shaking his head as he takes a step towards me.

"What are you doing?" I ask, pulse quickening.

"Do you want a trail of glitter running through the rainforest that shows everywhere you've been?"

I squint into the darkness, looking for any sparkle from the prolific glitter that supposedly trails me. Not a single glint.

"You didn't leave a trail when I carried you."

Heat rises in my cheeks as I realize that Warrick intends to carry me back. It was bad enough when he carried me here in the first place—but then, it was against my will in an ironclad grip meant to thwart any attempt at escape. To willingly allow him to carry me feels like…I'm a baby at best, his lover at worst. I'm grateful for the darkness as the flush in my cheeks fans brighter.

My gawping silence and hesitation are enough for Warrick to surmise my thoughts. "I'm not sure how you plan to explain the sparkly trail leading from your lodgings to the tunnel—but that's not going to escape notice. I don't have to carry you—it's your choice."

I get the point: my every movement is tracked. Another item on a growing list of problems I can't seem to fix.

"Carry me," I grumble.

"What was that?" I see the shadow of Warrick's head tilt to the side. He's enjoying my humble pie.

"Carry me." The words come out forced. There's good reason for him to carry me. It's also humiliating.

"Has anyone ever told you that it helps to say—"

"Just carry me," I hiss. *"Please."*

The last word is so venomous that Warrick chuckles. In one easy motion, I'm up in his arms.

Pressed against Warrick's chest, I marvel at his size. From this angle, I could probably see more of his face, but I don't dare. My gaze is steely and fixed straight ahead, willing the minutes to get swallowed up by Warrick's long strides through the rainforest.

We journey in silence—whether from prudence that we not garner unwanted attention or from stubborn, strong-willed discipline, I'm not sure. When Warrick steps onto the deck, I leap out of his arms.

"Thank you." The words sound pained.

"You're welcome," Warrick answers with some measure of amusement. "I'll be out here the rest of the night. Get some sleep."

I slink inside the cabin and find Emberlyn and Lenna exactly where I left them, none the wiser to my late-night wandering or the stealth intruders who canvassed the place. A whisper of a smile crosses my face as I slip into bed—it's a simple bedsheet that I pull over my body, but it feels like safety that I wrap around me.

That, and the fact that Warrick is standing guard outside, I realize. I didn't feel as secure when I first slipped into bed.

I close my eyes and shutter my mind to the array of problems Soulbourne has introduced. A new day may bring fresh perspective.

SIX

I've never been one to sleep in—a fact that usually annoys me—but today, I'm grateful. I'm not certain what time it is when I stir, but the angle of the light pouring in suggests that the sun hasn't been up for long.

Emberlyn is awake; Lenna is still asleep. My heart leaps in my chest when I remember last night—I wonder if Warrick still stands guard outside. I slip out of bed and draw a hand to my mouth to cover a yawn that speaks to my fragmented sleep. I have a headache.

Emberlyn sees me move and smiles, motioning for me to join her by the fireplace. It's not cold, but it's an inviting space and it's far enough away from Lenna that we can whisper without waking her.

"How did you sleep?"

"Okay," I admit, trying to decide how much of last night I want to share. "How about you?"

"Pretty well."

My gaze travels to Lenna. Her head rests on an outstretched arm, mouth open. Under her hand I see black leather and cheetah print and cringe.

Emberlyn follows my gaze and stifles a laugh. "She's trying to make a statement."

"I want to be invisible," I mumble, all too aware that this is the last thing I will ever be in Soulbourne.

Emberlyn shakes her head. "Too late. Everyone's curious to see the woman who crossed the threshold into Soulbourne...you may as well embrace it. You're here for a reason."

I don't know that I agree. I'm worried the reason might be as vapid as craving salt or scratching an itch. I haven't felt any pull or seen any glimmers since arriving in Soulbourne.

Lenna stirs, pulling me from my thoughts. She opens bleary eyes and seems a bit disoriented to find herself sleeping at the table atop a pile of fabric. "I think I finished your first outfit," she says.

I don't look at Emberlyn as I return her smile.

"I can't wait to see it," Emberlyn declares, maybe to save me from trying to find the right words.

Lenna smiles and tucks a stray hair behind her ear. "This outfit is for the Prosphora announcement."

I'm silent. Lenna's words are a somber reminder that I don't yet know what I face. I remember the scornful, haughty expressions of the leaders in the arena and I know I don't want to return in my ripped, dirty clothes. I'm not sure it's better to arrive in cheetah print.

"Back to our lessons," Emberlyn says quietly. "We still have Underworld and Overworld to cover."

I lean forward in anticipation. "Before we start—Lenna, you're from Boundless. Do you know many people there?" I pick at a nail and avert my gaze, afraid of what my eyes may give away.

"Boundless is a large domain," Lenna answers carefully. She throws a quick glance Emberlyn's direction—both girls are now alert. "I don't know everyone."

"Who do you want to know about?" Emberlyn asks, studying me carefully.

"It's not serious," I answer quickly.

"Who is it?" Lenna prods.

I blush. "Never mind." I should have known that an inquiry

would generate interest. I've been in Soulbourne less than a day—I can count the number of names I've learned on one hand.

"If it was nothing, you wouldn't have brought it up," Lenna protests.

"You can trust us, Andra," Emberlyn adds. "You haven't known us very long, but we came to help you. We're on your side."

"Who do you want to know about?" Lenna asks again.

I hem and haw, but ultimately try to keep my voice neutral as I say: "I'm just wondering if you know Warrick."

My gaze is downcast, but at the sharp intakes of breath it snaps up to take in the widened eyes and round mouths of the two girls as they look to one another. Apparently, *both* of them know Warrick.

Lenna clears her throat. "I don't know Warrick personally, but I know who he is, yes."

"*Everyone* knows who he is," Emberlyn corrects.

"There are probably lots of Warricks," I murmur, suddenly unsure if I want to hear more. "Let's talk about Underworld and Overworld."

Emberlyn tilts her head to the side, studying me like the scholar she is, trying to ascertain what this might all be about. "Why do you want to know about Warrick? Did you hear something?"

My nails dig into the palm of my hand to create sharp half-moon crescents. I shouldn't have brought Warrick up. My priority is to learn about the domains; I don't have time to indulge curiosity.

When I don't respond, Lenna's mouth drops open. "Did you—did you *meet* him?"

I don't know how to respond. I don't want to lie, and I decided about thirty seconds ago that I really don't want to continue this conversation. The result is a sequence of facial expressions and gestures that, I'm sure, tell a story of their own.

Emberlyn's mouth falls open. "When did you meet him?"

"I didn't say—"

"You met him," Lenna declares.

"Last night," I sigh, frustrated that I'm so easy to read. A pungent stench, a trail of glitter, and an abysmal poker face. Pathetic.

"*Last night?*" the girls squawk in unison. Their shock turns to interest. Lenna smirks.

"Not like *that*," I blurt. My face flushes red-hot.

Emberlyn's eyebrows rise. Lenna grins.

"Not like *that*," I insist. "I attacked him," I add, to get their minds out of the gutter.

The smirks disappear. Both girls lean forward, mouths agape.

"You *attacked* him?" Lenna's eyebrows scrunch in disbelief.

"I bit his hand and split his jaw," I answer truthfully.

Emberlyn laughs. She looks at Lenna, and she *laughs*. Lenna meets her eyes, her incredulity, and joins her. Both girls shake their heads and look at me as though I've sprouted a horn.

"I don't know what's funny," I gripe. So much for gleaning information. "Are you going to tell me what you know?"

"Are you going to tell *us* why you attacked him?" Lenna asks.

I do my best to appear nonchalant. "I heard a noise outside last night. When I went to check on it, Warrick surprised me and I attacked him." There: no lies, just major omissions.

"And then you…had a heart-to-heart on the porch?"

I snort my amusement. "No heart-to-heart. He told me I was in danger, like I didn't already know that."

"Did he explain why he was there?" Emberlyn asks.

I scoff. "To 'keep me alive.' He wouldn't answer any other questions."

There's a stretch of silence before either girl speaks. "Warrick is…" Lenna begins after a moment, but then stops short, struggling to find the right word. She glances at Emberlyn.

"…*complicated*? I think everyone in Soulbourne has heard of him," Emberlyn says.

I nod my head, waiting for Emberlyn and Lenna to share actual information that explains the "complicated" reputation.

"I've never spoken with him," Lenna says. "I've seen him—but

I've never spoken to him." She sounds star-struck.

"Warrick has an interesting status," Emberlyn interjects, trying to offer something of value. "He's from Boundless, but he has access to every high-profile individual in Soulbourne. I've never been able to understand why. His background is a mystery—he doesn't have records in Callings' repository like everyone else."

Her cheeks pink at this last revelation, and I realize that Emberlyn has intentionally looked for information on Warrick.

I frown, uncertain how to piece this information together. *Complicated* and *interesting* are both tantalizing and unsatisfying as far as descriptions are concerned. "But you don't think he's...bad?" The word sounds childish, but I'm not sure how else to ask. "Like Achlys?" My one interaction with Achlys was enough to last a lifetime.

"He's not like Achlys," Emberlyn is quick to agree. "There's nothing like Underworld."

The mention of Underworld sends a spasm of fear through me—both at the memory of what I saw in the arena, and at the fact that I still know nothing about the spirit domains.

"Sit here," Lenna instructs, pointing to a chair at the end of the table. "You can eat while I work on your hair."

The moment I'm seated, she starts brushing.

"Overworld and Underworld are different from other domains because of the spirits and creatures. You saw that." Emberlyn looks to me for confirmation, and I nod.

"No moving," Lenna barks. "Use your words."

"I saw," I tell Emberlyn, rolling my eyes.

Emberlyn smiles, but it vanishes with her next words. "The spirit domains are dangerous. Would you rather start with Underworld or Overworld?"

I clear my throat. "Underworld." This is the domain that scares me the most—the one I feel an insistent need to understand.

Emberlyn nods, her clouded hazel eyes reading the fear in mine. "Underworld is led by Achlys."

Achlys. The mere memory of his low, gravelly voice summons goosebumps on my arms.

Before Emberlyn has a chance to say more, horror strikes me like lightning. I remember Achlys' smoldering glare and words: *You may not leave.* What if...*Achlys* marked me?

Emberlyn shakes her head. "It could be," she says, reading my expression and guessing at my concern. "I don't think it was him, though. I don't know why he would do it."

This does nothing to warm the chill that settles on my bones. That there's a *chance* Achlys marked me for something is very bad news.

"Did you feel anything when you met him?" Lenna asks, pulling a pin from her pinched lips to contribute to the conversation. As soon as she's spoken, the pin returns to her mouth and a section of my hair is yanked into place.

"Fear."

It was pure terror that came over me when I saw Achlys and the Underworld section of the arena. Lessons aside, no one needs to tell me that Achlys is bad news.

"You'd think she would feel something from the person who marked her," Lenna thinks aloud. "Shouldn't she be able to sense who did it?"

"Not necessarily." The voice is one I recognize.

Emberlyn gasps.

I hear the clatter of a hairbrush as Lenna fumbles behind me. To her credit, she keeps her grip on my hair. I'm entertained at the reactions of the two—but amusement dies on my lips as I look up and take in all that I could not see last night.

Warrick's tall, but I could tell that much last night. He stands casually in the deck doorway and he fills most of the space. His muscled frame is relaxed, his arms crossed over his chest. I swallow hard as I take in the strong jaw, nutmeg-brown hair, and green eyes. He looks older than me, but not by much. I note the cut on his jaw and the bandage that encompasses his right hand.

Warrick holds my gaze before looking to Lenna and Emberlyn.

I can't see Lenna, but I can imagine she is a mirror to Emberlyn's gawking expression.

"Good morning, Warrick," I say, to put the ladies in the room out of their misery.

He nods in response.

"Hopefully you interrupted our lesson for a good reason." I nudge Lenna's arm to signal that she should continue working on my hair. Warrick studies me without saying a word.

"What do you want?" I ask, fidgeting in my seat.

"I don't want anything," Warrick replies evenly. "I told you last night: I'm here to keep you alive."

"I'm alive. You can go back outside."

I never speak to people like this. But Warrick ruffles my feathers, I can tell he does it on purpose, and I'm grasping for a way to put him in his place. The fact that he's handsome only makes him more irritating. I ignore Emberlyn's incredulous gaze and narrow my eyes.

"I think I'll stay and listen to the lesson," Warrick counters, moving inside the cabin and closing the door behind him.

Neither girl speaks—though Emberlyn nearly knocks the bowl of fruit off the table in an attempt to make space.

I groan inwardly—I genuinely need to learn about Overworld and Underworld, and if Emberlyn and Lenna are so affected by Warrick's presence, I'm not going to get good information. "Don't interrupt," I say with a glare.

"Do you…want anything to eat?" Lenna croaks.

I roll my eyes and grit my teeth.

"No, thank you. Carry on," he says, as though he were a fly on the wall and not a huge hulking piece of muscle that's distracting all of the women in the room.

Emberlyn nods. Her eyes meet mine, and I silently plead with her to carry on.

"Achlys is shrewd and merciless." Emberlyn glances over at Warrick nervously, afraid he might voice disagreement.

"What does he do?" I prod.

Emberlyn looks at Warrick, her gaze practically inviting him to answer the question. He gives her a polite smile and stretches out his legs.

"*Emberlyn.* What does he do?" I repeat.

"Sorry. He doesn't offer mercy to anyone; not even members of his own domain. He executes anyone who steps out of line."

"Turn your head to the right," Lenna tells me, gentle palms pressing against my face. "Almost done."

I'm obedient but begrudging, since this removes Emberlyn from my line of vision. She's falling apart at the seams with Warrick as audience to her lesson.

"Got it—ruthless murderer, steer clear." My attempt at light-heartedness falls short, even to my own ears. "Does he have any special talents I should know about?"

"He's the one who started the Prosphora," Lenna offers, her mouth now free of pins.

I look to Lenna in alarm, and she thumps me softly on the head in reprimand. "You're going to mess it up!" she complains.

"He offered protection from the spirits," Emberlyn confirms. "At a cost. The domain leaders brokered the agreement years ago."

"Pretty underwhelming protection, if you ask me."

Warrick's words are spoken as casually as a remark on the weather. I don't look his direction, but I can feel his gaze.

Lenna's hands go still. "What are you saying?"

I strain my neck ever-so-slightly to catch a glimpse of Warrick. My subtle movement reminds Lenna to finish my hair—her hands start moving again.

"There's nothing benevolent about Achlys." Warrick delivers the line without panache. "He operates solely for his own personal interests."

"What do *you* know about Achlys?" Lenna asks.

"I know enough about Achlys to write a book." Warrick doesn't elaborate.

"Great. Why don't you help us, then? How do we defend against

45

him?" I ask testily.

"There's not a five minute crash course on the most powerful man in Soulbourne. A good first step? Try never to encounter him."

I scoff.

"*Everyone* in Underworld is dangerous. The entire domain is crawling with dark spirits and creatures," Warrick continues.

"Underworld actually is *under* us," Emberlyn adds.

"Have you ever been there?" I ask.

Emberlyn shudders.

"No one goes to Underworld and comes out," Lenna answers for her. "Close your eyes—I'm starting makeup," she commands.

"And Overworld?" I ask.

"Overworld is also a spirit domain—people don't visit without invitation. Unless they're marked," Emberlyn says, arching a brow as she looks at me pointedly. "The leader is Justus. He rarely leaves his domain."

"Was he in the arena yesterday?"

"No. His son, Calum, was there on his behalf. Justus has him carry out most Overworld tasks."

"Overworld is *over* us, just like Underworld is *under*," Lenna adds.

"I'm not planning to go to either. I just want to go home."

"They're not going to let you go," Emberlyn reminds me.

"You leave *glitter* everywhere you go," Lenna adds. "Gold, sparkly glitter. You can't escape."

Warrick is mercifully quiet, surprisingly discreet in not revealing last night's attempt. My jaw sets. There has to be a way. I don't know enough about Soulbourne yet, but I will.

"Finished!" Lenna exclaims, startling me from my thoughts.

I blink my eyes open—without a mirror in front of me, I have no idea what I look like.

"Stand up," Lenna commands. She takes a couple of measurements before pushing me towards the washroom. "It's time for you to change."

I don't glance at the others. I hear Emberlyn prattle nervously from the other room as Lenna holds up black leather. "Your top," she says, gesturing for me to undress.

"That's—not very big." I search for the right words as I take in the swath of fabric. It's not that I don't think it will fit me, but how much of me I expect it will cover.

Lenna rolls her eyes and gestures for me to hurry up. "It's not the whole outfit. *Trust* me."

I'm not feeling any modicum of trust as I don the strapless black leather, which indeed hugs my chest but leaves my midsection bare. Lenna looks pleased as she holds up the cheetah print.

"Try it on. I might need to take it in a little."

At least the skirt covers more—it's tight, but it sits high on my waist and fits snugly. The ensemble feels too edgy for a formal appearance before domain leadership: it's asymmetrical with a high-cut slit on one side that tapers below the knee.

"Shouldn't I wear something more…conservative?"

Lenna waves me off. Instead of answering, she wraps a heavy gold bib necklace around my neck and slides a coiled serpent arm cuff above my elbow. She hands me simple golden sandals and stands back to assess the final product.

I still haven't seen myself, but I can see on Lenna's face that she's ecstatic with the outcome. I told myself yesterday that I would wear her creation, but after hearing about the domains, I don't feel like parading into the arena making a fashion statement.

"You look so, so, *so* fantastic. Amazing," Lenna gushes, clapping her hands together in delight.

"We want to see!" Emberlyn exclaims, though I suspect Warrick could do without a grand outfit reveal.

At the very least, I can walk out of a washroom in Lenna's design. Trying hard not to feel self-conscious, I emerge. I feel color in my cheeks and hope the makeup Lenna applied hides it.

Emberlyn's mouth drops open before a huge smile spreads across her face. I don't have the nerve to look at Warrick.

"You look incredible," Emberlyn gushes. "Lenna—nice work!"

"You don't think I need to be in something more conservative?" I wonder again, looking to Emberlyn.

"It's perfect." It's Warrick who answers. "It's a nod to your host, the Land domain, and it's edgy."

I'm not sure why it's good to look edgy, but I don't have the chance to ask. Warrick suddenly stands at attention, rigid before taking strides towards the back deck. "Good luck," he says before slipping outside.

My heart races.

When I first entered Soulbourne, I didn't realize what I was getting myself into. I was afraid in those first moments in the arena, but I didn't have time to worry.

This time, it's different. I have no idea what to expect, but my brain has prepared a million different horrible iterations of what could take place.

"You can do this," Emberlyn says.

"Don't show your fear," Lenna adds.

We all hear the footsteps before the knock on the door. This individual isn't trying to be stealth—there's no need. The summons has come. It's time to hear the Prosphora announcement.

SEVEN

An emissary with no notable attributes reads an edict. The words hover in the periphery of my mind. He can use whatever pretty words he wants—I know what I'm being called for.

As we walk, the emissary makes no attempt to engage me in conversation. The guard trails behind in a position that suggests he's better prepared to keep me from running than he is to defend me from a threat. I wonder if he saw the glitter in the rainforest.

As we near the arena, I take a deep breath. I want to present myself as dauntless, and right now, my knees shake.

You didn't mean to come to Soulbourne. Apologize for crossing the threshold, and appeal to their sense of logic.

It's the right pep talk, even if the words ring hollow. I remember the look on Achlys' face when he told me I could not leave—I can't imagine an easy exit.

The arena is more overwhelming now than it was yesterday. I'm surrounded by the eight domains—sitting in clearly delineated sections—and a crush of people. The energy of the crowd is palpable, a noise that swells and then dims as I'm led to the center.

The lights are focused on me, and only me, as I'm left by myself in the middle of the arena. I'm surrounded by the domains of Soul-bourne and I feel like I'm under a microscope. I'm struck by how haughty it is for the leaders to sit in the stands and look down on me. A ripple of anger electrifies my resolve.

I am innocent.

I should not be on trial.

I will not be bullied.

I have every right to leave Soulbourne.

I have a new appreciation for Lenna's bold design. Yesterday saw me startled and confused—I will not give that satisfaction today. My insides churn, but my head is high and my knees are still.

The arena falls silent.

I look to the domain leaders, locking eyes with each to let them know that I am not afraid. Achlys interrupts before I can look his way.

"You're dressed to make a statement." His face is utterly devoid of expression.

"Is that why you summoned me? To see what I would wear?" Achlys is the most intimidating of the domain leaders. To show that I'm not afraid of him sends a message.

Achlys smiles, and his artificially-white teeth remind me of fangs. There's no warmth in the smile—the light in his eyes speaks of a competitor meeting an interesting opponent.

"Just when we worried this might be boring. It would seem that our trespasser has some bite," Achlys murmurs. His voice stays low, the discordant, gravelly tone slow and calculated. It's the speech of someone who knows he's powerful and won't be interrupted.

I blink.

Achlys' smile widens. His gaze roves over my body and it takes everything in me not to squirm under scrutiny that I know is meant to make me uncomfortable.

I turn to the other leaders. "The announcement?"

I'm met with silence and hard gazes. In the end, it's Syphus who steps forward to answer.

"And-*ra*." Syphus nods his head in false deference. It's all a charade, and he's soaking up every second.

"Syphus."

"We have some questions for you. It's important you answer honestly," Syphus croons.

"To save us all time: I had no intention of coming to Soulbourne. I didn't even know this place existed. I would like to leave. I won't return."

There. It's so simple—the truth, basic and bare and matter-of-fact. I hear my message and agree with myself: *Yes, let Andra go. She didn't do anything wrong.*

I'm met with stony silence and a smirk from Syphus. He raises his eyebrows, scanning the arena to find the leaders' faces. "Well?"

"You cannot go." This time, it's Perrin who speaks. "It's no small thing to enter Soulbourne—you have no idea what you've done."

"What *have* I done?"

"You crossed the threshold to our realm," Perrin accuses. "You trespassed."

"You were asked if you wanted to cross the threshold," Tyra agrees. "You said yes. You made your choice."

"How was I to know what that meant?"

"Not to mention your marks," Elinarr cuts in.

"I don't even know what it *means* to be marked. I can't see or smell my marks—for all I know, you're making it up." Desperation creeps into my voice. "I want to know why I've been marked, too—I've been summoned into a death trap."

"We don't plan to execute you," Imara says. Her voice is light, like wind chimes in a summer breeze. "If you die, it will be your fault." If she intends for the words to bring comfort, they don't.

Calum is the last to speak. "We need to hear from you, Andra. We cannot make a decision without considering your perspective."

I wave a hand in resignation. "Ask your questions."

"Why did you enter Soulbourne?" Syphus asks.

I glare. He knows better than anyone that I had no idea what I

51

was getting myself into—he was there. I *tried* to peek past the threshold and I *tried* asking questions.

"I didn't know what I was entering."

"You never should have found the entrance to Soulbourne," Perrin says. He says it like my actions were premeditated, the result of a carefully-planned, nefarious scheme.

"The threat you present drives the intensity of today's questioning," Tyra adds, her face grave. "Your marks are cause for great concern."

"I won't come back," I promise. "I'm not a threat. I didn't even know this place existed. This is all a big mistake." I do my best to look harmless, but my ensemble and tongue aren't a convincing portrayal of meek and innocent.

"But you did come. And your marks incriminate you," Achlys says.

My frustration mounts, and with it, hopelessness. There's no way I can prove my innocence, and I'm going to be punished for it.

"Someone wants you here." Tyra nods her agreement. "We intend to find out who." The cool and assessing gaze she levels on me causes my blood to run cold. Here it is, then: the verdict.

"No individual has claimed responsibility for summoning you," Syphus proclaims, projecting his voice in thundering narrative that draws all eyes in the arena. He's enjoying this moment, this theatrical presentation at my expense.

"Andra presents a great risk to Soulbourne," Syphus continues, donning an impassioned, woeful gaze as he twirls to face every section of the arena. "Domain leadership has determined that the most pressing matter is to better understand Andra and the threat her marks pose. As such, the year's Prosphora will be unique." Syphus pauses to smile at me.

There's a cough in the audience, but no one says a word. My ears ring; I feel faint. I stand tall and proud and am the picture of resolute determination, but I look at Syphus and his smug grin and I know that I am about to take a fall.

"This year's Prosphora will not require tributes. The onus on the domains is this: each must prepare a test related to their domain—a high-stakes test that involves a fatal element," Syphus continues. "Andra alone will compete."

Fatal. High stakes. Each domain.

Words float in one ear and out the other, barely registering above my thundering heartbeat.

"We shall see for ourselves whether the prophecies are true, or whether Andra will lose her life in a test. This is the year's Prosphora."

Syphus pauses, and I wait to hear what will happen if I defy the odds and survive. But his oration is complete—I wait with bated breath for a second act that doesn't come.

The roar in my ears is deafening.

There's no need to concoct a hypothetical outcome for my victory, because no one plans to let it happen. Every domain is going to try to kill me. It's not a matter of *if*, but *when*, I will die.

"One test per week," Syphus continues, narrating the logistics of the verdict to the arena. Looking to me: "You may train and move about as you wish."

I fix Syphus with a glare that could cut stone. The fear inside of me yields to anger that rumbles, rippling in waves that threaten to overtake my body. I fan the flames of outrage and channel nervous energy to the more dynamic emotion of the moment.

"And when I conquer each test?"

I have the marginal satisfaction of rendering Syphus speechless. "You told me this wasn't a death sentence," I say, looking to Imara. "What happens when I beat every test?"

A flicker of hesitation, but Syphus will not be upstaged. "At the end of eight weeks, if you've survived every test, you will be free to go."

"And if someone steps forward in that time to admit that they marked me?" I ask. "Will they take my place? Surely if the culprit is found, I can return home."

Syphus doesn't skip a beat. "We will deal with that individual separately. Your task remains the same."

"That hardly seems fair." I raise my voice to make sure everyone can hear me. "I didn't ask for these marks. I haven't even heard the prophecies."

The arena is silent.

Syphus looks up to the leaders, and I know this is something they have not discussed.

"Conquer all eight tests, Andra. Then you can go home."

Goosebumps rise on my flesh at the sound of Achlys' sandpaper voice. The thrust of my shoulders and the lift of my chin suddenly feel fragile. Who am I kidding? The chances of me surviving one test—let alone *eight*—is slim.

"The Land test will be first—you will maintain your current lodging," Perrin declares. It is the closest thing to a dismissal.

I turn to leave and Achlys clears his throat. "I've received reports of trails of glitter throughout the rainforest. You've been here less than 24 hours, but you've been busy, Andra." He doesn't say more, but he watches me, his dark eyes rife with threat.

I don't deny it.

Let Achlys—let all of them—assume what they want. Anything I say or do now might offer information that they can use against me in their test. "Anything else?"

"Not for now. You are dismissed," Achlys says.

No one in the arena moves.

It's unnerving to leave. I wonder if the domains assess my stride, consider my muscle strength and agility as information to use against me in their test design. It's enough to set my teeth on edge.

Buck up, Buttercup.

It's Elara voice that pops into my head. My sister would shrug her shoulders and pledge her absolute confidence in my ability to conquer every test. No setback would impress her: every challenge would be understood to be met, overcome, and destroyed.

Buck up, Buttercup.

I channel Elara's strength as I walk away. Soulbourne's leadership *expects* me to die. It's not the first time I've been underestimated. I find comfort in the fact that they know very little about me.

I lack a great many things, but Elara's voice is a reminder that the most potent weapons I possess are facets of my character. In the absence of advantage, amidst dire circumstances, I still know how to fight like hell.

EIGHT

Lenna and Emberlyn are not in the cabin when I make it back, and Warrick is nowhere to be seen. I'm quietly thankful to be spared a conversation as I stumble towards the bed.

Along the way, I catch a glimpse of myself in the mirror. Lenna lined and lightly shadowed my eyes to make the ice-blue irises pop against dark lashes; my cheekbones sparkle with bronze dusting. My full lips have been painted bright red and my golden hair falls in waves down my back. I might not feel like a force to reckon with, but Lenna effectively dressed me like one.

I don't bother to wipe the makeup off before my head hits the pillow. Today has happened. I know the battle I face. It *sounds* like a death sentence, but I will find a loophole and I will find the courage to fight. Tomorrow.

Now, I just want to escape. Sleep is my willing ally.

When I do wake, it's with the disappointment that I must rise and acknowledge reality—sleep can only shield me from my circumstances for so long. Curled on one side, knees tucked close to my chest, I open my eyes and stare at the wall. I recall the words from the arena. *Fatal element. One test per week. Each domain.*

"Did you...sleep well?" Lenna asks when she sees me awake.

My deep sigh is answer enough.

Lenna offers me a sad smile. "I don't understand why they're doing this."

"They're insane."

"You can do it, you know." Her words are gentle and probing, testing to see where I stand.

"I don't even know what the tests will be. All I know is they're going to try and kill me."

"So don't die."

I look up with irritation. "Right."

"I'm serious. Don't make it more complicated."

"I'm *going* to try." The alternative is actual death.

"Don't just try. Win."

Lenna's ferocity catches me off guard. "Aren't you worried about being here?" I ask. "If they're coming this hard for me..."

Lenna shrugs. "I don't think anyone cares that I'm here. No one suspects me of marking you. I personally think your summons came from a prophecy and not a person."

"What do you mean?"

Lenna takes a deep breath. "This is really Emberlyn's area of expertise."

As if on cue, the door opens. I feel a modicum of relief when I see Emberlyn's hazel eyes and bright freckles.

"We were just talking about the prophecies," Lenna tells her. "Do you think it's possible Andra was summoned by a prophecy, and not a person?"

Emberlyn is silent for a moment as she considers. "It's possible," she agrees thoughtfully. "We should check the book of prophecies in Callings."

A chill creeps up my spine. "There's a book of prophecies? Who makes them?"

Emberlyn looks at me like I'm an idiot. "Prophets."

"But—how do you know they're legitimate? Anyone could say anything," I point out.

Emberlyn shakes her head. "*Prophet* is an esteemed position in Callings, Andra. Prophecies are recorded and when they come to pass, that's recorded, too. Frauds are rare."

"It's not like prophecies are made every day," Lenna adds.

"Not usually," Emberlyn agrees. "There are checkpoints in place to ensure prophets are authentic. Let's go to Callings. You can look at the book of prophecies and we can pick up materials to help you prepare for the first test."

"What does the first test have to do with Callings?"

Emberlyn shrugs. "It's the domain of knowledge—information is a good place to start."

Five minutes and an outfit change later, we're on the trail to Callings. The scenery changes quickly: the incline becomes steep and the path goes from well-finished to rough, with tufts of fluffy grass springing out from the cracks.

"You're taking us the back way," Lenna notes.

"I figured there'd be fewer prying eyes," Emberlyn explains.

"It smells nice." The scent of pine needles and fresh air is like Christmas and sunshine.

"So you *can* smell," Lenna remarks, shooting me a devilish grin. "Just not yourself."

Emberlyn smirks as I smack Lenna's arm, but she has the good sense not to say anything. The path stretches skyward with no sign of plateau.

"What *do* I smell like?"

"You're asking me as we walk up this hill?" Lenna complains. "Emberlyn, how much farther? You didn't mention anything about summiting a cliff."

Emberlyn rolls her eyes. "I'd hardly call this a *cliff*."

Neither Emberlyn nor Lenna answers my question, and I don't press the issue. The answer doesn't feel important—I'm just curious.

The next minutes are spent in silence, a chorus of huffs and puffs the only sound as we climb. I relish the burn of my thighs and the deep inhalations that clear out my lungs. The physical strain pulls my attention away from thoughts of the upcoming tests—I'm centered on the present, focused on the next step.

But then Emberlyn perches triumphantly at the top of the path, and Lenna and I close the distance to join her. We have an incredible view: blue and white wildflowers dot the dry landscape; the sun's warm rays shine on browned blades of grass to cast the hillside in swaths of gold. Even the dirt is pretty—reddish brown meets cinnamon and espresso in gradient swirls.

"Wow," Lenna breathes. I'm inclined to agree.

"It's beautiful, isn't it?" Emberlyn's voice is lush with pride.

Our silent gazes of wonder are answer enough. I marvel at the sound of buzzing bees and the *whoosh* of the wind as it threads through the long grass.

"This is...more remote than I imagined." My eyes rest on the single large building in the distance.

"The monastery," Emberlyn explains. She points to a path leading a different direction. "We're going to follow that trail through the forest to get to Callings."

"Let's keep moving," Lenna interrupts. "The monastery is beautiful, but it's not our destination."

The path down into Callings is difficult at first, but the steep descent and slippery rock eventually give way to a steadier path.

"Stick close," Emberlyn orders as we enter a thicket of trees. When neither Lenna nor I answer, Emberlyn glances over her shoulder. "And don't stare," she barks as we come out the other side.

The buildings in Callings are stone-gray and milk-white and the architecture radiates simple elegance. Heads turn as we pass, and

there's no subtlety to the craning necks and footsteps that pause—
some that stop dead in their tracks.

Heat travels up my body at the reminder that I leave a trail of
gold glitter in an otherwise-colorless backdrop. I'm grateful when
Emberlyn turns around. "Almost there," she promises.

We follow after her as she crosses the street and hurries up the
steps to a large building. I keep my gaze ahead, remembering not
to gawk.

"We're going to pass through security to get into the library,"
Emberlyn whispers as we near the door. It's made of solid white
marble with veins of cream and rose-gold.

I don't have time to question Emberlyn on whether security
might present a problem—Lenna and I exchange a shared look of
concern as Emberlyn heaves the heavy door open.

The energy in the hallway is electric. I feel it like a crack of
lightning the moment we step inside.

The walls are made of white marble; the floor made from a light-
er, purer shade of quartz. I'm not sure how much traffic the library
receives, but it's spotless: there's not a single footprint or speck of dirt.
These details are forgotten the moment my gaze falls upon security.

I'm not sure what I expected, but it wasn't a line of apex predators. A lion, a serpent, a warrior in white, and a winged warrior in
black stand a uniform distance from one another, neatly covering
the space between the front entrance and the door at the other end
of the hall.

"What is this?" Lenna whispers, face an ashy gray.

"Security," Emberlyn answers. "Guardians of the Library."

"How do we ensure they don't annihilate us?" Lenna asks drily.
I would laugh if I wasn't wondering the same thing.

"Can we have this conversation later?" Emberlyn's eyes cut to
the four illustrious figures standing at attention.

"You want me to just walk past?" Lenna asks, incredulous.

"Walk straight and don't make eye contact. Nothing will happen," Emberlyn advises. "They're here to guard the library."

There's a moment of weighty silence, during which the quiet seems to thunder and roar. It's hard not to sneak a glance at the guardians—four lethal figures who have so far not demonstrated any interest in us.

"Let's go, then," Lenna mumbles. "I'll follow you."

Even Emberlyn looks trepidatious as she walks through the chamber. Lenna is quick to trail her, so close to Emberlyn's heels she might trip over the scholar. I fall in line behind.

I keep my head down, nerves intact, for the first half of the hallway. We pass the guardian of light, then the snake. After passing the serpent, though, I become curious.

Contrary to Emberlyn's instructions, my head rises.

I regard the dark guardian first: he's dressed in a midnight-black ensemble of leather and velvet and his cold, steely gaze is directed my way. He doesn't move a muscle, but his hatred is *alive*—it crawls over his skin and heats his exterior; it is a writhing thing that grasps for me in the ten foot gap between us.

Electricity pulsates through my body, the threat noted and received. But I don't feel afraid. Of all the guardians, I find him the least intimidating. My neutral expression tells him as much, and I feel the tendrils of fury radiate anew.

The last guardian, the lion, watches me intently. He looks every bit like a beast of the wild, but as I pass, I know that he, too, is a spirit. There's a sturdiness to him, a dimensionality to his golden fur and regal mane that is at odds with the marble walls. I don't sense any threat as I pass.

As I near the exit, his stately figure shifts. The movement is so minute that for a moment I think I imagine it. But the lion's left paw is slightly raised, and there's something underneath. My gaze snaps up to take in the intensity of the feline's expression.

I don't know *how* I know to create a diversion, but I do.

I trip—on purpose—onto the floor. The fall is real, and the impact of my knees on the cold stone floor stings.

On the ground, from behind my curtain of hair, I see a marble beneath the lion's paw. In the half-second before Lenna and Emberlyn whip around in alarm, the lion nudges it forward.

My sweaty palm presses down over the cool sphere just as Lenna and Emberlyn regard me with wide, frantic eyes.

I scramble to my feet. "I'm okay."

Lenna's eyes stay wide and Emberlyn's mouth opens and closes without making a sound. Her cheeks are flushed and she's visibly flustered, but she waves a hand in gesture to hurry out of the chamber.

"You could have warned us," Lenna fumes the moment we pass through the marble doors. "That is *not* the usual security."

"Sorry." Emberlyn sounds moderately remorseful. "I forget what it feels like for other domains. When you grow up in Callings—especially if you're a scholar—you spend so much time in the library that you get used to it."

Lenna nods to Emberlyn dismissively, her eyes instead fixed upon me and regarding me with open concern. "Andra, are you okay?"

"I'm fine." My fingers curl around the smooth marble and I lie easily. "Just clumsy and nervous."

Lenna nods understanding before pinning Emberlyn with a pointed glare. Emberlyn scoffs but has the decency to look sheepish.

Privately, I wonder about the marble in my palm. *Why did the lion want me to have it? Does it have to do with my mark?*

I'm poised to ask Emberlyn about the guardians when I look up. Veined white marble extends up into the heavens; an enormous skylight bathes the interior with warm, natural light. A chandelier of crystals hangs from the middle, casting prisms of rainbow light across the marble walls in an awesome display of color.

"A gift from Rock," Emberlyn explains, following my gaze.

But my eyes are already wandering to the symmetrical built-in shelves that house row after row of books; books with spines of every color and texture and size. The diversity is striking amidst the uniform bones of the building and the marble staircases that swirl up in curlicues to the uppermost level.

"This way," Emberlyn instructs. The implied message: keep moving.

We follow the scholar up a staircase with neat stone steps that look like teeth. On the third floor, we walk a narrow pathway toward an alcove.

Emberlyn and Lenna don't notice the cat, but I do.

A slate-gray kitty with snow-white paws and sky-blue eyes curls around the nearest bookshelf, tail high and twitching.

I hesitate, reluctant to lag behind. I sense that there is something significant about the feline.

The cat ambles down the opposite path in tidy little steps that cause it to brush up against the titles stacked on the lowest shelf. She never changes course, but when those snow-white paws pause and those sky-blue eyes meet mine in a glance over her shoulder, I know I'm meant to follow.

I should know better by now.

After all, it was foolhardy intuition that landed me in Soulbourne in the first place. But I've come too far to turn back now—if my instincts led me into Soulbourne, maybe they can help me get out.

I don't say anything to Lenna or Emberlyn. In the span of five minutes, I've now made two decisions that would suggest I don't trust the two: first, hiding the marble and now, sneaking away.

I should probably feel a smidgeon of guilt, but I only feel a rush of anticipation and the thrill of intrigue as I break away.

NINE

The cat doesn't turn around.

Its steps are measured but hasty—graceful in the way that only cats can be. Lenna and Emberlyn are oblivious to my change of course. I'm near the periphery of the library when I become aware of voices.

The library is quiet, if not silent, but it's the urgency and tone in which the words are whispered that catches my attention. A bookshelf separates me from the speakers. I hold my breath and mindfully take each step so as to remain undetected.

"You were supposed to kill her."

The words come out in a hiss—a female voice I don't recognize. Goosebumps crop up on my arms and a lump forms in my throat: there's little doubt who they discuss.

"It's too early."

This voice is familiar. My stomach sinks. *Warrick.*

My brain buzzes; my arms and legs tingle as though I'm in a dream and not crouched behind a bookshelf eavesdropping as two individuals plot my assassination.

"The longer you wait, the messier it will get. If you'd killed her last night, we wouldn't still be worrying about the prophecy."

"If I killed her last night, we would still have to worry about the year's terms for the Prosphora."

A derisive snort. "Who cares about the Prosphora? A few insignificant lives is a pittance compared to the damage she'll cause."

I can't decide whether I'm flattered or offended that everyone thinks I'm a major threat with a diabolical plan.

Warrick's words are measured. "She's not going to have the chance to tear Soulbourne apart. Land will design a test that will kill her. If they somehow fail, the next domain will kill her."

"She does have a chance," the woman disagrees. Her voice is low; anger laces her words. "A small chance—an exponentially minuscule chance—but she has a chance. I don't want Andra to have *any* chances."

The buzzing in my head grows louder. It's hard to steady my breath. My heart pounds wildly, throbbing against my chest with such abandon that I half expect it to burst through my skin.

To this last point, Warrick does not have a rebuttal. I sidle up to the bookshelf and attempt to peer through just as the woman exhales sharply.

"We're getting rid of that chance. We'll need to be smart about it—especially now that the public is keen to have her serve as the year's Prosphora tribute."

A blanket of silence falls over the bookcase—the eerie, unsettling kind that comes right before something awful and foreboding happens. I peek through the shelves to find the back of a woman's legs and...Warrick's green eyes, watching me.

I don't have time to consider what Warrick will do; I beat a hasty retreat. My path will be riddled with glitter, I realize as I take a step backwards and land rather unfortunately on the cat's tail.

An angry, shrill meow and an affronted hiss cut through the air. The cat takes off running and I scuffle backwards, nearly tripping over my feet as I turn to run.

There is nothing peaceful or casual about the way I round the corner of the library wing—and collide with Emberlyn.

"Oof!" Emberlyn rockets backward, landing square on her bottom before looking up with irritation. "Where did you go?"

Sweat collects on my neck and armpits and the small of my back. I'm relieved to see Emberlyn and Lenna and I'm antsy to put as much distance between me and the two conspirators as possible. I can't decide if the woman would have the nerve to murder me in the middle of the Callings library, and I don't want to find out.

"I got lost."

I pull Emberlyn to her feet and whisk her down the corridor. Lenna's eyes meet mine in question, but she is quiet.

"I told you to stay right behind me," Emberlyn grumbles, nursing her elbow as she glares my way.

"Sorry."

It's a mumbled apology half-heartedly offered, but Emberlyn rolls her eyes and appears to accept the flimsy excuse. Lenna, on the other hand, does not. Her eyes pin me with a look that is easy enough to discern: *I'm not going to make a big stink about this right now, but I expect answers later.* To keep the momentary peace and to achieve my primary objective of safety, I nod my agreement.

Emberlyn wastes no time in guiding us to a secluded alcove where three hefty tomes sit atop a table. Emberlyn taps her fingers across the covers. "Perrin isn't very creative. I think Land will test your skills in the wild—you'll have to scavenge for food, build shelter, protect yourself...that kind of thing. You should start survival training."

"Some light reading," Lenna quips, nodding to the books.

"The fastest way to learn is to read," Emberlyn snaps defensively.

"But if she's trying to learn survival skills, she needs *actual* practice. Reading won't be enough."

Emberlyn and Lenna continue to discuss my training and preparation, but I can't focus. My eyes dart to the tops of the bookshelves: paranoia builds until I'm sure the two connivers will round the corner at any moment. They have a glitter path to follow, after all.

And Warrick...

"*Andra!*"

When I look up and see the irritation on Emberlyn's face, I know it's not the first time she's said my name.

"Lenna suggested you train with Warrick."

The blood drains from my face. "I have to go to the washroom," I blurt.

"*Now?*"

"Sorry." I don't offer further explanation. My brain and body need to make it onto the same page or I'm going to have a meltdown.

Emberlyn grumbles and points to the corner. I turn to make a beeline for the washroom when Lenna chimes in, "Me, too."

"Seriously?" Emberlyn gripes, and I'm sure her expression is dour. I don't turn around to check, nor do I wait for Lenna.

"What is going on?" Lenna's hair spills over her shoulder as she glances my way, stride long and rushed as she catches up to me.

I mumble a half-hearted excuse, but Lenna is undeterred. She steps in front of me and blocks my path. "Andra, what is it?"

My heart pounds in my chest. There's no way I'll be able to relax in the library, given what I overheard. I look up at Lenna and hold her gaze. Something in my expression softens her—Lenna's brows knit together with concern before she ruefully takes a step back. "Okay, Andra. Let's go to the washroom."

But the washroom is crowded. I pause fifty feet from the entrance and survey the swarm with resignation. Lenna is silent by my side.

I don't have to guess how things will play out. I'll attract attention, courtesy of my ubiquitous trail of gold dust. At no point will I be afforded the opportunity to collect myself.

Nervous energy bubbles inside of me, searching for release. My fingers find the marble in my pocket; I roll the sphere around in my closed palm as I think through my next step.

When a woman looks pointedly at me, I falter. When her gaze

stretches to the ground behind me, to the glittering trail that must extend beyond, I drop the marble.

I knew the marble was special—if for no other reason, because the lion gave it to me—but I am still surprised when it falls to the ground without making a sound.

Surprise turns to astonishment when the marble begins to move: not in a smooth glide, but in a slow and steady scoot reminiscent of a motorized toy. Even more surprising, the marble moves to the side—not straight ahead—to rove between two bookcases.

My eyes slide to Lenna; she meets my gaze and nods. Without speaking, the two of us slip between the bookcases.

The mystic properties of the marble grow undeniable in the moments that follow, when the diminutive sphere travels in zigzag pattern to lead us through shelves of books to finally stop in front of a dilapidated door.

"It looks like a supply closet."

I'm inclined to agree. The gorgeous, creamy white stone walls are severely juxtaposed with the decaying wooden door before us. The black paint is peeling and shards of sharp wood protrude like lances near the edges. The knob is heavily rusted and scuffed.

But the marble sits quietly before the door like a well-trained dog. My eyes meet Lenna's once again. We still don't speak. This time, there isn't as much as a nod exchanged. I pull the sleeve of my shirt down to cover my hand—the last thing I need is to contract tetanus—and grab hold of the knob.

I don't expect to be able to open the door without a struggle. My grip is firm and I'm ready to twist hard. Instead, the knob warms to my touch and opens easily.

My breath hitches, my heartbeat slows. Time suddenly seems dimensional, reduced to a singular plane. The atmosphere is nebulous, dark and thick and foreign and alluring. I feel the pull immediately, a metaphysical hook that sinks into my flesh and yanks me forward.

My prior concerns eviscerate like kindling in the face of a roaring fire: my singular fixation rests on the mystique that lies beyond the rotting door. I don't care about the Prosphora or planned assassination attempts or even Lenna's reaction to what is unfolding in the present moment. I scarcely breathe as I take the first step inside. A part of me is surprised when my feet meet actual floor.

The first thing that hits me is the smell. Wafts of fragrances ply my nostrils, some domineering, others gentle and tentative. The medley of scents is in no way coordinated or complementary, but it doesn't matter. The effect is intoxicating.

The second thing that hits me is the sound. All manner of competing noises trumpet, but just as with the smell, there is no clash. I'm cognizant of the delicate thrum of bumblebees' wings and the brash cry of a raptor and the haunting plucks of a harp string.

And then, in a sudden rush, I'm accosted with a myriad of tastes and tactile sensations. Cool mist and warm embers of flame and nagging itches and icy breezes raise goosebumps on my flesh. I taste cloves and grapefruit and carob and garlic.

The last sense to arrive is sight. The room itself is pitch black— and there's a texture to the room, a depth to the deep onyx that seems to permeate every square inch of space. This black is not a void and it's not a monochromatic backdrop meant to politely color empty space. This black is *alive*, moving and shifting in shades of sable and ebony and soot.

"What is this?" Lenna's question is a murmur, and still her voice sounds discordant against the symphony of senses that saturate the space.

I couldn't answer if I wanted to.

Instead, the room itself seems to respond.

A brilliant landscape of stars glitter above, twinkling white lights that range in size and position and shine. It's impossible to determine the actual dimensions of the room, but the space seems to defy structure—the dazzling sky stretches into the infinite.

There are millions of stars, but my eyes hone in on a particular one—a celestial body that burns with intensity. It seems to radiate light and energy meant for me.

Up until this moment, I've been transfixed, one step inside the door. Without thinking, I step forward, hand outstretched as though to grab hold of the radiant star.

A disorienting rush of things happen all at once.

Later, I will remember the violent rush of wind and the chill that struck my bones and the razor sharp blades that seem to penetrate my midsection and limbs. I will remember the sound of a mournful violin and the smell of roses and the panic that vibrates and rattles through every bone in my body when I hear a shrill cry for my sister, Elara.

I will remember the stars swirling above, an explosion of gold glitter, my eyelids fluttering, and lovely crystals of ice that form on my lashes.

And then, abject darkness.

"Andra."

Lenna's voice is soft, but my name is whispered with enough urgency—and fear—that it slices through the fog of disorientation.

My eyelids feel heavy and my limbs are numb and tingling. When I wrench my eyes open, a punishing headache is quick to greet me. My hand flies to my forehead on instinct, but it's quickly pulled away by Lenna. Her caramel-brown eyes are wide as saucers.

"Get up," she hisses. Her fingernails dig into my flesh, deep enough to break the skin.

I sit up and a wave of nausea roils over me, lurching me forward before Lenna places a protective hand on my lower back. "Stand up," she orders through clenched teeth. "Now."

Heat builds in my body, an awareness that considers what

transpired before I lost consciousness and what might unfold now. I don't waste energy looking; I take Lenna's outstretched hand and stand.

I feel Lenna relax; see the curl of her shoulders and hear the breath that is loosed. "Can you walk?"

I take a tentative step forward and find the nausea quickly ebbs. My gaze travels up to take in the decrepit door and then the illustrious bookshelves and long corridor. My eyes glide to Lenna's in question.

She shakes her head, lips tightly pursed. "I don't know. You just blacked out."

"Did anyone see?"

A small shake of the head. Then: "We've been gone too long. Emberlyn will wonder what happened."

My mind whirs with questions, wonderings that dance and jostle and wrestle for center stage. When my body suddenly stiffens, Lenna nudges me forward.

"Don't worry. I put the marble back."

My fingers fly to my pocket. When I feel the chilled sphere safely ensconced in my palm, I ease into stride alongside Lenna.

We walk the straightaway in silence, both of us left to ruminate over thoughts and questions that neither can answer.

"We won't tell Emberlyn," I say.

Lenna shakes her head. "No."

There's no judgment to her tone, but my heart still sinks. I'm accruing problems and secrets at the speed of light…and I have yet to unearth a single answer. The vestiges of a headache return.

Before we round the corner to Emberlyn, I remember my manners. Lenna pulled me out of that enigmatic room and helped me get back on my feet without attracting attention.

"Thank you."

Lenna's eyes meet mine in surprise, a look that quickly melts into a sheen of stubborn solidarity. "I'm on your side, Andra."

Lenna is one person—one individual from a disreputable domain and without any meaningful influence—but her words hit me deep in my chest. It might be foolish to trust Lenna, in light of the exposed betrayals of the day and the fact that most in Soulbourne hope for my demise, but I see truth in her brown eyes.

In the sea of enemies before me, I badly need an ally.

Emberlyn surprises both of us when she doesn't question us on what took so long. Perhaps we weren't gone for as long as we thought. I'm made to examine a few book titles—tomes Emberlyn determines I would be wise to study—before Lenna worries aloud that it's getting late.

"What about the book of prophecies?"

Now, more than ever, it feels paramount to understand what prophetic words have been spoken.

Emberlyn shakes her head, frowning. "I looked while you two were in the washroom. It's missing."

"What do you mean, it's missing?" Lenna blurts. "I thought the book of prophecies never left the library. It doesn't even leave its alcove."

Emberlyn frowns. "That's correct."

"So somebody took it?" Lenna presses.

Emberlyn bites down on her lower lip. "The guardians wouldn't let it leave the library." She speaks with authority, but there's an edge to her voice that tells me she's trying to convince herself that such a thing couldn't happen.

"Unless the guardians are part of the heist."

Lenna regards me with a solemn expression; Emberlyn looks affronted and then defensive. "The guardians are impartial. It's the reason they were chosen—they've taken a pledge of neutrality. Their only allegiance is to the sanctity of the library."

Emberlyn's proclamation is met with silence. Lenna doesn't yet know where I obtained the marble, but I have irrefutable proof that the guardians are, in fact, capable of biased behavior.

"Maybe it was misplaced," Emberlyn says a moment later, voice hollow. "We can check on the way out."

I nod absently. "Let's do that."

It's the right thing to say, though I know in my heart that the book's disappearance is no accident. Someone wants to deny my access to the prophetic words—and I know at least two library patrons that make for prime suspects.

Emberlyn leads us to an alcove of the library not terribly dignified or resplendent, but set apart for the fact that red velvet ropes secure the perimeter of the bookshelves. A stately podium stands before the entry, a wizened old woman stands guard. Before we can even make it up to the podium, she waves a withered hand in the air, shooing us away. "You can't come in."

"We were just coming to check on the book of—"

"You can't come in. Come back a different day." The woman waves her hand again, as though to shoo off an unwelcome fly.

Emberlyn looks offended, but she doesn't mount further protest. Lenna and I take our cues from Emberlyn, and so our group of three turns and walks towards the exit.

I feel the guardians' eyes shift to regard me the moment we step into the hall. I try to make eye contact with the lion, but while those amber eyes burn with intensity, they refuse to look my way.

The dark guardian is another story—his glower and undiluted hatred are so concentrated on my frame that my skin warms with adrenaline. I quicken my steps, accidentally stepping on the back of Lenna's shoe in my haste. I keep the dark guardian in my periphery, lest he make a move to attack me, but no such thing happens.

Outside, Emberlyn offers us a tight smile. "Stay close," she reminds us.

As we descend the staircase and pour out onto the crowded street, any doubt of being watched vaporizes. I feel a measure of dismay when I spot figures skulking and staring from the shadows. My insides rattle, but I steel my body and keep my head held high.

"Andra!"

My body hollows; the word seems to echo through my bones. I freeze in place before I can find the individual who has called my name. I see Emberlyn stiffen ahead of me; for a fraction of a second, she's still, trying to determine what to do. Lenna tugs on my arm, pulling me forward.

"Andra Bellemere!"

My eyes lock on a hooded figure clad in pearly white robes. His face is shadowed, but two gray-blue eyes shrouded with glaucoma bore into me. There's something arresting in his gaze, but it's not malice. It's not kindness, either.

"Let's go," Lenna hisses, yanking my arm harder. Emberlyn's eyes plead with me to move.

"Andra *Bretton*," I say to no one in particular.

I allow myself to be pulled, though I keep my eyes trained on the man. His words have drawn additional interest; a crush of people circle to hear what the man will say.

He is very, very old. Spit collects on his upper lip as he prepares to speak, his body vibrates in response to some unseen force. A single finger, gnarled and knotted near the knuckle, rises to point at me.

A hush falls over the crowd, and Emberlyn and Lenna finally stop walking. Emberlyn turns, dread written all over her features, to face the man. Lenna looks similarly grim.

"Andra Bellemere."

The man's voice is strong if a bit raspy, but he no longer strains to be heard. He's satisfied with the rapt audience surrounding him, with the fact that I've stopped and directly face him.

"Destiny pulls the woman with the bright star.
The prophetic landscape is true—the reason you were marked.
Beware the one who marked you—it wasn't done for your acclaim.
No matter how you move forward, the danger remains the same.
You will travel far, Andra, and you will do it alone.
You will need to go beyond if you are ever to return home.
Choose your help wisely: it is the difference between life and death
Without intervention, you will die in the Land test."

The air around me seems to be stripped of oxygen.

"Breathe," Emberlyn orders, her face gray. "Andra, breathe."

I blink.

I will die. Without intervention, I will die. The words roil through me with the vengeance of a hurricane.

"Walk," Emberlyn commands.

I walk.

The hairs on the nape of my neck stand at attention as we pass the throng of people.

They stare.

No one touches me, but by the time we reach the end of the street, I feel grimy and sullied, as though each individual personally defiled me.

"Can we walk faster?" Lenna asks.

Emberlyn doesn't answer, but she picks up the pace.

After we leave the main hub of Callings, the space between buildings widens and the clusters of people thin. There's no point at which I relax, but my chest isn't as heavy and my breathing comes easier when the crowds disappear. Then the distance between buildings grows larger still, and soon there aren't any buildings at all—only an expanse of grass that adheres to Callings' sandy-brown color scheme.

"Do you know who that was?" Lenna asks when we're alone.

"A prophet." Emberlyn doesn't elaborate.

"But do you *know* him?" Lenna presses.

"I've seen him before. I've never seen him prophesy."

The small elaboration changes the tenor of the silence. I contemplate what this might mean as Emberlyn drives a blistering pace back to Land.

"Did he—have to do that?"

I think of the milky, rheumatoid-ridden eyes that seemed to look right through me and the gnarled, knotted finger pointed straight at my chest. It felt personal.

Emberlyn's quiet at first. She looks over her shoulder to find my eyes.

"I don't know that he *had* to, but he likely felt *compelled* to. When a prophet gets something, it's like a burning rock in their hands. They're overwhelmed with sensation and the need to share their word."

"Who gives them the word?" Lenna glances my way before launching into her next question. "Who told him to say that?"

"Who tells a flower it's time to bloom? Who tells a human to fall in love? Who tells a person that they like one food, but not another? It's one of life's mysteries," Emberlyn says. "I don't pretend to understand it, but when you've grown up around it, you appreciate that it's real."

"Am I supposed to understand what he meant? Because that was about as helpful as learning that I've been marked." I laugh, but it's raw and shallow. "And he got my last name wrong."

Neither girl answers.

"We're not far from Land," Emberlyn announces instead.

"We're going to make it back before dark," Lenna says with relief, looking towards the sky.

There's no talking the final stretch back.

When we near the cabin, I barrel inside and stretch out on the rug in front of the fireplace. I don't want to stand up and I don't want to sit down and so I lay down on my back and begin to process the day's events.

Lenna and Emberlyn are politely quiet. I hear the sound of running water from the washroom and the *clinks* and *clanks* of cutlery as food is prepared. I stare up at the ceiling and try to empty my mind.

When darkness descends over the cabin, I shower. I'm grateful for the hot water that soothes my muscles and stings in delightful distraction from the cacophony of thoughts. I scrub my arms and legs, aware that I am doing more than just rinsing my body.

Someone—most likely Lenna—has set out a fresh set of pajamas. Enrobed in slippery silk, I feel settled at last.

I finally feel ready to discuss what happened, and it's a good thing, because Emberlyn and Lenna both sit expectantly at the dining table. There's a sizable spread of food, but nothing has been touched. I find my seat at the bench and accept the plate they pass my way.

"Okay. Let's talk."

TEN

"The guardians," I begin. The topic feels like a warm-up, something that isn't one hundred percent centered on me.

"Did you look at them?" Lenna asks.

Emberlyn looks up in alarm. "I told you not to," she scowls.

"Who appointed them?" I ask, ignoring Lenna.

Emberlyn's countenance is laced with suspicion, but she begrudgingly answers, "Two are from Underworld and two are from Overworld. I don't know how they were picked. They were instated for the library's protection a long time ago."

My fingers tighten around the marble in my pocket. I'm aware of Lenna's scrupulous gaze and Emberlyn's furrowed brow and work to maintain a blank expression. "What exactly do they guard?"

Lenna laughs. "The books, obviously."

Emberlyn's silence is loud. Lenna's laughter dies on her lips as she looks to the scholar with interest. "What else do they guard?"

Emberlyn's gaze is downcast; she clears her throat. "They *are* there to guard the books," she begins, and Lenna and I exchange a quick look. "But they supposedly guard other things, too."

My breath hitches and I feel Lenna's eyes bore holes through my forehead. I know what she's thinking, and I wonder the same thing: are the guardians there to guard that mystical room?

"Like what?" I ask, and my voice sounds scratchy.

Emberlyn sighs. "This is purely speculative." She waits for me to recant the question, but I'm too invested. Lenna sucks in a breath and Emberlyn continues reluctantly, "*supposedly*, there's a prophetic landscape somewhere in the library."

A prophetic landscape? What does that even mean?

Lenna and I sit in stupefied silence, a cue Emberlyn misreads. "Like I said, I haven't seen any of this. It's probably just Callings' lore." She laughs self-consciously. "No better than the tale that the guardians were appointed after Achlys' wife was killed."

I blanch. "Achlys was *married*?" I can't imagine the person who would catch the leader of Underworld's eye...and I *really* can't imagine an individual who would agree to wed him.

Lenna nods, though her gaze travels to the scholar. "Didn't he kill his wife?" she asks quietly. "That's the rumor that circulates in Boundless, anyway."

Emberlyn frowns. "There's no proof of anything."

Her meaning is abundantly clear; the implication chilling.

"But they found her body, right?" Lenna presses.

"They did," Emberlyn agrees. "Minus the—"

"Eyeballs," Lenna interjects. "Right? They found her body without eyeballs, and Achlys has been obsessed with eyes ever since."

A shiver of revulsion wracks my body. I look to Emberlyn with disgust.

"It's true." Emberlyn's grimace shows she finds the subject matter just as gruesome.

"Some say he's obsessed with eyes because they tell the truth," Lenna continues a bit breathlessly. "But it's actually because of what happened to his wife."

Emberlyn shoots her a pointed look. "That's a rumor."

Lenna flushes. "It's a *theory*," she corrects. "The *rumor* is that he

79

enlisted the help of a dark witch in Underworld to put a spell on the eyes, to preserve them forever and imbue them with magic."

My nose wrinkles. "Why would he do that?"

"It's *Achlys*. Your guess is as good as mine," Lenna scoffs.

One look at Emberlyn and her tightly pursed lips and I know I won't get an answer. I'm not sure what to make of all of Boundless' rumors, but I do want to better understand the guardians. Maybe it will help me to figure out why the lion gave me the marble.

"And the guardians stay in the library twenty-four-seven?" I ask, trying to get Emberlyn back on track.

The scholar studies me. "Did you look at the guardians?"

I'm saved from answering. The sound of boots on the deck sends nerves racing up my spine like lightning.

"Someone's here," Lenna hisses.

"It could be the guard," Emberlyn hedges half-heartedly.

Neither girl looks poised to move, so I grab a knife from the table and move soundlessly to the deck door. Another scrape of boots sends my heart to my throat. I force myself to take a deep breath, then another. I see the corner of a muddy brown boot and spring into action.

I launch onto the deck. The butter knife is thrust before me, firmly clasped with both hands.

It's Warrick.

Too late, I realize it's Warrick. The realization carries a myriad of emotions.

I have already jumped—and I now see the knife for what it is and how it looks: like I'm a five year old with a toy sword. But Warrick sees my face—and whatever is written on it—and knows that I was serious. That I meant to be intimidating.

His green eyes dance with yellow-flecked light and the corners of his mouth twitch. He doesn't move one inch as a result of my confrontation.

The adrenaline fades, and my fear is chased away by irritation when I realize that, whatever his ultimate motive might be, Warrick has not come to kill me. "Why are you prowling around on the deck?"

The twitching of his lips stops; it's replaced by a smile.

For a moment, I'm caught off guard—it's the first time I've seen Warrick smile, and he looks nice. Friendly, even.

He was hired to kill you, I remind myself.

"Is this butter knife some strange invitation to join you for a meal? Because I could use a bite to eat," Warrick quips. Lenna and Emberlyn giggle traitorously from inside the cabin.

My scowl darkens. "Why are you here?"

"I'm here to protect you, Andra," Warrick answers easily. "With more than a butter knife."

I roll my eyes and staunch the urge to call bullshit. He can't be so delusional as to think I didn't see him—we literally locked eyes in the library. There's scant chance he missed the trail of gold glitter. So what game is this that we're playing, and for whose benefit?

"Where have you been?" The words are casual, but Warrick's answer will be telling.

"I'll answer you, if you'll first answer me: after that hop and point maneuver, what exactly did you plan to do?"

My cheeks flame. "You're insufferable."

Warrick's mouth twists to the side in a smirk. I bristle as he takes a step forward, tense as his arm brushes mine. "You're not holding it right, anyway."

"She needs training," Lenna calls from inside. I take the opportunity to step back, creating a healthy distance between Warrick and me.

"That's the other reason I'm here," Warrick says. He shifts his weight away from me casually, but I know he understood the slight.

"You're going to train her?" Lenna asks, walking over to join us on the deck.

Cold dread sweeps over my body at the thought of alone time with Warrick—a notorious Boundless fighter with plans to kill me. "That's not a good idea."

"Warrick is the best. If he's willing to train you…" Lenna's eye-

81

brows rise to emphasize her point.

Warrick doesn't correct Lenna. His eyes flick to me in question. "No."

From the table inside, Emberlyn snorts.

Warrick levels me with his eyes. "Tomorrow morning. Five AM. Dress in athletic clothes—no clingy skirts and crop tops."

The skin on the back of my neck warms and my nostrils flare as I narrow my eyes at Warrick. "I said *no*."

"Lenna's right—Warrick is the best. You're not going to find anyone better." Emberlyn looks at me like I'm an idiot, but Lenna's gone quiet. She watches me silently, her expression hosting a litany of unspoken questions.

"It doesn't matter if he's the best if I can't trust him." My eyes glitter with intensity as I meet Warrick's gaze and don't look away.

Warrick's eyes hold mine. "If you're smart, you'll have realized by now that you can't trust anyone in Soulbourne."

A shiver of fear races down my spine; a reflex I do well to hide. Warrick didn't deny the fact that he couldn't be trusted—he just deflected.

"I'll be outside if you change your mind." Warrick holds my gaze. "If I wanted to kill you, Andra, I would have already done it." With that, he slips out the door.

For a moment, no one speaks.

"Do we know why Warrick is helping you?" Emberlyn asks carefully.

I sigh. If the last twenty-four hours have had any effect, it's to make me morbidly aware of how unprepared I am for just about *everything* in Soulbourne. I vacillate between wanting to give up—owning up to the fact that I am in way over my head—and fighting to believe I might succeed.

"He's outside listening," I remind her. I clear my throat and force a smile. Enough about Warrick—I need to prepare for my first test. "What can you teach me about survival off the land?"

Emberlyn, to her credit, reads the situation for what it is. "The

Land domain is split into ecosystems—Desert, Mountains, Jungle, Forest, Plains, Canyon, and Tundra." She pauses. "What kind of ecosystem did you live in back home?"

The next three hours are spent discussing crucial survival elements of Desert, Mountains, and Jungle. I'm relieved to find that some of the information is familiar—while Soulbourne itself is foreign, the land itself still operates on the fundamental principles with which I am well versed.

By the time we discuss Jungle, some of my confidence has been restored. There's a hum of hope in my chest as I brush my teeth and wash my face and then slip under the covers. I have a long ways to go, but I am not hopeless. Maybe I can do this.

A knock stirs me from my sleep. I'm groggy and bone-tired as I blink into pale gray light—the sun isn't up, but it will be soon. I pad to the deck door and find Warrick.

"Get dressed. Pull your hair back. No breakfast." Warrick's directives are crisp, as though I am a petty officer and he is my general.

"I told you yesterday: *no.*"

Warrick doesn't respond. Instead, there is a *thump* on the deck as he drops a pile of clothes.

Irritation prickles my spine. Who does Warrick think he is? I turn on my heel and climb back into bed.

It doesn't take long to realize that I won't be able to fall back asleep. I can lay in bed to spite Warrick, but it won't win me answers and it won't build my skills. I'd be a fool to trust him, but I don't imagine Warrick will dispatch me in plain sight. If I'm clever, perhaps I can play *him.*

I dress quickly in the leggings and loose cotton shirt left on deck.

I pull my hair back into a high, sweeping ponytail and step outside, where Warrick is waiting.

"I'm here for as long as I decide. If you pull anything, I'm gone," I warn.

"Yes ma'am. And, you'll run me through with a butter knife. Threat received," Warrick says with a straight face.

I cast a withering gaze Warrick's direction and roll my eyes.

"We'll run through Land, then pass through the arena to get to Boundless. Ready?"

If Warrick isn't going to give an inch, neither will I. "Ready."

Warrick doesn't waste time—as soon as the word rolls off my lips, he jerks his head towards the path and turns on his heel. With heart pounding in my chest, I follow.

Warrick is a taskmaster.

We run for over an hour—brushing past every ecosystem of Land—as Warrick narrates survival strategies and points out notable land features in diligent fashion that suggest he might actually want me to beat the Land test.

"That's strychnos." Warrick points to a tree with golden fruit. "It looks edible, but it's incredibly poisonous. If it comes into contact with your blood, it'll kill you. If you ingest it, it'll asphyxiate you."

I crane my neck to get a good look at the plant as we run past. Warrick doesn't slow down. "You're keeping up," he notes with approval a moment later. "Better than expected."

I don't have breath to spare for a snarky reply.

A wave of relief washes over me when Warrick slows his jog. Running itself was a challenge, but running through the ecosystems added complexity: some were arid, some frigid, some humid—as soon as my body adjusted to one, we moved into another.

The sun hasn't yet appeared, but the grays of an hour ago have brightened into hues of lemon and peach. Warrick nods his head to the tunnel leading out of Land. "We'll walk to Boundless." He throws a cursory glance over his shoulder to make sure I follow. "I want to cross before the sun is up."

We traverse the path in silence, but when we near the tunnel, I snap to attention. It doesn't matter that we're not headed into the actual arena; the fact that we're in the vicinity makes my blood chill.

It's a good thing Warrick leads the way, because none of the paths are marked. There are no signs in Soulbourne—the assumption is that you know where you're going or are with someone who does. After only 36 hours in the realm, I've learned enough to guess where each path leads.

Where Land has soft, nutrient-rich soil and Callings a smart, concrete path lined with neat curbs, Water has sand, Rock has smooth, speckled granite and Air has polished cloud agate that looks like the heavens themselves.

Boundless is distinguished by the chaotic crush of material that makes up its path. Chunks of asphalt, sand, broken shells, mulch, dirt, and who-knows-what-else lie at odds with one another, the path dimensional in a way that none of the others are. Boundless is a domain that doesn't fit a neat mold—even its path celebrates discordance. There are no paths to Overworld or Underworld.

"If we encounter anyone, don't talk." This pronouncement is followed by the crunch of gravel and asphalt under Warrick's boots.

The land is dry and rocky to start. Generally, the people we pass on Boundless' path don't pay us much attention. Most individuals travel solo, and there's not a lot of eye contact. A wide berth is given when paths cross. I find that *I'm* the one sneaking surreptitious, side-long glances.

There are dreadlocks and shaved heads and ponytails and long, tight curls. There are colorful smocks and loose trousers and tight mesh. There are chunky shoes and leather sandals and bare feet that don't flinch under the sharp path. Each individual is so unique that I find myself wondering about their back story. It's a foregone conclusion that everyone in Boundless has a story.

We pass concrete dwellings adorned with graffiti and beautiful plazas with large, classical fountains and two-story brick buildings draped with trumpet vines and honeysuckle and lush ivy. Each block seems to contrast with the next, the artistic juxtaposition curious. Boundless oozes character.

"This way." Warrick guides us down a dark alley with slate-gray cement slab walls and long shadows that provide a measure of cover before stopping abruptly.

"Is this where you plan to kill me?" The words are out before I have the chance to consider them.

Warrick flinches, a subtle tension in his shoulders that he is quick to hide. He turns slowly. "I already told you, Andra: I'm not going to kill you."

"Yet. You're not going to kill me *yet*."

A muscle in Warrick's jaw twitches. He regards me with a solemn expression. "You don't know what you saw in the library."

"Why don't you tell me what I saw?" I fold my arms over my chest protectively.

"You need to trust me."

I roll my eyes and shake my head in disgust, then glance over my shoulder as I consider whether I should just walk away.

"If you really thought I was going to kill you, why did you come with me?" Warrick's tone is matter-of-fact, but his green eyes smolder.

I don't answer at first.

It's a fair question—one I've already asked myself. I meet Warrick's gaze and hold it. "I'm not convinced it's preferable to die in the Land test." Not exactly true, but it's better to offer a pithy reply than to try to articulate the nebulous of my subconscious.

Warrick's expression is inscrutable. "What did you find in the library?"

I scoff; an incredulous huff that comes with arched eyebrows and a reproving shake of the head. "You can't be serious."

Warrick shrugs. "You want answers from me, but you're not offering anything in return."

"You are plotting to *KILL* me." I shake my head in disbelief. The conversation is so ridiculous that it should be funny, but instead I feel a pang of despair. My resolve might be ironclad, but I'm ill-equipped to vanquish Soulbourne.

"Quiet."

Warrick's word is sharp enough that I freeze in place. His eyes track the movement of something behind me; I twist to look over my shoulder. In the stretch of silence that follows, my nerves are wound tight as a boxer braid. I can hear my own heartbeat; I will my breath to submit to silence.

There isn't anything that I can see. The silence itself seems to serve as damning indication that something is amiss. Loathe to keep my back to Warrick, I edge up against the alley wall.

"Someone's here."

Warrick's murmur is low, his tone giving nothing away. The hairs on the back of my neck stand on end, my eyes work to make sense of the blank space in front of me. As much as I'd like to also perceive the threat Warrick ascertains, I don't sense a thing.

Warrick's movements are languid, his stride long as he closes the distance to the end of the alley, skulking along in a manner that opens a new vein of fear inside my chest. Before, it was up to my imagination to picture Warrick's threat; now, I have my first hint of just how much danger he presents.

For a moment, I consider running. But then a fist closes around my ponytail and a dagger is pushed against the soft skin of my neck. *Impossible*, I think, even as I feel the blade's tip chafe against the flesh below my jaw. *There wasn't anyone else in the alley.*

My assailant is slow to speak, though the implied directive of the knife is that I keep my mouth shut and stay put.

"Your test will take place in three days. Details will be given at a banquet tomorrow."

The voice is nondescript, the words spoken like a threat. I don't move. My brain works at a frenzied pace to try to understand what is happening and why.

From the end of the alley, Warrick senses something is amiss.

His shoulders tense and his frame goes utterly still before he whips around. A half-second later, he sprints towards us.

The knife at my neck is removed and I'm pushed forward. There's enough force behind the action that I barely have time to throw my arms out to cushion the impact against concrete. My head whips around to watch a figure scale the alley wall with the ease of a spider monkey, then jerks back when I hear a modest *plunk*. The fall dislodged the marble from my pocket, where it now buzzes to life to reprise the motorized scoot first debuted in Callings' library.

"Are you okay?"

Warrick stands above me, words tight and gruff. I throw a quick glance his direction to catch the consternation on his face and what looks to be genuine concern.

"Fine." I brush off my hands and watch the marble's journey with increasing anxiety. There's no way to reclaim it without attracting attention.

"I don't know who that was. Did you see their face?"

I shake my head and stand up, sneaking a surreptitious side step closer to the marble.

Warrick shakes his head, blowing out air as he runs a hand through his hair. "They might not be alone. We should—"

I don't have to look at Warrick's face to know he's spotted the marble. I know what the next question is going to be and I have about a second to decide my strategy.

"Where did that come from?"

My eyes drag up to meet Warrick's with reluctance. It doesn't matter what words come out of my mouth; my eyes have already incriminated me.

"My pocket."

Warrick's eyes flare slightly, the only sign of surprise before he schools his features into nonchalance. "Who gave it to you?"

He does not, notably, ask me *what* it is. I mark this fact as interesting and shrug. Warrick will know I'm dodging the question, but this answer feels far more scandalous than my first admission.

The marble continues its regulated path deeper down the alley, completely unbothered by the fact that no one trails behind. I still don't know precisely what the marble does, but it has undeniable power and I have no intention of letting it go. When I move to follow the marble, Warrick is right by my side.

Progress down the alley is marked by silence—the only sound comes from our scuffled footsteps. When the marble stops in front of a sewer grate, I lurch forward, fearful that the sphere will slip through the grating and disappear.

The marble doesn't budge, though—it's as though it's glued to the ground. My fingers pull and pry, but it's impossible to dislodge. It increases in temperature, too—the chilled sphere quickly grows uncomfortably hot. I squint between the lattices of the sewer, curious to see if there's something of significance that lies beyond. It's too dark to note anything of consequence.

When I turn back to Warrick, the first thing I notice is his posture: rigid like a statue. From my low position crouched on the ground, my gaze travels up to take in the pinched expression on his face. "What's wrong?"

But Warrick doesn't hear me. His glazed expression is fixed on the marble, or maybe the sewer grating.

In the absence of a response, my hand reaches out to jostle the bars of the grating, to see if it will move. The grate isn't large, but it's wide enough for a body to pass through.

When my fingers wrap around the grating and I start to pull, Warrick springs into action.

"Don't do that." His arm is on my shoulder, pulling me back.

"Why?"

"It's not safe." Warrick's expression is haunted, a fact that should register as a resounding warning. In light of the circumstances, I'm intrigued.

"Nowhere in Soulbourne is safe."

My fingers tighten around the grating; when I tug, it comes up easily. The marble moves forward an inch and I shift my body closer. I still can't see much—just shades of gray and black.

"Andra."

Warrick's voice sounds pained. Given everything that has happened in Soulbourne, I can't understand why my current position above a sewer grate qualifies as most distressing.

"You don't have to come."

The marble's message is clear, and I'm serious about wriggling inside the sewer to see what's below.

"It's Underworld," Warrick warns.

This, more than Warrick's reaction or the unsavory company of a few moments ago, gives me pause. I remember Achlys and the creatures by his side in the arena. I remember Lenna's words: *No one goes to Underworld and comes out.*

As if reading my thoughts, the marble hums to life once more, motoring towards the sewer. When it tips over the precipice, I don't hesitate.

ELEVEN

I'm plunged into darkness.

The descent is gradual—I slide more than I fall. It's damp. I feel a chill penetrate my modest attire, and when I take a breath, there's the distinct smell of smoke.

I land in a chamber cloaked in midnight black, my bottom crashing into stone and sharp, cantankerous gravel. In a space so devoid of light, it's hard to gather my bearings. The first thing my eyes spot is the marble—the smooth sphere seems to glow as it continues forward.

Not a second later, Warrick crashes into me. I let out an undignified *oof* as the upper half of my body snaps forward in response. I glare over my shoulder, trusting that the white slits of my eyes will send the appropriate message, even in the dark. My insides churn in response to the unsettling contrast of temperatures and the penetrating effect of total darkness.

"Try not to speak."

Warrick's murmur is low; the warmth of his breath sends an unwelcome shiver up my spine.

I stand and brush off the rubble affixed to my backside. The rock of the underground cavern is damp and chilly, but the smell of smoke is undeniable and the tang of burning wood—and something else—stings my nostrils and makes my eyes water.

I clutch Warrick's arm and point to the marble before taking a step forward. He doesn't protest.

I feel, rather than see, when we leave the chamber. The air becomes thicker. Long, lazy plumes of smoke tumble and somersault in intricate patterns. The graphite gray of the smoke is only marginally contrasted to the stygian black of the cavern.

When the marble makes a distinct move to the left, Warrick's revulsion is evident. "We shouldn't go that way." Warrick breaks his own rule to make this pronouncement in a thin, tight voice.

My eyes glance to the marble, assured in its motorized scoot forward. "If you know something I don't, now would be a good time to tell me."

In the silence that follows I can imagine Warrick's face—his jaw grinding in anguish and maybe irritation. In the end, he says nothing. Even without seeing him, I feel his diminished stature as we proceed.

When a set of eyes in the wall blink open, I gasp and jump a foot to the side—an action that sends me slamming into the opposite wall. I have no time to recover before a second set of eyes—this pair, inches away—blink open.

My skin crawls and my heart thunders as pair after pair of eyes blink open, jaundiced yellow orbs replete with melancholy. The irises are different, as are the size and shape of each pair. But the expression is the same: hatred mixed with deep despair.

The hallway of eyes is long, and as the irises glare, they give off enough light for me to see Warrick. He doesn't look surprised; his eyes meet mine with resignation. A wave of understanding washes over me. "You've been here before."

Warrick offers a resigned nod.

"When—how…" My words are fumbled as my brain works to pinpoint the most important question.

Warrick glances to the wall of eyes. "Not now."

"Do you know where we're going?" I whisper.

Warrick nods but doesn't say a word.

With downcast gaze, I follow the marble. I work hard to avoid meeting every pair of eyes, though I feel the judgment and hatred that each set projects.

"YOUUU!"

The word is screeched, the words quickly complemented by two scarred hands that wrap possessively around metal bars.

I yelp and jump back before reclaiming my dignity. I try to appear composed, but my limbs shudder.

"I know who you are."

The words are spoken like a threat, or maybe a curse. The woman spits her disgust and for a moment I am frozen in place, unsure whether the woman is deranged, lying, or if she really might know who I am and why I'm here.

"Keep moving, Andra." Warrick, at least, is unaffected by the display. "We're going to pass a lot of cells," he adds.

I cast a sidelong glance at the woman, the scarred hands that have my stomach in knots. *Focus on the marble. Keep moving.* I swallow hard and keep my gaze trained on the ground. My limbs tremble, and I rub my hands along my arms as though I'm merely cold and not terrified. There are no further outbursts.

Farther down the hallway, heat begins to build.

At first I think it's the result of adrenaline, my body's reaction to stress. When the curls of smoke become thicker, I know there's more at play. When a voice addresses me, all doubt vanishes.

"Andra. I wondered when we might meet again."

The voice sounds like chains and smoke and gravel—all elements I picked up on during our first meeting in the arena, but attributes that make perfect sense now that I've entered Underworld.

Achlys' effect on me in this moment is no different than when we first met—my blood runs cold and my heart stalls. I have the urge to run and hide and freeze all at the same time.

"You brought Warrick with you."

Achlys' next statement is followed by low laughter, a sound reminiscent of hissing snakes and the low growl of a predator. Beside me, Warrick is tense—but he's been that way since we first ventured into Underworld.

"To what do I owe the pleasure?" Achlys asks. I still can't spot the domain leader in the darkness.

"We're not staying." Warrick speaks for both of us, and though I may be scared sideways, he sounds regulated.

"Of course not. You'd have to be invited—or *imprisoned*—to do so. And who could forget your last visit?"

The words are spoken in low vibrato, and I'm suddenly light-headed from the smoke and the darkness and the uncertainty over whether I can trust my senses or my brain or really anything at all. That, and Warrick's silence is disconcerting.

When neither of us respond, Achlys laughs. The hissing-and-growl sound makes my blood pressure skyrocket. A cloud of gray smoke billows into the space between us; when it clears, the chamber is morbidly lit by eyes that peer out from the walls.

Across the room, Achlys sits on a throne of bones—a throne centered over a robust black flame. The gray smoke curls in all directions from the fire, the tendrils adopt moody and foreboding shapes before they settle like fog at the bottom of the room.

Achlys is still a shadow, but his smile is easy to spot. "Why did you come here, Andra?"

It seems unwise to ignore Achlys, though I don't have a great answer. I swallow roughly. "My marble?"

Achlys' smile grows wider. There's a blur of movement, and a moment later, the subtle lighting of the creepy eyes is enhanced by green and purple flames that materialize around the perimeter of the room. The eyes can now be placed—some belong to creatures and others to humans shackled to the walls.

A shudder of revulsion ripples through me. I take an involuntary step away from the wall—and the eyes—and find myself nearer to Achlys.

"Your *marble*."

Achlys nods his head to the floor below, to the smooth sphere just feet away. The marble is frozen in place, seemingly content to keep company with evil. I question whether I really want it, if it thought to lead me to *Underworld*, but I reach down to pluck it up. It comes easily, and I drop it into my pocket. Achlys watches my every movement with unconcealed fascination.

The attention of Achlys was disquieting in the arena, but it's especially jarring here, in the landscape of smoke and bones and tormented prisoners. "Who are they?" I ask.

Achlys doesn't register any reaction. His black eyes settle on mine and his hands grip the armrests of his chair—*bones.* He flexes his fingers before gripping the bones so tight that cords of muscle appear in each digit.

My breath catches. Beside me, Warrick stiffens. But then, for no apparent reason, the tension is defused and Achlys crosses one leg over the other in nonchalant fashion.

"Individuals who have crossed me."

I grimace. My fingers curl around the marble in my pocket, perhaps for strength to ask the obvious next question. "What does it mean to cross you?"

Achlys casts a disinterested glance to the figures shackled to the wall and sighs. A fat, yellow-and-black serpent slithers past his feet and up the leg of the chair. "Anything that causes my displeasure." There's no shame in his voice, no attempt to qualify his statement.

I'm suddenly very aware of the flames that encircle me, the eyes that watch me, the lethal creatures that I see and the ones that I don't that hover in close proximity to a man who oozes malice. The fear must be written in my eyes, because Achlys shakes his head. "If I wanted you imprisoned, Andra, it would have already happened. Ask Warrick."

My brow furrows. *Why spare me?* I have clearly caused Achlys displeasure.

"Ask the question." Achlys' voice is low but full of authority.

"What?" My voice comes out tremulous.

"We both know what you're wondering. Ask."

I hesitate. "Why haven't you imprisoned me?" The words taste like dust on my tongue.

Achlys smiles, cocking his head to the side and tenting his fingers before him like he's studying an ancient rune or maybe thinking through his next move in a game of chess. "Because I can't."

Of all the answers Achlys could have given, this is one I didn't expect. I stand in stupefied silence.

"I carry immense power in Soulbourne." Achlys speaks in slow, deliberate manner—his words laced with bitterness. "But even I am bound by the laws of our realm. You have been marked. At the moment, I cannot touch you."

My eyes pull away from Achlys' only to look to Warrick for confirmation. His jaw is tight, his features stern. He nods.

"Now that you've collected your *marble*, you may leave." Achlys' words are diplomatic, but the tone laced in each one is clear: Get. Out.

I turn to leave. We've used up our tenuous goodwill in Underworld and I can't wait to be above ground. Damn my marble and damn my curiosity. Warrick was right—we never should have come. "How do we get out?"

"Warrick knows."

Achlys' words are dismissive, and even before he's finished speaking the flames die down and a blanket of darkness cloaks the room once more. The sinister effect of Underworld is amplified when I consider that Achlys still watches us, though we can't see him.

"Keep your head down," Warrick mutters.

Achlys' laugh skitters over the dying flames, sending fresh plumes of dove-gray smoke swirling our direction.

"Think carefully before you make another trip into Underworld. These eyes will not forget your face—and they will hate you forever for the fact that *you've* been allowed to walk free."

With that, Achlys snaps his fingers. I didn't think it possible, but the darkness becomes even more absolute—even the gray tendrils of smoke disappear. Gnashing teeth and cries of despair steal the sensory spotlight as Warrick and I take our first step down the perilously long hallway. The warmth of the flames has vanished; it is replaced by a dank, bone-chilling frost.

Warrick reaches over to take my hand. "Let's get out of here."

TWELVE

The walk out of Underworld is a punishment, the path dark and foul-smelling and cold. The sounds and smells alone are enough to give me nightmares. When we emerge above ground, the taste of smoke and ash is thick on my tongue.

As we walk back to Land, I don't say much. My subconscious works double-time to process the events of the past hours. *Who held me at knife-point in the alley? Why warn me about the banquet? Better yet: why host a banquet at all? Is the marble an asset or a liability? Why did it lead me into Underworld? Was Achlys expecting me?*

My mind swims and my legs feel like lead by the time we make it back to the cabin. I still haven't said a thing to Warrick.

"We should talk."

The words belong to Warrick, and they catch me off guard. I look up, and Warrick meets my gaze with reservation.

"You think we should talk," I parrot back, tone flat.

Warrick shifts uncomfortably. "I'm sorry."

"For what?" I ask, and I genuinely want to know. Is the apology for collaborating to assassinate me, for withholding information, or for something else entirely? I don't even know where Warrick planned to take me before the marble hijacked our agenda.

"All of it?"

He's poised to say more, but I shake my head. "I need time to think." I climb the steps to the cabin without looking back.

The scene inside is comforting. Lenna and Emberlyn both sit at the dining table, Lenna stitching gorgeous, juniper-green silk and Emberlyn with her nose buried in a book.

Emberlyn takes one look at me and asks, "What happened?"

"I was held at knifepoint in Boundless—apparently, there will be a banquet tomorrow to announce the premise of the Land test." I deliver the update matter-of-factly, neatly omitting the detour to Underworld and the guidance of the marble. "I'm going to shower," I mumble before either has the chance to ask further questions.

Safely tucked in the washroom, I peel off my dirty, sweaty clothes and take down my hair. The first streams of hot water hit my body and I luxuriate in the steam and warmth and comfort. When I emerge ten minutes later, I feel fresh. Tired, but revived.

Warrick sits with the girls at the table eating heartily. Lenna nods to a plate that's been prepared for me. I sit at the table to eat food I don't have an appetite for. My gaze lands on the stack of titles Emberlyn has accrued for my benefit: books on poisons, edible plants, natural disasters, building shelters...

"You should start with the book on poisons. I flagged the pages I thought were most important," Emberlyn says.

The next hours are spent reviewing threats in the ecosystems. After I'm keenly aware of the many terrible, painful ways I could experience injury or death, we move to survival techniques.

Emberlyn is a patient teacher: she offers a high level summary before diving into specifics, then offers examples before moving to the next topic. Every so often she circles back to quiz me on a former concept. Lenna chimes in occasionally, but mostly she's content to sit companionably while she sews. I don't know what she has planned, but the fact that more fabric is involved is a very good sign. Warrick stands guard on the back porch, his silhouette illuminated as afternoon turns to evening, which turns to night.

By the end of the night, I've ingested a copious amount of information. Emberlyn is pleased.

"I'm going back to Callings tomorrow," Emberlyn says when I make for bed. "Are there any other books you'd like?"

I hesitate. "The book of prophecies?" I know it can't be taken from the library, but it holds coveted information.

Emberlyn is quiet. "I'll check to see if it's back," she promises after a stretch of silence. "If it's there, I'll copy down any prophecies that could be linked to you."

"*If?*" Lenna asks.

"I'm not sure the book of prophecies has been found," Emberlyn answers begrudgingly. "Last I heard, it was still missing."

"*Still?*" Lenna squawks. "That's, like, the most important book in the library, isn't it? The fact that it's missing is kind of a big deal."

"Yeah, well, in case you missed it, there are a lot of things happening in Soulbourne that are *kind of a big deal*," Emberlyn snaps defensively.

"I'll go with you," Lenna announces brightly a half-beat later. "We'll both check on the book of prophecies."

"Have you heard anything else, Emberlyn?" I ask, picking at my cuticles and trying hard to appear casual.

Emberlyn's rough exhale is answer enough. "There's another golden book missing," she admits.

Lenna's eyes snap to Emberlyn. "How many golden books does the Callings library have?"

"Three."

"*Golden books?*" I ask, looking from Emberlyn's scowl to Lenna's furrowed brows.

"Golden books carry special distinction—they're ancient tomes, said to carry magic within their pages. The book of prophecies is one," Emberlyn explains. "The pages are literally golden," she adds.

Lenna doesn't give me a chance to respond before she fires off her next question. "Which book is missing? Which book is left?"

"The book that's left is about time," Emberlyn begins, as though it's easier to articulate that which still sits inside the revered Callings library than that which is inexplicably gone. "And the book that's missing is on secrets."

"*Secrets?*" Lenna and I ask together.

"It sounds juicy, but it's essentially an encyclopedia of Soulbourne," Emberlyn tells us. "The book catalogs types of creatures, spirits, humans...and the different variations of each. There's a section on markings," she adds wryly.

One eyebrow arches in mock surprise as Lenna huffs her disbelief. It's hardly shocking to discover that someone is trying to learn as much as they can about me. Or, I suddenly realize, someone might be trying to keep *me* from learning about *myself*.

"Bring me the book on time."

Emberlyn's astonishment is loud. Her eyes flare and her head jerks back before she regains her composure and regards me with open curiosity. "The golden books are supposed to stay in the library," she says flatly. "It's one of the things the guardians protect."

"But they haven't been protected," I deadpan back. "They've been taken by someone who means to gain the upper hand. I want the last golden book."

Even Lenna's mouth is a little ajar as she looks from me to the scholar. Emberlyn's hazel eyes spark with intelligence.

"First of all, it isn't the *last* golden book. There are other golden books that exist in Soulbourne, though their locations aren't known. Second of all...I'm not sure it can be done. But I'll try."

I'm tired and overwhelmed as I climb into bed. Warrick stands guard outside; Lenna and Emberlyn will again stay the night. These are small comforts, given the questions and uncertainties I wrestle with. In spite of the circumstances, I'm asleep in less than a minute.

A hand on the shoulder wakes me.

I'm pulled from the depths of bottomless sleep in an instant; my eyes squint open to find a hulking shadow beside my bed. A hand clamps over my mouth, smothering any would-be call for help.

"It's me."

Warrick's words take a moment to sink in. "I didn't know how else to wake you. You didn't respond when I called your name."

I pull his hand away from my mouth. "I'm awake," I reply irritably. The electricity coursing through me is so strong I couldn't go back to sleep if I tried.

"We need to talk."

In the darkness, I can't read Warrick's expression. "In the *middle of the night?*" It takes effort to keep my voice calm.

"We'll have privacy."

"And you expect me to trust you?" I ask tersely.

Warrick doesn't answer right away. "Yes. You should trust me." He doesn't elaborate, but his words are rife with conviction and I feel concurrence in my bones.

With an exasperated sigh, I throw off the covers. There will never be a convenient time to converse, and Warrick's right—we *do* need to talk. "I'll meet you outside."

Five minutes later, I'm dressed and on the back deck, my arms wrapped around my middle to keep warm. The pale yellow in the sky tells me that it's not exactly the middle of the night—it's the early hours of the morning.

"About tonight..." Warrick begins. "Be on your guard at the banquet."

I scoff. Of *course* I'm going to be on guard.

Warrick ignores my rebuff. "I've seen the guest list. I don't think you'll have many...*friends.*"

I shoot Warrick a withering look. "The two *friends* I have are sleeping on the other side of this wall. Are we going to pretend this chat is about the banquet, or are we *actually* going to talk?"

"Andra, I'm serious."

"I'm serious, too!" I cry. "I haven't been able to let my guard down for one minute since entering Soulbourne. And this advice is rich, coming from someone who plotted to *kill me*."

My words agitate Warrick. "I'm trying to help you."

"Then help me. Answer my questions. Tell me what's really going on. *That's* what I need—not these cryptic, ambiguous warnings."

Warrick sighs in frustration and shakes his head. He shoots me a look of exasperation; even his posture looks vexed. "Let's train."

Hot irritation flashes through my body, but I manage to roll my eyes and shrug. I'm not going to let the topic drop, but maybe I'll have better luck plying Warrick with questions while we train.

Warrick sets a comfortable pace and the first strides are quiet, the duet of breaths the only sound against the early morning. Dawn breaks and our silhouettes gain color. The ache of my legs dissipates and the rhythm of my breath becomes fluid.

"How did you know your way around Underworld?" There's no easy way to wade into such a loaded conversation, so I jump headfirst.

"I've been there." There's no defense in the words.

I figured as much—Achlys overtly alluded to this fact—but it's still a struggle to keep moving when I want to stop and study Warrick's expression. "As a guest or a prisoner?" I ask.

Warrick sighs. "Neither."

My brows furrow in confusion.

"Achlys isn't allowed to hold me any more than he's allowed to hold you," Warrick says.

This strikes me as curious. The way Achlys presided over the arena, I can't imagine anyone in Soulbourne that's outside his jurisdiction—perhaps with the exception of Justus. What about Warrick renders him immune from Achlys' iron fist?

"Why?"

"I can't answer that."

I stop running. "You owe me an explanation." My hands find my hips and I glower. "You're expecting too much of me, if you think I'm going to blithely accept your word as truth."

"Let's not go there," Warrick says in a low voice.

"Why can you go to Underworld without consequence?" I ask again. I hold my breath and hope that Warrick will answer. "Why would you ever *choose* to go to Underworld?"

Warrick eyes me. "Why did *you*?"

I let out an annoyed sigh. We both know why *I* went, though my judgment in following a motorized marble could be questioned. "Are you going to answer *any* of my questions?"

"I am answering your questions."

"This is like pulling teeth, Warrick. Will you at least tell me who were you talking to in the library? Why did you agree to kill me?"

Warrick's laughter is harsh and discordant. "I don't want to kill you, Andra. I've told you that."

"Warrick, come on. I heard you in the library."

"Yes, you did."

"So..."

"I can't give you proof, Andra. I won't deny the conversation that you overheard in the library. You're going to have to decide if you believe me when I say that I don't have any plans to harm you. Like I pointed out before: *if I wanted you dead, I would have already killed you.*"

"Unless there's some weird rule in Soulbourne about timing," I grouse. "Achlys wants to kill me, but claimed he couldn't yet because of my mark. How do I know you're not just waiting for something to happen?"

Warrick shrugs. "You don't."

"How very flippant, considering this is *my* life we're talking about."

"I've been here, protecting you and doing my best to help you. I am never flippant about anything. I won't be able to make the case for why you should trust me, but I hope you do." Warrick holds my gaze before turning away. When he starts running, I know the conversation is over.

The annoying part is, I do.

I trust Warrick.

THIRTEEN

"You look *amazing.*"

Lenna's praise is predictable—she is the one who styled me, after all—but after I have the opportunity to see her handiwork for myself, I have to admit I'm pleased.

The dress is a rich shade of juniper green. It features a slit in the front that travels up to my thigh and tapers down to skim the floor in back. The silky fabric clings tight to my body, the neckline of the dress a low *V* that leaves my shoulders bare. Thin green vines made of velvet wrap around the dress in asymmetrical fashion. On my feet I wear wedged espadrilles with leafy velvet vines that twist up my calves. Gilt, leaf-shaped barrettes pin back the loose golden curls that tumble down my back. Only Earth tones have been used in my makeup, and my light-blue eyes look electric against bronze and copper eyeshadow.

I don't wear a lick of jewelry, which is a statement itself. Lenna was insistent that *I* would be the masterpiece tonight—no accessories or makeup would compete for attention.

"Are you nervous?" Emberlyn asks.

I shrug. "It's only a banquet, right?"

"Right," Lenna agrees, her voice falsely bright. She looks to Emberlyn, and the scholar offers a grim smile. I trust these women, even as I acknowledge the growing sea of secrets between us.

There weren't any remarks or questions when I returned at sunrise with Warrick, but I saw the pursed lips. Neither comments on Warrick's absence now. I'm not sure what I expected, but I'm surprised that he's not here to offer reassurance or the quiet comfort of his presence. That I even care annoys me.

Too soon, a carriage pulls up in front of the cabin. Horses nicker as the coachman slows to a stop. In another world, I might be Cinderella on her way to the ball. The irony is rich—I'm dressed like a princess, but I'm on my way to battle. A battle disguised as a banquet.

"You can do this," Lenna tells me earnestly.

"We'll wait up for you," Emberlyn adds. "And if we're asleep, wake us."

I hear the banquet before I see it. The sound of music, clinking wine glasses, and laughter floats through the carriage window. I inch closer to the side and peer out.

Perrin's mansion looks like something out of a fairytale. Long wooden tables run lengthwise underneath stately trees, their trunks encompassed with fairy lights and sparkly chandeliers. The tables are swathed with leafy garlands and flowers; elegant cream-colored candles flicker on top. The wooden chair backs are intricately carved, strings of colorful flowers woven through each. As the carriage draws near, there's a noticeable dip in noise. The moment I step out, silence.

I square my shoulders and look out at the crowd staring back at me. Perhaps the attention should intimidate; instead, it makes me feel powerful. I make my way into the forest clearing, carefully avoiding eye contact as my eyes sweep over the crowd. I don't make it very far when Syphus glides to my side.

"Someone came to play tonight," he croons.

"What do you want?" I ask stiffly.

"What are you playing at?" Warm breath tickles my ear, Syphus' tone light and predatory at the same time.

My eyes narrow. "I don't know what you're talking about." Syphus is poised to respond, but never gets the chance.

"Our guest of honor is here," Perrin announces over the din, bringing conversation and activity to a halt. "Please find your seats."

"We'll discuss this later," Syphus promises when a handsome man appears at my elbow. His shoulders are broad, his dark hair and brown eyes a mirror image of his father, Perrin.

"This way," he says, leading me to the end of the table. "My name is Tyrion."

Tyrion escorts me to a seat near Perrin. The other domain leaders flank either side: Calum from Overworld, Achlys from Underworld, Imara from Air, Elinarr from Water, Tyra from Rock. Two new figures, clad in the neutral tones of Callings and the edgy fashion of Boundless, are also present.

Tyrion takes the seat beside me, elegantly slipping in and scooting the chair forward with glib movements that tell me everything about his genteel, well-heeled upbringing. His eyes survey the company; his aloof gaze reeks of privilege and entitlement. He's done nothing to earn a place at the table, as far as I know, but he's here because he had the good fortune to be born the son of a powerful man. A truth that has escaped his notice, if one were to gauge the manner with which he carries himself. Syphus is not far away, and though I might not know ranking or title, I know I'm amongst Soulbourne's VIPs.

No sooner are we seated than plates and trays of food begin to appear. A string orchestra plays a soulful, haunting melody, and conversation begins.

In the first moments, most of the attention is on the food and drink. I accept the wine poured in my glass, though I have no intention of drinking it. I portion a little of everything on my plate. I don't *feel* eyes on me, but I'm no fool. I'm being watched. Some food I plan to fold into my napkin, some I will push around on my plate, and some I will slip under the table for animals to eat after everyone has left. I plan to eat very little.

I don't trust a single person at this banquet, and seeing people eat and drink from the plates and pitchers before me is not enough—Soulbourne's realm has defied my understanding and expectations in a thousand ways already, and I won't be played the fool.

"Do you have any guess what the Land test might be?" Tyrion asks. He looks smug.

"Isn't that why I'm here?" I ask. "To find out."

"Yeah, but you probably have some guesses," Tyrion prods.

This is a sport to him—I'm a source of amusement. My fight for survival is, to him, a game.

"Who designed the test?" I ask, ignoring Tyrion's question altogether.

He frowns, clearly unaccustomed to being denied, and doesn't answer. He glances in the direction of the domain leaders before turning his attention to the food on his plate. Our conversation is loud enough that it can be overheard by the domain leaders, but no one chimes in. The leaders are eerily quiet, by my mark—I watch them silently cut their meat and spoon their soup.

"So, Andra—what do you make of Land?" Elinarr asks. His tan skin and sun-bleached hair are distinct in the glow of candlelight.

This is a loaded question—if not for the words themselves, for the unspoken signal that is sent when forks are temporarily suspended in midair and side conversations extinguish on the spot.

I smile at Elinarr, lips closed as I finish chewing green beans. "Land is very beautiful." I gesture to the greenery that surrounds us. "Tonight looks like a fairytale. The food is delicious."

Elinarr looks disappointed—his sparkling blue eyes dull when he realizes I'm not going to offer any salacious gossip. In truth, Perrin is the only one who looks pleased by my remark.

When it becomes clear I'm not going to elaborate, side chatter resumes. Even when the entertainment begins—dancing, acrobatics, and musical performances—it isn't particularly rousing. I wonder, not for the first time, if Warrick is in attendance. Instinctively, I glance around.

"What are you looking for?"

The mere sound of Achlys' low, gravelly voice sets my skin crawling. My spine stiffens; I'm reluctant to meet his eyes. I can't do so without thinking of the gray plumes of smoke, the smell of rotting flesh and the rows of haunted eyes in Underworld. I wonder if Achlys told the domain leaders about my visit; I wonder if he suspects I'm looking for Warrick.

"Do you know where the washroom is?"

Achlys doesn't as much as blink.

"I'll take you," Tyrion volunteers. He pushes his chair back before anyone can protest and in one smooth motion offers me his hand.

I nod my thanks and stand. Aware of Achlys' watchful eyes and the heads that turn to watch, I take Tyrion's extended hand and allow him to escort me to the mansion.

"Doesn't it make you nervous that everyone's staring?" I ask, mostly because I feel uncomfortable walking in silence.

"They're staring because you're beautiful."

Tyrion smiles then, his handsome face crinkling. I know scant about the man, but his fluid movements and silver tongue remind me of an actor. He's charming *now*, but there is something cold as stone about the man.

I blush. "I'm a novelty," I disagree.

We pass the tables and climb the steps to the patio. Servants mill about and discreetly ignore us. Figures press against the shadows of the walls and disappear inside doorways; we're alone as we progress down the side of the building.

"The washroom isn't in there?" I ask, craning my neck to glance inside the mansion.

"I'm taking us the scenic route," Tyrion says easily. He pulls my arm in closer to his and warning bells chime in my head.

"I really need to go to the washroom," I protest, keeping my voice light as I pull away and towards the nearest door.

"Not yet," Tyrion mutters, his grip on my arm now ironclad. "I need a moment with you in private."

A servant walks out, sees us, and walks back inside. I am paralyzed by lack of understanding: I came into the night wary, and still I find myself continuously surprised by the scope of the game.

When Tyrion releases me, we're at the back of the mansion—still on the patio, but away from the lights. My heart beats fast. I take a quick step away from Tyrion to create distance; every cell in my body stands at attention. "What do you want?"

"You're beautiful." Tyrion's eyes rove up and down over my figure. "Unique, and powerful. We could make a good team."

"You want an alliance?" I ask uncertainly.

"This isn't a *game*," Tyrion sneers, though that's precisely what it feels like. "I want you to marry me."

Marry him? The idea is insulting, and preposterous. A sudden thought occurs to me. "Did you—did you...*mark* me?"

The air around us goes still.

Tyrion's body stiffens, his mouth turns down into a frown. "I didn't mark you. I want protection from you."

"*Protection?*" I ask, voice rising. "You think I'm going to come *after* you?"

Tyrion doesn't bat an eyelash. "You're the woman from the prophecies—better to be on your side than against you. What better way than to marry you?"

I stare at Tyrion—he's not joking. For all his idiocy, Tyrion sees the look on my face and recognizes the disdain.

"You're in a bad position—they're going to try to kill you," Tyrion explains, as though this point hasn't already been made abundantly clear. "If you marry me, you might not have to compete in the tests. You might not be the year's Prosphora."

His tone is earnest, but I catch the errors in verbiage. *Try. If. Might.* I may be new to Soulbourne, but I'm no novice to the English language. All words that hedge, none that carry the absolute power of a true heavyweight in Soulbourne. Tyrion has no more influence than a fruit fly.

"I can't imagine your father—or domain leadership—would agree to our union." It feels like the safest thing to say—an outright assault on Tyrion's clout would be foolish. Arrogant men go to great lengths to defend their pride.

Tyrion scoffs. "I'm a man. It doesn't matter what my father wants. I speak for myself."

Notably, these appear to be the most genuine words he has yet spoken. He *does* speak for himself: his actions narcissistic and short-sighted. He would take a wife to secure his own protection, with no regard for the well-being of any other citizen of the realm.

"Where is the washroom?" I try again. The sooner I can get away from Tyrion, the better.

Tyrion understands the redirecting question for what it is—a gentle denial. He shakes his head softly, shoulders hunched in defeat. His lips are curled into a snarl, his features saturated with scorn. He thinks me a fool: either because he imagines I underestimate the danger I face without him and his half-baked offer or because I don't properly grasp his star and what it would mean to be linked to him in marriage. Men like Tyrion can't fathom women that don't want them—their brains are too clogged with pride and stuffed with pomp to register that the world extends beyond their snowglobe of influence. Tyrion raises an arm as though to point inside. Too late, I realize his intention.

Tyrion's arm stretches out—not to point the way to the washroom, but to wrap around my neck and push me against the pillar of the patio. Cloaked in the darkness, he shoves his body against me, smothering me as his lips come down hard on mine.

My body freezes, unyielding to his touch. His tongue tries to push its way inside my mouth. One hand holds a fistful of my hair to keep me in place.

I'm not sure what Tyrion means to do—is this to intimidate me? He can't be idiotic enough to think this will somehow win me over, can he? I'm trying to wriggle loose when a voice sends chills skittering down my spine.

"So this is what you've been hiding."

FOURTEEN

Tyrion releases me immediately, pushing me away.

Syphus looks from me to Tyrion. A slow smile spreads across his face. "The washroom, huh?"

"I still need to go." My body shakes, not from fear, but from anger.

"Did you mark her?" Syphus asks. "I'm surprised you have the power. But perhaps, as your father's heir, with the right connections…did he do it himself?"

Tyrion shakes his head, face a bit pale. "I didn't mark her. My father *definitely* didn't mark her."

Syphus' smile lingers; he considers Tyrion and savors his squirming. Those slate-gray eyes dance with mischief when they turn upon me. "Andra. And-*ra*—is this what you were up to?"

My mind races.

I can't decide if it's better to pretend that Tyrion marked me or if it's better to insist I know nothing. In the end, I say nothing. I can't think of anything to say that doesn't carry potential to damn me. My eyes say plenty, though—I make no effort to hide the vitriol that burns from within.

"I didn't mark her." Tyrion's voice has gone up an octave, his eyes are panicked.

Syphus arches a pale yellow eyebrow. "That remains to be seen."

"It's her fault." Tyrion looks at me with scorn. "*She* caused this."

I can't hold back the burst of incredulous laughter, but I don't bother to defend myself. I'm not sure the truth matters. Syphus saw for himself the way Tyrion had me pinned against the pillar.

"I'm going to find the washroom," I announce coolly. I am shocked when neither man tries to stop me.

Perrin's manor is beautiful, but the elegant details barely register in my quest to find the washroom. When I do find it, it's mercifully vacant. My fingers fumble on the lock; once I'm safely shut inside, I slump against the door. A strangled sob escapes me; a sound I am wise enough to smother with my hand.

I don't know what just happened.

Nothing makes sense.

My sense of foreboding builds. Tyrion and Syphus are both my enemies. If they decide to team up against me...

It's not wise to stay in the washroom long.

I wash my hands and regard myself in the mirror—my makeup is intact and my hair is easily fixed—but the haunted look in my eyes is hard to shake.

I pull my shoulders back and tip my chin until my reflection looks composed and confident. The attempt is fragile. At some point I'll have to stop stuffing my feelings down, but that moment is not now. With one deep, measured breath, I exit.

Syphus and Tyrion are seated at the dining table. Neither looks upset. It takes effort to slide into the seat next to Tyrion, to stomach my revulsion and pretend like nothing is wrong. Tyrion doesn't as much as look at me—but Syphus does. He converses jovially with those around him, but I feel his insidious gray eyes bore holes through my forehead.

I don't know how much time passes before Perrin stands. He clears his throat and taps a knife against his wine glass—an irrelevant gesture in a crowd that has already fallen silent.

"It is time to announce the Land test, which will take place in two days' time." Perrin raises his glass and nods my direction. "Land will test Andra's ability in the wild. Five flags have been hidden in Land's seven ecosystems—Desert, Mountains, Jungle, Plains, Forest, Canyon, and Tundra. You have five days to survive the elements and find the flags."

The announcement is a relief.

The night has been horrible, but it will end. All nights do. The integral part of the banquet, the announcement of Land's test, is a boon. As soon as I hear Perrin reveal the parameters of the test, I know I can survive. I'll need some luck finding the flags, but I can do this.

"It's a giant game of Capture the Flag," Syphus announces with disdain. "That's the best you can do?"

I stiffen. Syphus doesn't look my way—he's up to something. Cold dread seeps into me.

Perrin reddens, flustered by the impudent remark baldly cast in front of all the most important figures in Soulbourne. "It is not a game of Capture the Flag," he sputters. "The test is deadly. Andra will have to stay alive in harsh climates. There are wild animals and beasts in each ecosystem. The flags are not easily acquired."

There are whispers, murmurs that ripple through the dining area. My skin crawls. The leaders of Soulbourne are stone-faced, expressions inscrutable.

When Syphus stands, I know things are about to get bad. Very bad. The crowd knows it, too—the whispers die and the audience sits in silence, waiting.

"I was hoping it wouldn't come to this..." Syphus trails off, playing to the crowd, milking the moment for every drop of drama. "I believe Land has intentionally planned an easy test for Andra. Just now, I caught Tyrion and Andra on the back patio—*kissing.*"

Gasps.

The buzz of gossip is immediate.

Perrin stands at the head of the table with a still-raised wine glass. His face is incredulous, then it is livid when he regards his son's white pallor and squeamish expression. Finally, Perrin looks afraid.

Truly afraid.

In all of this, I feel invisible.

Tyrion never once looks my way; no one whispers their thoughts to me. I don't know these people. They don't know my character; they don't know anything about me. It shouldn't matter. But I still care, and so I stand and clink my own knife against a wine glass.

The silence that falls over the crowd is deathly; there's not so much as a sigh or a sneeze as every eye turns to stare.

"I didn't kiss Tyrion."

I shake—visibly shake—with anger, my fists clenched at my sides. "I asked to go to the *washroom*. He led me to the back of the patio, and then he—"

I don't finish my sentence. Perrin's recovery is swift when he senses the damning proclamation I am about to make. His wine glass lifts an inch higher in the air as he shouts over me:

"There is more to the test! I have not finished." He rushes to get the words out. "Andra will search for the five flags hidden in the Land test, but she won't be alone. Achlys will loan us prisoners currently jailed in Underworld—one from each domain. Andra will have to evade or defeat them."

The roar from the crowd is immediate.

This time, it doesn't ebb—Perrin's additional test element whips everyone into a tizzy. I don't know who will be released from Underworld, but the haunted yellow eyes and inhuman shrieks are fresh in my memory. Syphus' glittering smile and conspiratorial wink solidify my understanding that Perrin has just handed me a death sentence.

"That worked out well for you," Tyrion snickers under his breath. "There's no way you'll make it out alive." The pandemonium is so loud and animated that no one hears him.

I don't honor Tyrion with any response other than my fist.

My angle is bad, so I can't throw my weight behind it—but there's enough force that Tyrion falls out of his chair with an undignified screech and grabs for his nose.

The leaders of Soulbourne all see—all *stare*—as I stand and lift my wine glass to Perrin. With everyone important watching, I pour the wine out on Tyrion's hunched figure.

"Thank you for the banquet." My words are tight. I've crossed a line, and there's no returning. "And for the very interesting *twist*."

My eyes shoot daggers at Perrin—his additional element of the released criminals was so obviously unplanned. But it doesn't matter—I will still be made to vanquish or evade the delinquents.

With the crowd still in an uproar, I turn on my heel and leave.

"What happened?" Lenna asks the second I return.

I don't respond right away. I have yet to find words.

Emberlyn takes one look at my face and grimaces. "Was it that bad?"

"I was seated beside Tyrion, near the domain leaders." I speak slowly, struggling to subdue the tremor of anger in my voice. Lenna and Emberlyn nod: they know Tyrion.

"I asked to go to the washroom, and Tyrion offered to escort me, but then he pulled me aside to ask me to marry him. When I said no, he forced himself on me. Syphus saw it. Perrin announced the test: a survival competition in Land's ecosystems. But Syphus suggested the test was easy on purpose, revealed that he found Tyrion kissing me, and to save face, Perrin decided that I'll also battle prisoners locked up in Underworld. I punched Tyrion in the face, poured wine on him, and left."

Lenna and Emberlyn's jaws drop in disbelief. The reaction affirms my fatigue and misery; I sink onto the bench and bury my face in my hands.

Lenna recovers first. "Well. I didn't see *that* coming."

"Tyrion asked to *marry* you? He *forced himself* on you?" Emberlyn asks, shaking her head in disbelief. "Is he *insane?!*"

"It would appear so," I sigh.

Emberlyn's nose crinkles in disgust. "Did he...mark you?"

"It wasn't him. Syphus seemed to doubt his authority to do so in the first place. Tyrion's reaction—and Perrin's—looked genuine. It's why Perrin was so quick to up the ante of the test."

"Who are they going to release from Underworld?" Emberlyn asks, face pinched with concern.

"He didn't say."

"They might not be human," Emberlyn warns.

Lenna's quirk of a smile keeps the moment from feeling heavy. "You punched Tyrion. I wish I could have seen the look on his face. Did you hurt him?"

"He fell out of his chair, curled up on the ground, and held his nose." The memory brings a measure of satisfaction.

"And then you poured your wine on him."

"At that point, it didn't feel like there was much to lose."

"Brilliant." Lenna's admiration is genuine.

"I hope you won't be punished," Emberlyn says quietly.

"How could she be punished more than she already has?" Lenna asks. "They've completely screwed her."

"I don't know," Emberlyn admits. "The pride of a domain leader is a powerful thing."

We're all silent.

"Did you see Warrick?" Lenna asks, and I shake my head.

"Isn't he supposedly protecting you?" Emberlyn asks.

"Yes," I say, and the weariness returns. I have no idea where Warrick was—I have no idea if he was even at the banquet. I can't begin to explain the complicated layers of what I've learned about Warrick to Emberlyn and Lenna.

Lenna's face is creased with worry. A moment passes and she declares, "You're still going to beat the test, Andra. We'll find out who they plan to release from Underworld."

I keep my thoughts to myself: I'm not sure it will be enough. I remember the prophecy: *without intervention, you will die in the Land test.* Words that gain credence with every moment spent in Soulbourne.

"You should get some rest," Emberlyn says softly.

I'm on autopilot as I put on pajamas and brush my teeth. When my head hits the pillow, I'm out.

When I wake the next morning, the sun is up. My eyelids are heavy as I squint into the day and my body aches. My head is little better—foggy, even though I slept through the night. Lenna and Emberlyn are awake and sitting at the table.

"How do you feel?" Lenna asks.

"Terrible." I don't bother to hide the truth.

Lenna nods, an action that makes me think that I look terrible, too. "Why don't you eat? Warrick's here—he's waiting outside."

I *am* ravenous—I was too upset to eat last night, but my appetite has since awakened. Warrick's appearance is both a relief and a source of irritation. "Did he say where he was last night?" I ask before taking a bite of muffin.

Both Lenna and Emberlyn shake their heads.

"I brought you books," Emberlyn offers, changing the subject.

My eyes drift to the texts neatly stacked on the table. In between history and geography books sits a volume with deep indigo cloth emblazoned with the phases of the moon cast in gold. My pulse ratchets when my eyes land on the gilt pages. "Is that…"

Emberlyn nods. "The golden book on time."

"How did you…"

Emberlyn shakes her head. "It's better that you not know."

Before I have a chance to thank her, Warrick appears. I lean back against the table, my body shielding the golden tome from view.

"I heard you were up. How long will it take you to get ready?" There's no mention of what happened at the banquet.

I finish my muffin with irritation. I want Warrick to address what happened last night—I want him to explain where he was, what he was doing, and I want him to acknowledge that it was horrible.

Warrick sees all of this and maybe more on my face. "Ten

minutes?"

My annoyance is great enough that I don't immediately respond. I grab another muffin and take an unnecessarily large bite. I wait until I've fully chewed and swallowed every last grain, then take a long drink of water.

Warrick's eyes never leave me. Lenna and Emberlyn are silent as they watch the exchange with open curiosity.

"I'll be ready."

I wipe my mouth with a napkin and push up from the table.

Eight minutes later, we walk the path to Boundless. Warrick's pace is steady, but his long strides require me to take extra steps to keep up. There aren't many people on the path at first, but this changes as we near the hub of Soulbourne.

"You'll have a lot of eyes on you today," Warrick warns after we pass the first pedestrian.

Sure enough, the people we pass gawk. I'm tense with each new cluster of bodies we pass, but Warrick appears unruffled by the attention. Even so, his stride shortens to match mine and his hands remain close to his sides—and his weapons.

"We're not going to talk about it?" I finally snap. "Were you there? Did you see what happened?"

"I was there."

When Warrick's eyes meet mine, I find anger. My own ire ebbs in the face of his—but it also gives way to new questions. *Why is* he *angry?*

"Don't expect the test to be fair." Warrick's first words have nothing to do with last night's banquet. "Try to avoid combat at all costs," Warrick continues. "If you encounter any Underworld prisoners, run. If you find yourself in hand-to-hand combat, you should know a few things."

"Do you think they'll be armed?"

"I don't know." His words carry too much force to be considered indifferent.

"I'm not allowed to be armed, am I?"

"Let's first see what weapons you're comfortable using," Warrick hedges. "Without knowing who they plan to release, it's hard to know how to prepare."

I think back to my brief time in Underworld, the decrepit souls with desperate, despairing eyes.

"They won't play fair," Warrick repeats. "If you encounter someone in the test, you'll have to kill them."

When the marble warms in agreement, I swallow thickly.

Warrick takes me to an empty warehouse in Boundless. We walk the same path as before, and my pulse quickens as we turn down the alley that last resulted in the threatening announcement of the banquet and subsequent trip to Underworld.

I hold my breath as we pass the unassuming sewer grating that leads to the degenerate domain and I'm immeasurably relieved when the marble is quiet.

A few minutes later, Warrick leads me to an unremarkable warehouse. The room is sterile and a little chilly: when Warrick unlocks the door, the waft of stale air is the first thing that hits me. Inside I'm met with concrete flooring and monochromatic gray walls. There aren't any windows. Weak, waxy light comes from fluorescent bulbs that hang from wires taped to the ceiling.

I find the space depressing, but I get the impression that it means something to Warrick. The pull of his shoulders is defensive, like he's made himself vulnerable just by bringing me here. As my eyes adjust to the artificial lighting, I note the weapons positioned around the perimeter.

"I train here."

I nod, waiting for Warrick to elaborate. Instead, he takes me on a circuit through the weapons in the warehouse. I'm awkward wielding every single one. Warrick offers correction after correction, a hint of frustration growing in his voice.

"At least *pretend* you care about surviving," he finally growls.

I stumble back in surprise. "What makes you think I don't want to survive?"

"You're holding that knife like a crayon," Warrick accuses. "Andra—they are going to try to *kill* you. You will not survive if you play nice, safe, or fair."

The words hang like a banner in the air. I am not a killer—but tomorrow, I must find a way to be. My life depends upon it.

"Isn't there something you would kill for?"

I don't answer Warrick's question—which is answer enough. He shakes his head and looks away. Not two seconds later, I am flat on my stomach.

My face is pressed into the ground, one arm is twisted and pinned. Warrick's knee grinds into my back and the knife I held two seconds ago is in my periphery, mere inches from my neck.

"Just in case you wondered how easy you are to disarm." Warrick doesn't make any move to release me.

"Let—me—go." The words are hard to get out—there's too much pressure on my lungs.

"Make me."

Anger floods through me—because Warrick put me in this position, because it hurts, because it's pitiful that it took him so little effort to do so, and because I don't think I *can* get out. Whatever point Warrick was trying to make, he made it.

I even my breathing and think about the parts of my body that are *not* pinned. My top half is restricted, but everything from the waist down is free. I need to get the knife away from my neck. I try to move my arm a smidge—to see if there's any possible leverage—and I don't get a centimeter.

"Not happening." Warrick has the audacity to sound bored.

I lay perfectly still, hoping Warrick will think I've given up. Then, I kick my legs back. They make it up in the air, but do nothing to set me free. I wriggle like an earthworm, but it's no use. I'm pinned.

A moment later, Warrick releases me.

"That's why you don't want to play defense." There's no smile or trace of amusement on Warrick's face. "If you have the chance to kill a prisoner, do it."

"Are you going to teach me how to get out of that, or are you just going to gloat?" I adjust my ponytail and wipe the dirt off my face. Tears of frustration sting the corners of my eyes.

Warrick meets my gaze and holds it. "That was *one* maneuver," he tells me evenly.

"Then let's make sure that *one* maneuver isn't the one that kills me in the Land test," I reply smartly.

Warrick's face is impassive as he teaches me a counter technique that I don't execute well. Time stretches on. I should head back to Land, to study from the books Emberlyn procured. In the end, it's Warrick that stops our training.

"I think it's time we called it a day." There's nothing readable on his face as he makes the pronouncement.

"I wanted to master that move."

"It's getting late."

Tears sting the back of my eyelids—frustration mounts within me and threatens to vomit up like a volcano.

"I still can't defend myself," I say quietly.

Warrick knows better than to lie. He studies me for a long moment, and then he walks towards the door. I follow.

The ache in my legs feels good. It's productive, somehow. Warrick doesn't say anything, but he allows me to set the pace back to Land.

"Elara."

Warrick's eyes snap up to meet mine. I don't need to include context—he knows I'm answering his question about what is worth fighting for...worth *killing* for.

"I'm sure she'd say the same about you. If you care about

Elara, you will kill in the Land test. If you don't, she's the one who will suffer."

We run the path back to Land in silence.

FIFTEEN

When we return, Emberlyn is waiting outside the cabin.

"We know who they released from the Underworld prison," she blurts. "Lenna knows someone who saw them come into Land an hour ago. She's out trying to get more information."

I hear the edge to Emberlyn's voice, but I can't muster any additional angst. I already know they will have picked the worst. "Who are they?"

"There are seven, not eight: a prisoner from every domain except Overworld," Emberlyn begins.

"Overworld doesn't keep prisoners," Warrick interjects. "There isn't anyone to pick."

"Yes," Emberlyn agrees, anxious to continue. "Here's what we know." She holds out a piece of paper with names scribbled alongside domains. "Agrona, from Rock."

The name means nothing to me—as expected—but Warrick's jaw sets and he shakes his head in disgust. "He's a hit man," Warrick growls. "And he's huge. He's the strongest man in Soulbourne—he could snap you in half like a toothpick."

I scowl at Warrick and his unnecessary comment. But Emberlyn nods voraciously, red hair falling into her face.

"They're all dangerous," she warns, turning back to her list. "Then there's Mercurius from Land. He—"

Warrick curses, cutting Emberlyn off. "Are you serious?" He scowls. "They literally picked the worst."

"I'm not finished," Emberlyn glowers back. "They're all bad. Don't erupt after each one. It doesn't help."

Warrick exhales heavily. He nods his agreement and stands stiff as a statue.

"Mercurius was put in prison for hunting people," Emberlyn finishes. She throws an uneasy look at Warrick, who is obediently rigid and silent.

"He...*hunted* people?" I ask.

"Like they were animals," Emberlyn says. "He tracked them, trapped them, and slaughtered them."

I shiver in revulsion. The hairs on my arms stand on end as though someone poured a bucket of ice down my back. "He will *love* hunting me. He won't have any trouble tracking my trail of glitter."

Neither Warrick nor Emberlyn respond. They don't have to. I know: I'm screwed. "Next."

"Dirce from Boundless. Lenna can tell you more about her—she hasn't been imprisoned for that long. I remember when she was sentenced...one, maybe two years ago. She's a spy."

Warrick clears his throat. "A spy who is excellent with knives."

Emberlyn purses her lips in solemn agreement. I nod my head in signal to carry on.

"Sarka from Underworld. I don't know as much about her, but she's known for voodoo and dark magic."

My hackles rise. They're all terrible, but some sound particularly chilling. At least if Agrona kills me, it will be quick.

"The prisoner from Callings is Brone—he was the leader of a cult. I don't know if he'll pose a physical threat, but he's manipulative and crafty. Kakarauri is from Water, and therein lies her threat. She knows a hundred different ways to drown you," Emberlyn warns. "And from

Air, there's Nox. He's incredibly stealthy—he worked as an assassin for over a decade. He's said to be as silent and quick as the wind."

"They all sound dangerous."

I don't know what else to say. I've lost my appetite for lunch and I can't imagine how I'll survive longer than an hour in the test. The silver lining—very *thin* silver lining—is that there weren't any creatures named.

"Lenna is trying to dig up dirt on their weaknesses," Emberlyn continues. "They've been in the Underworld prison for different lengths of time...and all of them *were* caught," she points out. "If we can find things to exploit, you'll have a chance."

"Thank you."

Emberlyn looks uncomfortable, like there is more she wants to say. "I'm sorry," she says, though none of this is her fault. "I wish we could help more."

"Let's study," I suggest. There's no time to wish and hope—I must do what I can with the tools that I *do* have.

Armed with the knowledge of my opponents, Warrick and Emberlyn lay out the map of the Land domain and suggest ideal locations for shelter and point out regions to avoid. The orientation of Land isn't too complex, and the fenced area in which the competition will take place is even more manageable to memorize.

Warrick is keen to run through hypothetical scenarios and how I should respond in each—we go through a few, but I worry that they won't be as valuable as he thinks. I eye the books stacked on the table, my gaze drawn to the golden text on time.

The afternoon wears on, Warrick and Emberlyn relentless in their quest to prepare me. When Lenna returns, she barrels through the front door without warning, cheeks flushed and out of breath.

"The prisoners are in the Land test. I saw them." Lenna's first words take my breath away—I'm silent and still as I wait for her to elaborate.

Emberlyn jumps up. "How'd you get to see?"

127

"I went to Perrin's mansion. It's where the competition starts and ends. Domain leadership was there, too. It looks like he's going to host them during the test."

"It's not like they'll be able to watch," Emberlyn grouses. The test begins at Perrin's mansion, but the ecosystems and the fenced area for the test is large.

"Maybe they want to be together for...news?" From the way Lenna's face twists at the end, I gather that "news" likely means the death of a prisoner...or me.

There's no further deliberation. Lenna moves around the table to lift up sleek black pants, a loose, long-sleeved cream-colored shirt, and an army green coat. There are woolen socks, a small pack, and brown boots, too.

"I don't want you weighed down," Lenna explains. "They're moisture-wicking and temperature controlled. You'll camouflage a little, depending on the ecosystem...but your gold dust kind of ruins that."

I run my fingers along the smooth fabric that Lenna holds out for my inspection. As usual, her handiwork is impeccable.

"Try the boots to make sure they fit," Lenna orders.

They do. They may give me blisters—they aren't yet broken in—but they fit snugly. When I lace them, my gaze falls to the inseam of the right boot.

"Look inside," Lenna encourages.

A small blade is neatly tucked through a loop that runs parallel to the length of the shoe. I pull it out and smile at Lenna's clever design.

"The flags are pretty big," Lenna continues. "I was worried Perrin would make them tiny, but they're about three feet wide."

"If the prisoners know where the flags are, they might camp out nearby," Warrick warns. "To ambush you."

"Try to pit them against each other," Emberlyn suggests. "There may already be bad blood between them."

There are countless dynamics to consider. Every suggestion is a good one, and I don't want to overlook a tip that could save my life. I've also reached the point where I am overwhelmed.

"You're going to survive," Lenna says stubbornly. Her brown eyes are wide and insistent.

"I will survive," I agree with lukewarm conviction. I glance outside and then at the time. It's after 10 pm. In less than nine hours, the test will begin.

"I'm going to read before I go to bed," I say, politely signaling that I'd like time alone.

"I'll be outside." Warrick stands up abruptly and makes for the door. "Sleep well, Andra."

Lenna and Emberlyn murmur their agreement, and I feel the eyes of both watching me as I make for the washroom.

It feels odd to get ready for bed—to wash my face, to put on pajamas, to climb under covers—when I'll be far from such luxuries tomorrow. I try not to think too much about the test.

Comfortably tucked beneath the covers, I pull out the text I've been most curious to read: the golden book on time.

The book starts simply enough, describing denominations of time (hours, minutes, days) and quantifying each measure in metrics I am familiar with. I begin to skim the text, but there's a paragraph that catches my eye. I have to read it twice to understand why my subconscious flags it as compelling.

"Time is an institution governed by the sun and the moon. Records of time have been kept for generations by the scribes and prophets of Callings. All of Soulbourne adheres to the same demarcations of time, though the monastery possesses a notable aberration."

The monastery possesses an aberration of time? It's an intriguing revelation. I remember passing the monastery on the way to the Callings library—I recall the peace and beauty of the place and also the pull, not unlike the one that drew me to cross the threshold into Soulbourne. When the marble warms, a shiver of anticipation crawls up my spine.

If I'm to survive this test, it won't be through physical strength.

It won't be a result of ruthless behavior or a fundamental under-standing of Soulbourne. If I survive, it will be the result of strategy and a cunning nature…and maybe a loophole.

With a burst of exhilaration, I make my plan.

SIXTEEN

I make my move at two o'clock in the morning, when Lenna and Emberlyn are sound asleep. My heart flutters in question: am I really going to attempt this?

My bare feet land on the floor in answer.

With more care than is probably needed, I dress in the outfit designed for the Land test and pocket the marble. I glance at the pack on the table and quietly slip the golden book inside before grabbing my boots and lacing them out on the deck. I wonder how long it will take Warrick to find me.

Like a moth to a flame, Warrick summits the steps two at a time. "What do you think you're doing?"

I don't look up from lacing my boots. "I'm not trying to escape. I'm looking for something. And I need your help."

Calmly, I lift my gaze. The full moon casts enough light that Warrick's face is shadowed with an eerie, green-gray hue. His expression is stern, but curious. "What are you looking for?"

"Let's go," I say by way of answer. "I don't have much time."

Warrick's lips press into a thin line.

"Please, Warrick."

Warrick shakes his head in docile resignation. "I hope you know what you're doing."

I offer no chance for reconsideration: my boots laced, I adjust the pack on my back and motion for Warrick to start walking. He looks pointedly at the ground beneath me, and I shake my head.

"I don't care if they see my trail. By the time they see the glitter, I'll be in the Land test. Let them guess what I was up to."

"Where exactly *are* we going?" Warrick asks, falling in line beside me. His voice is low; his eyes scour the darkness for any threat.

"Callings. To the monastery."

This answer drags Warrick's eyes away from the shrubbery. "Callings. The monastery. You have my attention, Andra."

I'm loathe to elaborate near the cabin, and Warrick seems to understand my silence. He nods towards the path and mutters, "Later."

Whether there are scouts or spies watching, I don't know. But I don't see anyone as we exit Land. It's only once we start on the side trail that I feel comfortable to explain. The dense forest is replaced by rolling hills of grass—if someone tries to follow us now, we'll spot them.

"The monastery has an aberration of time."

Warrick frowns, unimpressed.

"I read about it."

"And what's the significance of time?" Warrick asks. "Why are we trekking through domains in the middle of the night?"

"I don't know. It feels important. The marble agrees." I leave out the fact that the information was found in a *golden* book, since Warrick technically doesn't know I have the text in my possession and it was Emberlyn who took the risk to procure it in the first place.

Warrick's silence feels judgmental; he doesn't have to verbalize his thoughts for me to guess at them. When he does reply, though, it's with words that catch me off guard.

"I'm glad you asked for my help."

Surprise renders me self-conscious: there are layers of meaning to Warrick's statement that I'm not sure I understand and I'm suddenly eager to fill the silence.

"Emberlyn showed us this path into Callings. Have you taken this trail before?"

Warrick nods. If he guesses at my deflection, he doesn't show any sign. "I've been on most trails in Soulbourne."

Conversation stalls as we reach the steep incline of the path up to the monastery. Warrick and I fall into a synchronized chorus of heavy breaths; my heartbeat drums inside my chest in response to the difficult ascent. And then, the pale gray behemoth stands before us on the horizon: Callings' monastery.

Up close, the gray of the monastery is textured and varied, the stone thick in some places and worn thin in others. Proud Corinthian columns spiral up from the bottom floor; decorative inscriptions and statues protrude from higher levels. Altogether, the building is a work of art.

Warrick and I pass through a fragrant rose garden and a citrus grove before walking a tiled pathway to the main entrance. Low, flickering lights line the corridor. Tall walnut doors mark the entrance; together, the two doors make the shape of a teardrop. Two wrought iron ring pulls are all that separate us from the inside. I don't hesitate to grab a ring.

The door is as heavy as it looks—it takes effort to swing it open. Inside, a spiral staircase stretches up four levels. The ground floor is filled with wide pathways outfitted with marble statues and woven tapestries; wall sconces bathe the floor in warm light. The rich, complex aroma of incense is striking. Warrick stands quietly at my side, waiting for my cue.

I don't see anyone roaming the halls, but the monastery is not asleep. I take a slow breath and inhale the smell of frankincense and clove.

Left.

I try not to think too much as I take my first steps forward, boots quietly scraping against smooth stone. Warrick is right by my side; the two of us traverse the length of the hallway in silence.

When we near the end of the corridor, I feel a pull towards a side path: shadowed steps lead up and to the right. I don't know what I walk towards, but my anticipation mounts.

Warrick doesn't question me when I pause on the landing, nor does he say a word when I close my eyes and take a deep breath. I can still smell the tangy aroma of the incense from the first floor. I don't *think* so much as I *respond* to instinct.

We walk down a narrow hallway. No tapestries hang on these walls and I nearly graze the wall sconces that protrude on either side. For Warrick, it's a tight squeeze. There aren't too many decisions to make here—occasionally a choice to travel to the right or to the left, but mostly the corridor stretches on, deep into the belly of the monastery. When I turn the corner, I know we're close.

A set of double doors draws my attention, the grainy wood rustic and regal. My hand stops short of the iron ring. Warrick's face is inscrutable, features relaxed but attentive. He raises an eyebrow in unspoken question of what I might wait for. My heart skips a beat, the sweat on my brow suddenly cool with trepidation.

I open the door.

This room isn't taller than twelve feet, and its ceiling is flat—though beautifully painted with wispy white clouds and a powder blue sky. Tucked in the middle of the monastery, there are no windows and there is no sunlight—but the library is bathed in honeyed light that makes the books glow.

And oh, the books: they cover shelf after shelf after shelf, all built into the perimeter of the room. There are gilded tables and cushioned chairs with engraved arms, the fabric richly colored. There are globes and statues and even an exquisitely-carved chess set...but the books are so lovely—so *golden*—that it takes my breath away.

They are books, I tell myself as tears form behind my eyes. *Paper, ink, glue, and cloth.* It doesn't matter that they're anatomically simple—there is an *otherness* to this room, and a magic. I don't realize that I've fallen to my knees in awe until Warrick stands over me, looking down in concern.

Please.

I don't know what I ask—or who—but the thought is fired off in my mind. Without moving my lips or making a sound, I have sent a message. I don't know how, but I know.

My limbs tremble in anticipation, of *something* that I know is about to happen. I look at Warrick and accept the hand he offers to help me to my feet. His eyes carry intensity and I wonder if he feels the magic, too.

"Close the door." My voice is low and weighed with emotion.

Warrick does so without a second thought. I walk ten feet inside the library and wait.

The answer is swift, and the summons...incredible.

A bright light fills the library. A figure materializes on the opposite end of the room like a crack of lightning. Tall, broad-shouldered, and illuminated in white light, the man who appears is ethereal in every way. The alabaster white wings that protrude on either side are, oddly, the last thing that help me to identify him as a citizen of Overworld. His essence is powerful and immobilizing. Beside me, I feel Warrick stiffen.

My body murmurs with electric energy that supersedes any nerves. "Thank you for coming."

The words that first come out of my mouth sound like I'm welcoming a guest to a tea party, and Warrick's head swivels to me. He doesn't say a word, but his face says, *what the hell?*

"I need something here." I've figured this much out. The marble in my pocket warms in agreement.

The man nods. "I'm here to help."

Warrick clears his throat. "Galen."

The man nods in return. "Warrick."

I look to Warrick in surprise. "You know each other?"

Warrick and Galen exchange a cautious smile that looks a little like a grimace. When neither answer, I press on. "I'm Andra."

Galen's stern, statuesque features quirk with amusement. "Nice to meet you, Andra." He doesn't verbalize what his humor shows: I do not need an introduction.

Warrick still seems surprised by the fact that Galen is here. It's the second time I've seen Warrick unsure of himself—he adjusts his stance and seems fidgety.

"What do I need?"

My mental plea summoned Galen—that has to mean something. He came to help. I won't waste time asking the wrong questions.

Galen doesn't need to peruse the shelves: in the span of ten seconds he pulls a wooden chest from a low shelf and places it on the nearest table. "There are limits to the assistance I can offer," he says matter-of-factly. "I show you this at risk." Here, Galen meets Warrick's gaze and holds it meaningfully.

I look from the wooden chest to the two men before me. "What's inside?"

The question lingers in the air. Warrick is as still as a wraith beside me. Galen glances at Warrick before replying.

"If you open the chest, you will authenticate your mark. You will authenticate *all* marks."

I scoff—a sound that I am quick to silence when I see the solemn expression on Galen's face.

"This is bigger than you think, Andra," Galen answers. "You might not like what you find."

I look to Warrick, hoping his expression will offer some kind of clue. His green eyes are clouded with conflict.

"Do you know what's inside?" I ask him.

Warrick stands motionless. "I have a suspicion."

Inside my pocket, the temperature of the marble increases. What originally offered cozy warmth grows to uncomfortable heat and then begins to burn my thigh. I know what the marble demands.

"Open the chest."

Inside my pocket, the marble instantly cools to its former moderate temperature.

"You have to be the one to open it," Galen says.

Something solid forms in my middle, a resolve that I know isn't capricious or impulsive. I feel butterflies of nerves and anticipation, but my hand is steady as it reaches towards the latch of the chest.

The ease with which the trunk is opened defies the covert nature of the monastery's library and the contents within. My fingers pinch the gritty metal and twist, and the chest's lid pops open with a dusty exhale.

The smell of papyrus and patchouli strikes my nostrils; the cloud of dust causes me to take a step back and then to sneeze. Warrick and Galen are still.

My initial response is one of relief: I have yet to inspect the contents of the chest, but no cobra strikes and no poisonous gas pours out. My heart pounds ferociously as I peer inside.

A scroll of thick, textured paper lays in elegant folds. It looks like handmade paper—the viscosity and width vary subtly from one side to the other, and the edges are a cinnamon-brown where the middle is the color of cream. The paper is inked with elegant, spidery scrawl and a latticework of lines.

"What is it?" My eyes never leave the scroll.

"Soulbourne's genealogy."

The answer is a surprise—I look from Galen and his enigmatic smile to Warrick, who looks grim.

"Can I take it out?"

Galen nods, though he gently pulls the folds of the scroll out of the chest before I have the chance to do so myself. I watch with bated breath as he reverently lays the parchment on the table, unfurling the pleats to reveal graceful scrawl.

It looks like a family tree, but a complicated one.

The top of the scroll features a few couplings that split off into descendants—farther down the names become tightly packed; script extend to the cinnamon-colored edges of the paper. Rich black lines run from one name to another, though the text that catches my eye has a vein of glittery-gold.

My breath catches—not because my eyes land on any single revelatory component, but because I have the sudden premonition of what I might find.

"Soulbourne's lineage," Galen says.

My eyes track the names; there aren't any I recognize. I point to a name cast in glittery ink. "What does the gold mean?"

Galen gives the question room to breathe before answering. "Defectors, aberrations, and those who are marked."

My brow furrows, and I pull my eyes from the scroll to regard Galen.

"Since Soulbourne's establishment, its operations have been very carefully controlled. Individuals who do not match leadership's carefully-demarcated domains are eradicated." Galen points to a section of the scroll without any gold. "But there are always anomalies, defectors, and a few with mysterious marks."

Galen's gaze meets mine meaningfully before he unfurls a lower portion of the scroll, where Warrick's name is shadowed with buttery gold. It doesn't sparkle—the gold looks shy, as if it's uncertain it should be there. But it's in sharp contrast to the litany of names scrawled in coal-black around them. Notably, there are not any branches connecting Warrick's name to others.

"It's you." I look from Warrick's name to the man before me in confusion. "Why is your name in gold?"

Warrick says nothing. He clears his throat and won't meet my eyes. The response welcomes a host of new questions where Warrick is concerned, but his demeanor makes it clear I won't get answers now. My gaze is back on the scroll, searching for other familiar names.

For every few hundred names scrawled in black, there is one name lined in gold. Some names have extremely subtle gold detailing; others are easy to spot, the gold thick and brash. I search in vain for Emberlyn and Lenna's names. The only other names I recognize are those of the domain leaders—each written in bold black lettering.

When Galen unfurls the last of the scroll, my gasp is audible. There, in the left margin, in fat scrawl, is my name.

Andra is written in such glittery gold that it looks garish. At first, it looks like my name is by itself, a lone island amongst a robust archipelago of family lineages.

"Why am I on this? I'm not part of Soulbourne."

The subtle shake of my head that accompanies my dissent draws my attention to a shadow next to my name. There isn't any ink on the scroll, but a sand-colored impression, almost like tracing. I lean closer.

Elara.

My heart drops, then thunders like an elephant stampede. "What *is* this?" I demand.

Galen doesn't answer. He looks sympathetic when he says, "I didn't make this."

"Who did?" I'm angry now, disturbed by the appearance of my name, and especially my sister's name, on this lineage of a ghastly realm in which I want nothing to do with.

Galen looks to Warrick before meeting my eyes. "It's a living thing—it makes itself."

"What does that mean?" My heartbeat is erratic, my thoughts an anxious jumble. I'm grasping at straws, looking for the rationale that will explain this away.

"It's a prophetic lineage." Warrick looks solemn as he finally finds his voice. "The scroll constantly evolves and adjusts to match the prophetic landscape."

"But Elara isn't even in Soulbourne," I argue.

"That you know of," Warrick says softly.

Horror strikes me like lightning. "She's in here?" I whisper.

"I didn't say that," Warrick is quick to correct.

"The scroll is linked to the heartbeat of the realm," Galen says. "It doesn't err—but it is time-fluid. It shows what was, what is, and what is to come."

"How does this authenticate my mark?" I ask the question, but I'm not sure I want to hear the answer.

Galen holds my gaze. "Your destiny is in Soulbourne. Now that you've seen this, you're irrevocably a part of our realm. There's no way for you to go back."

The fear is sudden; a brick of ice that freezes my insides and shocks my system so acutely that it takes my breath away. When I am able to speak, I sound out of breath. "You mean for right now," I say, trying and failing to make the words sound casual.

Galen doesn't look away. His direct gaze, paired with stony silence, is all the answer I need.

The blood drains from my face and I'm shaking my head even before I have the wherewithal to speak. I have so many things I want to say, and I can find no words at all with which to say them. My brain works to form a coherent thought, then stumbles anew at the sight of the shadow of Elara's name on the scroll.

"Andra." Warrick's voice is low, but it's full of warning. "It's already past four thirty."

The Land test may seem trivial in this ethereal room, standing before a citizen of Overworld and poring over prophetic lineage, but it will come just the same. I need to make it back to Land.

"Will I see you again?" I ask Galen.

"Potentially. You *will* need to fight to survive, Andra." Galen's face goes dark as a thundercloud. "If you don't, you'll die. The danger is real."

"Can you see what will happen in the Land test?" I press.

"*Andra.*"

"I've interfered too much already," Galen answers, neatly folding and replacing the scroll in the chest.

"Andra, *please.*" This third time, Warrick sounds agitated.

I turn to Warrick with agitation of my own. "*Okay.*"

When I turn to thank Galen, he is already gone.

SEVENTEEN

"How do you know Galen?"

Warrick and I hustle down the path to Callings. I narrowly avoid falling—the rocky path and steep decline nearly take me down several times.

Instead of answering, Warrick asks a question of his own. "How do *you* know Galen? Did you ask him to come?"

I sent a plea in my mind, but I didn't send it to Galen directly.

"That was my first time meeting him. And I don't know."

Warrick turns to look at me, nearly slipping as he does so. "How did you know where to go inside the monastery?"

I shrug. "I followed my instincts."

Warrick exhales heavily and narrows his eyes.

"I can't explain what just happened," I say, working to keep my vexation at bay.

Warrick studies me before answering. "You still don't trust me."

"I believe you're on my side—for now. But yeah, there won't be much trust until I understand *why* you're helping me."

Warrick's eyes cloud with disappointment. "Seeing the scroll didn't help?"

"The prophetic lineage with your name in gold? Yeah, let's talk about that. What are you, a defector or an aberration?"

Warrick's laugh is harsh. "Why do you assume I'm a defector or an aberration?"

It's my turn to study Warrick. I arch my eyebrows in open appraisal as I fold my arms across my chest. "I don't see any mark."

"You can't see all of me." Warrick's answer is just ambiguous enough that it brings a blush to my cheeks. "And you can't even see your own marks. What makes you think you'd see a mark on me?"

I frown. "*Are* you marked?" If he is, I have a lot of questions about the flurry of attention and prophecies that have been hurled *my* way because of *my* marks while Warrick gets off scot-free.

Warrick scoffs. "Don't you think Emberlyn or Lenna would have told you if I was marked?"

He's right.

Emberlyn and Lenna *would* have said something. But Warrick's response is annoying—it's yet another deflection. I'm desperately searching for answers, for anything that provides clarity on Soulbourne and why I am here, and for someone who says he's there to help me, Warrick might just be the greatest enigma.

"I don't understand why you can't just answer my questions."

Warrick regards me a moment longer, eyes burning with intensity but not warmth. "Let's get back to Land." The words are stiff, a layer of bricks to further separate us.

I exhale my frustration and follow him down the path.

Dawn breaks as we near the cabin. I've mostly resigned myself to the fact that I won't get meaningful information from Warrick, but there is one question I think he'll answer.

"How did you learn I'd entered Soulbourne?"

It never before occurred to me to ask how this information was disseminated—Syphus intercepted me in the cavern, but what message was spread throughout the realm?

Warrick is tense—he's grown increasingly stiff on the return trip back into Land, and now his entire body looks tight. "What?"

"How did you know that I'd entered Soulbourne? Was there an announcement?"

Warrick looks tired. "We felt it. There was an earthquake."

This is not the answer I expected. "An *earthquake*? Did you know what it meant?"

"From what I've heard, there's only ever been one earthquake in Soulbourne before you arrived," Warrick answers. His words are measured. "Ask Emberlyn—it's probably the reason she packed up to come find you right away. There was an earthquake, and then news of your arrival spread. You interrupted the Prosphora, so it's not like you kept a low profile."

The cabin is within sight now, the sky awash in peony pink and tangerine orange. Lenna and Emberlyn will be awake soon, if they aren't already.

"Are you going to tell the girls about your trip?" Warrick asks. His eyes rove behind us to the trail of gold glitter that I can't see. I don't have time to think on it before Emberlyn opens the door.

"Where did you go?" Lenna demands, appearing at Emberlyn's side. Both scan the rainforest for signs that we are being followed as they motion us inside.

There's no reason to lie. "The monastery."

Emberlyn gapes.

"Why?" Lenna stares at me, trying to understand.

"I read about an aberration of time in the monastery. It was in the book you brought me, Emberlyn." I don't mention that it was the *golden* book, lest Emberlyn wants to keep that detail private, but I know she'll catch my drift.

"And?" Emberlyn looks both surprised and intrigued.

"I didn't find an aberration of time," I admit.

"What *did* you find?" Emberlyn asks. She's not hung up on the fact that I left them behind—something I can see Lenna will stew over for a while—but she wants to know what came of my efforts.

"I saw the genealogy of Soulbourne." I can't see any reason to keep this a secret, though I'm careful not to elaborate. "Someone from Overworld helped," I add.

"*Overworld?*" Lenna squawks. "Someone from Overworld met you in the monastery?"

"Who?" Emberlyn asks, eyes wide.

I hesitate. I don't have any previous experience with Overworld, but I get the feeling that my first introduction was rather significant. "Galen."

Emberlyn goes white as a sheet. Lenna stiffens, her eyes searching my face for any sign of jest.

"*Galen?*" Emberlyn asks, eyebrows high to the sky.

"Yes," Warrick is pleased to interject. "Andra *summoned* him."

I glare at Warrick. "Before you ask, I don't know how I did it. Seriously."

I'm met with a hush of disbelief.

"Is anyone going to tell me who Galen is?" I ask. It would be nice to understand why they're all in awe.

Lenna looks from me to Warrick, then back to me. "Warrick didn't tell you?" she asks, voice laden with concern.

Frustration bubbles. "No. He—"

"Didn't think it wise for you to trouble yourself with anything beyond the Land test," Warrick interrupts, leveling Lenna with a scowl.

Lenna's loyalty can be seen in the way she holds Warrick's gaze. She may swoon over his star, but she won't be cowed if it comes at my expense. Turning to me: "Galen is a spirit. A *powerful* spirit."

"He looked like a man," I tell her. "But he did have wings."

"That's how he chose to appear to you," Lenna says softly. "He can take many forms."

"You've seen him before," I guess, and the knot in my stomach loosens. "Did he appear to you with wings?"

"Oh no," Lenna gushes, eyes wide as she shakes her head with zeal. "I've never met Galen. He wouldn't visit me."

Lenna's angst is undeniable; my stomach clenches and my brows furrow in confusion.

"He's a spirit, Andra, but also a seer. He resides in Overworld, when he's in Soulbourne, but he's not controlled by the domain. He's not controlled by *anyone*. He moves between realms."

All of a sudden, my casual address and nonchalant demeanor in the monastery take on new meaning. I understand Warrick's tension and wonder again how the two know each other—Lenna's response has made it clear he doesn't often stoop to interact with citizens of Soulbourne.

"I don't know why he would do it, but he could have marked you," Lenna continues. "It would be easy for him to do. The fact that you summoned him so easily suggests there's a connection between you two."

In all of this, Warrick is silent. I'm stunned into silence myself, unsure if there's another reason Warrick wanted to keep Galen's identity hidden from me.

"I hate to cut this short," Emberlyn interrupts, and she genuinely sounds reluctant, "but you don't have much time. There are a few things we need to review before the test."

"You didn't even sleep last night," Lenna realizes.

"I wouldn't have slept any better had I stayed in bed," I answer honestly.

"I'll make breakfast. Start the review," Lenna orders.

The final minutes before the test are unsettling. I eat breakfast, but part of me wishes I didn't. I'm glad for the sustenance but I feel bloated and nauseous almost immediately. Lenna braids my hair and pins it back in a bun so it's out of my face.

In the last moments, Emberlyn reviews the list of prisoners. "Dirce, Sarka, and Mercurius are the biggest threats. Don't let them near you."

"Don't let *any* of the prisoners near you," Lenna says. "Not just those three."

"Find the flags and get out," Warrick advises.

It sounds so easy when they say it. It may calm *their* nerves to dispense last minute advice, but it adds to my anxiety.

Warrick is the first to hear the entourage approach the cabin. He stiffens, his face grave.

My time is up: the Land test is about to begin.

The crowd is small: domain leaders and a few others dot the grass in front of Land's grand mansion. Perrin steps down from his stately wrap-around porch to greet me. He's dressed elegantly in fir green and mahogany brown. His face is blank, if a bit wary.

The reminder that these people think of me as a threat energizes me. They don't have to know that I'm just Andra; Andra who likes hot tea and long books and dewy morning walks through the forest. Let them think of me as *Andra*, rife with danger.

The domain leaders watch intently as I approach. None of them make any move to draw near.

"Are you clear on the objective of the test, Andra?" Perrin asks, voice loud so everyone can hear.

"Retrieve the five flags."

Perrin nods.

"When I retrieve all five flags, does the test end?"

Perrin hesitates. He doesn't look behind him, but I can tell he wants to. He wants to see what his peers think; he wants to answer in compliance with the group consensus. Someone whispers on the porch behind and Perrin stiffens slightly.

"You won't find all five flags in less than five days. The task is a difficult one. When—*if*—you collect all five flags and make it back here, the test ends."

I don't ask what will happen if I fail to retrieve all five flags.

"You'll enter the test arena there."

Perrin points to a tall, wrought-iron gate at the edge of the forest. I'm to be locked inside like a caged animal. Worse—like a mouse offered as prey to seven serpents waiting inside.

I wonder if they're watching. If they don't know where I am now, they will soon. The trail of gold glitter will show them every step I take.

Perrin clears his throat.

"What time does the test start?" I don't plan to enter until I absolutely have to.

"Now," Perrin snipes.

My legs feel like lead as I walk towards the gate. I fight to keep my gait steady and even. If any of the prisoners *are* watching, I want them to see a confident woman. I don't want to give the domain leaders the satisfaction of witnessing my nerves.

Agrona, the hit man from Rock.
Mercurius, the hunter of humans from Land.
Dirce, the knife-wielding spy from Boundless.
Sarka, the dark witch from Underworld.
Kakarauri, the crafty siren from Water.
Nox, the silent assassin from Air.
Brone, the false prophet from Callings.

I don't know what any of them look like, but I've memorized their names and domains.

The dew on the grass makes the bottom of my boots slick. There's not much of a breeze, though the canopy of the tall trees keeps the air cool. I smell pinecones and loamy earth.

Try to stay hidden.
When you cover ground, stick to open spaces. When you stop, make sure to have a weapon in hand.
Don't worry about food, but pay attention to water.
Don't forget about the dangerous creatures in each ecosystem.

Watch your opponent's eyes. Don't willingly engage in a fight.

You can't sleep unless there's a storm, Andra—only water, dust, or snow will shield your trail of glitter.

Advice from Warrick, Lenna, and Emberlyn races through my brain. It's the last fact that troubles me most—there's no safe way for me to sleep. Adrenaline courses through me now, but how long will it last? I didn't rest last night...can I stay awake for five more days? If there isn't rain, snow, or a dust storm, I'll have little choice.

All too soon, I stand in front of the gate. I fidget with the straps on my pack to ease my nerves. Four guards—two on either side—watch me carefully but make no move to force me into the test. I know that the moment I enter the gates, I will be locked in.

The wrought iron allows me to see inside: I stand for a moment, scouring the land for any visible threat. The last thing I need is an immediate confrontation.

"Have you seen any prisoners?" I ask the guards.

Three of the guards ignore me, but one makes eye contact and offers a subtle shake of his head. It's so minute that it could be my imagination. He could be lying.

But I've hesitated long enough. I need to enter the test—there will never be a good time. The thump of my heart pounds so rapidly that I feel light headed, like I'm going to vomit.

Please.

I don't know how I sent the message last time, when I was in the monastery—but a similar channel in my mind opens as I take a deep breath and poise myself to enter.

Help me.

I enter the test.

EIGHTEEN

Warrick

As Andra disappears into the forest, I stand silent. Every sense is attuned: to detect a scream, a thud—anything that signals danger. All pointless, because I won't be able to do anything.

When the earth begins to shake, I first assume it's some theatrical element meant to commemorate the initiation of the test. The moment I see Syphus stand from his seat on Perrin's porch, I know differently. I sprint towards the hub of Soulbourne and hope I make it there first.

The path is mostly empty. Adrenaline and nerves work to my advantage, pushing me to run faster. Syphus notices me, and though no words are exchanged, he picks up his pace. I do the same. We reach the cavern at the same time, our heavy breathing the only noise in the otherwise-still cave.

I hear her first.

A lovely melody floats through the cavern: a light, airy arrangement that presents in short bursts—bursts that seem to coincide with footfalls. There's little doubt what this means: someone else has been summoned to Soulbourne, and this individual also bears a mark.

And then, I see her.

It's difficult to make out features in the dim lighting, but she's average height with a slight frame. When a smile stretches across Syphus' face and a macabre gleam glitters in his gray eyes, I know he's also spotted the newcomer.

"Welcome to Soulbourne," Syphus calls in a buttery voice.

"Who is that?" The woman's head jerks our direction.

Syphus waves, and the woman's attention snaps to his figure. She makes quick work of the descent. My heart races with each musical step taken—then drops the second I see her face.

Her features are delicate, her frame slender and petite. She has strawberry coloring to her shoulder-length golden locks and her eyes are a deeper shade of blue, but she could be Andra's twin. It's undoubtedly Elara.

"Ahhh," Syphus croons. "You've come for And-*ra*."

Elara's eyes flash with recognition. She fixes Syphus with a look of disdain. "Where is she?" The words are low and sharp, spoken in warning.

Syphus smiles. "We'll get to business soon enough. We haven't been introduced."

"Where. Is. She."

Elara's nostrils flare as she takes a step closer. The energy is palpable—rage rolls in waves over her body. Syphus is an intimidating figure—most find him unsettling, at the very least—and Elara looks at him like he's an ant she'd like to squish under her shoe. A moment ago, I was worried about protecting Andra's little sister. Now, I'm curious to see Syphus' response.

As though he can hear my thoughts, Syphus cuts his gaze to me. Elara's eyes follow. She regards me with little interest but repositions her body to face both of us. "I'm going to ask one more time."

"Andra's in a test," I say.

"Who are you?"

"Warrick. I've been helping Andra."

Elara holds my gaze, expression inscrutable. She turns to face Syphus. "Who are *you*?" There's a snarl to her tone that hints that she already knows Syphus to be an enemy.

Syphus inclines his head and smiles. "Syphus. I welcomed Andra into Soulbourne."

"You are *not* helping Andra." The words come out flat, a statement she dares Syphus to deny.

"None of us are helping Andra anymore. She made the decision to enter Soulbourne, and now she's in a test to try to win her freedom."

Elara's eyes narrow. "What kind of test?"

Syphus hesitates.

"What *kind* of test?" Elara asks again, louder this time. The timbre of her voice is unstable.

"I didn't make the test," Syphus replies, and this single statement tells Elara everything she needs to know about the nature of the test and Syphus himself.

Elara doesn't waste time with words: she chucks a fist-sized rock at Syphus' head. He ducks, and she uses the opportunity to hurl another rock his way. This one meets its target.

I'm dumbfounded—gleeful—and impressed.

When Syphus regains his balance, the look on his face confirms that this is the time to intervene.

I'm between them in seconds, pushing Syphus away and then pulling Elara to the side. I feel the anger that pulses like a live wire through Syphus, I feel the trembling of Elara's bones as she seethes with rage. I hear the lovely music of Elara's mark that sounds preposterous and out of place, given the circumstances.

"I'll kill you."

Elara says it like a promise. She looks over my shoulder at Syphus as she pushes against me like I'm a scarecrow and not a hulking mass of muscle.

"My dear, I think you'll have to hope for that opportunity," Syphus purrs, wiping a smear of blood from his lip. Elara's throw was a good one: Syphus' lip plumps and there's a faint shadow that promises a bruise just above.

"I won't rest until I do," Elara continues. The energy pulsing through her body is powerful enough that I know she does not over-sell herself.

"You might worry that I develop a mind to do the same," Syphus says sweetly. "Though I still don't have your name. All I've gathered is that you're very, very protective of lovely And-*ra*."

Elara's lip curls, her expression feral for a moment before she answers. "Elara."

I knew she was Andra's sister the moment I laid eyes on her. Hearing the confirmation still feels like a blow.

"You two could pass for twins," Syphus muses in an obvious ploy for information that Elara doesn't acknowledge. "Well, *Elara*—your timing is unfortunate. And-*ra* just entered her first test, and it's set to last five days. If she's alive at the end, I'm sure she'll be glad to see you."

Elara's body starts to tremble. I don't need to look at her to guess what will happen next.

"Elara, come with me."

The words are out before I have a chance to consider them. Elara studies me for an uncomfortable moment, then nods.

"You can't leave," Syphus snarls.

"You got to greet the first sister—I get this one." I don't wait for Syphus' response. "Quickly," I whisper to Elara as I point the way down.

To her credit, Elara is nimble. I keep close on her heels, checking to make sure Syphus doesn't follow.

"What's going on?" Elara asks the second we hit sunlight.

I shake my head. "You'll have to wait for answers."

I brace for Elara's protest—what reason does she have to trust me? Her older sister certainly doesn't. But those blue eyes see some-thing, because while her nostrils flare, she nods her assent.

And then I take Elara to the only domain I suspect might help us: Overworld.

I've been in Overworld a handful of times, and it never ceases to awe. The quartz path sparkles in the sunlight, rubies and emeralds glitter in lines on either side. Towering statues cast the only shadows, the blocks of marble meant to inspire reverence and a healthy measure of respect. The light of Overworld is intense; the decadence and opulence overwhelming.

Elara looks enthralled.

It's a normal response to Overworld, but Elara hasn't shown herself to be very normal in the short time I've known her.

"Anything I should know before we make it to wherever we're going?" A warning flashes in her eyes.

"We're going to try for an audience with Justus, the leader of Overworld," I explain. "He might help."

Elara's expression is full of questions, but she holds her tongue. I see the opportunity and take it. "You came for Andra."

"I'm *looking* for Andra," Elara corrects.

"How did you know where to go?"

Elara shrugs. "I felt a pull." Her words are casual; her gaze is anything but. She watches me, waiting to see what I make of her words.

I sigh. "Your sister said the same thing."

"Andra felt a pull here?" Elara asks, frowning. Her slim arms tighten, the muscles coil like rope. "What kind of test is she in? Why can't we pull her out?"

I run a hand over my face. "It's not that simple." And it's about to get much more complicated, when leadership learns that Andra's marked sister has made her way into Soulbourne.

"Let's *make* it that simple," Elara barks. "I'll suffer the consequences. Let's get her out. *Now.*"

"That won't work."

Mercifully, the words come from someone else.

We both turn to regard Justus, leader of Overworld. His hair is cloud-white and neatly trimmed and he's dressed in ethereal silver robes. Despite his prominent status, he has no guard.

Elara is temporarily stunned into silence, and I'm caught off guard by how quickly we found Justus. I was prepared to track the domain leader down, but it would seem he found us first.

Justus points to a bench made of quartz and rubies and motions for us to sit. We do. The light from the sun bears down with startling intensity, making it hard not to squint as I look up at the powerful leader of Overworld.

"We need to get Andra out of the test. We'll leave and never come back," Elara swears. I'm still gathering my bearings and Elara is coming in hot, completely undaunted by the surroundings and the formidable figure standing before us.

Justus shakes his head. "There are prophecies. No one comes here without a purpose." He inclines his head knowingly at Elara.

"*Me?*" Elara asks, bewildered.

"You're both marked." Justus appears indifferent as he drones on, "I suspect that you're not just here to save Andra."

A current of energy rockets through my body. I now understand the prophecy Andra was given while traveling back from Callings with Emberlyn and Lenna. *Without intervention, you will die in the Land test.* I just didn't expect *Elara* to be that intervention.

I clear my throat. "You'll help?"

Justus' expression is unreadable. "It behooves me to see Andra survive the first test," he answers smoothly.

This answer doesn't illuminate Justus' motives, something I will ruminate over later. In the moment, it doesn't matter what Justus' incentive for helping is—we aren't in a position to turn help down. I'll worry about the cost later.

"What do I need to do?" Elara asks.

Justus' violet eyes sparkle in the midday light. "You need to enter the Land test."

My head snaps up. I'm trying to save Andra *from* the test, not send her sister *in*.

Justus' gaze is fixed on Elara. "Your sister needs you in the test. If she's left on her own, she won't survive."

Elara's eyes bear the weight of purpose. "You don't have to convince me. Tell me what I need to do, and I'll do it."

It takes less time to exit Overworld than to enter. After receiving instructions from Justus, Elara and I waste no time. "You're not nervous?" I ask when we're alone. Elara looks unflappable. I don't know her well enough to know if this is an act or if she's actually insane.

Elara looks at me. Before she says a word, her eyes tell me that I'm an idiot. "Of course I'm nervous."

I nod, unsure how to respond. It was a stupid question to ask—it served no real purpose, and now I'm fumbling for the right words. "We're getting close," I say.

Elara's gaze is resolute. "I'm ready."

As we close in on Perrin's mansion, I note Syphus' presence. As I'd anticipated, he came straight to leadership with the news of Elara's entrance into Soulbourne. The domain leaders are engaged in heated discussion when they spot us. Our progress to the mansion is tracked, and when we're close enough that Elara's music can be heard, eyes widen.

Syphus, in a quick attempt to control the narrative, saunters to the edge of the porch. He opens his mouth to speak but Elara beats him to it.

"Release my sister at once." Elara makes eye contact with each domain leader as she summits the porch steps.

Syphus is caught off guard by Elara's audacity; he recoils a fraction of an inch as she sails past.

"How dare you speak to us like that."

Achlys' outrage is palpable—the porch seems to vibrate with the tenor of his low growl. He must have *some* effect on Elara, but she shows no sign.

"Are you the one responsible for putting Andra in that test?" Elara takes an aggressive step towards Achlys.

Achlys is stunned into silence—I can't imagine anyone has ever threatened him before. He doesn't know how to react—he's never *had* to react.

"Where is she?" Elara spits, unfazed.

"Like I said: she's a natural for Underworld," Syphus muses drily.

Achlys laughs. The notes of his laughter are discordant and ominous—my gut tightens in response.

"Well met, Elara. I would have enjoyed your company, if I did not have a warrant for your immediate arrest," Achlys says.

"*Execution*," Syphus clarifies, eyes wild with rage.

"We haven't decided that," Elinarr cuts in. He seems nervous to speak and looks to the other domain leaders to back him up. They do so with unease: tepid nods are offered alongside uncertain glances.

"What is your role in this, Warrick?" Tyra asks.

"She demanded to come to the test." I shrug, pretending I could care less what happens to Andra's sister. "You've seen her—she doesn't take no for an answer."

"She's about to," Syphus snarls.

There are murmurs amongst the domain leaders—a general sense of agreement that Elara should be questioned and punished.

"My father is coming," Calum announces.

A jolt of electricity ripples through the domain leaders at this announcement—Justus rarely leaves his domain. Calum is his known proxy, the face of Overworld. For Justus to leave...

"We shouldn't trouble Justus with this riffraff," Syphus says, but he seems rattled.

A flash of lightning causes two domain leaders to flinch. When the smoke dissipates, Justus stands in the clearing. He stands motionless for a moment, assessing the domain leaders in front of him before ascending the stairs.

"Justus," Perrin greets the Overworld leader. Quickly, the other domain leaders follow suit. Justus acknowledges them collectively with a nod before turning to Elara.

"You have trespassed not only into Soulbourne, but into Overworld," Justus accuses, violet eyes unyielding. "Furthermore, you bear the mark of a threat."

"We were just discussing that," Syphus jumps in eagerly. "We were—"

"Silence."

Justus doesn't raise his voice, but the tone is cutting and Syphus stops mid-sentence. No one dares speak as they wait for the leader of Overworld to say his piece.

"Elara Bellemere, for your transgressions, you will be punished. Effective immediately, you are a prisoner of Overworld," Justus declares. He looks to the other domain leaders, daring them to challenge this pronouncement. None of them move a muscle—not even Achlys, whose steely eyes flicker from Elara to Justus with interest.

Syphus looks dismayed, but he has no clout with which to challenge Justus—he will not get his pound of flesh.

"I understand the test has started," Justus continues. He doesn't even glance in the direction of the gate.

"Yes," Perrin answers nervously.

"Andra is to capture five flags from the seven ecosystems of Land?" Justus asks. His eyes betray no emotion.

"Yes," Perrin agrees. "There are seven prisoners—" he hesitates.

Justus inclines his head, beckoning for Perrin to finish the sentence he cut short.

"...one from each domain," Perrin finishes.

"Not *every* domain," Justus disagrees.

"We were under the impression that you did not have any prisoners," Perrin stammers, looking at Calum. Calum stays silent, eyes fixed on his father.

"Until very recently, Overworld did not house prisoners," Justus agrees.

"Yes," Perrin stammers, latching onto any excuse for a potential oversight.

"But we do now."

All at once, the domain leaders understand what Justus means to do. Achlys' lip curls and Syphus' mouth falls open with a squawk of protest.

"No one would deny Overworld's right to enter a prisoner into the Land test, would they?"

The domain leaders are silent.

When no one protests, Justus nods.

"Warrick, escort my prisoner to the Land test." Justus' pronouncement is final and delivered with authority.

My chest swells with the warm glow of victory as I grab Elara's arm roughly and pull her down the porch steps. It's all for show, but Elara doesn't protest. She doesn't say a word...though she can't help but throw a smug glance at Syphus on her way down.

No one mentions the fact that the test has already started. No one asks Justus why he descended from Overworld. Elara's lips curve into a smile the moment we have our backs to the domain leaders.

"Not yet," I snap.

We have won this round, but Syphus will not stand for humiliation and Achlys will not be played for a fool. Retribution is coming—and we have just laid out the terms for a complex, intricate challenge.

Elara restrains her smile, but her eyes twinkle with triumph.

"It's just beginning," I warn. "You're about to fight for Andra's life, but your life is on the line now, too." Elara's been briefed on the seven dangerous prisoners roaming the Land test—the worst is yet to come.

Elara nods, unbothered. "I'm going to find her, Warrick. We're going to defeat this test."

She says it with such confidence. I hope, with everything in me, that she's right.

NINETEEN

Andra

From the moment I enter the Land test, I have the feeling I'm being hunted. All my senses are on high alert; adrenaline pumps through my body.

Survive. Survive. Survive.

It's hard to know where to start. The stillness and quiet are crippling. Every branch and rock and lump of soil seems to watch my progress and judge my movement.

I need to move. Standing in place does nothing to secure my victory or safety. This doesn't mean it's easy.

It will get better, I tell myself as I take step after step across the loamy earth. I don't allow myself to consider the fact that it might *not* get better, that I have five days to survive, and if I manage to escape the Land test, it will just be a matter of time before I am plunged into the next fatal test.

While I walk, I keep my eyes peeled. Without knowing Perrin well, it's hard to imagine where he might think to hide the flags—will they be easily visible but hard to reach? Difficult to spot but simple to claim?

From what I've learned of Perrin, he's not very original. His test alone speaks to that fact—Syphus wasn't wrong in his pronouncement that the Land test is essentially a giant game of capture the flag. I expect the five flags to be evenly distributed amongst the ecosystems.

After an hour, my tepid progress through the forest thaws, my shoulders relax, and I begin to cover more ground. I've seen the physical features map of Land and the marked area in which the test takes place, so I have a general sense of where I am.

I plan to search Tundra first—I want to scour the ice while I'm strong. I also figure Tundra is not a place the prisoners will want to dwell. Of all the ecosystems, I guess that the prisoners will naturally congregate in Mountains, Canyon, Jungle, and Forest.

The sun rises high in the sky, then falls behind the clouds and finally drops low in silent goodbye. As brilliant oranges and pinks color the sky, panic sets in. I've walked all day, and I still haven't even *made* it to Tundra.

The first day is set to expire.

I'm going to have to cover ground and hunt flags in the night.

Every sound becomes larger than life: a crackle of twigs makes me jump, a gust of wind has me sniffing the air in panic. My own odor is a liability I cannot forget—while I'm busy trying to *guess* if there are prisoners around, my scent and glitter are a dead giveaway.

The forest grows cold, the wind more frequent and layered. I'm nearing Tundra, then. I saw the boundaries on the map but didn't understand the distance and the time it would take to travel from one ecosystem to the next until now.

I pledge to remain calm, but I've done the calculations in my head. I cannot keep my current pace and remain successful. I will not make it to every domain—much less track down every flag.

Travel at night, search in the day. I won't sleep.

I can make progress at night, when I hope the other prisoners *are* asleep, and then I will hunt like a fiend for the flags in daylight. When I find a flag, I will need to run to expedite the journey to the next ecosystem.

I'm not sure how long I have walked when I hit ice; and then, I keep walking. The frost chills every inch of me: even with my jacket pulled up around my ears and mouth, my body shakes and my feet go numb.

There's a chance that there isn't any flag in Tundra. There is also the chance that I will walk straight past a flag as I march across the ice in the dark night.

In the obsidian sky, stars twinkle like fireflies. So far away, I wonder if these stars are the same as those I would gaze upon back home—or are the stars different in Soulbourne, too?

When absolute black fades to the color of soot and then to graphite gray, I am alive. Freezing cold and shaking like a leaf, but alive. In the muted gray light of dawn, I see miles and miles of snowy mounds and sheets of ice.

My heart sinks. *It will take a miracle to find the flags.*

I can't keep the thought from pushing through, my mental defenses feeble after a night in the frigid cold. My boots keep moving; the crunch of snow and ice become an anthem.

Crunch. Crunch. Crunkkk.

The ice suddenly becomes slick, and when my boot lands in the wrong spot, I fall back onto my ass. Hard.

Pain shoots through my lower back and spine like a thunderbolt and tears spring to my eyes—tears that immediately freeze solid at the outer edges of my eyelids, making it difficult to keep my eyes open.

You're lucky you landed on your ass.

The fall is hard enough—the ice solid—that a landing on a less-fleshy part of my body would have ended badly.

If I were not in Soulbourne, in the Land test, fighting for my life, I would cry. Instead, I carefully shift the weight off my smarting tailbone and wait for my boots to gain purchase against the ice before attempting to stand.

It is there, in that juvenile crouch, that I spot the flag.

Pale blue, the color of clouds on a stormy day, it sits crumpled and frozen in a snowbank just feet in front of me.

I blink. Emotion roils inside me like a tidal wave.

It's a miracle: the fact that I walked this stretch of Tundra is a miracle in and of itself—but tripping mere feet from a flag, falling hard on the ground so that my eyes are level with the blue cloth and the snow it's trapped inside...

Tears blur my vision.

I will survive.

This time, the declaration isn't empty. I actually believe it. Someone—something—is looking out for me. Swiping at the crystallized tears hanging from my eyelashes, I dig like hell.

Ten minutes later, the pale blue flag is stuffed at the bottom of my pack. The skin on my hands is speckled red and white and green and—if I'm being honest, a shade of blue that looks unhealthy—but despite the stinging cold and throbbing of my hands and my tailbone and my feet, I smile as I walk across icy Tundra.

My optimism endures the first half of the slog through Tundra but fades with the rising sun. The bright light on the white ice is intense—without anything to shield me from its rays, I contract a migraine.

The warmth of the sun heats the entire top layer of ice, too—a constant hazard as I pick my way across the snowy expanse. It's technical work to navigate each footfall and assess the slope and depth of each square foot, and I'm exhausted.

I entered the Land test physically fatigued and compromised from a sleepless night...and now I've spent an additional twenty-four hours without rest. I haven't needed to run or climb or fight—but the nonstop walking and lack of a respite wear on me.

I'm so locked into a mindless, numbing march that it barely registers when I see a clump of grass through the ice. Next, the *crunch* of ice becomes more pronounced—it's no longer solid and slick but clumpy and a little bit muddy.

The shadow of my body and the position of the sun suggest it is early afternoon. I see trees in the distance. I hurry—I need to make it out before night falls. I don't want to spend the night in Forest—that and Jungle are the two ecosystems I imagine hold the most danger.

With bleary adrenaline I enter the copse of brush, eyes burning and eyelids heavy. I blink back fatigue. The shade of the trees brings some relief, but it also brings a chill—I no longer walk on blankets of ice, but I don't have the direct impact of the sun's rays to warm my body.

I'm determined to make it to Desert before the sun sets. Also: I'm hungry, my body hurts, and I'm tired.

I don't have the luxury of rest in this test, but I feel my energy fade. I don't know how much longer I can function without sleep.

I make it through Forest before dark. I can't spot the sun through the towering trees, but the long shadows and filtered light tell me enough. I stop shivering. I'm just cold now, not freezing-can't-think-of-anything-else cold.

I haven't seen any prisoners. The thought weighs on me.

In the beginning, I startled at every disturbance—sure that imminent death lay just ahead. Now, I hope that my consistent movement and ground coverage keep me out of harm's way.

The dense trees become loosely clustered and then spartan; the foliage on the trees transitions from lush to haphazard. The wind picks up, ushering in goosebumps on my arms and legs.

Aware that the wind will only pick up the closer I make it to Desert, I cinch the jacket as close to my body as it can go, folding my arms across my chest and tucking my hands in my armpits for warmth.

When I see the reddish-orange sands of Desert, the otherworldly mounds that rise and fall in craters that look more like another planet than an ecosystem, I run. Not to get away from anything in particular, per se, but to exit Forest without incident.

The expanse of sand in Desert is not unlike Tundra: though there's some variation in elevation, you can see far into the distance. I will be exposed for the first couple of miles, at least—besides the trail of gold dust, my figure will be easy to spot against the backdrop of red and orange sand.

Flashes of pain shoot from my tailbone down my legs as I run, courtesy of my fall in Tundra. My legs feel like blocks of stone. The pack jostles on my back uncomfortably, throwing off the careful cadence I built through steady strides.

The light-headedness is another matter.

I stayed fully hydrated in Tundra, but I didn't stop for water in Forest. I have a skin of water, but it's half gone, and I don't dare to chug it now, just before I enter Desert. I realize too late that it would have been prudent to seek water before leaving Forest.

Yellow specks cloud the periphery of my vision, pesky dots that blur and then shift position when I blink. I have some almonds in my bag that might help, in case it's my blood sugar that's low and not the fact that I'm dehydrated—but I'm loathe to stop to retrieve either. Right now, I need to disappear.

It's with bleary, yellow-spotted consciousness that I stumble through Desert. When the sand becomes soft, my progress slows—and when it becomes too much work to lift my already-fatigued legs, I stop running and walk.

It should be a reprieve.

Instead, the world before me swirls and spins.

My eyes search for something to anchor my awareness, but it's hard to tell which direction is up or left or right or down. And then the world goes black.

I regain consciousness slowly, in gentle waves that draw me nearer and nearer to awareness. I feel sensation in my fingers and toes: a

numb, fuzzy tingling. My midsection feels heavy and my brain like a hunk of lead. Little fingers of thoughts press into me, reticent and unsure. I suppress them at first, reluctant to leave the land of tingling sensation for the real one.

But awareness dawns and I begin to remember my entry into Desert and the lightheadedness that precipitated whatever it is that I'm in right now. In a panic, my eyes fly open.

My head pounds, my throat dry and chalky, and my eyes look up to behold a sky full of brilliant stars. The incredible beauty of the universe above is in stark contrast to my state of being—just the act of opening my eyes is enough to summon nausea. I roll on my side and vomit. It's only then, when I go to push the stray hairs out of my face, that I realize my hands are tied.

Panic rears its head a second time, this time with a sense of foreboding that clings to my bones like a spider web. My body won't release me from the nausea and my physiological response can't be contained. I vomit when I should be looking around to gauge the situation. My life may depend upon it.

"Andraaaa."

I'm still not over the waves of nausea—my head stays bent, my stomach churns and heaves. The errant hairs of my braided bun are soiled as I work to steady my breathing and control my stomach. When I'm able to do so, I lift my head.

It's a woman—I don't know if it's Dirce, the Boundless spy, Sarka, the witch from Underworld, or Kakarauri, the siren from Water. Whoever she is, she watches me intently from the distance of ten feet.

A fire blazes. I see my pack near the woman's feet and can tell from its lumpy appearance that the contents have been rummaged through. My feet are tied, like my hands, but I think I'm otherwise unharmed. I don't feel pain, at least.

In the flickering fire light, I study the woman. She has silver hair that sparkles in the warm glow of the fire. As impractical as it may be, especially in the desert winds, she wears it down. She's dressed in dark robes—the flames don't reach close enough to reveal the color.

165

But her eyes—her eyes look to be wholly white. I don't see any pupils, and that is most unnerving.

"Who are you?" The words come out raspy, my throat ragged and dry both from dehydration and retching.

The woman stares at me for a moment, considering. Her limbs, hidden in her robes, stay frozen in place. An arid breeze lifts her hair, gently sweeping it up and sending wayward strands into her face. Even then, the woman does not move.

"Sarka." The word sounds more like an oath than an introduction.

My brain feels like it's been attacked by a sledgehammer, but I probe my memory for every detail Emberlyn and Lenna and Warrick told me about Sarka. *She's a witch—she loves the darkness. Something about voodoo...*

The fuzziness clears and I scan the fire for any sign of foul play. Sarka has me tied up—but for what? I suppose I'm lucky that I haven't already been killed—Agrona, the hit man from Rock, would likely have polished me off in seconds. I imagine most of the prisoners would have done the same.

"What have you heard about me." Sarka doesn't move as she speaks—she is wholly fixed on my face and watches my every move.

"You're a witch—from Underworld."

Every word hurts—it feels like rocks scrape against the inside of my throat. I don't want to mention voodoo.

"What else."

"I—I don't know that much," I stammer before breaking into a coughing fit.

Sarka's eyes narrow.

I keep my head lifted but my gaze down. Most of my hair is pulled back, so I'm not able to hide behind a waterfall of tresses, but under the cover of my lashes, my eyes gather every detail of my surroundings.

I've already laid eyes on my pack and the fire. I look to see what weapons Sarka has...to see if there's anything I might be able to leverage to my advantage.

But if the witch has any weapons, they're concealed beneath her robe. There isn't anything strewn about near the fire. We're in the middle of Desert, surrounded by sand and rock and open space.

My eyes land on the frayed edge of a rope sequestered under a large rock. It's taut and extends upwards at a forty-five degree angle that tells me it's linked to something. It's far enough from the fire that I can't tell what it is.

"Who marked you."

Sarka's voice doesn't follow traditional speech patterns—the way she chunks syllables and manipulates tone makes every word sound like she's chanting a lethal incantation. Every sentence ends flat, as though she won't degrade herself by raising her voice in question.

"I don't know who marked me."

Even here, in this confounded test, I'm asked about the mark. Even a prisoner from Underworld wants to know. I can't decide whether this makes me want to laugh or pull out my hair.

"*Liar.* Tell the truth!"

The word is hissed with such venom, with such intensity and shrill that the hairs on my arms stand at attention. My heart races; Sarka's white eyes seem to glow and vacillate in size.

A shifting of feet and a dust cloud of sand win my attention. My head snaps up to peer into the darkness between Sarka and me.

It's the rope—the rope holds someone else captive.

"Who is it?" I ask. The words burn as I nod my head towards the rope.

Sarka glowers. Her eyes squint and her chin juts out as she grates her teeth with displeasure. She moves closer to the rope, movements lithe and slippery and more animal than human.

I hold my breath. Is the prisoner gagged? A cold dread sweeps over me, but I can't look away.

Sarka stalks to the rope, then stops. She crouches low, her face close to the fire so those chalky-white eyes reflect flames and illuminate every pore on her ashen face.

I want to recoil—my body does, in fact, pull back and away—but I have nowhere to go. My arms are bound and my legs are bound and I'm stuck with a front-row seat to whatever monstrosity is about to take place.

Eyes fixed on mine, Sarka's long fingers encircle the rope, stroke the coarse cord gently before exacting a powerful jerk. There's a grunt of pain—Sarka's eyes glow with sadistic pleasure at the sound—and then a camel's head and neck come into view.

My heart sinks.

Not only because I feel pity for the captive camel, but because there isn't another human with whom I might conspire to win my freedom. If Sarka had captured another prisoner, I might have negotiated an escape. But this desert beast with chocolate-brown eyes is just as doomed as I am.

"You thought you had a chance to escape."

There's a timbre of delight that pulses through Sarka's words—she takes pleasure in my despair, feeds off of it.

I don't answer. I lock eyes with the camel before looking down. I don't have any ideas of how I might free myself, much less the camel. Without the use of my arms and legs, I'm not much of a threat. I'm still working to clear the haze in my brain.

"You—and this beast—are going to die a slow, miserable death," Sarka says. It's not a threat—it's a promise.

My pulse quickens—not so much at the mention of death, but at the thought of slow, drawn-out pain.

"Why kill something useful?" My cracked voice is pitiful even to my own ears.

Sarka laughs, a sound utterly devoid of mirth. The tone is all wrong. "How useful is a girl who won't answer questions." Her white eyes are alight, enthralled by the bargaining and groveling she anticipates.

"I meant the camel, not myself."

Sarka's face freezes for a moment—she's caught off guard. "You're a disappointment."

"Why didn't you kill me already?"

I'm desperate to buy time. Maybe the roaring fire will attract the attention of another prisoner. Maybe, if I'm lucky, the two will fight over who gets to kill me and I can somehow wriggle free. It would take a miracle to get out of this predicament, but I've already gotten one. Maybe I can get another.

Sarka considers me, gaze disdainful like I'm scum between her toes. Every bone in my body is tense, wary—ready for lightning-quick reflexes to deliver punishment. But Sarka doesn't draw near.

"I thought you would be interesting."

Sarka's answer surprises me, though I try not to show it.

"The woman from the prophecies...the one with the bright star." She finishes in her usual flat way, but this time it feels personal—like an indictment that I am a flat *person*, utterly devoid of intrigue or dimensionality. "You don't have to tell me who marked you. I already know. And I don't know what Achlys sees in you."

This last comment strikes me—my head snaps up and I stare at Sarka with open confusion.

"Why would he summon you," Sarka asks. For the first time, there's a hint of emotion to the words. She sounds almost...*hurt*.

I swallow. My throat still feels like sandpaper, but the pain barely registers. I'm more interested in what Sarka has implied. She thinks *Achlys* marked me...that *Achlys* is the one who summoned me to Soulbourne. The idea is revolting.

"What are you hiding." Sarka asks. "What is so special about you. Why would Achlys give you his prized possession. Why did he let you visit Underworld without punishment."

I hesitate.

Sarka didn't intend to, but she's given me insight—some potential leverage. She cares what Achlys thinks. I can't imagine *why*—Achlys is a certified psychopath—but I may be able to play this to my advantage.

"How do you know Achlys?"

Sarka surprises me by answering. Maybe, for all her loathsome character traits and depraved state, she is still human enough to want empathy. "He used to love me." Pride glitters in her eyes, and I know that whatever is playing out right now, it is rife with real emotions.

I don't know what to say. Though I am silent, my eyes carry some message: a dark gleam flashes in Sarka's eyes and her eyebrows slope angrily.

"I don't want him back anymore. Not after what he's done. I don't care what happens to him."

But it's not true.

I look at the sharp edges of her face and the way her chin points in the air and I know that she is still deeply, deeply wounded. She might murder Achlys before admitting she still has feelings, but Sarka is anything but apathetic where the leader of Underworld is concerned.

This realization clears the fog from my brain. I don't have a plan, exactly, but I have the threads of an idea.

"Why did he betray you?"

Sarka glowers and stares at the flickering flames. "Because he could."

Whatever Achlys did to Sarka, I don't doubt that it was cold, hard betrayal. Achlys is evil—even this dark witch was used and abused by him.

"Don't pity me, girl. You're the one who will suffer. Every drop of blood, every whimper and cry will serve as a reminder of your weakness. Achlys will be just as repulsed by you as I am."

The hurt in Sarka's eyes has vanished, replaced now with a depravity that makes my blood run cold. I scoot back and away from her, bottom dragging across the sand as I near the fire.

Sarka rolls her neck and shoulders like she's preparing for strenuous exercise. Reaching deep within her robes, she pulls out a long, thin blade. It's as long as her shin; it looks like a butcher's knife.

I gag.

I don't have to delve deep into my imagination to guess how she might use the blade. I'm close enough to the fire now that it stings— embers lash out and burn the hairs on my arms, but I don't pull back. I would rather die in the fire than at the hands of Sarka. The flames will consume me; Sarka means to torture me.

The camel makes a noise, twisting against the rope in agitation at the sight of the blade. Sarka throws her a menacing glare and a growl that suggests the camel will be next before taking a step towards me.

It's instinct to scoot away.

Back to the fire, I feel the flames and can't bring myself to pull away, because that would mean moving closer to Sarka. My brain trills with deafening bells of alarm and adrenaline courses through my body without outlet.

I am trapped.

My senses are acute—I smell the iron in the rippled red sand dunes and I smell acrid fear in the sweat beading my forehead and neck. I smell...*smoke?*

I subtly move my arms behind my back, aware of Sarka's slow stalk as I test to see if the cords have become loose. I'm still bound. The smell of smoke has faded—whatever was smoking before is not now. Ignoring the blaze and danger, I scoot back one more time, drawing my wrists close to the flames.

Without eyes to gauge my progress, I drag my hands too far— the flames lick the heels of my hands and a blanket of black passes over my vision, prompting another wave of nausea. This time, there is nothing to send up—only spittle is produced in the reflexive heave, and it dribbles down my chin.

Sarka now stands before me, blade raised high.

She couldn't care less that I burned myself—she looks down at me with unadulterated hate and derision. To Sarka, I am weak and pathetic, a poor excuse of a human and a scapegoat for Achlys' maltreatment.

I don't want to see Sarka and her enormous knife. My eyes squeeze shut, expecting the worst, when I feel a hair plucked from my scalp. Then, a shallow cut on my forehead. I'm kicked in the stomach and feel a glob of spit hit my cheek.

"Idiot girl. I told you I was going to kill you slowly."

I open my eyes then, heart pounding as though it might burst from my chest. Blood trickles down my face.

From beneath her robe, Sarka pulls out a small doll.

I fight to stay composed in the wake of the low dread that settles like autumn mist in my belly, the shallow breaths that encourage hysteria as I watch Sarka secure the long golden hair on the top of the doll's head. She brings the doll to my forehead and smears it across my blood.

Sarka is a dark witch who excels in voodoo.

I pull and twist my arms away from one another, desperately working to break through the ropes. I kick my feet and squirm.

But Sarka has receded into herself—there's a sheen to her eyes and a pallor to her skin that suggests she is not wholly human. Her breathing becomes low, like a pant, and when she begins to chant I feel the cords on my wrists break.

The second my hands are free, I reach for my feet. If I can break those cords—if I can release all of my limbs, I can fight.

Sarka's eyes undulate with rage. Her lip curls and she thrusts the blade into the chest of the doll.

White light strikes my body, so sharp it takes my breath away. My eyelids flutter and I teeter on the edge of consciousness. I feel the blade twist through my organs and slice through my midsection. My gaze travels down to my chest, fully expecting to see Sarka's blade wedged inside.

But there's nothing.

My fingers flutter against smooth, unmarred skin. I'm not physically cut, but the pain is excruciating. I writhe and gag, hunched on all fours as I try to reclaim my breath.

Even in the depths of pain, I know I need to do two things: release my legs, and get rid of the doll. If I fail to accomplish either task, I will die.

Still gagging and shuddering from pain, my hands reach for my ankles. *My boot—I have my own blade!*

Remembering Lenna's ingenuity and the life-saving design of my footwear, I struggle to get my hands on the blade. I feel another sharp pain, this time in my lower abdomen.

I don't know how voodoo works, but I feel the blade and the slicing of my organs and muscles and the release of my blood as though it were spilling out on the desert sand. I cannot deny the physical reaction of my body to these attacks—the recoiling and curling and heaving and gagging and low groans.

I crawl away.

It makes no difference whether I'm close to Sarka or far from her. As long as she has that infernal doll, I am hers.

I crawl to the camel—without raising my eyes, I take in the cord of frayed strings and feel the agitated huff of sour, putrid breath. I slash quickly, hoping to cleave the rope with a single blow. Instead, I am met with a new agony.

This time, it is not a cut.

My feet feel like they're on fire—a pain that consumes my brain as I writhe in agony. Just as suddenly as it began, it stops.

In front of the fire, Sarka grins. The doll is in her right hand, the bottom charred. She's pulled it from the fire only to show me what she's doing, to offer me a moment's respite before she does it again.

I don't have time to think.

I steel my resolve and swipe at the cord a second time, and this time, it breaks. I don't have time to celebrate the camel's freedom, because my feet are on fire again.

I scream.

On some level, I'm aware of my shrieks and cries, of the way my body jerks and bolts and shakes in response to the furious licks of flame. I can't escape the pain.

The next time Sarka stops, I writhe towards her.

I need to get that doll out of her hands. I don't care if the doll drops into the fire—it would at least end my agony. The camel is nowhere to be seen—so at least one life was saved.

Sarka showed no interest in the camel's release—she's so enraptured by my pain that she can focus on nothing else. She holds the doll forward in expectation.

"Please."

It's my own broken voice, pleading for mercy. Mercy I know I will not get—mercy Sarka does not know how to give.

173

Sarka doesn't acknowledge my plea. Her arm flutters close to the fire, ready to administer the next round of pain.

I twist, wiggle and scoot towards Sarka. I take my small blade and hurl it at the witch.

By some miracle, the blade lands in the fleshy part of Sarka's upper arm. She hisses in response, her eyes flashing momentarily with pain. I don't wait to see how she will respond—I scoot closer. Before she has time to pull herself together, I kick her legs out from under her and knock her to the ground.

Now, it's a dogfight. Very aware of the stakes—and what will happen should I fail to kill Sarka—I crawl forward with intention.

But Sarka has two blades now, not one. She's on the ground, but she doesn't have bound arms or legs. My only hope is to keep her down, to wrestle her so that she can't use the blades or the doll.

I grab for her ankles and bite.

My teeth sink into flesh, hit her ankle bone, and I don't let go. My teeth are the only weapon I have at my disposal, and I will not die at the hands of a dark witch in the middle of Desert without at least putting up a fight.

A flurry of stomps catches my attention; thunderous pounding shakes the ground. I squint my eyes shut as sand and dust swirl.

When Sarka's body stills, I release my bite.

I spit out the repulsive taste and the disgusting instinct that may have saved my life. Waving away sand and dust, I brace for battle. Instead, my eyes fall on Sarka's motionless body.

I recoil in horror.

Sarka's head is cracked open like a cantaloupe. Blood pools at the skull and lifeless eyes stare straight ahead. My gaze travels to the camel standing just behind, legs shifting with agitation.

The camel stomped on Sarka's head like it was a grape. The camel just saved my life.

Camels are smart. They remember a human's face their entire life...and they hold a grudge for just as long. If you wrong a camel, they will remember. And they will take revenge.

Emberlyn's words float through my mind as the fire blazes on. The voodoo doll is half-buried in sand and now, Sarka's blood. The camel doesn't leave. She stays put, brown eyes studying me.

I retrieve my blade from Sarka's arm, trying hard not to look at her as I do so. I've emptied the contents of my stomach a dozen times today, and I'd rather not find another reason to hurl. With a few deliberate swipes of the blade, the ropes securing my feet are shorn. I am free.

I rise slowly, taking inventory of the new places that hurt and the old places that hurt. I note the residual damage that has been exacted on my body, then adjust my clothes and re-braid my hair. I wipe blood off my face using the bottom corner of Sarka's robe. These small gestures restore my humanity, remind me that I am Andra and *I will survive this test.*

Sarka didn't take anything from my pack. Likely she founds its contents as disappointing as she found me. I shoulder the pack and look to the camel. She's still there, waiting. I've lost time, tied up in Desert, but I may make up ground now.

I bury the doll in the sand, then drag Sarka by the feet to the fire and watch her body burn.

When I approach the camel, she kneels, allowing me to climb. I hiss in pain at the movements required to mount her, but I am able to do so.

Without another look back, I take off across Desert, the brilliant, white-bright stars lighting the way.

TWENTY

At some point I fall asleep, because I wake up with a stiff neck. I'm relieved to still be sitting atop the camel. I feel wretched, but I'm rested enough that I feel human again. I can think. I don't expect I'll be lucky enough to find another flag in my path, but I keep a keen eye. Though it's night, the stars illuminate the sand.

When dawn beckons, my throat is so dry it hurts to swallow. My tongue feels engorged and rough as sandpaper—it's thick and obtrusive in my mouth. *The average human can survive about three days without water.* My physical activity and current arid surroundings don't help.

It's impossible to know how far I've traveled, but I'm alert when I catch sight of monolithic red rocks. Two large pillars made of tomato-red sandstone flank a pathway—and this seems to be where the camel is headed.

Most of Desert has been open and expansive with plenty of opportunity to spot a threat. The same was true of icy Tundra. But here—we're about to pass through a tall, slender passage that would be the ideal spot to host an ambush.

"Easy," I mutter to the camel.

With bated breath and a jackrabbit heartbeat, we enter. Even in the dim light of dawn, the color of the stone is remarkable—shades of tangerine and pepper and hibiscus. From a distance, the rock just looked red—up close, it's a work of art.

I *feel* a change, too. It's cooler in the passage, and in the shelter of the great rocks, resilient weeds pop out from cracks in the sandstone. As we draw deeper, the weeds grow more prolific. There are even a few plants in the otherwise-austere ecosystem, leading me to wonder if the camel is guiding us to water.

Soon, the camel's steps feel sturdier. It's hard to discern in the low light, but the ground looks different. And then, the passage suddenly ends in a fishbowl-shaped space. My eyes snag on a tree. An actual *tree*. Lying just beneath the tree is a glorious pool of water. The camel looks back at me triumphantly.

Don't drink water too fast, I hear Emberlyn's voice in my head. *You'll get sick—and you'll have the worst stomach cramps.*

I drink with great restraint and stop before my thirst is sated. I'm scooping water to clean the dirt and dried blood on my body when I notice Agrona.

I've never seen a picture of Agrona—but I remember Emberlyn's description and I especially remember Warrick's face as Emberlyn described the hit man from Rock. The man Warrick warned was the strongest in Soulbourne, the one who could snap me in half like a toothpick. The man sleeping on the other side of the pond, hidden behind a cluster of boulders, can be none other.

His fist alone is as large as a pumpkin, his neck nearly as thick as the trunk of the tree he sleeps beneath. Dense ropes of muscle twine every square inch of his body. He sleeps heavily—Agrona's chest rises and falls like an elevator; his mere breath sounds like a forceful gust of wind.

I should turn around.

I should turn around and creep out of the passage and pray that Agrona doesn't hear me flee; pray that the sun doesn't rise enough to rouse Agrona in the two minutes it will take for me to retreat. The camel was a nice, temporary perk—one I should not stick around to keep secure. I should get to safety, immediately. And I would...if it weren't for the flag suspended from the high branches of the tree above Agrona.

I wonder what the prisoners were told.

Were they promised a reward if they captured flags? Were they incentivized to kill me? I'm not sure if Agrona sleeps below the flag by coincidence or by design. Either way presents a problem, but if he's there by design, to trap me...then I'm *really* in trouble.

The bottom line is the same: I need the flag.

Warrick warned me not to go against Agrona's strength; he instructed me to run at the first sign of him—but my options are limited. Maybe, just maybe, I can nab the flag before Agrona is any wiser to my presence.

I scan the water, tree, and surrounding rocks for any sign of a trap. The light of day grows brighter. I mentally map my steps around the pool to avoid potentially-slippery rocks and take my first step when Agrona sighs.

My body stiffens on reflex; I hold my breath.

Agrona's chest rises and falls again, and I relax, but only a smidgen. Agrona still sleeps, but that sigh signaled what I already suspected: my time is limited.

My first steps are cautious—I gingerly shift my weight from one place to the next, tepidly testing the space before committing. My heart thumps wildly as I near the tree—and Agrona.

Mere feet from the giant, I will myself into utter silence—I don't dare to swallow or even breathe wrong. My eyes flit between the tree above and Agrona's hulking frame, which is even more intimidating at close range.

His size alone is difficult to process—I don't know that I've seen a man *half* his size. I'd been warned this was the case—by Warrick, by Emberlyn and Lenna—but it's one thing to hear it and an entirely different thing to see it. I try not to stare.

I look to make sure I understand the situation and what I am up against, but then I focus on the flag in the tree.

I give Agrona as wide a berth as possible in my steps to the trunk. The tree is an acacia—this particular one isn't more than twenty feet tall, though the flag is tied to a branch at the very top. The lowest branches protrude a couple of feet off the ground, making it easy to climb—a plus for me, since my upper body strength isn't the best.

The bark is as sharp and rough as it looks. I bite my lip to silence the wince as I take hold, vigilant of Agrona's slumbering frame as I take my first step up. I lean against the prickly bark and pray that my weight holds, that the bark doesn't flake off and fall to the ground and wake Agrona.

A marginal sense of relief is awarded me when I make it to a limb about ten feet off the ground. From here, the branches become more prolific, spawning out and up to distribute their yellow-green leaves. I'm preparing my next maneuver, thinking how to navigate the dense maze of branches, when the camel moves.

No. Please don't come.

It doesn't matter what I think or wish—the camel ambles through the edge of the pool, feet gently splashing through water.

She wants to eat the acacia leaves, I realize.

For a moment I'm frozen—I watch the camel and I watch Agrona and I wonder what it will take for him to wake up.

I twist through branches now, doing my best to ignore the piercing pricks of the thorns and the trickle of blood that runs down my arm in response. I don't have much room to do so, but I pull the fabric of my jacket up and around my face to shield me as I reach the uppermost branches.

I'm close to the flag now—I can see the lavender hue and the periwinkle stars clustered in the upper left corner. One more step, maybe two—and I will be able to reach it.

A rustling causes me to freeze in my tracks.

The camel is almost at the tree...and Agrona stirs awake.

My heart thunders and incentivizes an antsy step up—a step that is not carefully planned, because the branch snaps in two and hurtles downward. My hand desperately grips the nearest branch.

The pain is immediate. Acacia thorns plunge into the soft flesh of my palm. Yellow stars dot my vision, but I do not let go.

Agrona's consciousness is not marked by noise, but silence.

The expansive exhales cease. When I look down, hazel eyes stare up at me—two tiny orbs in the massive expanse of Agrona's body.

He doesn't move; his body is frozen in supine position. It's more unnerving than if he had jumped up and started hollering—this silent, watchful gaze has me worried that Agrona has mental cunning to match his brutish strength.

I don't know how I'm going to escape with the flag, but I do still need it. This is the thought that propels me forward, to make the final reach to pull the flag from the branches of the acacia tree. I'm met with some resistance, but a sharp, defiant yank frees the flag. It rips—a shredding sound dispels the silence as it flutters down.

Agrona's eyes watch my every movement as I stuff the flag in my pack. Ruby blood from my palm mars the light blue and purple cloth, but Perrin never said anything about returning the flags in pristine condition—I only have to procure them.

The moment the flag is tucked away, Agrona moves.

He shifts on the ground—that action alone is enough for me to feel the tree vibrate. I could shimmy down the tree and run, but I have no idea how fast Agrona is. I'd have to make quick work of the descent, move out of reach with similar speed, and then hope to outrun him. In my current condition, I'm doubtful I can do it.

The camel happily munches leaves, totally oblivious to my plight. As attuned and committed to my survival as she was in Desert with Sarka, she's wholly unconcerned now. She doesn't cower or otherwise move as Agrona stands—she doesn't even shift feet or change position to make room for the giant.

Perched in the acacia tree, I wait. My brain considers options, but I don't want to make a move until Agrona does. I plan to play defense in a situation with no clear offense.

Every muscle in my body tenses when Agrona takes a step towards me. He must be over seven feet tall—with arms outstretched, I'm not far from his reach.

I suspect he's going to grab for me. I cling to the branch and root down with my feet, toes curling to solidify my position. But when Agrona reaches, it's not for me.

He stoops over and stretches giant, sausage-like fingers around the trunk. My blood stills and my heartbeat is a crescendo that threatens to explode.

In one motion—*one* single motion, as though it is easy—Agrona rips the acacia tree from the ground. He doesn't even show evidence of exertion—there's no grunt or bulge of muscles or even a sparkle of sweat on his brow.

Suspended in the branches of an airborne, thorny tree is a very bad thing—exponentially worse when said tree is in the beefy palms of a notoriously lethal hit man. I don't know what Agrona plans to do next—*bash the tree against the rocks?*—but staying put is a death wish.

I have three choices, although only two of them hold the possibility of survival. I've already eliminated the option of staying put. I can jump from the tree and hope that I land cleanly, and away from Agrona…or I can jump from the tree to the rock wall. I'm not sure how stable the red sandstone is, but it's layered and protrudes in a way that makes me think I have a chance of securing a hold. Then, I can climb.

With only a second or two to decide, I make my choice. When the tree moves, I jump to the side.

My left knee is the first to connect—I feel a sharp pain and a flare of heat travels up my spine. My hands claw for purchase on the sandstone. My entire body is tense; I cling to the rock wall like I've been glued on. I land high enough that I'm out of Agrona's reach.

There's a growl of anger from below—the first sound out of Agrona—but I don't look down. I don't wait to see Agrona's next move; I climb.

A *thwack* captures my immediate attention. Rock crumbles and part of the sandstone wall caves. My fingers claw desperately to the rock; red sand and dirt collect under my fingernails.

Agrona swings the felled acacia tree like a baseball bat against the rock wall. He wields a *twenty foot tree* like a *baseball bat*.

His aim is not very accurate in his first blow, or his second. Neither leave me feeling very safe, though—chunks of rock come loose and threaten to clock me in the head. My hold isn't secure.

I'm afraid to climb while the acacia tree thunders towards me, but if I stay put, I'm a sitting target.

With gritted teeth, I ascend. When a moment—then two, then three—pass without the *thwack* of the tree trunk against the sandstone wall, I dare to look down.

Agrona has abandoned the tree, tossing it to the side like a discarded tissue. He strides to the wall and begins to scramble up. I feel his weight and I hear his grunts and the sound of shifting rock. I pray that Agrona slips and falls—that his size and weight work against him—because if he's an able climber, he will close the distance between us quickly.

The next rock I grab is poorly-planned.

When I attempt to pull myself up, it falls loose, sending a small shower of stones along with it. My body reacts quickly: I press into the wall as my right hand searches for a better placement.

You could throw rocks. An aptly-placed hit from a rock could be debilitating to Agrona.

The thought is truncated, immediately, when I gaze in front of me and inside the hole created from the fallen rock.

Eyes. Beautiful, golden eyes flecked with smudges of espresso brown and a thin vertical line. Eyes surrounded by brown and beige and tan and golden scales that look like flat shells layered in neat, symmetrical patterns. When a forked, coal-black tongue shoots out, I scream.

I stifle the sound, willing it to die, but even as I bite my lip so hard I draw blood, a strangled cry emerges. Loud enough, raw enough, that it will win Agrona's attention.

The horned viper.

Horned *vipers*, actually.

The greatest danger in Desert, after exposure to the elements and risk of dehydration. Thanks to Emberlyn, I'm well aware of the peril. And from the looks of it, I've uncovered an entire nest of the serpents.

Every instinct and reflex in my body begs me to let go—to push away from the viper-infested portion of the wall. I gag; my body physically roils in disgust and fear at the sight of the nest.

I can climb up, or I can climb down.

To let go is to welcome death—though I'm not confident that the vipers will let me move at all without punishment. The disruption of their home has agitated them—thick, swollen, sepia-toned scales swirl as vipers twist and slither over one another. None of them look coiled to strike, but that could just be a matter of time.

Vipers aren't aggressive towards humans, but they will attack if they feel threatened.

One bite will incapacitate you, but it won't immediately kill you. Your blood will clot, your body will swell, and it will affect your heart. Among other things.

A viper usually rattles its tail in warning before it strikes. Sometimes you can also hear it rustle its scales.

Facts flood my mind, narrated in Emberlyn's tight, controlled voice. I'm not the horned viper's preferred prey—but if I upset one, I'm not immune from an attack.

Rock crumbles below me.

Agrona is closing in—the sandstone mostly holds under his weight, and he hoists himself a considerable distance with each step.

Death by vipers, death by Agrona, death from falling. What a list of options.

I will survive, I tell myself, though I'm not sure I believe it. Not now, while I'm precariously perched forty feet off the ground above a gargantuan hit man in front of a nest of vipers and above packed desert sand that stretches as far as the eye can see.

I wince and shift my weight, avoiding the glowing amber eyes of the horned vipers. I pray they don't find cause to strike. My breath loosens when I don't feel fangs.

So far, so good.

When I make the next few steps successfully, I feel relief— both feet are above the viper nest and out of striking range. Death by

Agrona and death from falling are still viable options, but I have escaped death by vipers.

Agrona is close enough now that I can hear his breathing. His progress is fast and reckless—the movements of a man who doesn't need to exercise caution. He's Goliath in every face-off, and it is this comparison that inspires an idea for how I might take him down.

"Hey!"

My voice alone is enough to startle Agrona—his head jerks up in surprise, hazel eyes narrowing with suspicion.

"What did they tell you to make you come after me?"

I take another step up, aware that I am playing fast and loose with the safety of my climb as I keep my eyes on Agrona.

The giant's eyes are now trained on me, but he continues his ascent. He doesn't answer my question.

I try again. "What did you do to become a prisoner?"

This question agitates Agrona—I see it in the way his body tenses. He continues to climb, narrowed eyes trained on me.

"Did they hurt you?" Another step or two, and I will be within Agrona's grasp. "I bet it was fun to see the big, powerful giant taken down. Did you beg for mercy?"

I have really poked the bear now. If my plan doesn't work, there's no doubt that my death will be at the hands of Agrona, who practically foams at the mouth as his face turns eggplant purple. His snarl sounds feral as he swipes for his next handhold, massive fists slamming hard against the rock in anger.

Against rock, and against the viper nest. The movement is so perfectly placed it's like poetry. Lethal, gruesome poetry.

Agrona is so consumed with ire that he doesn't see it coming. His first cry is one of surprise—he's stunned by the fangs that sink into his meaty flesh. But his second, his third, and his fourth cries—those are from pain.

Keep moving, I tell myself as guilt balloons inside my gut. *You did it to save your life. There wasn't another option.*

Agrona's cries become louder.

184

I want to climb higher, and higher, and higher—away from Agrona and away from the horned vipers and away from the horrible cries—but rock that I climb up is rock that I must eventually climb down.

With eyes tightly closed and body pressed against the rock wall, I do my best to shut out the noises of Agrona's agony.

It is only when I hear a reverberating *thud*—the impact of Agrona's body on Desert floor—that I allow myself to look down. Without looking closely, I can tell from the angle of Agrona's neck and the pervasive stillness of his body that he is dead.

With careful movements, as though I'm embroidering a scarf or braiding Elara's hair, I pick my way down the wall. I veer far from the viper nest and don't relax until my feet touch the ground. The camel, for her part, is still after the acacia leaves.

Even though I have no taste for it, I stop for a drink at the pool. I fill my water skin. And then, without the aid of the camel, I limp down the pathway and off into Desert.

TWENTY-ONE

Hobbling across Desert, my progress slow against the resistance of shifting sand, I consider who is left.

Mercurius, hunter of humans.

Dirce, spy with an affinity for knives.

Kakarauri, crafty siren.

Nox, silent assassin.

Brone, cult leader.

It's impossible to know who poses the greatest threat—so much depends upon the context in which we meet.

I'm in moderate but not unbearable pain. I don't think I have any lasting damage: Sarka's voodoo didn't actually cause internal harm, and the cuts and bruises accrued in Desert will heal. My tailbone still smarts from my fall in Tundra. Now that the adrenaline is starting to wear off, my brain fogs. Mental, physical, and emotional exhaustion hang off my bones like drying laundry.

My hunger is another issue.

Discomfort is one thing, low blood sugar another. The human body can go days without food, but I'm exerting an incredible amount of energy and I'm not replenishing the vault. I finished my almonds hours ago. There's no food in Desert, but it needs to be a priority when I hit the next ecosystem.

The sun rises higher.

I'm not certain where I am—without knowing which direction the camel led us last night, I'm turned around—but I hope to hit Canyon or Plains next.

Two hours later, I see the edge of Desert.

Though I can't make out specific features, I see the terrain bleed from rust red to nut brown in the distance.

As I near the transitional space between ecosystems, I remain alert. The ground is flat and the shrubs are few and scattered, but my eyes are peeled for a flag or signs that a prisoner has passed through. My own trail will be easy to follow.

I'm scanning the horizon when my gaze falls on a strange-looking bush. It's darker in color than the others, and there's something unusual about the shape.

When the bush stands up, I stop. It waves.

I can't very well turn around and run. I don't want to go back into Desert, and I don't have the energy, anyway.

Now that I've been spotted, there's no point in hiding. I stop for a swig of water and pretend to tie the shoelaces of my boot. As I do so, I remove the knife and hide it in my palm.

The prisoner doesn't walk towards me—something that could be interpreted as a good sign or a bad sign. At a closer distance, I can tell that it's a man...it's either Mercurius, Nox, or Brone.

From what I know of Nox, it doesn't seem like his style—he's notorious for stealth. It's not the kind of behavior I expect from Mercurius, either—he delights in the hunt—but perhaps this is the opening act of a twisted game? That leaves Brone.

My palms are sweaty as I approach.

The man stands casually, as though I'm a neighbor dropping by for a porch-side chat. His hair is gray and he is slight of frame, but I know better than to let appearances deceive.

I stop a good twenty feet away, close enough to make out brown eyes, olive skin, and an easy smile. "Are you Brone?"

The smile grows wider. "We've both heard of each other. Hello, Andra."

Though I'm relieved it isn't Mercurius or Nox, I'm wary of Brone. *The others could be here,* I remind myself. *The prisoners could have formed an alliance.* My eyes are trained on Brone, but I'm attuned to activity around me.

"Well then. Not in the mood for pleasantries." Brone's summery smile sparkles.

I haven't seen my reflection in two days, but I can imagine what I look like. It's not an aesthetic that warrants a shiny smile—that much I know.

"What do you want?" There are a hundred iterations of this same question that I could ask, but I decide to be direct.

Brone chuckles, shaking his head like I've just said something silly. His charm is turned way up, which in turn drives my anxiety way up. He's playing a game, but I can't see it yet—I don't know what he's up to.

"An alliance."

The words catch me so off guard that I recoil. "How can we possibly form an alliance?"

"The best alliances are the ones that no one suspects," Brone replies smoothly.

"I'll repeat my earlier question: What do you want?"

"Your people skills could use some work. Most people engage in a little chitchat before getting down to business."

"Most people aren't in a test fighting for their life. Most people haven't had to go two days without sleep or food. Most people haven't killed two people in the past twenty-four hours."

188

Brone's smile never fades. When I mention the two deaths, a flicker of surprise flashes in his eyes. "All the more reason to form an alliance."

"Give me one reason why I should trust you."

Brone's hands fly up to his sides, palms raised in innocence. "I haven't killed anyone in the past twenty four hours. How do I know I can trust *you*?"

"You can't." I don't have to think about my reply. "I'm not the one asking for an alliance."

Brone's head tilts to the side. "You don't even want to hear what I have to say?"

I shrug. "Why did you lead a cult?"

Brone's nose wrinkles. "Is this your idea of chitchat?"

"What did you expect? Talk of the weather?"

Brone shrugs. "I'd be interested to know your initial thoughts on Soulbourne."

"That's a very general, open-ended question," I point out. I keep a distance of six feet between us. "And not that different from asking about your cult."

"You can answer the question however you want," Brone smiles. "I'm curious what you think."

His concession is marginal, likely intended to finesse the way for me to give him what he wants.

"A question for a question," I negotiate.

Brone's lips temporarily form a thin line, a subtle signal of frustration that he is quick to erase. "You're stubborn." He says the words playfully, but I understand the edge that lies beneath.

"I'm not going to be played," I correct.

Brone nods with grace and elegance, a genteel mannerism that feels out of place in the wilderness. I remind myself of the danger he presents—his affect and figure both appear so harmless that it's easy to forget what he's capable of.

"Soulbourne is different than where I came from. The domains are interesting."

Brone considers me, giving space for my words, and then he sits down. My stomach rumbles traitorously as he reaches into a bag and pulls out a hunk of cheese, bread, apricots, and dates. I have no idea how he acquired them.

Brone tears off a piece of bread and a sizeable chunk of cheese. He takes a generous bite of each before throwing a handful of dates into his mouth. "Please," he insists, waving a hand in invitation for me to partake. "And it wasn't a cult."

It's exactly the kind of answer a duplicitous, conniving false prophet would give. My face says as much.

"Is there anything I can say that would alter your impression?" Brone asks.

I don't answer. I tear off a hunk of bread and grab an apricot, covertly sniffing each before taking a bite. Brone watches carefully, even when he pretends to tear off bread or chew cheese. There are levels to this interaction, and I need to be wise to all of them.

"Why did you come to Soulbourne?"

I can tell by the way he asks that the answer means a lot. This is the question *everyone* wants to know the answer to.

"I was drawn here. I don't know how, I don't know why, and I don't know who did it. But I won't deny the pull." This is the most I'm going to give Brone, the full extent of my good faith effort.

He nods; apparently, my answer passes muster. "I learned some unsavory truths about Soulbourne. My discovery was not well received by domain leadership, and I was framed as a false prophet."

"What did you learn?"

Brone stops eating and casts a pointed look my way, but he answers my bonus question without verbal complaint. His voice drops an octave as he speaks. "The Prosphora is unnecessary. The spirit realms rule in deceit."

A sense of foreboding cloaks the atmosphere. This, I know to be true. Is it possible that Brone might actually be an ally? Or is this part of his master manipulation?

Brone licks his lips and lifts his chin. "There are many realms outside of Soulbourne, though communication was cut years ago. Domain leadership uses this to their advantage: they don't want people to know what the realm could become. Then, people would want change. They'd expect more."

My heart pounds, but I school my face into passive neutrality. I haven't decided yet if Brone's full of shit.

"Justus and Achlys are powerful," Brone continues. "They enjoy uncontested authority as leaders of the spirit domains. Two domains enjoy a sanguine lifestyle while the others labor and pay tribute."

Heat creeps up my spine at the implication behind Brone's words. He is a known master of deception—it's the lethal skill he's known to possess—and still the words strike a chord.

"Soulbourne has been carefully crafted. It's a powerful realm, but one that rests upon the compliance of eight domains. Even a moderate disruption of the order would yield serious impact. Don't let the democratic pretenses fool you—Achlys and Justus run Soulbourne, and they have a vested interest in making sure that the spirit realms reign supreme. To contest their arrangement is to end up like me." Brone smiles, but the light never hits his eyes.

"There's no way for me to know if you're telling the truth."

"Maybe not right now," Brone agrees. "But let my words settle. You'll see the truth. If not now, in time. Hopefully, in time to save yourself."

"How dramatic." My unblinking gaze meets his. "Now I'm especially interested in the alliance you think we should form."

"We could help each other. We both want to get out of Soulbourne."

"You're a prisoner. I'm competing for freedom. Neither of us are coming from a place of strength," I point out.

Brone smiles. "Strength comes in different forms, Andra. Strategy and cunning happen to be my two preferred weapons. Let's overturn Soulbourne."

"You're assuming I came here to overturn things."

"Why else would you come?" Brone asks.

"I'm not a revolutionary. I didn't even mean to come here."

"That's a neat cover story, but do you really believe that?" Brone keeps his face neutral, but I know he weighs my words.

"I don't have grand aspirations where Soulbourne is concerned," I say drily. "I'm trying to survive and leave."

Brone temples his fingers in front of his face. I have no idea if he believes me—I don't know that it matters.

"I think you're going to survive, Andra. I'm betting on you."

I huff my skepticism, though the words open a vein of hope. "I have the feeling I still don't know what you *really* want."

After I speak, I reach for another hunk of bread and a wedge of cheese. Our conversation could end at any moment, and I could use more sustenance.

Brone doesn't hesitate. "I want a place in the new order—after you overturn things."

I blink. My bewilderment is so complete that I forget to mask my face.

"I'm serious," Brone says softly.

I'm not sure how to respond. I can't give Brone what he wants—I can't promise it, at least. Even with the topic on the table, I can't digest it. It's so far out of reach.

"I don't know that I can do that," I say carefully.

"You don't have to decide now," Brone assures me.

Our conversation has seemingly run its course. Brone rubs at the back of his neck and I take the last apricot.

"I can't promise anything," I repeat. "I'm not thinking past the Land test."

Brone nods. Apparently, this is a satisfactory response. "And I won't kill you."

I stand up and brush the dirt from my pants, signaling to Brone that I am ready to take my leave.

Brone doesn't stand. His slight frame appears even smaller when I look down at him. "Don't forget what I said, Andra."

"I won't forget," I reply, voice testy.

"It's interesting that you didn't mention the trees," Brone says. He throws the words out casually, as though they're superfluous.

"What trees?" I ask, though my body is tight. I haven't mentioned the marked trees in Holostown to anyone.

"I asked you why you came here, and you said you were drawn. You left out the part about the trees." Brone's eye contact is intense.

My throat is dry. The apricot I've just eaten leaves a chalky aftertaste, and it has nothing to do with the genus of the fruit. I don't know what to say—it's not possible that *Brone* marked me, is it?—so I'm left to stare back at the disgraced prophet.

Brone shrugs and takes a bite of apricot.

"It might be a good idea to keep the trees a secret—I can't say." He holds my gaze as he finishes chewing. "Just thought I'd leave another card on the table, so you have an idea of the value I bring to a partnership."

"They labeled you a false prophet," is the only thing I can think to say.

I hold Brone's gaze a moment longer. It's impossible to tell if he's a mastermind manipulator or innocent whistleblower—I need time to digest what he's said, and even then, I might not know.

My legs are stiff as I take my first steps away from Brone. I deny the instinct to shift my weight to my good knee and hobble—I will not let Brone see any weakness.

The prophet's watchful eyes bore holes into my back as I walk away. I look over my shoulder once, to make sure he doesn't follow me. Alone with a cacophony of thoughts, I walk into Canyon.

I have a flag to find.

TWENTY-TWO

If there's a flag in Canyon, I can't find it.

The glow of morning fades into fully-fledged daylight—not as intense as in Desert, but still without much shade. The ground here is dry and cracked, rigid where the desert sand was soft and yielding. There isn't a flag buried underneath the stiff ground of Canyon. My bleary eyes canvass the terrain in search of any anomaly or variation that might signal the presence of a flag, but there aren't any.

Just when the landscape starts to get interesting—elevation change, an established tree line, color variation in the dirt—I become aware that I am being watched.

Goosebumps prickle my arms and legs; the hair on the back of my neck stands at attention. I glance casually over each shoulder to see if I can spot the individual, but I don't spot a single element that warrants suspicion.

But I *am* being watched.

Entering the prolific chaparral of trees, I am sure of a few things. One, I'm nearing the heart of Canyon—there must be water nearby to support the vegetation. Two, there are now many places that a flag could hide. Three, there are now many places that a *pris-*

oner could hide.

I try not to be jumpy, but there's wildlife to match the abundant foliage and every snap of a twig or chirp of a bird first strikes me as a malignant omen. There are bears in this ecosystem, I remember—cougars, too.

Neither present danger commensurate to one of the remaining prisoners. There were never any "good" prisoners to encounter in the first place, but there's a pit in my stomach as I consider who might stalk me.

I suspect it might be Mercurius, Dirce, or Nox. All three are masters of stealth and evasion.

There's a strong compulsion to sprint through the trees, to flee from watchful eyes that make my skin crawl. But without spotting the threat, I don't know which direction leads to safety.

I'll walk with purpose and stay vigilant, I tell my racing heart. As though intention will somehow protect me from ruthless assassins, hunters, and spies.

When I hear the low, drawn-out *ziiing* of a blade as it is sharpened, my mouth goes dry. It's not Nox. It's Mercurius or Dirce—and whoever it is, they're playing with me. They *want* me to know that I'm being tracked. Fear bubbles to the surface, but anger does, too.

I guess it is Mercurius. There's a chance it's Dirce—she's known for her prowess with knives—but a spy doesn't seem the type to flaunt an attack. Frightening and intimidating a target you plan to corner sounds a lot like the behavior of the lunatic human-hunter Warrick and Emberlyn and Lenna warned me about.

"Mercurius!"

I stand in a thicket of trees—hedged in at every direction—and my voice echoes through Canyon. I will not be hunted like some stag; Mercurius will be made to fight. My small knife is likely no match for whatever blade Mercurius has singing against the whetstone, but he will have to face me. I will fight back.

"Mercurius!" I shout again.

Birds trill in the treetops, indifferent to the drama unfolding on the ground below. A twig snaps and I whirl around to face my stalker—but there's no sign of anyone.

My palms sweat; I wipe them on my pant legs and as swiftly as I can, bend down to free the knife from my boot. A pounding heart and rush of adrenaline amplify my senses—I'm aware of every sound, smell, and even the tangy taste of the air around me.

The longer the silence lingers, the harder it is to stay put.

He wants you to run, I remind myself. *Mercurius wants you to run away. That's part of the fun—he wants to chase you. He loves the hunt.*

This last thought triggers an idea. A risky idea, but an idea nonetheless. I hesitate, consider the prudence of such a chancy action. And then I remove the pack from my back and lay down.

It's counter-intuitive, to relax like this. It's *insane*.

I rest my head on the pack like a pillow and curl my knees up towards my chest. If Mercurius is looking for a hunt, I will deprive him of one.

I position myself so I am a ready, easy target—I lay in plain sight, where there is no challenge. My action will either enrage Mercurius into a confrontation, or he will wait. And I could use the rest.

I'm so tired.

I initially intend to fake falling asleep. But the sun on my back is warm, the cushion of the backpack under my cheek too similar to a pillow. *I'll just close my eyes,* I lie to myself. *I'll listen for any sign of Mercurius.*

I wake up refreshed.

My brain is no longer foggy and my headache has disappeared. The sun is on its way down, the long shadows of the trees signal that it's afternoon. I don't see any sign of Mercurius, though I don't doubt that he watches me, quietly waiting for the right opportunity.

I scour the vicinity for signs of a trap—when I can't spot any, I consider what would be the least thrilling pursuit, then walk in the open. My path takes me out of the trees and to the lip of Canyon, the major feature for which this ecosystem has been named.

Canyon goes deep—at least a few thousand feet—and while there isn't a path to the bottom that I can see, there's a whitewashed river with foliage on either side. It would be a good place to hide a flag.

Retrieving the five flags was always an enormous task, but standing above the vast, gaping canyon, I'm struck by how futile it all might be. I was incredibly lucky to find the first two flags. In Canyon, there are literally a million spots a flag could hide.

The nap was refreshing, but it didn't shake the weariness from my bones. I'm aware of every ache and pain both of my body and spirit as I skirt the edge of Canyon, a careful distance from the edge so I don't fall.

"You're ruining all my fun."

Mercurius' voice jolts me from my thoughts. I spin around to find the hunter standing ten feet behind me.

He's tall—but I expected that. Broad-shouldered with a muscled body, but I expected that, too. His thick brown hair is flecked with gray and tumbles in a neat wave over his scalp; his eyes are the color of chocolate ringed with amber—they'd be beautiful if they didn't look so cold and conceited.

"Mercurius."

He curls his lip in place of a greeting; his eyes glitter with malice. "I said, you're ruining all my fun."

I look to Mercurius in disbelief, then fold my arms over my chest. "I'm not here for your entertainment."

In the blink of an eye, Mercurius shoots forward and grabs a fistful of my hair. Face inches from mine, his handsome features contort into something hideous. Spittle collects on his lower lip as his fingers pull tight. "You would deprive me of the hunt. But the challenge elevates the kill. That water woman learned the hard way."

Water woman?

I don't know who Mercurius is talking about, but it doesn't matter. It's not wise to antagonize the man—Mercurius' overt mental instability marks him as both a physical threat and a wild card that I would do well to avoid.

"I killed her," Mercurius adds, as though this detail were not already heavily implied.

My pulse skitters at the thought of death at this madman's hands, but when Mercurius leans close to murmur some new threat in my ear, I'm ready.

My head jerks back, slamming into Mercurius' chin. A strangled cry is my only encouragement; I twist enough to knee him in the groin and sink my teeth into his forearm like a wild animal. When he cries in pain and releases me, I don't run. I pull a safe distance away and face Mercurius, ready to fight.

"I'm going to kill you." Mercurius' words are low, trembling words that spark with rage. His eyes promise death; his taut muscles agree.

I should feel more fear than I do. I shake my head and don't break eye contact. "You all say that."

Maybe I am powerful, too. I don't have the hulking frame of Mercurius, but there is something far more dangerous inside of me right now—anger. I am tired of playing the victim. I will not run. My focus is concentrated; adrenaline pumps through my body as I prepare to fight.

"Did they tell you to hunt me?" I ask.

Mercurius doesn't hesitate. His scoff is laced with derision: "No."

"Then why go through the effort? What's in it for you?"

Mercurius' face flushes with anticipation; his pupils dilate with enthusiasm. "Because it's fun."

I wait for Mercurius to pontificate. He doesn't.

"Wow." My tone and disparaging glance provide context for how to interpret the single-word reply. Mercurius really is an unhinged psychopath.

The response is immediate. Mercurius lunges.

I barely elude the hunter's grasp. When I catch the glint in Mercurius' eye, I question whether he still values the game over my life. I have antagonized him enough that now I suspect he just wants to kill me.

That does change things. For all my provocations, I actually *do* want to get away from Mercurius. And now, he will get the hunt and chase that he wanted all along.

I sprint.

The pack is clunky and bounces on my back. I pull the straps tight, then fold my arms like grasshopper legs to keep them in place and stop the bouncing. The ground is uneven—I scan the earth for holes in which I might twist my ankle or land unevenly, but mostly I just sprint like hell.

I have no plan as I run the rim of Canyon.

Every so often I glance down into the deep ravine and then up ahead to see if any land feature sparks inspiration. I hear Mercurius behind me, his breath heavy but even. I have his years as a prisoner in Underworld to thank for the fact that he isn't in better shape. He hasn't yet caught up to me, but I'm not losing him, either.

In the distance, I see a bridge: wooden slats supported by two ropes that traverse the wide chasm of Canyon. I consider the blade in my boot—if I cross the bridge before Mercurius, what are the chances that I could hack away the rope before he finished crossing?

Moderate, I decide.

My blade is sharp, but small. The ropes holding the bridge look thick—they won't be easily cut. But I don't have a better plan: I have to try.

It's only when I get closer to the bridge that I notice a second incentive to cross: waving in the breeze on the other side of Canyon is a small green flag.

TWENTY-THREE

I don't know if Mercurius sees the flag. I don't care.

I can do this. I've been lucky—there is someone or something looking out for me. I survived Sarka; I survived Agrona. I can survive Mercurius and win this third flag, too.

My gait is steady and my steps do not fail. Every stride is a risk: one misplaced foot, and I could go down. But I do not misstep.

The bridge looks secure—there aren't any pieces missing or dangling loose. But there's a small space between each slat—if I land wrong, there's enough room for my foot to become wedged in between or to fall through.

I hear Mercurius' breathing behind me. I can't slow down. I run straight up to the bridge and take a giant leap.

The bridge wobbles immediately, absorbing the impact of my weight and quavering in undulating motion that travels like a sound wave. My sweaty palms grab for the ropes on either side as I ride the wave, stomach knotted and tumbling in somersaults.

I have to keep moving. I can't wait for the motion to pass, because Mercurius is either going to chase me on foot or pause at the edge of the bridge to shoot me down.

The bridge continues to undulate as I shuffle my feet forward. I cling to the ropes so tightly my palms burn.

Not two seconds later, the bridge trembles anew. Nausea rises within me like a raging beast: two figures now roil on the bridge like miniature boats on the high seas.

Mercurius' breath is hot on my neck—he's close enough to grab me, but he doesn't. Without looking over my shoulder, I guess it's because he's holding onto the ropes of the bridge, too.

It's too difficult to walk with the movement of the bridge, so I lower myself onto my hands and knees and scurry across. It's easier to move forward with a low center of gravity—I'm better balanced—but now I can't help but look through the two-inch slats of wide open space. I feel a fresh wave of nausea when I see the ground and the river and the trees sparkling in the distance. The very, very, *very* great distance.

A hand grabs for my ankle and I kick violently. My boot connects; I scramble forward. I don't know how far I've made it across the bridge—I don't risk looking up.

My wrists hurt. They snap and click in response to the continuous impact as I crawl, and then my hand misses a slat and sails through. My cheek hits the plank with a thud and there's a tight pinching on my upper arm as the soft flesh becomes wedged in between chunks of wood.

I look back.

Mercurius' handsome, predatory face shines with sweat and anger and the promise of suffering. When he sees my arm stuck, he smiles.

The slat has been twisted into vertical position and my arm is firmly wedged in place. The ropes are strong and don't budge, no matter how hard I pull. I estimate I have seconds before Mercurius will be upon me.

I yank wildly, pulling with everything I have. When my arm breaks loose, I lurch forward and scramble to my feet. I run. Mercurius clambers to his feet, too.

I feel the bridge shudder, the center of gravity shift to accommodate Mercurius' displaced weight. I'm surprised he hasn't caught up to me yet and I risk a glance behind.

Mercurius has a bow out, a feathered arrow nocked.

A shiver races up my spine. While I freed my arm, Mercurius armed himself. He stopped to pull out a weapon. Because Mercurius likes the hunt, and this is a production.

I run faster.

Or maybe I just imagine I'm going faster, because my footfalls are reckless and I've thrown caution to the wind. I'm only halfway across the bridge. I have to survive.

When my instep lands funny, my ankle twists and I slam to the ground. Hard. The bridge roils and rumbles, the ropes groan but hold. The whistle of an arrow passes overhead and I wonder if a moment of clumsiness just saved my life.

I need to get off the bridge and onto solid ground, where I can use obstacles to evade Mercurius. I'm faster when I'm up and running, so I stand again. Maybe I have adrenaline to thank, but my ankle doesn't hurt. I jump to send new undulating rolls through the bridge and throw Mercurius off balance. Then, I run.

"DUCK!"

My knees hit the slats without hesitation. A second arrow whistles past.

I'm close to the end of the bridge now—if I sprint one more time, I should make it to the other side. The gap between Mercurius and me is wider now—I might actually have time to cut the ropes.

I scramble to my feet and run past the green flag—I'm not insane enough to think I have time to free it *and* keep my life.

"DUCK!"

I fall flat.

This time, the arrow nicks my ear. It penetrates a wooden plank inches from my face with a *thwaacck*.

Too close, says the blood trickling down the side of my neck. *Too close*, say the raised hairs covering my arms.

"Get up and go! You're close!"

I look up to see a figure flying across the opposite edge of Canyon's rim, stride long and elegant. For a moment, I'm stunned into immobility.

My body is frozen, my brain confused. *Am I in Soulbourne, after all? Have I died?* The figure skirting the rim of Canyon, sprinting towards me, looks exactly like Elara.

"Andra, MOVE!"

This frantic plea, bellowed over the cacophony of squeaking slats and groaning footsteps and labored breaths, mobilizes me.

When my feet hit solid ground, I turn to find Mercurius close behind. *Run*, my mind entreats me. Instead, I take my small blade and hack at the rope.

The knife slices through the first rope faster than I expect. I don't look up as I begin to saw through the second one. When it begins to give way, I hear the *ziing* of a final arrow that doesn't meet its mark.

Mercurius' tumble with the bridge to the bottom of Canyon is unremarkable. He doesn't windmill his arms or adopt an expression of horror. He doesn't cry out. His figure fades into the chasm in strangely peaceful descent—a marked contrast to the deaths of Sarka and Agrona. I collect my wits in time to close a fist around the green flag before it disappears with Mercurius into the abyss.

At first, the flag threatens to pull me down.

The green rectangular cloth and part of the bridge are temporarily suspended in midair, held in place by tension. But then, a dramatic rip fills the air and I shoot backwards with three-fourths of a flag in my right hand.

"Are you hurt?"

I blink. By all accounts, it looks like Elara standing above me. But I'm in Soulbourne, in the Land test. There's no way that Elara could be here.

It's not until she's bent over me, eyes flared with concern, that I know it's not a hallucination. It *is* Elara.

I burst into tears.

I wipe at my eyes and stare at my sister in stunned silence. Elara is in Soulbourne—I can't decide if it's a good or bad thing.

Elara's own eyes fill with tears. Not a word is spoken, but in our gaze, a thousand words reside, the deepest sentiments pressed from one heart to the other. I stand up and hold my little sister tight, my arms easily encompassing her petite frame.

"Are you okay?" I pull away to look her over.

"I'm fine. Are *you* okay?"

I laugh, the sound rough and jagged. I can imagine what I look like. "I'm okay," I assure her. "Most of the blood isn't mine," I add, considering the rust-red stains on my clothes.

Elara studies me.

"I wasn't trying to hurt anyone. I had to kill to stay alive."

Elara nods soberly. "You'd be insane not to."

It's my turn to consider my sister. "How did you get in here?" My throat is tight. Elara's presence gives me new cause for worry. As much joy as my sister's presence brings me, this scenario is one I deeply feared.

Elara ignores my question, nodding to the contents of my right hand. "How many flags do you have?"

I look down at the torn green cloth. "Three."

Elara's eyes widen and she nods in appreciation.

"I've been lucky. We have a lot to talk about." I shift my attention to the afternoon sun that sits low in the sky. There are only a couple of hours of daylight left. "We should keep moving. I have the flag from Canyon, so there's no reason to stick around."

Elara nods in deference—she'll follow my lead.

"We need to look out for Dirce, Kakarauri, and Nox. Dirce is a spy and knife-wielder, Kakarauri is a siren, and Nox is an assassin. There's another prisoner still out there—Brone—but I don't think he's a physical threat. I've already encountered him."

Elara's face is grim, her countenance resolute. What most find daunting, Elara welcomes as a worthy contest of her fortitude and mettle. "You've killed three of the worst, then. I know what this test is, Andra. I've been briefed."

"Are you going to tell me how you got in here?" There are a dozen questions I want immediate answers to, but this is the natural entry.

Elara snorts. "I was looking for *you*. I didn't know this place existed until I was drawn inside."

Elara answers as expected, and still, it foments fear. Before I entered the test, I sent up a silent plea for help. Did Elara answer?

My sister watches me. "You want the details, I know. But I'm here now—there's no changing that. We still need to find two flags."

"There are four ecosystems I haven't explored," I tell Elara. There are many, *many* things I want to know, but my sister is right. Our first, and only, priority is to find the flags and end the Land test.

Elara's jaw sets; her blue eyes flash in anticipation of a challenge. "Where have you already been?"

"I have flags from Tundra, Desert, and now Canyon. I came in through Forest—is that where you entered the test?"

Elara nods.

"You didn't see any flags on your way, did you?"

Elara shakes her head.

"Prisoners?"

"None."

"How did you even get into Soulbourne?" I ask, leading us away from Canyon's edge and into new territory.

"I crossed the threshold," Elara tells me matter-of-factly.

I laugh, a mirthless sound that rings hollow to my own ears. "Please don't tell me you had the pleasure of meeting Syphus."

Elara's grin is wicked and tells me exactly what she thinks of the man. "Oh, I met Syphus. He doesn't like me very much."

My giggle is genuine. For a moment, the conversation takes on a tone so natural that I forget the deep aches and sharp pains that scourge my body. I forget the nerves and pressure I wear like a thick woolen coat and feel my body relax in anticipation of a delicious Elara-sass story. My favorite kind.

"Please tell me everything. Don't leave any details out."

Elara's bright smile is all the assurance I need.

Elara and I keep a brisk pace as we walk through Canyon. We're in the Land test, but we might as well be back home. Conversation never ceases—Elara and I fill the space with stories and insights and the nuanced details and impressions we both know the other will care about.

When the sun disappears from the sky, we're skirting the edge of Canyon's ecosystem. Beyond Canyon lies Forest—the most familiar of the ecosystems. I don't know if there are prisoners hiding in Forest, and I don't know if there are flags—but I can anticipate the flora, fauna, and animal life that exists within.

"Are we traveling through the night?" Elara asks.

"That's what I've been doing. Although now that there are two of us, we could switch off taking watch while the other sleeps."

"There are a lot of places someone could hide in Forest," Elara speculates with unease.

"And I leave a trail of gold sparkles," I remind her. An owl hoots in response.

"I still don't see any glitter. But to your point—let's keep moving…as long as we can," Elara suggests.

"Agreed. Keep your eyes peeled for a flag."

Elara bobs her head in agreement, a pale flash of strawberry blonde against the charcoal gray sky. We fall in step together, voices silent in unspoken agreement to remain alert.

When dawn breaks, Elara and I are still walking.

We never stopped to sleep—at no point during the night did it feel safe to do so. Also: I can't shake the feeling that we're being tracked.

For too many hours, the only sounds in Canyon were the snap of twigs under feet and the asynchronous chorus of our breaths. Now that birds chirp the start of the day and pale yellow light shines through the branches of the trees, I feel relief. I don't trust my other senses nearly as much as I trust my eyesight.

"I'm really tired."

Elara's words are the first in hours—we trekked through the night in companionable silence, only talking when necessary. Now that I look over at my sister, I see the fatigue that marks her face—fatigue I'm sure is also etched in mine.

"Let's find a spot to rest," I suggest. "I'll take first watch." I ignore the shrill cry of anxiety that insists there is no time for rest—no time for anything but hunting flags. I have three ecosystems to explore, and only two days left.

Elara wastes no time: she sits at the base of the nearest tree and curls into the fetal position, her bicep twined beneath her head as a pillow. A moment later, she breathes heavily.

I rub my eyes and roll out my neck. I can't stand still—I'll grow thick with fatigue. My eyelids already feel too heavy to keep open. Removing my pack, I stretch my limbs and canvass the area, careful not to trail too far from Elara. If I'm to stay awake, I might as well make myself useful—I can scrounge for nuts and berries.

There isn't anything in the direct vicinity, but as my eyes sweep the greater region, I notice a bush flush with berries. It's not *that* far away. I can jaunt over quickly, just to see if the berries are edible.

I don't leave myself time to overthink.

Moments later, I smile in victory: the thorns and brambles I saw from a distance protect dark, bloated blackberries.

I don't hesitate to pluck the black fruit off the bush—dark berries, especially those with brambles, are the safest to eat. Only half of red berries are safe, and only ten percent of white berries. The risk factor here is low, and Elara and I badly need sustenance.

I'm laying the berries on top of my jacket, collecting a substantial mountain of the fruit, when the shrill whistle of an eagle stops me in my tracks.

There's nothing innately alarming about the cry—there are all manner of birds in Forest, and Elara and I have heard hawks and robins and sparrows since we entered the ecosystem. But there's something about this eagle's call that makes my spine stiffen.

My first instinct is to crouch down, which is stupid. If I haven't already been spotted, then the trail of gold dust will give away my exact whereabouts. My gaze snaps to Elara—she's sound asleep under the tree, the rise and fall of her chest uninterrupted.

But there's someone here.

Something is wrong with the scene before me, though my brain is slow in identifying the aberration. My pulse quickens and my eyes rove Forest before drifting back to my sister. My gaze travels from Elara's small frame to the tree above, where my breath stills.

A "0" is carved into the trunk of the pine, neat and small, the scrawl familiar. I close the distance to the tree in a daze, my eyes never drifting from the mark.

Up close, my complementary senses confirm what I hoped I misperceived: the mark on the tree has been freshly carved. The pads of my fingers trace the moist bark, dread crawling from my midsection to take up residence in every extremity. I'm aware, not for the first time, of how small I am. How unprepared.

My limbs shake as I reach down to pull the blade from my boot, then to nudge Elara awake. I can't identify the danger, but it is rife—omnipresent and suffocating. I clamp a hand over my sister's mouth in warning.

Elara wakes in a second; her bloodshot eyes widen with alarm and confusion. I raise a finger to my lips, certain my eyes carry the warning that my lips do not utter. For a moment we're still as statues, every sense attuned to the rhythms of Forest.

When the moment lingers on without any clear danger, I waffle. We can't very well stand in one spot all day. I'm loathe to move without understanding who marked the tree...and for what purpose. It unnerves me that the individual was so close, so near to Elara as she slept—and it's deeply unsettling to know that I've either been followed from Holostown into Soulbourne...or someone in Soulbourne knows my background—and summons—intimately. My nerves turn to ice at the thought that the mark on the tree and the mark that I bear might be related.

A bush rustles and a brown bear clambers into view, nose quivering as it nears the mound of blackberries atop my jacket. The bear regards the boon and proceeds to inhale the fruit in seconds.

Elara looks at me out of the corner of her eye and I shake my head. It wasn't the bear that spooked me.

"I feel it," Elara whispers. "Something's not right."

My sister's response is all the confirmation I need. Our eyes locked, I offer a resolute nod. "Let's move."

Elara dips her chin in agreement, the action nearly imperceptible. Both of us are unsettled, reluctant to make noise.

Our first movements are away from the bear, our angle negotiated so that we're able to keep an eye on the beast's movements. Not once does he look up—after devouring the berries on my jacket, the bear continues pillaging berries still on the bush.

When we're a safe distance from the bear, I look to Elara. Even without saying a word, my sister knows what I suggest. I'm reluctant to leave my jacket, but considering what may lurk in Forest, the concession is marginal. We break into a run.

An hour later, I start to feel light-headed.

I need water. I need sustenance, too. I'm running on fumes. I slow to a stop, and Elara is quick to do the same.

"Someone marked the tree that you slept under." Now miles away, I explain my unease.

Elara doesn't say a word, but her bright blue eyes snap up to meet mine. She waits for me to continue.

"It looked the same as the carvings in the trees back home, before I was summoned to Soulbourne," I explain.

Elara's wise enough to follow the literal conversation and also absorb the context for everything I do *not* say: her face reads every nuance of expression. "The person who marked you is here," she whispers.

It's easier to hide from the truth when it's buried inside; much harder to face when the facts are baldly stated. I swallow roughly, reluctant to acknowledge the reality. My throat is dry, and the action sets me to coughing.

"Let's find water." Elara doesn't wait for my response—she begins to skirt around felled logs and bushes in pursuit of hydration.

I follow, and soon we find ourselves before a meandering creek lush with ferns and vegetation. I no longer feel the thrum of panic, but I'm no idiot. I might not see the threat, but it still exists.

The water in the creek is so clear and light that it looks like liquid diamonds. I'm on my knees in seconds, shins sinking into moist earth as I cup my hands and drink deeply. The water is cold enough to suggest it melted from ice—perhaps we are close to Mountains.

When my thirst is sated, I scoop another handful of water—this time, to wash my face. Dirt and sweat and dried blood coat my skin, and I shiver with pleasure at the feeling of the cool liquid. I'm reaching for my second scoop of water when I meet eyes in the reflection.

My hands freeze, my pulse hammers. Beside me, Elara is hunched over, drinking contentedly. I elbow her in the ribs and stand.

He shouldn't be here.

It's the first thought—wildly unhelpful—that I can't shake. For someone who has entered a foreign realm chock full of ridiculous procedures and traditions, the anomalies and discrepancies should no longer surprise me.

We never would have been evenly matched—not when we first met, in the marble corridor of Callings' library, and especially not now, when I'm dusty and sleep-deprived and hungry and injured in a dozen different places. I know better than to expect pity.

The dark guardian is still clad in midnight-black leather and velvet, but it's the glittering malice in his eyes that I would recognize anywhere. I take a step nearer to Elara.

"Andra."

The greeting is perfunctory, the tone disdainful. The guardian simmers with tightly-coiled wrath, but he is too proud to bypass formalities.

I don't know his name, and I hardly think he'd appreciate the moniker of "Dark Guardian," so I keep quiet. I nod my head curtly, matching his gruff tone. My body feels sluggish and dull, but curiosity blunts the sharp knife of fear as my brain tap dances through hypotheticals.

"I'll make this quick. You have something that doesn't belong to you. Give it back.".

TWENTY-FOUR

"I don't know what you're talking about."

My palms sweat and my pulse quickens, but the words come out measured. The truth is, there are many things the dark guardian might reference. I *think* he's talking about the marble tucked in my pocket, but only because it was given to me in the Callings library... by a different guardian. The marble has been notably quiet since my entrance into the Land test—I wonder now if that has anything to do with the man before me.

The guardian sneers. "Did you really think we wouldn't notice its absence? *Every* title is carefully catalogued, and you took a golden book."

The book. He's talking about the book—not the marble.

My thoughts turn to the volume packed in my bag, the golden book on time. Until now, it's just taken up space.

"You saw me walk out of the library. I didn't carry any books past you." Until I have the chance to organize my thoughts, I'm not giving anything away. Elara is wise enough to stay silent.

The guardian's jaw clenches. His single responsibility at the library is as guard: he doesn't want to admit that someone slipped past him.

"The golden books are still missing?" I guess.

The guardian's face darkens, his olive complexion deepening to a moody eggplant. "You dare to ask *me* questions?"

"We're both capable of asking questions," I answer coolly. "I'm surprised they allowed you in here. Perrin had more twists planned for the Land test than he let on."

"Perrin is a pawn," the guardian spits out scornfully. "Nothing more. He doesn't give the orders, he takes them."

"He's a domain leader," I point out.

"A *pawn*," the guardian is quick to correct me. "Complicit and obedient with whatever orders the spirit domains dictate."

"I don't believe I caught your name," I say neutrally. "Or who sent you."

"You may call me Guardian. And I didn't tell you."

Elara snorts derisively, the first action she's taken since the guardian's arrival. His steely eyes flash to her now, glittering in anticipation of a challenge. My stomach twists—even without looking over, I can imagine the expression on my sister's face. It's not going to placate the guardian.

"Guardian. Of what, exactly?" Elara asks. Her voice is saccharine, falsely sweet and unnaturally high.

The guardian glowers, understanding Elara's slight. He raises his chin in defiance—he will not admit to failing in his duty to guard the Callings' library.

"Seems more appropriate we know your actual name, then." Elara's words are neat, her smirk saturated with condescension.

"Don't talk down to me."

Elara feigns surprise. "I'm half your size. Of course I don't talk down to you."

The guardian's legs twitch, and I worry he is on the brink of attack. It's a wonder he hasn't assaulted us already.

"You want something from us, but you can't harm us without incurring the wrath of the domain leaders," I guess. "Do you propose a trade of resources?" I'm eager to redirect the conversation to a useful end—a battle of wits and barbs between the guardian and my sister is something I'd like to avoid.

The dark guardian scoffs, but he takes a moment to respond. His pause confirms my thinking: he hasn't been sent here at the behest of the domain leaders.

"Give me the book."

"Or what?" Elara asks.

"What will you offer in return?" I'm quick to add.

"You are in no position to bargain." The guardian looks us over with disdain. "Give me the book, and no harm will befall you."

I'm shaking my head even before he finishes speaking. "Who sent you? Or did you come on your own?"

Thin lips press together to make a tight line. "If you don't give me the book, things will get worse. It will be better for you if you just give it back now."

Elara laughs. "That's your best pitch? Surely you can lie better than that."

"What, exactly, will happen if I don't?" My head tilts to the side in question. I'm not patronizing the guardian—I actually want to know what he imagines will happen if I don't return the book to him.

"It's dangerous to be in possession of a book of gold." The words are offered begrudgingly, through clenched teeth. My question remains unanswered.

"Books themselves are rarely dangerous: what harm can paper and ink do?" Elara is having too much fun cutting this guardian down to size—she's missing the plot of what I'm trying to accomplish.

"What do you mean?" I ask. My fingers press against the pocket that holds the marble on instinct, but it is unresponsive and quiet.

"Stop wasting my time," the guardian barks. When I'm quiet, he exhales in exasperation. "If—if you're caught with the book of prophecies, you will have sealed your own fate. No victory in any domain test will save you."

My breath hilts. "I don't have the book of prophecies." My words are quiet, and something in my expression tells the guardian that this is true.

His rage ebbs, his sharp features melt into furrowed brows and then a frown. He looks lost. "You don't have it." His words are as quiet as mine as he searches my face for any indication that I'm lying.

I shake my head slowly. I would open up my pack to prove it, but I don't want him to see the other golden book I have in my possession.

The dark guardian doesn't look angry anymore; he looks frightened. He glances over one shoulder, then the other, as though the book of prophecies might suddenly materialize. I know we're both wondering the same thing: who took the book, and why?

"Why did you think I took the book?" I ask. The guardian has no reason to stick around—he's going to leave any moment. If I hope to have any questions answered, now is the time.

"You're new to Soulbourne, summoned by someone powerful. Your motives for coming here are unclear; there are prophecies written about you. You visited the library, and went to the alcove where the book is kept...I saw the trail of gold myself."

I nod. The logic checks out. I wonder if the heist was made to look like my work.

"This is bigger than I realized." The guardian's words do little to ease my nerves.

"Do you have any idea who it might have been? Could it be the same person who marked me?"

The guardian stares at me as though seeing me for the first time. "You don't know who marked you." He looks surprised.

Our time with the guardian is rapidly winding down, a point Elara also picks up on. "How *did* you make it inside the test?" she asks. "No outsiders are allowed."

The guardian blinks, slowly drawing his gaze from me to my sister. "Is that what they told you?" His voice sounds far away. "And who do you suppose the rules are made for?"

It's the last thing he says before he disappears.

"We're playing a game inside a game," I tell Elara the moment he's gone.

"Inside a game," Elara adds.

I sigh heavily, interlacing my hands on top of my head as I think about what we just learned.

"You don't have the book, do you?" Elara asks, eyeing me from the side.

I shake my head. "I tried to go see it—with Emberlyn and Lenna—but it was already missing by the time we got there."

Elara nods slowly, piecing information together. "So we don't think that...guardian...was the one who carved the tree?"

My eyes meet my sister's. "No."

"Right. Then we'd better keep moving. We may be playing a game inside of a game inside of a game, but this present game is the one we can see. And we're running out of time."

Time.

"Wait."

Elara hesitates.

"I do have a golden book...on time. It's not the one the guardian was looking for, but it's one of the special books he warned us about having in our possession."

Without waiting for my sister to respond, I shrug off the pack. I wipe my palms on my pants to divest myself of the layer of grime even the creek water didn't dislodge, then retrieve the text. The feel of the book alone sends a hum of anticipation through my bones.

The gilt scrawl on the cover feels ostentatious now, the gold deep and rich and decidedly contraband. I've held the book in my hands before, but this time, it feels heavier. More important. When I look up to Elara, I find her still. Her deep blue eyes survey everything with guarded curiosity.

I open the book.

The world around me slows and my senses sharpen. I've already read much of the book, but my fingers trace the first page of text with reverence as I search the yellowed paper for a clue. I flick through pages in silence. My eyes don't land on anything noteworthy and so I skim faster, thumb fanning the pages so they riffle past.

Elara still doesn't say a word.

I know what she's thinking: we need to move. I can't crouch in the middle of Forest and read. This book might be golden and it might have special qualities, but those are mysteries I can solve later. We still have to hunt flags.

I make to snap the book shut when a thick paper falls from the folds. Elara's head jerks sharply as the rough, milky-white sheet dances on the wind and gently lands on the grass.

It could be nothing, I tell myself. My heartbeat quickens, my eyes find Elara's before I pluck the paper from the ground.

My eyes devour the slanted scrawl, the thick black ink and letters that curl in ornamentation. Every word is precise. There is no mistaking what I've discovered, if the title is true.

My face is pale and drawn when I look up to Elara. Her eyes and nostrils flare at the mere sight of my face—she knows I've found something wonderful or horrible. Maybe both.

"What."

I swallow, then take a deep breath. "Tell me what you think," I say, offering her the paper.

"Do you think it will work?" Elara asks a moment later.

"There's only one way to find out."

Elara nods, then shrugs. "It's worth trying."

"It seems like a game-changer."

"Do you think they'll punish you?" Elara asks.

It's my turn to shrug. Maybe I should care more, but I'm bone-tired and mentally exhausted. I want to survive this damned test—I want to make sure *Elara* survives this test. There doesn't seem to be a "right" way to do anything.

"We need to do it together," I say.

Elara nods her agreement.

My hands are steady, though sweaty, as I smooth the creamy paper. It's a simple stanza—a few foreign words, but nothing that will cause us to stumble. The simplest words are those that appear at the top of the page, slightly larger and underlined for emphasis.

How to Stop Time.

"On three," Elara suggests, reaching for my hand.

The moment we speak the words, there is a shift in the atmosphere. A warm breeze blows, a caress that riddles my arms and legs with goosebumps. Golden light sweeps the perimeter of my vision, turning the forest into something enchanted and fuzzy. My voice—Elara's voice, too—sounds like it's traveling through a tunnel. I feel very far away from myself...detached somehow.

And then, with sparkling clarity, it stops.

The fine lines and details of the world are in focus, but all movement is suspended. The flight of a bumblebee, the descent of a leaf from a tree, the current of the water are all frozen, caught in time. The lack of sound is what makes the surroundings feel truly eerie.

Absent any noise, the world feels surreal: unnatural and unsettled. I'm thankful for Elara's hand in mine, the physical connection and reminder that I am alive and not a ghost.

"It worked," Elara breathes. Her voice is soft, but in the stunning void of other sound, it sounds obnoxiously discordant.

I nod, stunned at what we have done. We have stopped actual time. I look to the paper wedged between my thumb and forefinger, a smear of sweat marring its otherwise pristine surface. The title and the stanza are the only things written—there's no explanation for how long time will stay frozen.

"Think it will stay like this until we say the spell again?" Elara asks.

I shrug. It would make sense, but common sense doesn't always comply with the preternatural characteristics of Soulbourne.

The suspension of time has made me cautious and contemplative, reluctant to make any sudden moves. It's made Elara jumpy and fidgety, as though she can somehow outrun the effects of what we've done.

"Let's go, Andra."

"We *are* going," I insist. I take a tentative step forward. My mouth drops open and a shiver of delight creeps up my spine at what I see trailing me.

Gold glitter dust.

The gilt, glittering trail that I could never see before—I see it now: slick gold that sparkles and twinkles with blinding brilliance in the morning light. I hate being marked, but this is beautiful. Gorgeous. Maybe even ethereal. It's splendor that takes my breath away.

Elara sniffs, her freckled nose scrunching with interest and then delight. "Do you smell that?"

The golden trail isn't just for show—it smells like night blooming jasmine and sandalwood and frankincense. It's floral and dimensional and earthly and regal, and the scent is thick as it clogs the air around us.

I'm speechless.

I'd always assumed my mark had a *bad* smell. No one told me the olfactory trail left in my wake smelled divine. I look to Elara. "Your turn."

I look to the ground as Elara walks, chin lifted so I'll catch a whiff of my sister's fragrance. But there isn't any trail that follows her and there's no perfume. Instead, there's music.

It's a symphony of dreams, a sound so lovely it summons tears. I close my eyes to better hear the sound, to dull my dominant senses into submission to the mellifluent melody. It's wordless—the instruments work in synchronization to evoke hope and passion and beauty in a single score.

When I open my eyes, it's to look at Elara in wonder. Her own eyes shine. For a moment we stand and marvel, both content to revel in the awe and glory of our respective markings.

"I wonder what it means that we can perceive our marks. We stopped time, but it seems like we did something else, too."

Elara looks my way, so I know she's heard me, but she continues twirling to keep the dazzling melody alive.

"We still need to find the flags," I say with reluctance.

This captures my sister's attention. "Lead the way." Elara takes a graceful step forward, beaming at the music that pours forth.

Out of Forest and into Mountains we go. The sun stays in its same position in the sky, bright and radiant. Our progress is relaxed and the warmth of the sun causes my body to unwind and embrace the fatigue I've been fighting.

"I'm tired."

Elara takes one look at me and nods. "You're never going to have to convince me to sleep."

My gaze lands on a patch of moss beneath a giant tree, filtered light streaming through its branches. I remove my pack and snuggle up against the trunk, body singing with glorious anticipation. Now that time has stopped, it finally feels safe to rest. Not another word is exchanged before I fall into a deep sleep.

When I dream, I see Galen.

I'm in the monastery library in Callings, sitting at a table reading a book. When Galen walks in, I look up. His face is grave, countenance riddled with warning.

"Spirits are not bound by the rules of Soulbourne."

I put my book down, then press my elbows on the table and lean forward to ask him what he means.

But Galen is already gone.

When I wake up, I'm relieved to find Elara sprawled out in sound slumber. It's strange to wake to a world that is silent, and I'm grateful for Elara's soft breaths.

Everything feels heavy as I make my first movements—even my eyelids feel like iron shutters. It's impossible to know how long I've slept—the sun hasn't changed position. The sameness feels spooky. Before, it offered comfort. Now, it strikes me as unnerving.

I nudge Elara, and my sister's eyes blink open. She groans and gives her surroundings a bleary scan before closing her eyes and hugging her arms across her chest. "Ten more minutes."

"We both know you're not going to feel any more rested after ten minutes," I protest. "You're just going to ask for another ten minutes."

"Maybe if you let me sleep for six rounds of ten minutes, I'll feel better," Elara murmurs.

"You're doing math—you're not *that* tired. I had a weird dream," I add.

Elara's eyes flash open. "What about?"

"It wasn't long," I hedge, but Elara's eyes never leave my face. "I was in the monastery library, reading."

"The one you went to with Warrick?" Elara asks, recalling the synopsis of my time in Soulbourne.

I nod. "Galen—from Overworld—appeared. He told me that spirits aren't bound by the rules of Soulbourne. Then he disappeared and I woke up."

Elara's face is unreadable, but goosebumps prickle her arms. "It's a warning."

"There's a spirit in the test," I murmur.

Elara's eyes lock on mine. "*Spirits*, more like it. And they're not bound by the spell on time."

The realization hits me like a penny dropped in an empty well: a small epiphany, but with resounding, shrill impact. Spirits are crawling around inside the Land test. Elara and I are not the only ones conscious.

Elara is up in a second. She stretches and scans our surroundings—something I've already done—and comes to the same conclusion I have: there's no visible threat.

"Let's walk," I suggest, ignoring the apprehension that crawls up my spine like a spider. I jerk my head in the direction I think we should walk: deeper into Mountains.

Our first steps are a chorus of grunts and hisses as our bodies remember their present ailments and shortcomings. I grit my teeth in the beginning, but as the blood starts to flow and my muscles warm, the edge is taken off.

"What was that?" my sister demands.

"What?" I ask, head swiveling to understand the threat Elara perceived.

"I heard something." Elara's body is tight and slightly hunched as she moves forward with caution.

A cool breeze floats by: a crisp, wintery wind that awakens the senses and invigorates the soul. Our eyes travel in the direction of the draft to find a cinnamon-brown flag ruffling in the breeze, resting between two gloved hands.

My heartbeat thunders in my chest as I look from the gloved hands to the shadowed face obscured by an expansive hood. The body is motionless, but it could be a trick. A skilled assassin who is known to move like air could easily hold such a pose.

"It's Nox," I guess.

Nox's reputation has been built upon his prowess for killing and slinking about in abject silence. My breathing suddenly seems as loud as a stampede, my whisper a shout.

"I can't see his face," Elara whispers back.

I grab the nearest pinecone. When I chuck it at him, he doesn't move. A promising sign, but my stomach is still coiled in knots. I'm not confident that Nox is truly frozen in time.

Elara senses my hesitation. "You think he's faking it?"

I shrug. There's a slimy sensation in my gut—intuition that beguiles and annoys me.

"We're not going to have an easier shot at the flag," Elara points out, voice loud against the void of silence.

"I know," I hiss. But something is off. There's something amiss, and I'm not seeing it.

Elara huffs and crosses her arms over her chest. Another breeze ripples through, and my sister makes a move towards Nox and the cinnamon-brown flag. It's in that moment that I realize: there should not be a breeze.

TWENTY-FIVE

"Don't!" I cry, but Elara has already thrown back Nox's hood.

I recoil, sure that we're about the meet the unrestrained wrath of the silent assassin. My worry is for naught: Nox is immobile, frozen in time.

"I thought..."

There were two breezes—two more than there should have been. Since Elara and I stopped time, there haven't been any disruptions to the ecosystems besides that which we have manufactured. And that breeze was a crosswind, not something that could have been created by our own movement.

I'm unsettled as I look to Nox.

His figure is slight but muscular; he doesn't stand much taller than Elara. This works to his benefit as an assassin, I'm sure—it's easier to escape notice and prowl around at an inconspicuous height. I see why he dons a hood, though—Nox is not the kind of individual who blends into a crowd.

His face is a true white—not beige or honey or peach—actual white. His skin is so paper-thin that it appears translucent: I see the fine web of veins and capillaries that run in cross-cross pattern from his neck to his face. His eyes are a light, watery blue that could pass for colorless if not juxtaposed to his *truly* colorless skin. His lips are thin and his flaxen hair clings to his scalp in fine clumps.

Elara regards him, same as me, and she must come to the same conclusion, because she takes a step back. There isn't one feature about Nox that marks him as disquieting, but the sum total of all his parts leaves a distinct, unsettling impression.

"What did you think was going to happen?" Elara asks.

"There was a breeze."

Elara's face scrunches in confusion.

"What caused the breeze?" I ask. "Everything is suspended in time."

Elara stares at me, paling as she realizes what that means.

"I have a bad feeling," I add. Even the low oration of words feels like a gaffe. "Let's get the flag and get out of here."

The rough canvas is easily pulled from Nox's gloved hands. I hand it to Elara, who makes to put it away. She moves my braid to open the pack when I hear a rustling.

My body goes ramrod straight, my fingers latch onto my sister's free arm with a hawk-like grip. My warning is redundant: Elara has heard the noise, too. Icy fear and dread tiptoe up my spine, taking their time as they claim every inch of my body.

I don't have to say a word.

Elara slowly lifts the top to my pack. I feel every movement as she stuffs the flag inside and secures the flap once more. Each movement is more haphazard than the last. When the flag is safely buried, she moves my braid back over my pack and gives my shoulder a squeeze. Neither of us say a word before we start running.

Footsteps follow us.

I don't waste precious time or energy to look behind—Elara and I take off up the mountain.

The air grows thin and the incline is significant. Elara and I draw deep breaths. Neither of us acknowledge it, but I know we both wonder how far we'll be able to run before we need to stop. I don't allow myself to consider my reservoirs of energy: the most important thing right now is to keep moving.

"Shit."

I hear the curse a half-second before I hear a heavy thud. A hot flash of panic strikes as I whip around to find Elara on the ground. She scrambles up as though nothing is wrong, but the grimace on her face and the darkening maroon stain on her knee tell a different story.

"I'm okay," Elara mutters as she takes my hand and allows me to pull her to her feet.

In a different circumstance, I might insist we take the time to assess my sister's injury. But even if Elara isn't okay...she has to be right now. In the seconds we're down, I don't see any sign of Dirce. I don't need to. I *know* it's Dirce out there—I can feel it.

We run.

I'm painfully aware of Elara's hitched breaths and the fact that we're slow. Anxiety mounts inside of me like a tower of bricks. When we reach a plateau and there's an opportunity to descend, I don't hesitate. "This way." I point to the path that slopes down and away from the mountain peak.

A flash of confusion crosses Elara's face, but she doesn't question me. She's careful with her steps—the decline may be easier cardio, but the technical work is more demanding. One misplaced step could twist an ankle or cause a second fall. In Elara's case, that could really end badly.

As it is, the blood stain blossoms through her pants and spreads until it wraps the circumference of her knee. She moves well enough, though she clearly favors her healthy knee. The tight expression and gritted teeth tell me all I need to know about the pain. There's still no visual sign of Dirce.

"It hurts more going down," Elara complains.

"We can't go up. We won't outrun Dirce—she'll catch us." The words come easier now that we're no longer climbing.

"Dirce. The knife-wielding spy," Elara muses. "That's who you think is chasing us?"

225

"Yes."

Elara stops long enough to meet my eyes. "Only one flag left." The words themselves are matter-of-fact, but I know what she's saying. We're close. We can do this. We can beat the Land test.

"I'm taking us to Jungle," I tell my sister. "Our marks will be harder to track and I think we'll find the last flag there."

There's no way to know for sure where the last flag is hidden: we don't know where Nox found his flag, and I haven't yet set foot in Plains. I didn't find a flag in Forest.

I wait for Elara's rebuttal, but it never comes. She must have run through the options herself and come to the same conclusion. Either that, or she's in a lot of pain.

"I don't hear Dirce," Elara says after a few minutes.

"Me neither."

"Do you think we lost her?"

I shake my head. "No. She's a spy…she's going to be quiet and hard to detect."

Elara sighs. "I hate being hunted."

I raise my eyebrows in silent agreement. I don't say what I think: it's much worse that we leave trails of glitter and perfume and music everywhere we go—literal beacons to attract every element of danger in the Land test.

The constant light causes time to pass strangely. My body knows that it should be night, but the sunlight that corresponds with morning throws me for a loop. I'm disoriented, hungry, and tired.

I remember the map of the ecosystems and recall that Forest is in the center—you can pass through Forest to get to any other ecosystem. But without signposts or markers, it's impossible to gauge distance. Now that time has stopped, it's even more difficult.

"How's your leg?" I ask Elara when we stop for water. Both of us gaze towards her knee.

"I'm afraid to look. As long as we're moving, it's okay. I have a feeling it's going to stiffen up once we stop."

"We can do this," I remind her.

We're exhausted but close—one flag to retrieve and then we can put this hellish ordeal behind us. Elara's eyes glitter with similar determination.

There's slightly less urgency as we continue on—I no longer feel Dirce trailing us, though I'm not foolish enough to think she's given up. Tension curls its claws around my insides. "I think Dirce split off on purpose. I'm worried it's a trap."

Elara is silent as she considers. She's poised to speak when we turn the corner. The landscape stretches far in the distance—we can see for nearly a mile.

At the edge of that view is Jungle.

The relief I feel upon entering Jungle is profound.

Glorious, dense vegetation abounds, rich tropical fragrances aromatize the moist air, and the cloying nature of the humidity is an unusual comfort after the arid lands we've passed through. Hydration won't be an issue—and neither will food. I've already spotted clusters of mangoes and bananas in the trees above.

But the neutralization of former poignant threats comes at the materialization of a new host of elements which merit concern: namely, progress through Jungle is slow and laborious.

"You don't think there's a path anywhere?" Elara asks when we first engage with the thicket of vines, ferns, and spindly trees.

I stumble over an unruly root and curse.

"If there's a path, it's long gone or far away," I reason. I don't add that we wouldn't want to take any well-paved path, anyway—it would be too easy for Dirce to intercept us.

We walk on.

The warm embrace of humidity starts to irritate. The baby-fine hairs on the nape of my neck are slick with sweat and curl in unruly, rebellious fashion; my clothes stick to my skin like glue. When I hit my head on a low-hanging tree branch, I grit my teeth and bite back vulgar words.

"This is miserable," Elara says for both of us.

Heat creeps into my face as I consider my sister's peaky pallor and drawn expression—she hasn't complained, but she must feel terrible. She *looks* like she feels terrible.

"How's your knee?"

Elara shrugs in an unconcerned manner that I know better than to buy. She doesn't have to say a word for me to know that it's gotten worse, she feels like shit, and she needs to rest.

My fingers attempt to smooth the hairs clouding my line of sight. There aren't any natural resting places in Jungle—just verdant foliage for as far as the eye can see.

"Why don't we take a break?" I point to a small clearing. It's not ideal, but…nothing in the Land test is.

Elara offers a silent nod rife with fatigue; I note the grimace as she bends down. She takes a couple of deep, centering breaths that I know are in response to pain.

I slide alongside my sister and kneel. Without asking for permission, I rip the fabric of Elara's pant leg, then pull on each end to widen the tear. In all of this, my sister is silent. My stomach turns as I lay eyes on the wound.

"Your nostrils flared. How bad is it?"

My eyes go wide in innocence, but Elara shakes her head. *Don't even think about it*, her eyes warn. She wants the truth.

"It's…bloody."

It's hard to assess the damage beneath the congealed layers of blood. The mottled red and nightshade are the cause of my revulsion—I've never been a fan of blood, and the bright colors and torn flesh look garish.

"I'm going to find water," I announce. This shouldn't be elusive in Jungle, and we need it both for hydration and to wash. It will help to assess the true damage done to Elara's knee.

It takes little time to spot a pool of water in the distance. It's far enough that I don't want to venture over without Elara by my side, but I move close enough to qualify that the water is clean and the area safe. A small river feeds into a pond—the ideal place to drink.

"Over there." I nod in the direction of the pond.

Elara makes to stand.

"Use me," I suggest, squatting low so my sister can use my shoulders for leverage. She grunts in pain, but stands.

Together, we hobble towards the pond.

"Bananas." Elara gestures to a tree weighed down with the bright fruit.

"Let's get water first—then we can worry about food." I keep my voice light to hide my concern. I want to wash away the blood to see how bad Elara's wound really is.

When my sister is perched on a low, flat rock at the water's edge, I gesture towards her knee. "I'm going to wash it a little bit," I warn before scooping water between my cupped hands. Elara's shoulders tighten and her nostrils flare in anticipation.

A few washes later, I relax.

The cut on Elara's knee is nasty, but it's not bone-deep and there's no infection that I can see. To my inexperienced eyes, it looks like a painful wound...one that looks much better after the dried, cakey blood has been wiped away.

"Thank goodness," Elara breathes before I've given any verbal report. She's seen the answer on my face. "It just hurts, then."

"I'm sorry it hurts."

"Can you wrap it?" Elara nods to the bottom of her pant legs. Minutes later, the task is done: her pants are an inch shorter and the fabric encircles the wound at her knee.

"Does it feel any better?"

"It feels better knowing it's not a big deal."

My smile is tight. This entire Land test, I've bubbled with adrenaline and anxiety and fear. Elara's entrance into the test likely saved my life…and gave birth to my greatest nightmare.

"Should we start time?" Elara asks a moment later.

The question catches me off guard. We still have a flag to find, but we don't know whether it's in Jungle or Plains. We've frozen time—for most. Not all. If Galen's warning in my dream was real, then the spirits remain active…and stopping time isn't the boon we originally believed it was.

"Andra?"

"I don't know. I think the final flag is here, in Jungle."

"So…start time?"

"I don't have any gut feeling about where it is in here," I warn.

Elara shrugs. "We'll figure it out."

Even without articulating her reasons why, I can tell that Elara wants to restart time. Maybe we both feel uncomfortable knowing that the biggest threats—*the spirits*—still crawl around.

A few moments and a paragraph of words later, time ticks once more. The sound of insects buzzing and birds trilling is a relief. The fragrant scent and golden glitter and mellifluous sound of our markings are obfuscated from our senses once again.

Our progress through Jungle is steady, if slow.

Thick vines and obtrusive foliage make for cumbersome travel—not only do we negotiate over gnarled roots and under heavy ferns, but we keep our eyes fixed on the floor, on the trees, and in the branches above for any poisonous creature. Every step requires analysis, and it's exhausting.

The sticky, cloying humidity hangs like a second skin. Puddles of sweat accumulate around my joints in particular—my knees, elbows, and armpits seem to serve as veritable pools that fester and disgust me to no end. More than once I'm tempted to shed my garments altogether.

Fortunately, Elara's knee holds up. Even as we crouch and squat, she doesn't complain or wince. She's likely uncomfortable, but her mobility is a big win.

"What will they do when you pass this test?" Elara asks.

I pause in the gummy mud long enough to glance at my sister. "You do realize you're part of this mess now, too?

I haven't given much thought to what might happen when the Land test ends. But Elara is right to think of the next step, especially as we've restarted time and there's only a day and a half left in the test.

"I'll have a few days—maybe a week—before the next test begins. We need to worry about what they might do to *you*."

Elara's response is swift and direct. "I won't leave you."

"No," I'm quick to agree. "We won't be separated." Butterflies swirl in my stomach: I have little doubt domain leadership will try to do exactly that.

"Achlys seemed irate that I got to enter the test. But he didn't argue with Justus' logic." The way Elara says it, I can tell she thinks Justus trumps Achlys.

"Don't underestimate Achlys."

"I'm not underestimating anyone," Elara answers.

"Wise words, indeed."

The female voice is surprisingly light, and I know instinctively that it is not the voice of Kakarauri. My hand reaches for Elara. She has stilled, too—we're both frozen in place, poised to react.

Dirce steps out from behind a tree, her movements lithe and unbothered. She wears a thick, fitted vest and beige pants riddled with pockets. Some straps and folds secure sheathed blades, others bulge with contents left to the imagination.

The spy is petite—much of her body is covered, but her small wrists and slender frame are easy enough to gauge. Her angular eyes are the color of coffee and her unblemished skin the color of porcelain. Silky black hair is pulled back into a tight braid, and even the tendrils that have come loose look elegant. I have to remind myself that Dirce is lethal—if not for the many blades that adorn her stealth uniform, I'd sooner imagine her royalty.

231

"You found us."

Dirce's eyes rove up and down my figure and then Elara's. "It was only a matter of *time*," she agrees.

I cringe.

"How did you do it?" Dirce asks, eyes narrowed.

I cast a nervous glance in Elara's direction—the only time my eyes leave the spy. The movement is quick, but it mobilizes Dirce. She takes a step forward.

"What do you mean?" Silently, I beg Elara to stay quiet.

"Time. How did you stop it?" Dirce asks.

"Stop *time*?" I scoff. "How could we stop time?"

Dirce's expression is a mask, her features smooth and unwilling to yield. Her silence calls for further explanation, but I bite my tongue.

"We made a deal with Achlys," Elara says.

My head snaps to my sister. Dirce does the same.

"Go on." The spy's chin juts out in expectation.

"And in exchange?" Elara asks, one eyebrow arched.

Dirce coughs a laugh. "Are you looking for protection?"

Elara shrugs. "Is that the best you have to trade?"

"Isn't that what you're worried about? That I'll kill you?" Dirce asks.

"I think there are many things to worry about," Elara answers carefully.

Dirce's eyes narrow. "Are you threatening me?"

"There was no threat mentioned," Elara responds coolly. "Only a reminder that you don't have all of the information."

"You have to get out of the Land test alive," Dirce parries.

Elara folds her arms over her chest. "We've done a pretty good job of that so far."

I chew the inside of my cheek. Elara is playing loose and fast, and I'm not sure it's the right way to interact with Dirce. But the spy regards us carefully, brown eyes quietly assessing the threat we pose.

"I know you've killed prisoners," Dirce says. "But not all of them. If you tell me how you stopped time—about this deal with Achlys—I'll kill one of the leftovers for you."

A wave of cold revulsion engulfs me. Dirce's attempted negotiation of lives—*human lives*—sounds as casual and practical as a sale of goods at market. Even knowing full well her profession, I'm struck by how unnatural and irreverent the action is.

As much as I don't want to interfere with whatever it is that Elara is spinning, I feel compelled to clarify our position. "We're not trying to kill people."

Dirce smirks. "It must have been you who killed them, then."

I open my mouth and close it. I don't meet Elara's gaze—I'm sure there will be a glare waiting for my interference.

"How many flags do you still need?" Dirce tries again.

"We don't need your help," Elara interrupts. "But we don't want your opposition, either."

Dirce frowns. "You're not going to give me what I want unless I hurt you."

"There are two of us and one of you," Elara says softly.

Dirce breaks out a wicked smile. "More fun for me."

"You're not worried what Achlys will do to you?"

This elicits a response—Dirce scoffs and shakes her head. "You're insane to work with Achlys," she mutters.

Elara waves a hand in the air as though the matter is of little concern. "We needed his guaranteed protection."

Dirce hesitates. Her jaw protrudes and then retracts. Elara doesn't give an inch, so I don't either.

"What did Achlys tell you?" Dirce asks a moment later.

I wonder what fabrication Elara will spin when Dirce's coffee-brown eyes flare. A moment later, she disappears.

"What—" Elara doesn't finish her sentence—her words die on her mouth as her own eyes widen with alarm.

"You have something that belongs to me."

The reason Dirce slipped away is suddenly apparent. Since we restarted time, Nox has wasted none in tracking us down.

TWENTY-SIX

Nox's face is covered in shadows—his hood reinstated to its original position so I'm unable to read the expression on his face. He's obviously upset.

"I don't believe we've met."

Nox snorts. "Are introductions truly in order, Andra?" Nox's voice is low and cold, but his intonation and enunciation convey unexpected refinery.

I ignore Nox's scorn and wave a hand towards Elara. "This is my sister, Elara."

Anyone who lays eyes on us immediately suspects our shared genetics—with Nox's honed repertoire of skills, this will not have escaped his notice. The assassin offers a sharp nod, face still hidden within the folds of his hood.

Elara looks nervously over one shoulder. We don't know where Dirce went—we don't know if Nox *saw* Dirce—and we can't guess how Nox might try to reclaim the stolen flag.

"Don't think about running," Nox declares, misjudging the furtive glance.

"What do you want?" Elara asks. We likely know what he

wants—the flag…maybe the two of us, dead—but I understand why she asks.

Nox doesn't answer straight away.

His gloved hands flex, but there's no other sign of movement. My heart beats light as a butterfly and the hairs on my arms and legs stand on end, even in the heat of Jungle.

I can't see within the folds of Nox's robe. I have no idea what diabolical weapons are strapped to his person; I know little about the man who has earned the reputation of fearsome assassin. His color-less appearance now seems to suggest he is absent a soul—like his personhood couldn't even contain pigment, much less a moral code.

"Where did she go?" Nox asks.

The question catches me so off guard that it takes a moment to respond. Elara and I exchange a glance before I look back to the shadowed figure.

"I don't know."

Nox seems to accept this answer, though it's hard to know in the moments of stillness before he moves. There's a slight tilt to his chin and I hear a deep inhale. Then he's in motion, lithe and graceful as a dancer and limber as a gymnast as he leaps over vines and swoops under branches and disappears from sight.

The moment we're left alone, Elara looks to me with wide eyes. The hairs on my arms and legs continue to stand at attention; the danger has not passed. My sister looks over both shoulders, trying and failing to spot the spy or assassin. She scoots close to my side. "We should make a break for it—we're not going to get a better opportunity."

My body, chock-full of nervous energy, *wants* to run—but something tells me we should stay. Not for the first time, I wish the marble would send a signal. Even a mere whisper or hint of how to proceed would be deeply appreciated.

"What?" Elara asks.

My face scrunches. I don't have words to articulate the feeling that tingles my bones, lighting up my nerves like glowworms.

"Should we stop time again?" Elara whispers.

I shake my head. To stop time would work against Nox and in favor of Dirce—and while it might eliminate one threat, it doesn't solve the problem.

"She took off."

Nox's words hit me before I see the man return—a move I believe to be intentional as he swings his frame beneath a vine and lands before us. Our chance to flee is gone.

"She would have killed you," Nox says a moment later.

Elara and I are silent.

"I don't know what she told you, but she was going to kill you," Nox repeats.

I throw a quick glance in Elara's direction. The plot continues to thicken and I'm not at all confident that we're playing things correctly. "You say that like you're not."

Nox hesitates, then slowly tugs his hood back so we can see those expressionless, watery-blue eyes. He winces at the light before settling eyes on me. "I will kill you if I need to, but it's not my objective." The words are delivered so directly that I'm inclined to believe him.

"Dirce tried to negotiate with us, too," Elara cuts in. She doesn't elaborate—just lets Nox know he's not the only one playing a game.

"...and you're an assassin," I add.

Nox nods, stretching his fingers in his gloved hands before they settle at his side. "I *am* an assassin," he agrees. "It would be a mistake, however, for you to presume that it's all that I am."

Nox doesn't carry himself with bravado, though there is a quiet confidence to him. I wondered before whether the long layers and cloak were to obscure his appearance; I realize now that this is unlikely. My gaze travels to the neck of Nox's shirt: the flesh is marbled in coloration, a blend of pig-pink and white. It looks textured, like stretched dough. I find myself wondering what lies beneath his gloves and sleeves.

"Are we meant to guess what else you are?" It's the kind of sassy remark that would typically fall off Elara's lips, but the words are mine.

Nox laughs, though there is no smile. "I'd hoped the Bellemere sisters were as tough as I'd heard. I don't know what you did to take the flag from me," Nox looks from me to Elara, "but it's clear that there's more to you than meets the eye."

Elara opens her mouth, probably to tell him that our last name isn't Bellemere, but Nox holds up a gloved hand.

"I'm not asking you to tell me how you did it. I'll learn in time, whether or not you deign to share your secret. Whatever you did, it will have caught the attention of Justus and Achlys. Nothing escapes the notice of the leaders of Overworld and Underworld."

My expression remains neutral, but my heart rate increases. When we made the decision to stop time, we didn't consider what would happen *outside* of the test. The last thing we need is further attention from the spirit domain leaders.

"What do you want from us?" Elara asks. Apparently, she's not hung up on being called by the wrong last name—maybe she thinks it will work to our advantage.

"I'm going to help you make it out of the Land test alive. In exchange, you will assist me in the moment that I ask."

Of all the schemes and requests I considered, this didn't cross my mind. I study Nox, consider his mottled flesh and colorless eyes and wonder what he truly stands to gain from such an unusual alliance. He's the second prisoner to believe I have clout, that I will somehow carry influence outside of the Land test.

"How are you going to help us?" Elara asks skeptically.

"What kind of assistance do you expect?" I add, concerned that Elara is only focused on one dimension of the potential agreement.

"Dirce can't live," Nox answers matter-of-factly. "Whatever you did back in Mountains, she knows about it and she will use it against you."

"I thought you said that Justus and Achlys already know," I point out.

"The domain leaders will demand answers. Dirce knows definitively. Doesn't she?" Nox asks, an eyebrow arched in question.

I swallow, remembering Dirce's demand that we tell her how we stopped time. I nod.

"So I'll kill her," Nox answers simply.

The blood drones in my ears. Dirce won't be the first prisoner to die in the Land test. To delegate the task to Nox seems preferable to killing her myself, but there's a metallic bitterness in the back of my throat.

"How?" Elara asks.

Nox shrugs. "That's my problem. I'm sure you'll be able to find out after the test, if you're interested."

It's abhorrent to let Nox kill Dirce. I also don't see how we can refuse him. It will eliminate a major problem and allow us to focus on finding the final flag and ending the test.

"She's not the only one left," I murmur. Dirce is the greatest threat that remains, but Brone and Kakarauri still wander around.

"Brone isn't going to attack you. He's two ecosystems away," Nox answers swiftly. "Dirce is the only remaining threat."

"Kakarauri is still out there," I remind Nox.

Nox shakes his head. "Kakarauri isn't wandering anywhere—I came across her body in Plains. Looked like Mercurius' work." Nox's expression remains impassive, but I see the subtle flare of his nostrils and guess that it was not a clean death.

I feel a jolt of horror and then a trickle of relief. I am shamefully grateful that Elara and I do not have to worry about encountering Kakarauri, though I shudder to imagine how Mercurius killed her. I don't need to glance at my sister to know that she will feel the same.

"Can you be more specific about the favor you're going to ask for?" Elara asks, glancing my direction. In doing so, she assures me that she recognizes the weight of what we might agree to. We both brace for a costly transaction.

"I don't know what I will ask for. When the time comes, and I need your help, you extend it."

I suck in a breath. "That's pretty broad."

"You're in a desperate situation."

"There will be limits to the help," I say. "Help can't come at personal expense. Nor will I hurt an ally to help you."

Nox regards me with an ever-neutral face and solemn eyes. "Understood. The request will not compromise your well-being or that of a loved one or ally."

I look to Elara. We're not in a place to negotiate, but I don't want to enter into a fool's bargain. Elara shrugs her slim shoulders, her pretty pink mouth twisted to the side in a way that suggests she can't think of any other caveats.

"We have an agreement," I say tentatively, glancing toward my sister. Her expression is calm and she offers a hesitant smile.

Nox nods. There is no smile. "Good. In a moment, I will leave. You will not see me again in the Land test. Once you retrieve the last flag, get out. We must not intercept each other."

"We never met in the Land test," I say, picking up on Nox's train of thought.

"We never crossed paths," Nox agrees.

"How do we explain the flag?" Elara asks.

"Concoct whatever story you'd like. My fingerprints are on the flag—they might learn that it was once in my possession. But I could have lost it anywhere," Nox answers.

I nod as I consider other loopholes. "How do we explain Dirce's death?"

"Don't. I'll handle that. There will be reason and justification for my pursuit of her."

I swallow and try not to think about what the assassin has planned for Dirce. Nox seemed repelled by the death Mercurius exacted from Kakarauri, but will his assault on Dirce be any cleaner? It's not something I can trouble myself with, especially as Elara catches my eye and nods her assent.

"Why?" There is so much I could ask Nox, but I confine my question to one weighty word.

"I'm more interested in long term gains," Nox answers. "Far greater spoils lie outside of the Land test, perhaps outside of Soulbourne."

The words raise goosebumps on my arms. Nox wasn't lying when he suggested that there is more to him than meets the eye—I'm not sure what kind of future he anticipates, but I'm clear on the fact that he means to be a key figure. I can't decide whether to feel flattered or concerned that he believes these next steps hinge on my success.

"We will remember you and make good on our bargain."

"Find the flag and get out," Nox says in response. And then he is gone.

TWENTY-SEVEN

When Nox disappears, I feel a weight lift from my shoulders. The task is finally within reach. Elara and I can find the flag and get out. We don't have to worry about prisoners hunting us.

An hour later, Elara and I both shine with sweat. We've been trekking through Jungle relentlessly and we still haven't found a thing.

"It doesn't feel like we're making progress," Elara mutters, swiping irritably at a low-hanging vine.

"We're covering ground. It won't feel like progress until we've found the flag, and then it will be done."

I don't disagree with my sister, though—jungle trekking is not enjoyable. Our boots sink in sticky mud and the fragrant air is thick and suffocating and the hum of mosquitoes is in constant refrain. There are a host of bumps dotting every expanse of exposed skin that I try hard not to think about. My legs are tired.

And then the sun sinks in the sky, contributing yet another element of stress as the fourth day comes to a close. The stakes are the highest they've been, and the fact that we've made an alliance with Nox has upped the ante further.

"It's all starting to look the same," Elara confesses, pushing a stray hair out of her face.

"It's not the same. Let's make a final push before dark."

Elara doesn't answer. We both pick up the pace: though fatigued and irritable, there's a ferocity and intentionality behind every step and swipe of vines.

My eyes soon water from overuse. I blink profusely to try and steady my vision. It's taxing to study the ground and the trees and the plants—there's so much foliage and so many gradients of color that snakes and spiders might use to camouflage.

When the light hits at a deep angle and the rainforest is bathed in warm, golden rays, I know we're going to need the fifth day.

"I think it's time."

I'm first met with stubborn silence. Neither of us are thrilled about the fact that we're down to the wire where time is concerned. "It would have been really nice if we'd found the flag," Elara grumbles.

I ignore my sister's complaint. "We're not going to find the flag in the dark—let's find a safe spot for the night."

The sun is low in the sky and the lighting dim. The atmosphere is ash gray: shapes and shadows are all that remain of the vibrant colors of Jungle, but it's not so black that sight is rendered impossible. With every step I take, my boots cling to gummy mud, making progress slow and laborious.

I'm leery when we happen upon a shallow cave. It looks to be an ideal resting place, but I worry that serpents and other poisonous creatures will have come to the same conclusion. But the alcove is vacant, and it extends back ten feet—enough space for Elara and I to lay down.

Elara sighs in pleasure as she drops to the ground and pulls off her shoes. "I am so disgusting." She holds up a sock caked in dirt to punctuate this point.

"I'm not taking anything off," I answer, grimacing at the thought of what I'll find when I finally shed layers. We have one day left in

242

the test: I can endure the grime a little longer. It will be bliss to scrub caked dirt and blood and sweat off my body, but I worry now about blisters in my boots and the fit of my outfit if I take it off and then try to put it back on again.

My hair is another matter.

I unravel my braid and work my fingers like a comb through the gnarls. It's slow progress, but after it's detangled and then neatly braided once more, I feel better.

"I know I shouldn't complain, but I'm hungry," Elara says. We were so focused on our quest for shelter that we didn't procure food. Now that it's dark, neither of us are going anywhere.

"We'll find something in the morning." I pause. "We need to talk about our strategy for the final day," I add.

"Find the flag and get out. The faster we do it, the better."

"Not *just* that," I'm careful to reply. "We need to think about what happens when we make it out of the test. We won't have time to strategize in front of the domain leaders."

I have Elara's full attention. She hugs her knees close to her chest, waiting for me to elaborate.

"We need to think about what to say if Achlys or Justus question us. We don't know what they know," I begin.

"We can't deny it all and claim to be innocent?"

I bite my lip. "I don't think it will be that easy."

Elara sighs heavily. "At least Justus is on our side."

I shake my head. "Justus helped you get inside the test, but that doesn't mean he's on our side. We don't know why he did it."

Elara tilts her head in invitation for me to continue.

"The Land test isn't the greatest danger we face." It's a truth I've been slow to recognize. "We still don't know how far-reaching this plot is."

"We beat the Land test, then. We pass the first obstacle."

I nod. "They might try to penalize us. We should be prepared that they don't accept our victory." It's the outcome that brings me the most anxiety: we survive the Land test only to emerge and be told that it doesn't count.

"What do you propose we do if they deny our victory?"

This is where I falter—I can't think of what we should do.

"We could stop time again," Elara offers.

"If we dare to stop time in front of them, it will be a death sentence." On this point, I have strong opinions. "I think we need to do something about the book on time. The dark guardian suspected we had the book of prophecies—if they search us and find the golden book, we'll be in trouble."

"If it's that dangerous, we should destroy it."

I grimace. To destroy a golden book feels immoral.

Elara sees my face and suggests, "We could hide it, then. Leave it here in the cave."

I chew my lower lip. It's not an airtight plan, but it might be the best option. I expect that our belongings will be searched the minute we exit the test—it's too dangerous to keep the book.

"I think you're right."

Elara can tell from my tone of voice that I'm less than thrilled. "It's going to be risky no matter what we decide, Andra."

"I know."

"Someone's been looking out for us this long," Elara adds.

I blow out a deep breath. I'm grateful for the aid that has come from unlikely places and in timely fashion, but it's another layer of mystery. I wish I understood the source and the reason for the help.

"I just want to finish the test and go home."

Elara's slim shoulders hunch forward. "I know. But we can do this, Andra. We're close now."

I pull my sister close. "I love you."

When Elara pulls back, she wears a tired smile. "I love you, too. Let's look at this golden book before we hide it away for good."

I nod my agreement and pull the pack open to retrieve the text. And then, by the light of the moon and the stars that dot the night sky, we read.

There's nothing particularly enthralling in the first chapter, but there's something cozy and familiar about snuggling up to Elara and reading together. Tucked in the cool enclave of the cave, cicadas and frogs provide the symphony of the night.

At the start of the second chapter, Elara yawns, her body slumping against mine. "I'm sleepy."

"You're not even trying to stay awake," I complain, though I can't help but smile. Elara has always been the queen of sleep—a stint in Soulbourne will hardly impede years of training.

Elara's reply comes in the satisfied smirk that graces her lips. If I asked her to, she would stay awake and muddle through the text alongside me. But she knows I won't ask. A sneaky smile traces her lips as her breath quickly hitches into arrhythmic cadence: Elara's song of slumber added to the background music of the night.

My own yawns become consistent. A fog hovers around my mind, but I dutifully slog through pages. Sheer will compels me to read on; I wonder how much of the information I'll retain. There's a sense of relief when I stumble upon the last page.

Time is the ultimate ruler: it wields power to interrupt, delay, or hasten destiny. Though typically an impartial governing body, its ambassadors can, at times, be persuaded to act roguishly. One must carry a firm conviction of necessity and boldly summon the ambassadors of time to make their case.

I blink hard, then rub my eyes gently for good measure. My addled brain is past its prime for the day, and even simple sentences are difficult to parse out. But when I read the excerpt a second time, and then a third...

Until this passage, time was described in typical fashion. Now, a shiver of trepidation wriggles up my spine. It doesn't seem likely that there's been a sudden change in author: the writing style and tone are still the same. But the personification is strong. Either this is the strangest literary conclusion to an otherwise factual account of time, or...

My brain swims with ideas, saturated with thoughts that make sense and thoughts that make no sense at all. My best cognition doesn't take place at night—I know better than to try to unpack weighty statements in the midnight hour. After a night's rest, the text will appear lucid.

I survey the mystical words a final time, puzzling over the last line. *"I boldly summon the ambassadors of time to make my case?"*

The words are orated without hope of an answer. Jungle pulses; the night holds still. But the question from my lips will be carried into my subconscious, canonized in the peripheral echelons of slumber. Perhaps my subconscious can make sense of the riddle. My head lays to rest on the pack.

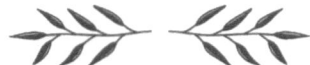

"You cannot have meant to summon us only to have us watch you sleep."

The words float gently as a flower petal—a lilting, buoyant descent that does nothing to rouse me. But when the words permeate my subconscious and settle, the wistful quality ebbs.

Surprise draws my eyes open, my pounding heart at odds with the serenity of the night. Even before my eyes land on the spirits, I sense their presence in the cave. The air is heavy with importance, fragrant with the scents of citrus, eucalyptus, and clove.

Even with my brain fogged, I have the sense to sit up quietly. Elara's chest rises and falls in soft cadence—she's in the comforting thrall of sleep. Predictably, the arrival of nocturnal visitors has done nothing to wake her.

It's with inherent calm that I consider the spirits. I'm not sure how it's possible, but there's a charge to the atmosphere that assures me that they are not a threat.

The spirits are the size of a dragonfly, with lovely pearlescent wings so light and delicate as to appear translucent. Even in the starry, moonlit darkness I see the intricate webbing and patterns that embellish paper-thin wings. The whorls and designs are different on each spirit, and while everything is cast in shades of cream and gray, there's a beautiful palette of colors on display.

The wings are as large as the spirits themselves, their thin frames swathed in silk the color of milk and ash and ink. Some of the spirits have iridescent whorls on their cheeks, others do not. And while their hair color and skin color and outfits are all unique, each spirit has half of their figure bathed in light and the other half of their figure cloaked in darkness.

"I didn't know you were coming." It's the only honest thing I can think to say, since the onus is on me to speak and it seems banal to ask who they are.

"You summoned us," one of the spirits counters.

I remember the moments before I fell asleep, the words that escaped my lips. *Ambassadors of time*—that's who I've summoned.

"I didn't realize you were real."

The spirits don't scoff—their faces are wholly neutral and non-judgmental. "Everything is real," one says.

I blink.

"Like your gold glitter," a female spirit says kindly. "*You* can't see it, but others can. With the right lens, everything is tangible."

I don't know if this is good news or bad. It certainly reinforces my belief that Soulbourne is complex and multi-layered. "Are you... omniscient?"

The spirits look at each other, uncertain. "We exist outside of the parameters of your reality," one answers. "As ambassadors of time, we exist in everything and we are beholden to nothing. There is no beginning or end for us. You have many delineations of time."

I nod, though I'm not sure I understand. "So you don't interfere with...reality?"

Another pause. "We don't meddle of our own volition," one of the spirits clarifies. "But when summoned, we sometimes answer."

Sometimes.

It's not a detail I wish to clarify in the moment, but I mark the distinction as important. A small part of me feels the warmth of pride—they deigned to answer *me*.

"We didn't just come because we support you," the female spirit says. Though phrased as a rebuff, my encouragement grows as I catch the weight of her words—they *wanted* to come.

"You have a special assignment," another adds. "A significant task...especially for someone new to Soulbourne and just learning about herself."

I frown. "I know about mys—"

"You know enough to get started," the spirit cuts me off. "But you have much to learn."

"I know myself," I say, a stubborn edge to my voice.

Another smile—one I would find condescending if it was plastered on any other face besides an ambassador of time. "You're just getting started, Andra."

The use of my name seems intimate, and though the smile feels a touch patronizing, I recognize that these words are spoken in kindness. The spirits mean me no harm. The words are meant to encourage me, but I feel the exhaustion that settles into my bones. The words carry expectation.

"I'm tired," I confess.

"Two opposite things can be true at the same time," the spirit says softly.

When my gaze meets his, he shifts his face to the side so that I can take in the juxtaposition that exists on either side of his body.

"Our figures represent the sun and the moon—the orbit of the earth that marks the passage of time...for humans. We are not darkness, and we are not light—we hold both, at the same time. You can be exhausted and you can be strong at the same time, Andra."

The words are so pointed, so poignant, that my chest tightens. Tears pool at the corners of my eyes. The truth of the statement resonates—I am so, *so* tired, in all the ways a body and soul can be weary...and I haven't given in. I keep imagining I've hit rock bottom only to find that the well goes deeper than I ever imagined. Perhaps this is what the spirits mean when they say that I am learning about myself.

As though they've intuited my thoughts, one of the female spirits smiles. "It's in the deepest, darkest places that gemstones are buried and pearls are formed. The darkness has its role to play."

My throat bobs as I swallow the emotion building within. "I don't think I have any need to manipulate time," I say, circling back to my summons.

"Not anymore," one spirit quips. "Who do you think stopped time for you?"

My eyes widen. "That was—I didn't see any of you."

"Your eyes are *one* facilitator of sensory input. You would do well to remember there are others. The fact that you didn't see us doesn't mean we weren't present." The spirits nod together on this point. "But you directly summoned us moments ago, and we wanted you to glimpse the spirit world."

"Why?"

"You will need the conviction of this moment in the future."

"With your eyes, you see a fraction of the world," another spirit adds. "We thought this visit might help you to imagine all that is taking place in any given moment and at any given time."

"There are ambassadors of time everywhere," I breathe.

"Not *just* ambassadors of time. There are other spirits besides the ones in Underworld and Overworld. They're concealed to you now."

"Who else can I summon? How do I do that?"

"Not every spirit is kind. There are those you will not want to meet."

The response is oblique, a dismissal of my original question in favor of answering the question the spirit believes I *should* have asked. I nod my understanding, certain that if Underworld is included in the retinue of the spirit world, there are some spirits I should like *never* to meet.

"I need to learn how to summon the right kind of spirits and avoid the bad ones."

A pregnant pause, during which a few knowing looks are exchanged amongst the ambassadors of time. "To educate you on this matter would qualify as interference. You must learn on your own."

"Can't you help me at all? It was random that I spoke those words out loud—what are the chances that I'll invoke the right circumstances again?"

"*Random* is what humans say when they don't understand the interworking elements of the universe. Nothing that has happened to you in Soulbourne has been *random*, Andra," the spirit chastises.

My mouth opens to protest, then closes. My brows knot. I can't decide if it's a comfort to know that there's a method to the madness or terrifying to learn that I'm living out a reality in which I hold only a sliver of control.

"Knowledge is power—and your instincts when it comes to books has served you well." A wink—so quick that I wonder if I imagine it—is the closest to a clue that I will get. "But even knowledge on its own is sterile and finite. It is only when intellect and intuition converge that true magic appears."

The words are spoken evenly; my brain absorbs each with reverence. The spirits speak with intention—they will have chosen their words with careful precision.

Before I can ask another question—before I can thank them, before I have the chance to wake Elara to behold the beauty and mystique that is the ambassadors of time, they are gone.

TWENTY-EIGHT

I don't remember falling asleep, but I do. When I wake my body is stiff, especially my neck and the shoulder that lay nestled against the cave floor, but I feel rested.

My sister is the first to rise. "Good mornahhh." The second half of Elara's greeting is lost in a yawn and stretch.

"Good morning," I respond absently. My mind is already ablaze with logistical analysis: there are many tasks that must be accomplished, and this is the last day of the Land test. Anxiety-induced adrenaline releases into my bloodstream and I'm eager to get moving.

"Pack up and go?" Elara asks, reading my body language.

I nod my agreement.

"And find food," she adds. "I'm hungry."

It takes less than a minute for us to pack our belongings.

"I think we need to head east. We've covered most of the southern and western regions of Jungle," I tell Elara.

"Agreed. And we'll keep our eyes peeled for threats," my sister adds.

"Or for Dirce or Nox," I say quietly. We can't rule out the possibility that Nox might be playing us.

Elara studies my face; her thoughtful expression asks a question that never leaves her lips.

"No gut feeling. Just normal worry."

Elara's shoulders relax. "I wish we knew the color of the flag."

"We found the other flags without knowing their color—we'll find it." For all my worrying, I am awash with conviction, inspired by the spirits' visit. That a force is acting on our behalf is undeniable.

"Where should we hide the golden book?" Elara asks.

We both glance around. There's really only one spot that makes sense: the back of the cave wall, while damp, has loose rock. I press a palm flat against the wall and when my fingers graze rocks that feel insecure, I pull.

It takes effort to wedge the book in the space—it doesn't lie completely flat, and the corner protrudes even when the rocks have been replaced in the wall. But it's inconspicuous enough that I doubt it will be spotted by the casual observer.

I'm antsy but confident as we leave the cave. It's possible that I will have a proper bath and a warm meal and a comfortable bed by the time the sun sets tonight. I will see Emberlyn and Lenna and Warrick. Anticipation rumbles through me like thunder—I am ready to conquer.

Elara doesn't say anything, but I see the corners of her mouth tick upwards and I know we're both on the same page. I want to tell my sister about the ambassadors of time, but I want to get moving even more. We'll have plenty of time to talk as we traipse through Jungle.

"Something interesting happened last night," I say after we've procured a bunch of bananas and a papaya.

Elara's eyes snap to mine as she peels a banana.

"When I finished the book on time—"

"You found something after I fell asleep?"

"It was confusing at the end," I answer. "The last page talked about time as a ruler and made it sound like a kingdom."

"That's weird." Elara bubbles with energy for the epiphany she knows is coming.

"The last line said something about ambassadors of time and how they might be summoned." I pause. This next part is going to generate a strong reaction.

Elara levels her gaze, nostrils flaring slightly.

"I read the last line about summoning the ambassadors of time out loud and...spirits showed up."

There's a half-beat of silence. When Elara does speak, her voice is unnaturally calm. "What kind of spirits?"

"Ambassadors of time. They're just one kind of spirit, apparently. These ones were small—the size of a dragonfly."

"Did they talk to you?"

"Yes."

"You didn't think to wake me?" Elara's question isn't an accusation, though it could easily turn that direction.

I shake my head. "They weren't there for very long. There wasn't anything I learned that couldn't wait until the morning."

Elara nods—a good sign. "What did you learn?"

"There are spirits everywhere—we just can't see them. The ambassadors of time were the ones who stopped time for us. They warned me to be careful summoning spirits."

Elara is thoughtful, her gaze stretching to the horizon as she digests this information. I watch her nose scrunch and then her eyes narrow. Her next words are wildly off topic. "Does that eagle look familiar to you?"

I follow Elara's gaze to the bird perched on a low branch, its plumage an impressive array of espresso, mahogany, and toffee that lightens to the hue of honey and ale around the nape of its neck. Its golden eyes are bright and alert, set above a lethally-hooked beak shaped like a scythe.

"It looks...out of place," I say carefully.

Elara nods. We slow our pace. My eyes don't leave the eagle.

As if it knows what we discuss, the raptor cocks its head to one side. Both Elara and I stop talking to watch as the eagle adjusts its stance on the branch. Silken feathers ripple and fluff as the bird stands tall to reveal mustard-colored feet fitted with massive, slate-gray talons. But the raptor doesn't move in agitation—his shifting weight reveals more than just formidable talons. In its grip, the eagle holds a scroll of paper.

"Elara," I whisper.

"I see it," my sister murmurs back.

We both wait in deferential silence. There's a moment in which nothing happens—all three of us stand still, regarding one another quietly—before the eagle extends its leg.

It's Elara who makes the first move to retrieve it. The eagle stands as still as a statue, one leg extended with aplomb.

I tense as Elara reaches a careful hand up to the parchment. But my worry is for naught—when Elara's fingertips graze the surface of the scroll, the eagle releases the paper. His errand complete, he launches himself from the branch and into the sky in a display of power and grace that arcs high over the canopy of the jungle.

Elara unfurls the parchment and reads. Her jaw sets and she swallows—actions that summon dread in my own body. My sister reads the scroll a second time, her deep blue eyes moving rapidly over the words on the page, before she hands it to me.

They know you stopped time. Under the pretense of looking for the unauthorized spirits in the test, domain leaders are sending in their worst. Make no mistake—no one is coming to catch spirits—they're coming for you. Get that last flag and get the hell out.

P.S. It's yellow.

I read the letter twice. "Shit."

My sister nods. "And this is from…"

"Warrick. I think it's from Warrick," I answer, suddenly worried that we might not be able to trust the dispatch. "It could be a ploy to mess with us."

"It sounds real." Elara doesn't offer evidence, but I'm inclined to agree.

"We need to move." This much is obvious—of course we need to move. We *were* moving. But now that we've received the eagle's ominous message, we *really* need to move.

"At least we know the color of the flag," Elara says, working to find the silver lining.

I nod in silent agreement. "We're close. We're going to make it out." The words are as much for my benefit as Elara's.

"Yes. We are."

A crow's cry startles us both. The sound is discordant against the melodic backdrop of Jungle, and though I'm no ornithologist, it sounds like a warning.

A flock of birds shoots up from the forest canopy, every color of the rainbow represented in the thousands of wings that suddenly take flight. These birds fly with purpose—their wings flap and propel them away from Jungle.

Absent the birds, Jungle falls quiet.

The frogs and cicadas are silenced—only the leaves dare to rustle in the breeze. When the ground begins to shake and vibrate, and the sound of howler monkeys screaming like dinosaurs fills the air, I feel sheer terror creep into every nook and cranny of my body.

One glance at Elara tells me she is just as petrified. There's no strategy for direction or consideration of the location of the missing flag in either of our horror-stricken faces.

"Run."

One syllable, and it comes out easily. All caution be damned, my sister and I run at breakneck speed through Jungle.

TWENTY-NINE

It's a relief to move.

Anxious energy burns like pine needles as we rip through Jungle. Where before Elara and I slowed down to assess our footfalls—*are there snakes? Is there a protruding log?*—we now fly past obstacles, trusting speed and luck to keep us from falling. Vines snap across my body and leaves slap my face and branches jab my arms and legs, but the pain doesn't register in the wake of my great fear.

The sound of the howler monkeys resounds through Jungle, but it's difficult to tell if it's louder, quieter, or the same. Elara and I drown out most sound: our heavy breaths and the crash of trampled leaves and branches are anything but quiet.

"We need to climb!" I cry out.

Elara glances over. Her blue eyes flash with understanding: we need a better vantage point to see what we're up against.

Plenty of the trees around us reach far into the sky, but many are too skinny or crooked to climb. Of the trees that look capable of bearing our weight, many lack branches in the lower region of the trunk.

Elara and I spot the tree at the same time: a vine-wrapped behemoth, thick and gnarled. There are no low branches, but there are spindly roots that encircle the tree like boa constrictors—these can serve as footholds.

"Be careful of snakes." If we have singled the tree out for its favorable qualities, other creatures will have done the same.

"Be careful of everything," Elara mutters.

Adrenaline ensures quick progress up the tree. The soft flesh of my palms quickly turns pink with irritation; I engage my core and upper body as I negotiate my weight and wedge my feet in between gnarled, upraised roots to reach for the lowest branches. These limbs are sturdy and thick—there's no chance that they'll snap under our weight—but that makes it difficult to earn a solid grasp.

"I can't get a good grip," I complain to Elara as her torso joins mine to press flat against the trunk.

My sister clings to the tree like a praying mantis; she breathes heavily. Her eyes drift to the branch I'm attempting to climb. "It's too thick."

I shake my head: that's not the problem. "It's smooth on top—there's no place to get a good grip." I hesitate. "Climb me."

"*Climb* you?"

"You'll be able to reach the branch if you stand on my shoulders. I'm taller," I add, just in case there's a rebuttal on my sister's lips

"By two inches."

"We don't have time to argue. Just climb."

Elara gives me a pointed look. If we were not in a stressful, high-stakes situation, we would definitely argue these points—but she removes one hand from its leech-like hold of the trunk and wriggles her body closer to mine. "Sorry if I hurt you."

I nod my head towards the branch and Elara begins to climb. She's cautious at first, her movements slow and painful. When her feet press down on my shoulders, it's mere seconds before her entire weight is lifted off my body and up onto the branch. Elara reaches down to offer me a hand, and soon we're both atop the limb.

"We have a long ways to go," Elara sighs.

I follow her gaze.

I can't see to the top, but it's a long way up to the canopy line. Branches are plentiful now—climbing will take time, but it won't be too rigorous. Twenty feet off the ground, I already feel safer.

"We need to hurry," Elara worries aloud. "The test ends today. We don't have time for detours."

"Then start climbing."

An hour later, we're close to the canopy line. I note the sun's position in the sky—directly above us, which means we've burned through half of the day.

"Can you see anything?" Elara calls from below.

"Not yet. But we're close."

I heave myself up to the next branch. My upper body aches, but it's my hands that take the brunt of the ascent.

The moment I break through the canopy line, I can see to the ends of Jungle and even into the ecosystems beyond. The wind rushes past, no longer blocked by the wall of foliage.

Elara makes it up a moment later. So high in the sky, every sound and sight feels eons away. It's not a place we can stay, but it's worth a moment of peace.

"I don't see any threat," I confess. Most of Jungle is obscured by dense flora. I can't discern any irregularity in the rainforest below, but I can *feel* that something is amiss.

When my eyes narrow on a swath of yellow suspended from bamboo, I pause. Blink. Then squint. "Elara." My sister's name is uttered in low decibel; I resist the urge to inject excitement. I could be wrong.

"What?"

Elara's not fooled by my nonchalant delivery—her head whips around to take in my expression and the direction of my gaze.

"That yellow spot." I point. "What does it look like to you?"

Elara presses her body close to mine in order to create a line of vision as similar as possible. Her eyes narrow. When I feel her body stiffen, I know she sees it. We climbed the giant tree to search for threats, but we have just found something better: the final flag.

"How far do you think it is?" Elara asks.

There's an electric current of anticipation in the air now that we've spotted the flag—a lemon-yellow rectangle that sits idly in the branches of a bamboo stalk.

"It's not far…but getting the flag will be tricky."

I eye the position of the flag, the trophy that could end it all. The bamboo stalks are tall and slender and silky and branchless.

"Go to the bamboo, get the flag, and get out," Elara suggests.

She makes it sound so neat and simple—*too* simple.

"Do you see anyone guarding the flag?"

Nox knew it was our final flag, and even Warrick, well outside the boundaries of the Land test, knew. If this is common knowledge, I worry about who *else* has been hunting the final flag…if only to clash with the sisters from Holostown.

"I don't see anything," Elara answers slowly, words stretched out in an unspoken disclaimer.

I exhale heavily. "Me neither. Elara, I don't think this is going to go smoothly."

"The plan is simple."

"Yes, but no. How are we going to get the flag? We can't climb the bamboo. It's too slippery."

Elara shrugs. "We'll cut it down."

"With what?"

"We'll find something."

"That's my whole point—we don't know what's waiting for us down there. Once we're out of this tree, I don't want to hesitate. We get that flag and we get out." My heart pounds with anticipation.

"Okay," Elara agrees. "Use your knife."

"The knife isn't strong enough to saw through the whole bamboo stalk."

Elara shakes her head. "It won't have to. If we make a cut, we can leverage the weight."

"Go on."

"We find a strong vine, position it in the cut on the bamboo, leverage our weight against it, and pull it down."

I bite my lower lip. Physics has never been my strong suit. I think Elara's plan sounds clever, but I'm not versed in the theorems and laws that might substantiate such an action or otherwise undermine it. We won't know until we try.

"It could work," I say, and that's all the encouragement Elara needs.

We begin the descent, testing the weight of each branch and securely anchoring our center of gravity before making the next move. Unease crawls along my skin like an army of ants.

"You're quiet," Elara muses.

I swallow, reluctant to verbalize my worry. I don't need to foment paranoia in my sister. "Just nervous."

Elara doesn't respond at first. I hear the scuffle of feet on bark hitch and I know she has stopped. "Andra."

I ignore my sister and continue down. *It's just nerves.* All my feelings are amplified now that we're so close to the end.

"Andra, stop."

I slow before yielding to a complete halt. I sigh heavily, then raise my eyebrows in question.

"Why are you nervous?"

"For the obvious reasons. Nerves."

Elara studies my face. "Do you think this is a mistake?"

I meet my sister's gaze with reservation. "We don't have a choice."

It's true—we don't. This isn't a market filled with options, where we can elect to forego this yellow flag in lieu of another. Our task is straightforward: retrieve each of the five hidden flags. There's no skipping the final one.

Elara's silence is loud.

"It's nerves," I repeat, this time with words stiff as concrete. Fear will get us nowhere. I summon an encouraging smile for Elara's sake. As grateful as I am to have my sister by my side, her presence magnifies my fears. It was one thing to face Agrona or Sarka on my own, to know that I might not prevail. But with Elara…there isn't anything I wouldn't do to assure her safety. There isn't anything *she* wouldn't do to assure *mine*—and therein lies the deepest fear of all.

It was *my* decision to enter Soulbourne—the consequences of my actions should fall squarely on my shoulders. The idea that my sister might somehow suffer…

I know Elara and her no-questions-asked, defiant loyalty. A gift I don't deserve; a burden I'm loathe to bear. If my sister dies in Soulbourne, I will never recover.

A disturbance in the bushes below sends lightning up my spine. Elara hears it, too—all movement beside me halts. My eyes scan the cornucopia of greens of the foliage below. My breath is shallow, my fingers and toes curl around the bark of the tree so hard that the soft flesh beneath my fingernails bleeds.

Another rustle.

A hand extends from the dense curtain of leaves and vines and I stiffen. Every sense sharpens with lethal precision: I smell decaying leaves and the iron in the nutrient-rich soil, I hear the song of cicadas and the thump of my heart. I feel blood thunder through my veins and the texture of the bark beneath my fingernails. I taste fear, I feel the humidity that tastes like mold and leeches to my body like a parasite.

The hand moves higher, revealing a thick, muscular arm and then the top of a head that I recognize.

Warrick.

The tension in my body eases, my muscles unspool as the familiar figure climbs towards us. The relief flickering through me bates the moment Warrick's eyes meet mine. His jaw is set, and those piercing green eyes glitter with intensity…and warning.

"It's an ambush," Warrick says by way of greeting.

"Why are you in here?"

My eyes search Warrick for clues. I pull my gaze only to survey the rainforest: there's still no visible threat, but the news of a planned ambush seems to explain the oily feeling in my gut.

"You got my note?" Warrick's muscular frame hugs the tree like a koala—a position at odds with his sober expression.

"We got it," Elara interjects.

"Why are you here?" I ask again.

Warrick already sent a written warning...there must be some other reason he thought to traipse through the Land test. My breath halts for a moment as I remember Warrick's dealings in the library—has he come to make good on his bargain and kill me?

"It's a free-for-all," Warrick says with a scowl. "Perrin knows you cheated, but he doesn't know how you did it. He doesn't want you to leave the test alive."

A chill settles on my spine. "It's not *just* Perrin. All of them want me to fail."

This truth, surprisingly, doesn't bother me. Those who hate me don't know me. Their loathing isn't personal, it has nothing to do with my character. It's what I represent that they despise.

Warrick doesn't answer. "The test still stands: get the final flag and make it out of the gate before time is up."

Elara nods her head towards the lemon-yellow flag hovering in the bamboo. "It's right there."

Warrick follows her gaze long enough to spot the flag but turns back to me, unimpressed. The look on his face is solemn, worry written in his stiff countenance. His concern is genuine, his thinking clear. We've found the last flag, but it might not be enough.

"Help us get the last flag and get out." Elara shifts her weight on the branch above. "We're wasting time."

"I can't help you get the flag." Warrick's voice sounds distant. "This is Andra's test. She has to be the one to commandeer the flags."

I grasp the implication and gravity of Warrick's remark, but Elara pushes for more. "Okay, so guard us while we grab the flag. Help us get past the ambush."

The light in Warrick's eyes flickers.

"He can't," I say for him, my words slow as molasses. Warrick meets my eyes for a moment—clouds of something brew in those green irises—but his gaze is quickly averted.

"I shouldn't even be in here," Warrick says through gritted teeth. He looks ready to say more, but stops himself.

"How did—"

"Your glitter and your scent," Warrick answers, reminding me of the sensory impediments that cloak my every move. "And now, music." This last comment is made with a nod towards Elara.

My heartbeat ratchets in anticipation. I meet Warrick's gaze, and this time, he doesn't look away. "Do you know what's waiting in ambush?" My eyes drag to the flag in the bamboo.

Warrick shakes his head. "It doesn't feel human."

The hairs on the back of my neck stand at attention, as though the baby-fine fuzz will somehow arm me against the evil lurking below. "It. You think there's only one?"

Warrick's nod is tight. The message is clear: get your ass moving before others come.

"You can't help us defeat that spirit?" Elara asks again.

Warrick's eyes are on my sister, but he notices my flinch at the word *us*. His eyes lock on mine once more. "I can't help."

"We need to move," Elara decides. She's none the wiser to the silent communication unfolding before her: I hold Warrick's gaze—only to make sure he understands what I ask. His eyes carry a heaviness, but he musters a slight nod.

With stealth, the three of us descend.

As soon as Elara's feet hit the ground, she nods her readiness. "Let's go," she declares, taking the first step towards the flag. She stops when Warrick and I make no move to join her.

"I love you," I say, forcing myself to offer her the dignity of eye contact. It's a punch to the gut to watch the confusion that passes over her ocean-blue eyes, the fear and the desperation that quickly join. "Warrick's going to get you out," I say, throat tight with guilt. I look away as soon as the last word is out.

"You can't—"

Elara's baffled enough that her rebuttal is hitched. I don't need to look at my sister to know that the hurt of betrayal will be written in a thousand ways on her face.

"You can't get the flag, Elara. It has to be me. I need to know that you're safe. Warrick won't let anything happen to you." I'm upset enough that my words are short and direct.

Warrick understands the assignment—his strong arms lift my sister and carry her away. I feel each of Elara's pleas as though they were daggers in my side, but I look away. *Warrick will protect her*, I tell myself. *Elara is safe.*

Soon enough, Jungle is quiet.

With a pit in my stomach—Elara will never forgive me—I hone my instincts. The days in the Land test have sharpened my senses: it's with lithe, animal-like movements that I close in on the flag.

The feeling of *otherness* hangs in the air and my senses are laser-focused; I'm attuned to every sound and smell. I trust my subconscious to do its job as I skulk towards the prize. I won't overthink this.

I close the final distance to the flag, pausing only when I reach the nearest clearing. As Elara and I had assessed from our perch in the canopy, the flag is tied high in the bamboo. The yellow stalks are dense enough to obscure a threat—another reminder that I will need to move quickly. I want to capture this flag without the challenge of additional rivals.

For a moment, I crouch low in the brush. My fingers trace the vine wrapped around my shoulders, then move to my boot to release the blade hidden within. My eyes stay zeroed in on the flag. I take a deep inhalation to steel my nerves and bring every fiber of my being to attention. And then, I move.

With a predator's ease I slide into position at the base of the bamboo stalks. My movement with the blade is swift: I make a clean, shallow cut. I'm pulling the rope from my shoulders when a gray-green hand encircles my bicep.

Immediately, my senses are accosted.

There's the smell of rotting wood and the cool feeling of dampness that defies the heat of Jungle's ecosystem. Neither compare to the nails that retract from the gray-green hand: jagged, flint-colored protrusions that threaten to pierce my skin as the creature's grip tightens.

The hand alone is terrifying: the nails look like rusty scythes and the gnarled, ghoulish-colored hands cannot possibly belong to a human. The size alone is wrong, the proportions off. The fingers are too long, especially the part after the knuckles. Each digit is swollen and thick. There is a settling deep inside my belly—this is my ambush, then. I am freed from the agony of the unknown.

A low, guttural hiss penetrates the silence and I feel the creature's weight shift behind the rustling branches. It stays hidden behind the dense bamboo but moves enough that I can see eyes: two dark, glittering, beetle-shaped slits that rest at forty-five degree angles above a long, pointed nose. Coarse, crow-black hair hangs over either shoulder, accentuating the sharp lines of her face and the hunch of her green shoulders. A crown of branches wreathes her head, an unruly array that holds errant hairs hostage. She's slender and not very tall, but the musculature on each limb says plenty about the strength she wields.

The creature opens her mouth to hiss again, revealing two sets of pointed, reptilian teeth. Small teeth, considering the wide mouth they outline. It's a mouth that looks capable of swallowing someone whole.

"What do you want?"

I'm crouched low to the ground at the base of the bamboo stalk. My knife is in my right hand, one length of the dried vine clutched in the other.

The creature considers.

Her long face tilts to the side, further accentuating the harsh angle of her jawline. Her beetle eyes open and shut like shutters, layers upon layers of inky black narrow to assess me. I know better than to move—as fearsome as this creature appears, her presence doesn't radiate violence. If I'm lucky, she's curious.

Slowly, with intention, the creature twists my arm. Apprehension skitters the length of my limb as her nails push my sleeve back to consider the expanse of soft, moon-white skin. Her nails caress the silky underside of my arm, the jagged edges of the creature's nails at complete odds with my unmarred flesh.

My breath catches and my shoulders tense—both at the possession and intimacy of the movement and at the markings it reveals on the creature's own arms. Primitive designs are deeply etched into her limbs, the patterns midnight black and plum colored against the unsightly green of her skin. The designs are gouged, the patterns cut out of her flesh.

The creature notices my gaze and lifts her arm so I can better see the scarred flesh and dried, raisin-colored blood—just another marker that this is no human. Thin, bloodless lips part again, this time to curl upwards in a smile.

"I can hear your heartbeat." The creature's voice is thin and scratchy.

I'm momentarily stupefied, too shocked to do anything but watch as the creature presses her nose right up against my arm and inhales deeply. Her eyes close and a soft moan escapes her lips. I'm wise enough to panic.

The creature senses this, too—her black eyes glitter with delight as a snake-like tongue shoots out, the eggplant-purple appendage licking the space between my wrist and elbow. I bite down on the whimper of fear that warbles deep in my throat, the bile that churns in my stomach and the acid that stings my tongue.

"What do you want?" I ask again.

The creature ignores me at first. Scythe-like nails dance up and down the length of my arm. "If you take from the bamboo, you must pay tribute." The creature's answer is straightforward, her words a surprise.

I look down to the base of the bamboo stalk, the cut that speaks of the damage rendered. Why this creature cares about the bamboo, I have no idea. But if her motive is to protect...

"I don't need to cut the bamboo," I say carefully. I'm aware of every inch of space between me and the creature, and I subtly try to draw my arm back.

The creature hisses through her teeth, immediately curtailing the action. "You have already damaged the bamboo," she growls, words clear even in her feral delivery. "You must pay tribute."

I steady my breath, ready to try again. "The bamboo will heal," I say, confident in this knowledge and the reading I did with Emberlyn before entering the Land test. "I wasn't trying to harm it. I just need something." A risk, to reveal that I am after the flag.

"You must pay," the creature seethes, beetle eyes narrowing with rage.

"What do you want?" I ask again. My breath hitches—I'm afraid to hear the answer.

The creature huffs through her nostril slits in sign of her displeasure...and possible appeasement. Her nails slide down to encircle my wrist and she presses her nose close to inhale my scent another time. The rapturous expression on her face is disturbing.

"For this cut in the bamboo," the creature slides her eyes to the stalk in question, her gaze lingering over the cut at the base and then sweeping upwards to knowingly rest on the lemon-yellow flag waving near the top. "An eighth of a pound of flesh."

My stomach tightens, my wrist flinches in a reflexive attempt to come back to safety and tuck in at my side. The creature's grasp is ironclad. My wrist snarls against her nails.

"I'll let you pick the design, if you like." She means to carve my flesh—to use her rusted nails to cut a design in my forearm.

I try again to wrench my hand back. "You can't do that."

Mirthless orbs of black narrow, eyes so dark there's no distinction between the pupil and iris. "It's too late for that. You cut into my flesh, I cut into yours."

I blink. Consider the creature's words. "I didn't cut into your flesh. I cut the bamboo."

Face inscrutable, the creature stands to her full height, the motion forcing me to rise alongside her. One hand firmly wrapped around my wrist, she uses the other to push her coarse hair to the side.

Her body is heavily tattooed. While her arms mostly feature whorls and primitive, decorative designs, her bare midsection reveals cuts of a different nature. The green flesh looks scarred in some places, the serpentine skin crusted and raised in charred ridges.

But the mark her long, curved nail points to is not deep at all. It's a shallow, neat slice—an arc that stretches from one side of her small torso to the other like an inverted rainbow. The creature's eyes look to the mark, then rise to meet mine. There's no damnation in those eyes, but there's no forgiveness, either. Flesh for flesh.

"You're connected to the bamboo," I breathe, wondering how such a thing might be possible.

The creature eyes me suspiciously, unimpressed. I lean forward to take in the other markings on her flesh, but she hisses her disapproval and falls back into the shadows.

"Let us complete the transaction," she grunts.

My mind spins.

The creature is unnerving, but she is not evil. She's justified in her logic, alarming as it might be. I believe she will release me after she takes her eighth of a pound of flesh. She hasn't been waiting to ambush me. And that means…

My head whips around. I felt an unsettling presence: if it wasn't this creature, then something else lurks in Jungle.

"Have you ever killed someone?" I ask, taking a step into the bamboo forest towards her.

If the creature is surprised, she hides it well. Her face gives nothing away, though her feet shift to accommodate my presence. "Yes." She doesn't elaborate.

"Quickly?" I ask, throwing a glance over my shoulder before taking yet another step into the stalks of bamboo.

This time, the creature's eyes narrow. "I'm not going to kill you. That's not how this works. I take what is owed—I carve for retribution."

"Yes. I understand." My voice is breathless as I piece together a plan.

"I grow tired of waiting. Will you choose your design, or shall I?" The creature's words are laced with warning. I am going to have to play this very, very carefully.

"I know the design I want. It's part of the decoration on that flag." I point up, to the flag hanging heavy in the humid air.

"I don't see a design." The creature's voice is flat.

"Can I get it, to show you?" I ask, distancing my words from my body. Earlier, the creature noticed my irregular heartbeat—I will my every breath and muscle to stay at ease.

The silence stretches. "Maybe you'd rather get it," I shrug. "If you're worried I might damage the bamboo."

More silence. Silence that is palpable and anxiety-inducing. I yawn, if only to busy myself and push out the stale air building in my body. The creature's eyes surveil the flag, likely searching for the design that does not exist, before sliding to meet mine.

"I will not be denied my eighth pound of flesh," the creature announces. The implied message: *no trick will work on me.* She still considers my request, then. My eyes are wide and innocent—I go so far as to proffer a tepid smile.

"I assume I'll have the mark for my entire life," I say blandly. "I'd like it to be something pretty."

The creature's hesitation lasts a moment longer before she grunts disagreeably. "I'll get the flag."

I package my enthusiasm in my chest, careful not to display any expression that might give away my ploy. The creature throws me one wary, scrupulous glance before releasing my hand and trading her ironclad grip of my arm for the stalk of bamboo. The bamboo holds her weight—it does not so much as bend as she climbs in movements so fluid she seems to glide.

She's halfway up the stalk when I notice the numbers.

I see a *3* on her calf and a *7* just above her elbow. My breath hitches. *It could be a coincidence,* I tell myself, but I know it's not. The size and structure of the numbers are too similar.

My heartbeat ratchets with the creature's next step, a movement that reveals a *2* on her ankle. I don't need to see any more numbers to know: the same person who carved a countdown in the forest of Holostown has marked the bamboo in the Land test.

I don't dare to look anywhere but at the creature. My mind pulses with confusion, but the carvings don't matter at the moment.

The flag, Andra. Focus on the flag. I feel my heartbeat build. My timing has to be just right...and I need an incredible amount of luck.

When the creature yanks the flag free from the bamboo, I feel like my heart might explode. Now. Any second now.

"I don't see any pattern." The creature frowns at the flag as she slides down the stalk.

"It's along the perimeter, in the stitching," I lie. The truth won't matter in a moment.

The creature is only a foot off the ground when I hear movement from behind. I twist and crouch, looking for the threat I gambled would appear in exactly this moment.

"Give me the flag and the girl," a low voice commands, its timbre laced with authority.

Even without seeing the face that the voice belongs to, my blood chills. Luckily, the creature is caught off guard. Her lithe frame is off the bamboo and hunched in contemplation, her confusion punctuated by the tilting of her head.

"Give that to me," the voice rages.

The creature hesitates. The cogs of her mind spin, trying to understand why the flag is contentious and what, exactly, is unfolding before her.

This moment of hesitation serves as the lynchpin for my luck. Impatient and provoked, my would-be aggressor takes a bullish step forward, snapping bamboo and trampling branches as he does so.

The creature is a flash of green as she snarls in warning, the flag forgotten as she rushes to avenge the destruction of the bamboo.

It's with the tiniest seed of guilt that I pluck the flag from the ground and stuff it in the waistband of my pants. I don't want to waste time stashing it in my pack.

Careful not to harm any bamboo, I weave a hasty path through the maze of stalks. My heart races and adrenaline surges, but I make no effort to tamp either.

When the bamboo ends, I don't hesitate. I break into an all-out sprint, hurtling over felled branches and around trees and vines. I'm dimly aware of agony-laced cries that speak to the clash between forces taking place in the thicket of bamboo. But I follow only one instruction: *Get that last flag and get the hell out.*

THIRTY

Jungle is alive with the song of birds and the rustle of leaves, but with the last flag pinned to my midsection, every sound merges to become a low, gentle hum.

I'm tired—from physical exertion, from jolts of adrenaline that electrified my body before abandoning it just as suddenly, from lack of food, and from emotions weighing heavily on my subconscious, begging to be unpacked.

My exhaustion has succeeded in one way: I've tapped into a survival mode that is more primal than anything I've ever experienced. I ignore the groan of muscles and labored breathing and fatigue. My knife is out, ready to engage any threat. If I fall or otherwise misstep, I might impale myself. Normally, I would never take such a risk. My situation isn't normal.

Tendrils of hair escape my braid and stick to my forehead and temples, now slick with clammy sweat. I run with abandon, hurtling over and under and around without checking for predators. It's momentum that propels me along, shoving me towards victory. If I stop—if I slow down—I might not be able to start back up again. My body knows what to do to keep me alive; I fly through Jungle.

When the scent of pine hits my nostrils, my heart soars. Forest is nearby...and once I hit Forest, it's not far to the gates. The Land test is large, and Forest is the largest ecosystem, but I estimate that I have less than five miles separating me from victory.

I can be done with this wretched test in an hour. Less than, if I hurry. *Elara. Warrick. Emberlyn and Lenna. A hot shower. Food. A bed.* Each thought is tantalizing in its own right, a delicious motivator that spurs my legs to pump faster.

They know you stopped time.

My breath hitches at the reminder, my gait altered just enough that I nearly trip.

Focus, Andra, I scold myself.

A hot flash of anger roils through me—to fail this close to victory would be shameful indeed. But I do need to have a story ready.

Too late, I realize that Elara and I have not coordinated on this point. If Warrick successfully marshaled my sister out of the Land test, I hope he was also able to shield her from the domain leaders. And if not...I hope there will be some way to stall until I can glean Elara's stated reason for why time stopped.

I'm in Forest now, lungs rejoicing at the fresh, cedar-scented air. My footfalls are soft, the main obstacles the thick trees that spear the land. I no longer hurdle logs and vines. I see a fence and know that I skirt the perimeter of the Land test, and since I am already in Forest, I am close. Very close.

My run is a crescendo, a musical score that has enough tempo and reverberation that it cannot be undone. I couldn't stop if I wanted to—my arms and legs move in swift, choreographed motions meant to propel me to the gate. My thoughts have turned back on, but intuition rules my body—my automated movements are proof.

When I see the gate, a bubble of air constricts my breathing and sears my lungs. My emotions feel tight and powerful. Relief makes my legs wobble, my breathing shaky.

I note Perrin's expansive mansion and the solemn figures who watch from a distance. Every domain leader looks to be present. Elara and Warrick are notably absent.

273

My eyes shine with tears of relief and exhaustion as I run the final stretch. I'm vigilant for any last-ditch attempt to foil my victory, but none comes.

The sun sinks behind the pine trees as I run through the wrought iron gates of the Land test. I don't stop at the gate—I run all the way to Perrin's porch.

It's an effort to stop—my legs burn and buck at my attempt to pull up before the domain leaders. The low position of the sun outlines their figures with light; their silhouettes are dark.

I wobble.

Bright light that has nothing to do with the setting sun flares in my mind and nausea roils deep in my gut. I have denied my body and its intrinsic systems long enough—they will exact their punishment now, presumably together.

When the light ebbs and the black curtain in my brain is pulled back, I blink into Perrin's face. It's tight with rage. He's said something—I can tell from the twisting of his lips and the anger swimming in his eyes.

"What?"

The word sounds strangled; the mere effort it takes to utter the single syllable brings me to my knees. My stomach heaves. I can't decide if it's fortuitous or unseemly that nothing comes up—my body is a cornhusk, too dried out and empty of food.

I steady myself, palms settling on my knees as I sway like seaweed before Perrin and the other leaders. My vision is fuzzy, too hazy to register gratuitous smirks or other slights of countenance.

I attempt to focus on Perrin when he addresses me again. He sounds like he speaks from underwater—the noises are distorted and unintelligible. My eyes narrow on his lips, squinting as I try and discern the words.

My effort is in vain.

I shake my head to clear the fog that has settled in the upper chambers of my brain. The movement disorients me, throwing me off-balance. My palms hit the ground, sending shocks of pain through the delicate bones of my wrist.

At this point, I'm fighting to stay conscious. Sheer will brought me out of the Land test and to the domain leaders, but now that the immediate danger has passed, my resolve melts faster than a popsicle on a summer's day.

"Get her out of here."

These words pierce the veil of my stupor, perhaps due to the danger laced within. My head shakes back and forth in protest, prompting a new wave of nausea. I drop my head lower, letting it hang between my legs. My body feels so heavy.

Not yet, I bark.

I have fought through five days of the Land test—I've watched people die and I've been the reason people died and I've summoned spirits and I've pushed my body to the brink of exhaustion. I've defied Perrin's test—I won't have my feat negated or otherwise questioned. I'll be damned if I'm denied victory now.

One palm rests on the ground, fingers outstretched and curled around dry earth and blades of grass in an effort to keep me upright. The other palm pulls the first flag—the lemon yellow flag won in Jungle—from my waistband. I toss it in front of me before shrugging the pack from my shoulders. It falls with an irreverent plop. Trembling fingers root around in the pack for the various fabrics of the four flags within.

"One," I say, pointing to the lemon-yellow rectangle crumpled in the grass in front of me.

"Two." I pull the second flag, the one stolen off of Nox, and lay it beside the first.

"Three." The flag from Canyon, the one I acquired just before Mercurius fell into the chasm.

"Four." The flag from Desert—the one pulled from the acacia tree above Agrona.

"Five." The last flag—the first one to enter my thrall. Attained in Tundra by sheer luck.

My eyes rake over the five flags, still brightly hued but crumpled and soiled. Some sport unseemly patches of blood. Five stupid rectangles of fabric; emblems of my triumph. Despite the sweat that coats my skin and the bruises that tattoo my arms and legs and the general knowledge that I'm sunburned and weather-beaten and sleep-deprived and look like shit, I smile.

"We know how to count," Perrin scowls.

I open my mouth—to say what, I don't know—but finally, my body finds bile. Summons it with stunning speed and no advance notice so that a thin, sticky stream of vomit lands atop the closest flag...and dangerously close to Perrin.

The sound of dark laughter and a snort of disgust is the last thing I process before slipping unconscious.

I wake in a cold room. Nothing looks familiar.

The walls are dove gray and barren; the only furnishing is an unframed mirror. In its reflection I see my glazed, cloudy eyes and tousled hair, the pink cheeks that could be a result of sun exposure or fever. My skin is clean and I'm dressed in a sleeveless, cream-colored nightgown. My hair looks to have been washed and there isn't any dirt beneath my fingernails.

The Land test. Five flags. Elara.

The memories of the past week float through my mind like pollen on the wind, utterly impossible to pin down. When Lenna walks in, I practically melt with relief. Her smile is broad, but her movements are stiff enough to communicate caution.

"You're in Boundless. There was an argument over where to take you—this was the only place everyone could agree on," Lenna is quick to tell me.

"Am I...in trouble?"

Lenna pauses. "I'm so glad you're safe," she says, pulling me in for a hug. With her lips pressed against my ear, she whispers: "War-rick got Elara out. The domain leaders didn't intercept them."

"They're safe?" I murmur.

"They're safe." Lenna pulls back and offers a smile that doesn't reach her eyes.

If Warrick and Elara weren't intercepted, my sister hasn't had to deny or otherwise explain how time stopped. The domain leaders will demand answers from me, and not just about time. They'll want to know where Elara is, too.

Every story I consider has pitfalls. My best bet seems to be to feign complete ignorance—to wholly commit to the idea that I know nothing.

It would be an easy lie. Perrin has probably already sent his cronies into the Land test to retrace my steps—a gilded path I pray fades by the moment—but there isn't any damning evidence. There's no way to prove the interaction with the ambassadors of time or the conversations with Brone or Nox. If Dirce survived Nox's assassination attempt, we can deny her account. The only artifact that presents a problem is the golden book—the text Elara and I did our best to conceal behind the rocks in the cave.

"How do you feel?" Lenna asks, leaning her weight against the side of the bed.

I shrug. "I'm fine." In my eyes lie further questions: *What are you doing here? Is it safe? Are* you *okay? What's going on?*

Lenna misses none of this, though she's wise enough not to answer. "I was authorized to dress you for the banquet."

"Banquet?" I can't keep the frown off my face.

"I believe it's in your honor," Lenna says smoothly. Her breath hitches at the end, like she's ready to say more but doesn't.

"It sounds like a trap." There's no way the domain leaders want to celebrate my success.

"I have a few different designs for you to choose from," Lenna continues, a warning laced in her oblique response.

"When is the banquet?"

Lenna's chocolate brown eyes hold mine. "Tonight."

My eyes widen. "Am I...allowed to leave this room?"

"Yes. We'll get ready at my place and make our way to the banquet together." *We'll be watched like a hawk*, her expression adds.

"You're coming to the banquet?" I'm unable to hide my relief. To have an ally—a friend—makes the banquet far less terrifying.

"I'm coming."

"Who else will be there?"

"We have a long walk ahead of us," Lenna responds, neatly deflecting. "I brought you clothes to change into; then we can get out of here."

Two minutes later, Lenna leads us down a corridor, expertly navigating a maze of hallways that all look the same.

We don't encounter anyone on the way out. I keep my mouth shut and Lenna doesn't bother to make small talk until we climb a flight of stairs and push open a door to reveal the daylight beyond. Even in the sun-drenched square, our first steps are silent. We're in a largely vacant plaza with only a few unmarked buildings.

"This is the official Boundless quarter," Lenna says, nodding to the nondescript buildings around us.

"It's very...sterile," I decide. Large swaths of pristine concrete seem to emphasize the flavorless nature of the square, foreboding in the absence of any greenery or decorative motif.

"It's ugly," Lenna answers matter-of-factly. "Stay close."

It takes all my self-control not to bombard Lenna with questions. I'm sure we're being watched, but when I can't spot our tail, I sidle close to Lenna's side. "How bad is it, really?"

Lenna knows, implicitly, to begin with matters of the heart.

"I haven't personally seen Elara, but I have it on good authority that Warrick got her out safely." She pauses for a half-beat. "The domain leaders couldn't agree on what to do with you. They expected to see Elara with you, for one. And the time thing threw them for a loop—it cast suspicion on Boundless, Overworld, and Underworld, and it ramped up fears over what you're capable of." Lenna's eyes meet mine.

"I have no idea how it happened," I lie. I note with interest that Boundless escaped the effects of the spell on time—Overworld and Underworld were not the only domains immune.

"It's weird that you didn't get frozen in time with everyone else." It's as close as Lenna will come to calling me out.

I laugh drily. "I don't understand Soulbourne—don't ask me how it happened."

Lenna's quiet—either to process what I told her or to give me time to redact my story—before she continues. "The Land test is done, and no one's arguing your victory, but…you're going to face a lot of questions."

Dread coils in my stomach. "I expected as much."

"Not just about Elara and time. Agrona, Mercurius, Sarka, and Dirce are dead. Kakarauri is presumed dead, but her body is missing. Nox won't say a word about what happened in the test, and Brone is smug to no end—though he hasn't been formally questioned yet."

"I'm not responsible for them," I snap, affronted by the idea that I should have to answer for the prisoners put in the test to kill me.

"I know." Lenna throws up her palms to show she has no say in the matter. "Nox and Brone are back in Underworld's prison. Achlys promised to personally oversee their questioning. I'm just saying… be on your guard."

Be on my guard—as though I would otherwise waltz into the banquet like it's a cheerful soiree. Everything in Soulbourne has been a test—there hasn't been a single moment of rest.

"Emberlyn?" I ask, switching topics.

"Keeping a low profile in Callings. She high-tailed it out of Land as soon as the test ended. She's the one who learned that Warrick got Elara out safely," Lenna adds. "Though she wouldn't tell me how she knew."

The ambiguity around Emberlyn's practices should be disquieting, but it brings a strange wave of relief. I have no idea how Emberlyn procured the golden book on time, but it was an impressive feat. That's she surreptitiously moving behind the scenes now inspires hope that she might have a plan when I do not.

"What—what was it like when time stopped? Out here, I mean." I fumble for the right words. If I'm going to be questioned, I need to understand.

279

Lenna's silence is pensive. "Strange. People just...froze. Everything went quiet. I was by myself, and the thing that tipped me off was the silence. It quickly became clear that not *everyone* was affected—it was creepy that some people froze mid-sneeze or mid-stride and others carried on like normal."

Lenna regards my sober expression before continuing. "It was... interesting to see who froze and who didn't. Boundless, Overworld, and Underworld weren't affected. And not every individual in the other domains froze. There's a lot of speculation over why—if these individuals have been deceitful about their true origins...or if some people have power that the others don't."

My eyebrows rise. I don't tell Lenna, but I'm relieved to hear there's so much dissent and confusion—it will make it easier to feign ignorance.

Lenna leads us down a major artery of Boundless, where the eerie silence is traded for hustle and bustle. The lively activity is substantial enough that no one notices us. Either that, or they don't care.

After a few crowded blocks, Lenna leads us down a side street. My head is drawn up by the brightly colored homes with quirky décor: most of the houses sport chipped paint and sinking beams, but there's personality in spades.

Vines crawl around dilapidated porches, flowers burst from baskets and boxes, gingerbread trim outlines the second stories, floppy-eared dogs nap on porches, and fat cats sit atop Dutch doors left ajar. Here, the streets have cracks; dandelions and weeds boast their robust existence. The smell of banana bread and hyacinth perfumes the air and even Lenna adopts a skip in her step. When she sees my open admiration, she smiles.

"Almost there," she says proudly.

"I like it here."

Lenna nods happily, stopping once to pet the top of an orange-haired cat who rubs up against her legs.

Her home is at the end of the street, a yellow house with white trim that sits before a densely-wooded forest. The house isn't large, but it's tall—four stories that seem to sag to the side like a birthday cake left too long in the sun.

"I'm on the top floor," Lenna says, opening the white gate into the front yard. The latch clicks behind us and we walk the cracked front steps past sunflowers and peonies and fistfuls of grass. Lenna wiggles the oversized key into the lock, jiggling it back and forth and lifting the handle at an angle before throwing her shoulder into the door. It wheezes open with a sigh, dust particles airborne and illuminated in the sunlight warming the entryway.

I follow Lenna up the wooden staircase. There are no decorations on the walls—just a simple banister that twirls up all four stories of the building. Every third step seems to squeak or groan in protest. By the time we make it to the fourth floor, the air feels stuffy. Lenna fumbles with another key.

When she pushes the door open, it's to reveal the most chaotic, cluttered, colorful mess I've ever seen. Lenna throws me a knowing smile before tossing her key on the table and opening the large window overlooking the woods. The sunlight mixed with fresh air makes the room lazy-warm, the perfect temperature for a nap.

Every color has a place in Lenna's home: there's a green couch and a yellow chair and a faded purple loveseat that sits beneath framed landscape paintings and impressionistic portraits. An entire wall is devoted to artistic inspiration: a series of canvases sit perched atop stands, some swathed with blocks of color, others with pencil-fine outline and still others that are blank. Sketches and cuts of fabric are pinned to the wall alongside articles and pages ripped from books. Expansive swaths of fabric hang over the chair and the couch and even the kitchen table. There are sewing scissors, a pincushion, and pins haphazardly stuck into the various cloths.

For all the artistic mystique, there's an impressive library, too. My feet guide me to the shelves, where tradition meets innovation in dusty, cloth-bound texts. I eye each tome with appreciation, unable to keep my fingers from gliding along the spines.

"Make yourself at home." Lenna kicks off her shoes and pads into the kitchen. "Do you want anything to eat?"

My stomach grumbles in response.

Lenna laughs as she pokes her head through the doorway. "Is a sandwich okay?"

"Sounds great. I can help." My fingers still graze the surface of the books.

Lenna shakes her head. "Look around. It brings me joy to see you appreciate my home. Not everyone does."

I do poke around. I try to see Lenna's flat through impartial eyes: it's messy and cluttered, with seemingly no rhyme or reason to where things are stashed. But for an artist—for anyone with an imagination, really—this place is a sanctuary of color and texture and light. Every square inch of Lenna's home dares you to dream, imagine, and explore.

My fingers drum the spines of the books, dancing over titles that lean heavily towards artistic function. Texts on painting techniques and pastry baking and an enormous glossary on textiles.

Agents and Origins of Beauty.

The title is rose-gold, the raised lettering a complementary contrast to the olive-green cover. It looks similar to the text on time and the other golden books I was warned about.

Intrigued, I pull the volume from the shelf. My fingers delight in the thick, rough pages porous with color and intricate design. I flip through chapters on nature's enhancements—pigments and oils with impressive properties. I scan pages of beauty folklore, tales of spirits and creatures responsible for amplifying or siphoning off beauty.

Lenna says something from the other room, but it doesn't register. My blood throbs with anticipation, my senses tingle like they did in the cave of the Land test when I read about time. My eyes are glued to the page.

Many spirits appreciate beauty, but some create it. The prism people and the illusionists are two such spirits who thrive on beauty, inherent and superficial.

I have tunnel vision; the world around me is a roar of white noise. I read the words aloud. My fingertips trace the fine lettering, swoops of midnight blue that shimmer in the rays of silver sunlight.

I'm dimly aware of Lenna's cool hand on my arm, her gasp of surprise as my fingers pull up golden steps—or maybe it's my voice that does it.

Without hesitation, I raise my foot to the first gilt step that glistens in holographic fashion. The step winks in the sunlight, but as my foot comes down, it meets solid ground.

I take another step.

I'm higher on the golden staircase, further on my way to who-knows-where. I'm obliquely aware of Lenna's movements, her steps that follow mine as I ascend to the shimmering gold door above.

THIRTY-ONE

The gilt door is filigreed in a delicate pattern reminiscent of spider webbing. A gauzy curtain sways in the breeze and the gentle notes of a harp play in the distance.

I pull the door open and the curtain is soft against my cheeks, its feather-light touch an indulgent, jasmine-scented kiss. Inside lies a moss-covered path lined by a tunnel of trees, the leafy branches twisted to allow sunlight through their intermingling limbs. Ferns and songbirds and butterflies abound; there are waterfalls of turquoise and diamond. Lilies and lotuses float on ponds, gardenia and wisteria crawl up trellises.

Rolling hills in every shade of green loll on either side; majestic, snow-capped mountains lay just beyond, their tips shrouded by a thick layer of mist. In the shade dwell lightning bugs and glow worms, their bodies warm and resplendent with otherworldly light. In the sunshine the colors are so vibrant that they seem alive—never before have I seen such intense, concentrated color.

A gentle breeze blows from the east, dragging my attention to yet another section of loveliness, this one bursting with glorious foliage of gold and russet and crimson. Leaves larger than my palm fall, twirling in whimsical fashion to land neatly on the footpath below.

The sounds, the sights, the smells...there are enough intoxicating sensations that I could stay fixed in this one spot for the rest of my life and never grow bored. I could renounce food and forget my own identity to stand in this space and bask in such incredible beauty.

"Did you know this existed?" Lenna's words are a whisper, mild against the backdrop of perfection.

I shake my head slowly. "No. It was your book, Lenna. You have a golden book."

For a moment, we stand in silent wonder, our bodies still.

"Andra..." Lenna's brown eyes are wide with wonder and fear. Her freckles are pronounced against skin leeched of color.

"This is incredible," I say, a tad defensive.

"We shouldn't be here," Lenna replies gently.

I turn to look at her. "Why?"

Lenna's been defiantly optimistic in the face of every challenge and threat. Syphus and domain leaders like Achlys are far more foreboding than this fairytale-come-to-life. If the danger lies in possession of a golden book...Lenna's had one on her bookshelf for longer than I've been in Soulbourne. But Lenna's gaze holds mine.

"This is a spirit realm," she says quietly. "This place—it's not part of Soulbourne."

"Does it matter?"

Lenna looks pained. "How did you summon the entrance?"

"It was the book. I read a line of text out loud, and these stairs appeared."

Lenna looks at me as though she is seeing me for the first time, and it worries me. I trust Lenna, but not her fear-drenched logic. Fear can make good people do bad things.

"I know very little about Soulbourne," I add drily. "Add this to the list of things I don't understand."

"But you don't seem surprised." It's not an accusation—Lenna's face scrunches like she's genuinely trying to understand.

"Lenna—you've lived your entire life in Soulbourne. The creatures and the spirits and the different domains and the Prosphora all make sense to you. They're *insane*—but you don't think of them that way because they're familiar. Consider my perspective; think about everything I've gone through. This is just another crazy element... and this one is beautiful."

Lenna holds my gaze. "Yeah. Okay. This is still really dangerous," she adds.

"*Everything* I've done in Soulbourne is dangerous."

Lenna's face is pinched, leading me to believe that on this point, she doesn't agree. "We can't be here long."

It's the closest Lenna will come to a concession, and I don't argue the point. Instead, I lead us to a path that draws near a mountain before disappearing inside. The last time I ventured into a cave, I found myself in Soulbourne. The irony is not lost on me as we take our first steps inside.

"Hello."

The voice belongs to a boulder the size of a child. It's a colorful orange rock that resembles a geode, with hexagon facets for eyes and a pentagon nose and a long rectangular prism for a mouth. The voice sounds feminine, though the bulky, prism-like body doesn't retain any gender-specific traits.

"My name is Clementine," the rock-like creature continues, turning to the side so that white light refracts from her body to erupt in shades of tangerine orange. "Welcome to Prismea."

"Prismea," Lenna whispers, jaw slack with shock. Her voice is laced with disbelief.

"The one and only," Clementine agrees, blinking her hexagonal eyes open and closed. Her entire body is a thrill of geometry—every limb and facial feature perfectly proportioned. Only straight lines exist on the plane of her body, which stands about four feet tall. Clementine tilts her head to the side to survey the two of us before gesturing us closer. "Come inside and meet the others."

There's no reason not to.

I take a step forward, Lenna close on my tail. The chamber

boasts an oversized chandelier dripping with crystals; light refracts from each prism to hit the craggy sides of the cave and illuminate colorful geodes. A river runs through the chamber, where geometric figures of all colors and sizes and shapes sit in chairs and on canopied chaises. My eyes flit to a series of pathways that lead away from the chamber, into the darker recesses of the cavern.

When we enter the chamber, all eyes turn to consider us. Conversation continues, but it's clear that we are the center of attention as Clementine guides us to an empty alcove and gestures for us to take a seat on crystalline stools. From this position, I notice the multi-colored entourage that makes its way towards us.

"Welcome, Andra and Lenna." It's a male who speaks—his voice is low and his geometric facets seem sharp. He shines like aluminum.

"You know our names." Lenna's voice makes clear she's not entirely sure how she feels about this revelation.

"My name is Sterling," the spirit says, ignoring Lenna's comment. "This is Blanche, Jade, Noir, and Garnet." Each spirit nods his or her head at the introduction, each geode resplendent in a hue corresponding to their moniker.

"Are you…illusionists?" Lenna asks. She sounds nervous.

"We *have* illusionists in Prismea," Sterling responds. "But we're prism people."

"Prism people? Who are you? What is this place?" I ask.

"What we do depends on you," Clementine answers soberly.

"We're gem spirits: hewn from intense pressure and shaped from incredible heat. To stand in this chamber today, we've spent years in uncomfortable solitude. The process is long and painful—but it equips us with gifts of great value," Sterling explains.

"If the legends are true, you make people better," Lenna says reverently.

"We enhance," Sterling corrects. "We do not manifest that which does not exist—that lies in the wheelhouse of the illusionist. We only shape and refine."

"How do you do that?" I ask.

"It varies by individual. Some transformations are relatively painless; others are extensive," Sterling answers.

"And the illusionists? What do they do?"

"The illusionists create," Sterling answers. "They introduce new elements that didn't originally exist."

"At a cost," Clementine adds.

"It doesn't cost anything to work with prism people?" I ask.

"There's no *cost*—but no transformation is possible without sacrifice," Clementine answers.

"And the results are always an improvement?"

"Most certainly."

"We don't have time," Lenna mutters, guessing at my train of thought.

"How long does it take?" I ask.

I feel, rather than see, Lenna stiffen.

"That depends on the individual," Sterling answers.

"I'd like to try."

"You don't even know how they might transform you," Lenna protests, aghast.

"Are you sure?" Clementine asks. She doesn't as much as glance at Lenna.

I nod. I don't give myself the chance to overanalyze—if this is an opportunity to level up, I'm taking it. I want every advantage possible when I face the domain leaders at tonight's banquet.

"Come with me."

Clementine leads the way; Sterling and the cadre of prism people follow. I fall in line behind. Lenna tries—and fails—to catch my gaze.

Clementine leads us to a raised platform, the floor a smooth and polished milky-white. It's not private—I look down at a chamber full of prism people and shake off any self-consciousness.

"It's been a while since we've had a human visitor," Sterling says as the spirits fall in line along the wall.

"I can't imagine many know how to get in here," Lenna replies drily. She's taken up position in my shadow. She leaves space to show that she won't be participating, but she's close enough for me to know that she's got my back.

"Not many do," Clementine agrees. "Only the marked can summon the entrance."

Lenna and I exchange a glance as the sparkling geode wall parts for Sterling. The room it reveals is small—the size of a closet—and it sports mirrors around the perimeter.

"Who was the last human to visit?" Lenna asks.

Clementine's tone is clipped and tight. "Warrick."

My head jerks back in surprise. "*Warrick*? But he's—he isn't—I didn't think he was marked." My gaze flies to Lenna, who looks just as bewildered.

Clementine nods, suddenly busy shifting geodes into place and shooing prism people into position. Sterling doesn't say a word.

"Did he see you or the illusionists?" Lenna asks. No one is fooled by her innocent tone—the answer to this question matters.

"He worked with me," Sterling answers. "End of questions. We don't gossip—it's not our place to discuss. Just like we won't prattle about your visit today." Sterling fixes us with a pointed look.

"Step up," Clementine instructs.

I do as she says, taking the step into the recess so that I'm surrounded by angled mirrors. Every square inch of me is reflected back in one mirror or another. What is about to happen is significant, but I'm fixated on the fact that Warrick is marked.

How? It's not surprising that I didn't discern Warrick's mark—I could only see my own mark, and Elara's mark, after we had stopped time—but why didn't anyone *else* perceive it? Lenna and Emberlyn would have said something if they'd noticed a mark on Warrick. The citizens of Soulbourne must not know, either...or else why have I been singled out and targeted? It doesn't make sense.

"The prism people have different strengths," Sterling says, drawing my attention back to the present moment. I can puzzle over Warrick's mark later. "We each have the proclivity to draw out different things."

"We'll start easy," Clementine interjects. "We'll see how you do with the first couple of spirits before we advance to more difficult territory."

"How do you do that?"

"Garnet will go first. He'll tease out trivial idiosyncrasies and bad habits," Clementine explains. "Noir will take over from there. Each of us will dig deeper."

"You're going to take chunks out of her?" Lenna looks horrified.

"Laser light removes the undesirable elements," Sterling answers. "It burns," he adds.

"And she can stop at any point," Lenna continues, chewing on her lower lip.

"She can stop at any point," Sterling agrees. "I'll be the last one to work with you," he adds, geometric eyes roving up and down my frame. "If you make it that long."

My throat suddenly feels dry. "Do—most people last that long? For you to work with them, I mean?"

Sterling's gaze is withering, despite the fact that he has no eyebrows or pupils to punctuate his expression. "No. They do not."

"But Warrick did," Clementine chirps before shoving Garnet forward. She keeps her back to Sterling, though she surely feels the glare he sends her way. "Whenever you're ready, Andra."

Lenna and the other prism people stand just outside the recess, where the geode doors have been pulled inward to create an octagonal room of mirrors. Perhaps I should feel more nervous. I don't give myself the chance to back down. I nod to Garnet.

After I signal my readiness, ruby light radiates from Garnet's figure. The red lasers circle my body like hawks circling prey. The lasers are polite at first, tentative rays that travel over my skin with a feather-light touch. But when they focus, the areas start to chafe with irritation. It's tempting to move, to shift my body to elude the lasers. I grit my teeth instead.

It's a sight to behold: snarled clusters of unidentifiable matter hover just outside my body—within orbit of my frame, but loosely attached.

I don't know how much time passes before the ruby lasers retract. The masses stay suspended in midair. Garnet takes a step back, hands at his side. A concentrated beam of ruby light encompasses my body. I can't help the cry of surprise that escapes my lips as my body burns, like a bad sunburn and then a horrible sunburn and then like sandpaper is being scratched against the sunburn. My throat is tight and I try to calm my breathing and then it's over.

The ruby light is gone. The snarling masses are gone.

Garnet nods at me, then walks out. I'm working to assure my nervous system that we do not need to launch into fight or flight when Noir walks in.

I'm subjected to shadowed black laser light, then milky white, then vibrant green, then tangerine as Blanche, Jade, and Clementine follow Noir. Each time, the process is similar—though it ramps up in intensity.

Each spirit seems to draw deeper from the sensitive areas that have already been probed and cut. The concentrated beam of light at the end hurts more with each spirit's visit. The light penetrates deeper. In the shadow of the pain, there is satisfaction. Immediate satisfaction. So when Sterling walks in, I feel ready.

Sterling studies me for a moment, considers my tender areas and my confident smile. There's warning laced in those gray octagonal eyes, though it only lasts a moment before searing pain shoots through my body.

Shit.

I don't have time to gasp before another beam sluices through me, carving my insides like roast beef. I stiffen, then arch in pain.

Stop. The word is loud in my head, but I don't have breath to get it out.

Stop, I think again, my panic palpable.

I was told that I could stop whenever I wanted, but I can't find the breath to tell Sterling. One look in his eyes, and he knows. He knows, and sends another fiery blast my way.

Where the other lasers teased and pulled, Sterling's silver light explodes. The masses that come off in the wake of his light are like chunks of volcanic rock blasted by dynamite—there's nothing precise about his light. I can't understand why he's last—his light feels reckless in the aftermath of his fastidious predecessors.

But the blasts keep coming, and I'm knocked senseless. I stop trying to summon breath to call for Sterling to stop. I dive deep inside myself and look for the place in which I might take refuge.

Disassociate, I tell myself.

"Don't do that," Sterling growls. "Don't hide."

Warrick endured it.

I hunker down. I am nothing if not competitive, and apparently, Sterling hasn't cut this part out of me. If Warrick was able to endure Sterling's worst, then I will, too.

"Look."

It takes a moment for the word to register. But my gaze lifts and I see Sterling survey his work with satisfaction. There are so many snarls it's impossible to believe they all came from my body. They fill the recess, clogging up space and sucking air from the room. Silver light separates the snarls into two groups. My body echoes with pain and sensitivity, and he hasn't even gotten to the worst part yet.

A blistering beacon of slate-gray flashes. My body feels like it cracks into a million pieces. I shake, then pant for air. When I look up, there are still snarls in front of me.

"What happened?"

Sterling doesn't answer, but Clementine walks into the room. Noir, Blanche, and Garnet follow.

"What's going on?"

"These faults of yours," Clementine begins somberly, "are also strengths."

My eyes narrow in confusion—the only gesture I can muster in my present state. "What are you going to do?" The fear in my eyes is genuine.

The prism people don't answer. Instead they extend their laser lights, colorful rays that pass through a prism before rushing to meet the snarls above my head. It's over before I have a chance to fear it.

"These faults also serve as the foundation for your greatest virtues," Sterling says. "You retain these flaws, but they exist in a prism capable of absorption, deflection, and perspective. Take in that which serves you, deflect that which is meant to harm you, and remember that a perspective shift can cast light in a whole new direction to reveal a hidden truth."

Sterling's poetic speech finished, the prism people file out of the recess. Sterling and Clementine are the last to leave—the former offers a nod of respect before departing, the latter places a rectangular hand on my shoulder.

"There's one more spirit you should meet."

THIRTY-TWO

I feel, rather than see, the spirit arrive. An electric current runs through the air, an icy charge that carries with it the smell of patchouli and jasmine.

She looks like a human.

Onyx black hair falls in silken sheets down to her waist, thick and lustrous as a waterfall. Her eyes are icy blue ringed with violet, her lips full and blood-red. She's voluptuous and dressed in plum-colored silk that hugs every curve on her body. She looks at me, one perfectly manicured eyebrow arched in invitation to appreciate her beauty. Everandina may *look* human, but I know she's not.

"Andra," she purrs.

"Hello." My voice sounds loud and brash even to my ears.

"My name is Everandina. I'm an illusionist." Everandina's violet eyes scan my frame; her expression remains aloof.

I nod and Everandina takes a step closer, tapping her pale pink nails against the soft silk of her dress. "I've come to offer my services."

"What is that, exactly?" I ask. I recall the words of the prism people: illusionists work at a cost.

"Illusionists can do many things. I amplify beauty."

I hesitate.

"Most people would covet this opportunity," Everandina snipes, red lips pouty. "Especially since I'm not charging."

"There's no cost?"

"Not from me," Everandina clarifies.

A blanket of silence falls over the room. I'm enveloped in the intoxicating fragrance and chill that is Everandina's aura as I weigh her words. I wish I understood more.

One of Everandina's perfectly sculpted eyebrows arches. "You don't trust me."

"I don't know much about illusionists."

"I'm a master of perception and deception," Everandina admits, "but I don't lie. I offer my services as a gift—for withstanding my brother's brutality."

My eyebrows shoot up. There isn't any resemblance I can see between Sterling and Everandina.

"Andra." Lenna's voice is tentative from outside the recess.

"Yes?" I ask, aware that Everandina judges my every move.

"I'm worried about time." Lenna's voice is polite but firm. I can tell from her tone that she's eavesdropping and worried about more than just the time.

"It will be quick," Everandina shrugs. "If you choose it."

I hesitate. I don't like making decisions on the spot; I loathe missed opportunities more. "It doesn't sound like there's any reason not to." I'm still searching for the loophole.

"An upgrade is a change. Not everyone appreciates change."

"You won't ask me for anything," I clarify.

"Not a thing."

"And it won't hurt?"

Everandina's dark lashes flutter as she closes her eyes and gently shakes her head. "Not a bit."

"I'll do it," I say, and I hear Lenna suck in a breath.

Everandina's full lips part in a smile. "Close your eyes."

I do as she says. I feel the petal-soft caress of Everandina's hands on my cheeks, but nothing more.

"Done," Everandina breathes moments later.

I open my eyes carefully and meet my gaze in the mirror. It's me—it's definitely still me—but every feature has been enhanced. My hair looks like silk the color of a golden sun, my light blue eyes are ringed with deep sapphire and fringed with heavy, dark lashes. My lips have more pigment, my skin is impossibly smooth. I find Everandina's eyes in the mirror.

She smiles. "An outer makeover to match the internal one."

I reach a hand to my satin-smooth cheek. "Thank you."

Everandina shrugs, as though the transformation is of little importance. "Enjoy it." And then she's gone.

"I'm coming," I tell Lenna, admiring myself one more time in the mirror.

Lenna's eyes widen in appreciation when I emerge, but she doesn't stop to comment or consider the specific changes. She drags me out of the cavern and back down the path to the golden staircase.

"I hope this wasn't a mistake," Lenna says as we descend the first golden step. She smiles ruefully.

The moment we set foot in her flat, I close the golden book. The gilt staircase evaporates as though it were a figment of the imagination. With care, I replace the book on the shelf.

"We were gone two hours," Lenna announces. I follow her as she pads to the kitchen, where she gestures to a plate holding the sandwiches we'd intended to eat before visiting Prismea.

"I would never have guessed Everandina and Sterling are related," I say to Lenna between bites.

"Mmm," Lenna answers, anxiety evident in her clipped tone and tight movements. She's clearly not in the mood to speculate. She takes a bite of sandwich and makes for the door. "Ten minutes, Andra. You have ten minutes to eat, and then it's time we got ready for the banquet."

It would seem I'm not the only one traumatized by the disaster that was the first Land Banquet, because while Perrin did not turn down the honor of hosting, tonight's function is in a new location.

Lenna is noticeably silent in the walk to the wharf. The night is warm—we hug the river for the cool breeze that lifts from the water. It was Lenna's suggestion—*pointed* suggestion, with no room for disagreement—that we travel by boat to tonight's banquet.

Lenna's logic followed that it's a considerable distance to walk to the venue and there are certain to be a host of prying eyes: some curious, others with mal-intent. On a boat, we enjoy relative privacy.

The sunset along the water is fantastic: a brilliant ensemble of purple and pink and orange that looks like sherbet in the sky. Despite the beauty of the evening, there aren't many people out walking.

After our visit to Prismea, Lenna was all business: we ate, and then she pulled out a golden gown. A dress so pretty I hadn't even wanted to look at the other options.

"You're really quiet," I say. I'm trying not to make too much of the matter, but it's starting to unnerve me.

Lenna doesn't answer. Her strides shorten as we near the boat. She carries two garment bags heavy with our gowns; I carry a smaller bag with our shoes.

"This is it," Lenna tells me, craning her neck forward to identify a small vessel with peeling green-and-white paint.

A moment later the boat's captain pops out. She and Lenna exchange smiles; the woman gestures for us to come on board before disappearing to complete nautical tasks. I'm relieved she doesn't engage us in conversation—there will be enough idle chatter at the banquet tonight.

"I'm nervous," Lenna admits once the boat starts moving.

I don't reply. Instead, we stare out at the navy blue water that reflects less and less of the creamsicle sunset.

"Believe me—I know your situation is harder than mine." Lenna's sardonic laugh does nothing for my nerves. "It just feels like the danger is getting...real." She looks my way, her brown eyes large and vulnerable, beguiling in the waning light.

The words are a blow I work to hide. "When did things change for you?" I ask.

Lenna picks at a loose thread. "I think when you went into the Land test."

She doesn't hesitate to answer—so while she says "I think" I know that this *is*, in fact, when things changed.

"What happened?" I ask gently. I know so little about what took place outside the bounds of the Land test—something I can't imagine will work to my advantage at tonight's banquet.

"I watched you go in," Lenna begins.

My heart pounds in my chest—for a moment, I'm back on the grass, refusing to look at Perrin as I began the pitiful march to the gates of the test. I was petrified...but I can't think of anything that happened that would scar Lenna.

"There was an earthquake, and Warrick took off. Emberlyn left for Callings to investigate something—she wouldn't say what. When time stopped, things really began to escalate. There was a lot of speculation and not much clarity—everyone spun the story for their own personal agenda. I'm worried where it's going to land us. All of us." Lenna's troubled eyes meet my own reluctantly.

"And this morning—after so much arguing, the domain leaders allowed me to take you home. They were quarreling and quarreling about what to do with you, and then they just suddenly agreed. I don't know what that means." Lenna shoots me a pointed look. "And then you summoned a staircase into a spirit realm."

"It's been a lot," I say quietly.

"Not to mention the prism people and the illusionist," Lenna adds drily.

"Oops?"

"I don't regret helping you, Andra." Lenna holds my gaze so that I can see the truth in her eyes. "But I'm scared. For me, for you…for Elara and Warrick and Emberlyn and whoever else might come into the line of fire. This is getting big. Pretty much everyone is going to come for you tonight," she warns.

I offer Lenna a tight smile. "I know."

"Perrin is still trying to save face and the other domain leaders are riled up about what happened with time. Most of the people in Soulbourne are livid you're still alive. They're going to look for any excuse to take you down. And…" Lenna looks away. "Elara."

"What?" I ask sharply. My pulse ratchets and my fingers choke the railing on the boat. "What's wrong with Elara?"

"I don't know," Lenna says quickly. "When we were in Prismea, Clementine told me that she was in trouble."

"What else did she say?" I ask, thinking over my time in the spirit realm. I wonder why Clementine told Lenna and not me.

Lenna is silent.

"What did she say?" I ask, a pit of dread blooming in my stomach. I hear the desperation in my voice, see my knuckles go white as they strangle the brass railing in front of me.

Lenna's fidgety fingers rip the seam of her dress, but she doesn't notice. She's too busy avoiding my gaze.

"Lenna. What did Clementine say about Elara?" It's taking everything in me to keep my voice controlled, my tone even.

"We don't know that this is true," Lenna hedges. She still won't meet my eyes. "Clementine said that she was taken."

White noise begins to roar in the vestiges of my mind. My body warms and my limbs begin to shake. "Who took her?" I ask dully.

"I'm not sure." Lenna hesitates. "Clementine said something about a trial."

My stomach drops. There was no good scenario for Elara's capture, but if she had been seized by a rogue renegade from one of the human domains, we might have mounted an operation to get her back. If there's a trial…it seems certain that the domain leaders are involved.

"For what?" My voice sounds broken, my horror exponential. Elara's greatest crime is devotion. *I'm* the one who committed crimes in the Land test—Elara's conscience is clean.

"Where is she?" I ask. The answer to this question is what *really* matters. My first question is irrelevant. It doesn't matter that Elara is innocent. If Syphus or Achlys or any of the insidious domain leaders have a say, they will have trumped up phony charges.

"Did she say anything about Warrick?" I add. He got Elara out of the Land test, but where did he take her? Why didn't he stay with her? Does his mark have anything to do with what's happening?

"I don't know, Andra," Lenna begins, as though it might stop the waterfall of devastation about to crash down on me. "But if she's waiting to be sentenced, there's only one place she could be. There's one domain that holds prisoners."

She doesn't have to name the domain; she meets my gaze with remorse and my heart lurches. For a moment, I'm back in Underworld myself, skulking past curls of smoke and legions of eyeballs that glow eerily from the mildewed walls. I remember the serpents and the throne of bones and the depraved cries that I don't think I will ever forget.

My sister.

Achlys' domain.

Underworld.

"We have to get her out."

Lenna studies my face, her lips drawn in sympathy. She swallows hard, and I know she's about to say something I won't like.

"We have to get her out, Lenna." My tone is firm, the words insistent. Lenna is going to offer an argument of reason, temperance, and prudence…and I don't want to hear any of it. None of it matters if my sister is stuck in Underworld.

"Andra…" Lenna's eyes find mine. "The best thing you can do for Elara right now is to show up at the banquet. We don't know what they're going to announce. I'll help you get Elara out of Underworld—if she's even there—but let's wait to see what we're up against first."

Lenna's right.

She's right, and I hate it.

The banquet is about to start. I haven't seen the domain leaders since I fainted on Perrin's lawn—I have no idea what they've plotted. It would be impulsive and foolhardy to make a move right now. If I'm lucky, Warrick will be at the banquet. Maybe Emberlyn will be in attendance, too. They can help me free my sister.

I hope.

I'm troubled by the realization that I don't know where Emberlyn or Warrick stand. Lenna, my most constant source of support since entering Soulbourne, is now questioning her involvement. Who's to say that Emberlyn won't do the same? Perhaps she already has—Lenna said she'd taken off for Callings at the outset of the test... there's no way to know now what she thinks or how she intends to align herself.

And Warrick.

He whisked Elara out of the Land test—Lenna, repeating what she'd heard from Emberlyn—said he'd eluded the domain leaders. So how did my sister end up as a prisoner of Underworld? Where is Warrick now? Why did he hide the fact that he was marked from me? What *is* his mark?

I don't have to articulate my agony to Lenna. She sees my face, and she knows. Her russet eyes are sympathetic. There's a moment of respectful silence before she claps her hands together, pulling me from any spiraling thoughts. There's no time for morose speculation as Lenna points to a dock one hundred feet away.

"We've arrived."

THIRTY-THREE

When we exit the boat, I'm dressed to kill.

I'm ensconced in a dress of golden feathers that fall in tessellating fashion: the glittering appendages cling tight to my body and then billow out in a bell-like train that sparkles with every movement. Around my waist, the feathers flare. The neckline is low, the perfect complement to the ribbon of amethysts that hangs from my throat.

Lenna looks incredible herself—her crimson gown is covered in soft, nude-colored mesh and it's decorated with tiny roses. The fabric is a rich red satin, the mesh train embellished with golden cross-hatch stitching. Her lips are a deep red; a single ruby hangs at her throat.

"Are you okay?" Lenna asks.

I hesitate.

We both know I'm not okay, but I know the question Lenna *really* asks: am I up to the challenge ahead? I am about to descend into a pit of lions…I need to have my wits about me.

"I'm ready."

Lenna's eyes are full of concern, but she doesn't press the issue. Instead she leads us inland, farther from the quay to uneven cobblestones. I walk a half-step behind, head down. We're soon joined by others whose whispered conversations are impossible to discern over the clip of shoes on stone.

"There," Lenna whispers in my ear. Her head is conspiratorially close as she leans in and loops her arm through mine. Her chin juts forward and to the right, to a small queue of elegantly-dressed individuals. "Our transportation to the top."

We slip into line, and my senses immediately register the guests as upper brow: pretentious perfume and impeccable posture hold the air. I keep my heartbeat in steady rhythm at the sight of a satyr surveilling the crowd. Close by is a beast with leathery black wings and pale yellow eyes.

"Guards," Lenna explains, but her body's gone stiff, too.

"This is Perrin's banquet, right?" The presence of such creatures strongly suggests this is Achlys' shindig.

Our arrival earns the immediate attention of both.

The winged beast doesn't move, but I feel the intensity of his gaze as though it were a laser pointed at my forehead. I feign indifference in the wake of the creature's open consideration, my chin raised in false nonchalance. The satyr is less smooth—his pupils dilate with recognition and then his nostrils flare. His lips peel back to reveal sharp canines. In the unwanted attention of the creatures, Lenna doesn't answer.

You haven't done anything wrong, I tell myself.

This logic is too easy to rebuff—the rules of Soulbourne are expansive and oddly-formed, and as designated enemy #1 of the realm, I'm not sure *any* rules apply.

They won't kill you here, I try again. *If they wanted an easy kill, they would have done it already. They invited you to the banquet to put on a show. You may die tonight, but it won't happen right here, while you're standing in line.*

Under normal circumstances, this would account for a lousy pep talk. But the logic holds: these creatures may terrify, but I can walk forward without fearing for my life.

The creatures continue to stare—their eyes gleam with horrific delight and intensity that is hard to shake. I focus on the color of the cobblestones, the musky scent of cologne, and the whirring of the contraption before us.

We're close enough now that I can see the mechanism—an elaborate pulley system that features gondolas atop thick cords. A team of grunts continuously turn a giant wheel, propelling the gondolas up and out of sight.

My heart stills at the sight of the man at the front of the line ticking names off a list.

Syphus. It may as well be a flesh-eating dragon.

"Andra, *relax*," Lenna hisses.

It's hard to relax.

My body wants to turn and run from evil incarnate; instead I traipse *forward*, towards the threat, like an animal led to slaughter.

I straighten my spine. It's too late to avoid the fear that has taken up residence, but perhaps I can prevent Lenna from succumbing to the same fate.

There are eight people ahead of us when Syphus spots me. His imperious, condescending expression shifts away from his clipboard of names and his slate-gray eyes meet mine. His body goes still with predatory intent, like a cat who has spotted a mouse.

The smile that spreads across Syphus' face is slippery, the light reaches his eyes and transforms his entire face into something from a nightmare. The people at the front of the line are talking to him, but his attention is on me.

When the woman repeats herself, Syphus waves her off with a disdainful flick of the wrist. He knows the guests won't dare try to sneak into the soiree with Achlys' henchmen on guard, so Syphus launches off the raised platform and moves his body through the crowd like it's the parting of the Red Sea.

"And-*ra*," he purrs in his familiar, entitled way.

"Syphus." I'm grateful for the heels Lenna selected, the extra three inches that mean I'm able to meet Syphus' gaze head-on.

If Syphus feels the rebuff in my words, he doesn't show any sign. If anything, his eyes sparkle with challenge. "You leveled up."

To the unknowing eavesdropper, Syphus' remark is benign. I know better—the words are a veiled threat, a way to tell me that he knows something has changed.

"It's a shame you haven't."

My eyes flick past him, to the guards standing before the gondolas, to the sweaty men enjoying a brief respite from the hard work of hauling people up the lift, and then to the clipboard wedged between Syphus' elegant fingers. "Did you need something from us, or can we make our way to the banquet?"

Syphus' smile never falters. This man has been my primary opponent since day one. Elara's, too. The thought of my sister, and the trouble she may be in, makes my eyes darken.

"By all means," Syphus intones, bowing low and sweeping a hand in broad gesture towards the waiting gondola seat. I offer Syphus my own arrogant smile and pull Lenna forward.

The people in line give us a wide berth.

I ignore their open-mouthed stares and whispers. I don't spare a glance for the creatures standing guard. I don't acknowledge *anyone* as I take a seat in the gondola and smooth the train of my gown. My throat bobs once—the only sign of insecurity as the overworked men reluctantly resume their rigorous task.

In the quiet of the journey up, in the navy blue evening light that twinkles now with fireflies, Lenna's hand finds mine.

"I'm okay," I tell her somewhat defensively.

"I didn't say otherwise. We also haven't arrived yet," Lenna replies carefully.

My eyes find hers. A little bit of bravado slips away. "It's going to get worse," I acknowledge through gritted teeth.

"Probably," Lenna agrees, not unkindly.

I take a deep breath. We sit in silence and watch the sky: ombre shades of light blue that yield to indigo.

Too soon, the gondola slows. I take another deep breath, my fingers finding my hair this time for reassurance. The clinking of wine glasses and the song of crickets mixes with the laughter of guests. My stomach is in knots in anticipation of who—and what—may be at this banquet. And then the gondola rises over the lip of earth to drop us at the banquet's locale.

We're on a patch of fern-green grass, but just beyond is an expansive garden with neatly-trimmed hedges and colorful, fragrant flowers. Each neatly-manicured section boasts its own personality and still somehow synergizes to magnify the castle beyond. Perrin's first banquet was exquisite, but this is...regal.

The whitewashed stone of the castle stretches up into the clouds, the turrets and pinnacles so high up they look to reach the heavens. Elaborate gargoyles perch on the tallest parts of the castle; archers stand strategically in the crenellations. Guests frolic to and fro in the gardens: through the apses to the courtyard beyond, and into the castle itself.

For a moment I'm relieved that there is not one concentrated area of interest. There are so many people—and so spread out—that it might be easy to avoid creating a scene. Perhaps the night will go better than I expect.

"Let's walk through the gardens."

Lenna doesn't argue as I guide her towards the closest, high-hedged plot. We're hardly invisible behind the box hedge, but I feel safer tucked behind the greenery and away from prying eyes.

"This is bigger than I imagined," Lenna admits. She looks similarly enraptured by the grandiosity on display.

"How many of these people do you recognize?"

Lenna blows out a breath. "Not many."

"Do you think you could go mingle? To try and learn what people were told about tonight's banquet? We're flying blind."

Lenna nods, though she doesn't look thrilled. "What am I supposed to say when people ask why *I* was invited?"

I'm too nervous to offer any creative suggestions. I shrug. "Make something up. You're clever."

Lenna grumbles, but she disappears from sight.

"Don't be gone long!" I call after her.

Tucked behind the hedges, I begin to consider the layout of the castle grounds when I'm distracted by low voices.

"It's a surprising move—if it's true," a woman whispers. Her voice is thick with disapproval and the thrill of juicy gossip.

"A serious break of tradition," her companion agrees. "But nothing has been announced yet. It's just a rumor at this point."

The first woman is reluctant to forfeit the conversation. "A rumor with substantial grounds. Why invite us all to this banquet? It can't *just* be about the girl. I heard her sister is here, too."

The second woman sighs her disagreement or displeasure—it's impossible to know which without seeing her face—and I'm left to consider what it all might mean. My heart leaps at the mention of Elara. Is she really here, at the banquet?

I'm filled with adrenaline as I exit the garden. Lenna will have to find me when she's done snooping—I can't hide behind box hedge now that I know Elara might be at the banquet.

I'm painfully aware of every crunch of pebbles under my heels in the slow progress to the castle. I love my golden gown, but in this moment I wish for a dark blue or black dress that might better blend with the night. Every sconce light and hanging lantern makes my dress sparkle—paired with my trail of gold dust, I'm hardly inconspicuous.

Heads turn as I pass, but there aren't gasps or other dramatic reactions. No one seems surprised by my presence, though I feel their gazes track me with interest. I blaze a straight path to the stone steps leading to the apse and the courtyard beyond. I don't see any sign of Elara, but she may be sequestered in some fortified crevice of the castle.

In the bright light of the courtyard, I mark the open-mouthed surprise and appreciative gazes of guests, a mixture of elegantly-dressed humans and the occasional creature that sip champagne from flutes and nibble on artistically-arranged hors d'oeuvres. I don't linger long enough for anyone to engage me in conversation: I'm a blur of gold as I glide through the first floor of the castle, peering into rooms and dark recesses with an urgency that negates any indifferent countenance I'd hoped to project.

There's no sign of Elara.

Just how much trouble is my sister in? Where is Warrick? The *click-clack* of my heels on stone becomes more pronounced: even my shoes scream in outrage.

When I feel a settling in my bones, I know that Elara is present. I don't see her yet, but I can feel her.

I slow my pace.

There's a hum of energy in the air, a magnetic pull to a corner alcove. I hear voices—none distinct, none that sound like my sister—but I know she's there.

I round the corner with a bland smile that freezes in place when I regard the nine individuals who sit around a chestnut table. Every domain leader is there: Justus, Achlys, Perrin, Imara, Elinarr, and Tyra. Justus' son Calum is there, too...as are two individuals I surmise sit on behalf of Callings and Boundless. Elara sits in an upholstered chair in the corner, Warrick stands by her side.

Every head whips my direction.

The expressions are variable, each tells a different story. I can't absorb them all fast enough; I don't have the context to understand what each means.

My gaze lands on Elara. I plan to apologize with my eyes and signal contrition every way I know how.

When I see my sister's face, this intent vanishes.

I know Elara, and I know the look written in the set of her jaw and the flicker of her eyes, the nostrils slightly flared and the angular tilt of her jaw. Even her hands tell a story: the neatly stacked palms on her knee a sure sign of icy rage.

But it's not the ire that scares me. It's the resignation in her eyes. The tilt of her jaw that signals bravery to the world watching, but that tells me just how scared she is. She looks lovely in a pale blue gown... and she also looks small. Vulnerable.

My blood freezes in terror before thundering through my veins with reckless rage. I don't know what they've done to my sister, but this expression isn't one Elara adopts easily. I barely register the look of warning Warrick shoots my way as my anger builds to something everyone can see.

"Elara." My voice is high and false, my eyes trained on my sister. "Do you want to go walk in the gardens?"

Elara doesn't move an inch. She doesn't even meet my eyes.

"Elara? Let's take a walk in the garden."

Achlys looks to Elara before arresting me with a hateful gaze. "I don't think she wants to go."

"Elara?" There is no denying the desperation in my voice. I take a step forward, prompting my sister to look up.

"I'm sorry, Andra."

The words stop me like I've walked into a brick wall. "What do you mean, you're sorry?"

When Elara doesn't answer, I turn to the leaders sitting around the table. "What have you done?" My eyes rove the room with predacious intent, ready to sink teeth into the first figurehead who looks guilty.

Perrin sighs. "I would be careful throwing out accusations. We've done nothing to your sister, though we have legitimate grounds for action."

"Something is going on," I insist. I'm tired of the games within games and I intend to address the domain leaders directly. "You wouldn't sit here if you didn't have an agenda. What have you done? Why throw this banquet?"

The domain leaders are silent. Warrick stares at me, trying and failing to establish eye contact.

"Your quarrel is with *me*. I'm the one who came into Soulbourne… Elara came because of me. Don't take it out on her. Let her go."

"If you had played your part as intended, we might take greater leniency," Perrin states sourly. "But that stunt with time—and then your decision to enlist the help of the prisoners to assassinate others—all very distasteful."

Distasteful?

Disbelief sweeps over my face. My behavior in the Land test was all to survive—to survive a test *he* created, to meet the objective *he* set forth—and he thinks *I'm* the one who is distasteful?

My scoff of disbelief is all that makes it out before Syphus enters from behind, gliding in to take the space right next to me. "Did you notice her little glow-up?" he asks, eyes flicking up and down to regard me once more. "Let's not forget to add that to the list. I'd love to hear her explain that."

"I thought she looked different," Imara says, leaning forward to get a better look. "It's more than just makeup, then. What did you do?"

Hypocritical. Petty. Unbelievable. Small-minded.

My impressions of the domain leaders are damning, but they do nothing to negate the fact that I am beholden to their laws as long as I reside in Soulbourne. Since I cannot foist my way out of the situation, I must resort to diplomacy.

"What is it that you want from me?" I walk forward until my fingertips graze the edge of the table. The leaders sitting closest look uncomfortable, but they don't shrink back.

In the silence that follows, I grow more confident. What was it Emberlyn told me when I'd first come into Soulbourne? *They don't know what to do with you.*

"I was summoned into Soulbourne." My fingertips tent on the smooth oak as I lean forward to address the group. "Marked by a powerful individual with gold dusting and a scent. You determined that I must prove myself in eight sadistic tests.

"The Land test was horrible. Not only did I have to survive in the wild, but I was hunted by seven notorious psychopaths, strongmen, assassins, and masterminds imprisoned in Underworld. Five days I spent wandering inhospitable terrain. And yet, I survived. I found all five flags."

My hands shake with rage—I make a point to stare down each individual sitting at the table. "I found all five flags. I brought them back within the required five days. I did it. I did your bullshit test. And now—after I nearly died doing all that you asked—it's not enough? Because what? Because I beat a test you didn't think I could beat? Because I'm stronger than you thought I was?"

So much for diplomacy.

"Do you admit to murdering members of Underworld and to conspiring with prisoners against domain leaders?" Perrin asks from behind clenched teeth.

"You listened to exactly nothing that I said." Turning to my sister: "Elara. We're leaving."

It's an authoritative command. I'm banking on years of sisterhood, of trust, of learned communication patterns and history to get Elara up and out of that chair and walking towards me.

For a moment, it looks like Elara is going to do just that. But Justus intervenes.

"No one is going anywhere until we've made the announcement."

THIRTY-FOUR

Elara is quickly flanked by armed sentries as the leaders rise. Perrin goes first, smoothing his coat and raising his chin indignantly before ascending a spiral staircase.

Justus and Calum go next, followed by Tyra, the two ambassadors for Callings and Boundless, Achlys, Elinarr, and finally, Imara. The leader of Air is the only one who looks my way. Her violet eyes hold mine and promise that there is more to discuss. She is bothered by my elevated beauty, of all things.

"What's going on?" I hiss the moment the leaders have left. I look to Warrick with expectation and thinly-concealed outrage.

He doesn't answer.

When the sentries usher my sister into the front courtyard, I follow. Warrick does, too.

I grab his arm roughly, knocking into the corner of the table in my haste to cut him off. "*What happened*? Where are they taking her?"

Warrick still doesn't answer.

I yank harder, goading Warrick to respond; to give me *something*. My nerves can't handle the toxic ambiguity. In the ensuing silence, I sneer: "I know you're marked."

Warrick whips around so fast it nearly knocks me off balance. "Never repeat that," he snaps. "You don't know what you're saying."

"I don't?" My brow wrinkles with anger and hurt.

If Warrick truly intends to help me, now is the time I need him most. "I don't understand why you wouldn't tell me, especially given my own mark...Warrick, *what* is happening?"

Warrick looks at me with such sympathy it makes my gut roil. He swallows hard, his other features so fixed that he could be made of stone. "There's nothing we can do."

"What. Is. *Happening?*"

Warrick doesn't have to answer. Trumpets sound, winning the attention of the guests promenading the garden and chatting over hors d'oeuvres. Those roaming the bottom floor of the castle pour out and tip their heads up to the sky to regard the nine prominent individuals standing atop a high balcony. Trumpeters stand in full Land regalia, a row of sentries at their back.

Perrin steps forward, his smile the polished veneer of a slimy politician. "Welcome to Land. We are pleased to host you on such an auspicious occasion.

"As you are all aware, Soulbourne has had a few surprises this past week." Perrin pauses long enough for the crowd to find me and stare. "Besides the intruders," a pointed glance my direction, "we've had prophetic words, an unexplained aberration in time, and heightened activity of the spirit realm."

The crowd is silent. Their collective anticipation eats at my frayed nerves.

"Andra did not die in the Land test. The terms of the Prosphora have not yet been met." The crowd grumbles, and Perrin raises a hand to indicate he has more to say. "There are seven more tests—she won't make it out alive."

I know the words are meant to demoralize me, and still my arms and legs tingle with forbearance.

"If by some *miracle*," Perrin glowers at me to show me exactly what he thinks of my stunts in the Land test, "Andra is alive at the end of the last test, her sister Elara will satisfy the Prosphora's debt."

My knees knock together. The oxygen in my lungs rushes out; I begin to fold like a limp balloon.

Finally, Elara's silence makes sense.

She finds me now, our blue eyes connecting across the crowd for the briefest of moments before my sister raises her chin in defiance. Her frosty exterior is an act: she doesn't want my empathy; she wants me to beat every test. I'm not even sure it's possible, but I won't try. Not if it signs Elara's death sentence.

My dismay is the crowd's jubilation: there is genuine uproar at the announcement. When Perrin raises a hand for silence, it takes time for the crowd to settle. His eyes meet mine and hold them in unspoken threat. My stomach bottoms out. I'm not sure how it's possible, but there's more.

"The Prosphora exists to ensure that Soulbourne's safety is preserved." Perrin takes a breath. "Overworld and Underworld work in concert to protect the realm from any threat—external or internal—and all they ask in return is a token of allegiance: the Prosphora tribute."

The speech sounds like straight propaganda, but Perrin isn't finished. I saw the threat in his eyes and I know there is more.

"To remind the citizenry of the threat they are protected from, domain leadership has determined that Underworld will design the next test." My skin crawls and my heartbeat ratchets. "Achlys has pledged that Underworld's test will be his own design, and he further promises that the test arena will be neutrally located so that citizens from every domain can witness Andra's fight."

The silence is deafening. The *crickets* sound obscenely loud—brash and inconsiderate in their continued symphony against such jaw-dropping news.

The edict delivered, the domain leaders disappear from the castle's upper ledge. When they emerge in the garden, I'm quick to close the distance.

"Why do you think I'm such a threat? I don't want anything to do with Soulbourne—I literally just want to go home." The words come out soft and cracked, the sound pitiful, like that of a broken toy. In the vacuum of noise, they're heard by all.

Syphus' lips twist into a smile and I know I've played into their charade. For all my strategizing in the Land test, I've proven inept at playing their larger game.

"You cheated in the test. You worked with outside spirit realms. You stole from the spirit domains." Achlys' gravel voice carries easily on the night. In the presence of Soulbourne's most intimidating figure, no one speaks.

"I didn't steal anything."

On this point, I am indignant. The only thing I stole was the flag from Nox, and I later received his blessing.

"You stole Truth-Teller."

Achlys' accusation strikes me like lightning. The hair on the back of my neck stands on end, but I raise my palms in innocence. "I don't even know what that is. I don't have *Truth-Teller*."

"Not anymore," Achlys agrees. "It's back with its rightful owner." He's smug as he pulls a small sphere from the folds of his clothes, lifting it high so I can see the heist for myself.

It's a marble. *My* marble. The one that led me to the prophetic landscape in Callings' library and the one that led me to Underworld. Even from a distance I spot the idiosyncrasies of shape and color that confirm that the marble is the one I once held in my possession. I can't imagine how Achlys got a hold of it. If it truly was his to begin with, I can't imagine why the lion, guardian of the Callings' library, gave it to me. Was it all an elaborate set-up?

"You don't have proof of any of this."

I don't know how much they *can* prove, but I can't stand silent. If I'm going to go down, at least I will put up a fight.

"You were seen in Underworld with Truth-Teller. By *me*." Achlys' eyes simmer; he dares me to contradict him.

"It's a *marble*." My own outrage kicks in: my limbs shake with rage and my face flushes.

"Truth-Teller?" Justus frowns and shakes his head like a disapproving father.

"It's an *eyeball*," Perrin declares with disgust. "You stole the *eyeball* of Achlys' dead wife."

Disbelief thaws into horror, which quickly transitions into revulsion. I recall the rows of eyeballs lining the cavern walls in Underworld and then recall Emberlyn and Lenna's account of Achlys' suspected murder and his obsession with eyes for their ability to convey truth, and I know Perrin speaks true.

"Why...do you have your dead wife's eyeball?"

There are many questions I should ask, such as, *why does your dead wife's eyeball move, and what makes it sentient,* but this is the question that prevails upon my brain for an answer.

"It's a memento," Achlys answers, as though it is a photograph or ticket stub and not the decayed body part of a deceased human. His *wife*, no less. "She betrayed me," he adds.

I remember my conversation with Lenna and Emberlyn and a shiver travels up my spine. "Did you...kill her?"

Achlys leans forward. "She *betrayed* me."

My throat tightens. Achlys answers as though her death was justified—further proof of his depraved, soulless manner.

"She was foolish: she didn't think I'd find out," Achlys sneers. "That I wouldn't know she'd helped an enemy realm."

Another chill skitters across my vertebrae. Somehow, this has to do with me. With *us*. I can feel it.

"As illuminating as this conversation has been, I think we're starting to bore our guests. Let's not tax them with domain prattle," Syphus croons, slipping between Perrin and Achlys.

Perrin nods stiffly before waving an aristocratic hand in signal for someone to do something. A trumpet blasts and waiters spring into action carrying flutes of champagne and new platters of hors d'oeuvres.

"Let's continue this conversation inside, shall we?" Syphus asks. His fingers encapsulate my upper arm like a vise as he nods to the sentries on guard.

"It doesn't sound like we have a choice," I growl.

Syphus doesn't disagree. His fingers pinch my upper arm as he pulls me forward. No one says a word until we are safely tucked inside one of the castle's lower level chambers. The door is closed and a sentry stands guard.

"You're not in a place to make bargains, Andra." Justus' warning is cold.

"Don't humiliate yourself by groveling. You're a fool if you think you can persuade spirits," Imara adds.

"Leave my sister alone." My words are emphatic. "I don't care about the Prosphora or your stupid tests. You want to kill me? Fine. But keep Elara out of it."

There are tears in my eyes now, liquid pooling so thickly that it won't be long before my desperation is made clear to all. It likely already has—my voice shakes and goosebumps cover my flesh.

Syphus picks at his lapel before surveying me with cool indifference. There's no sympathy in his eyes; he looks disgusted by my emotion. "Your *sister* chose to involve herself, so that won't be possible."

"One of you *will* die," Perrin adds harshly.

My heart breaks in the moment Elara opens her mouth, her eyes full of shadows. Even before a consonant is uttered, I know what she will say. I don't think I'm strong enough to hear it.

"You can't lose in the Prosphora, Andra. It has to be me. I need to know that you're safe."

The words are so similar to the ones I said to her in the Land test that my breath hitches. I'm deathly still as I feel the words rumble through my body with a vengeance.

"Elara..."

My voice breaks into a sob; my last attempt to go after my sister foiled as she is pushed out the door. Her last look isn't to me, but to Warrick—a solitary, traitorous nod.

It takes less than a second for me to push my way out of the room, past domain leaders and sentries to chase after Elara, to convince my sister that she's making a mistake. My thoughts are as wild and frenzied as my actions; no one attempts to stop me. But

Elara is gone—swallowed by the crowd or whisked away by the sentries or ensconced in another room, I don't know.

My dress suddenly feels too tight.

I'm outside, in the fresh air, and still my lungs gasp for oxygen and threaten to regurgitate the scant contents of my stomach.

Elara. My sister. I have to find Elara.

My eyes land on Lenna, who has finally made her way back to me. Her brown eyes are wide with astonishment, her brows knit together with concern. She says something, but it doesn't register.

My body is in shock.

The world around me looks like a dream: faces blur to indistinguishable shapes and everything spins. I can't tell which direction is up or down or right or left. I think I might faint and I hope that I do, if only to wake up and find that this has all been a terrifying nightmare and not reality.

I am obliquely aware of Warrick as he comes to my side and lifts me unceremoniously to carry me like a sack of potatoes across the grass and back to the gondolas. I don't have the spirit to protest; my resolve has evaporated faster than a puddle on a summer's day. Lenna walks beside Warrick as he transports me all the way back to her flat.

There, Lenna takes over. She helps me to undress, then helps me to step into a spare pair of pajamas before she lifts the covers for me to crawl into bed. I don't have the strength to do anything but comply. I hear Lenna speak with Warrick in the other room before she pads to the other side of the bed and climbs in beside me.

The Land test didn't break me.

Killing another person didn't undo me.

Pushing my body to the limit didn't take me down.

But the domain leaders taking my sister...

Tonight, I feel broken.

Tomorrow, there will be hell to pay.

THIRTY-FIVE

My feelings the next morning are ambivalent, two warring factions that threaten to usurp all resolve before I even make it out of bed.

I am determined to do whatever it takes to get Elara back.

I am utterly exhausted and despondent, a hollow shell of the woman I need to be right now. I have no strategy.

Lenna coaxes me to the breakfast table and offers me oatmeal I have no intention of eating. Warrick joins us—it would appear that he spent the night on the couch—and I feel both of them stare at me as I look down at the bowl of mush.

"Please tell me there's a plan."

The silence is deafening, telling me everything I need to know.

"I'll do what I can to help."

Warrick's words are low and insistent, leaving no doubt of his honorable intentions. But they're not the words I want to hear: absent a plan, we're just a few individuals against a powerful realm.

Lenna anxiously taps fingernails against her mug. "You know I'll do whatever I can to help, too."

"How many days until Underworld's test?" Really, I wonder how much time I have to free Elara.

"Three days." Lenna's nails click against the ceramic mug at increased tempo.

I eye Warrick suspiciously. Elara's nod suggested she trusts him…to do what? Keep me safe? Prepare me for Underworld's test? This is a man who conspired against me; a man with a mark—whatever that means.

"Why are you here?" I demand. "What happened after the Land test? You were supposed to protect my sister."

"I didn't have anything to do with this," Warrick insists.

I glower. "I don't even know what *this* is. You've been keeping secrets since I met you. I have no reason to trust you," I fume.

"He's had opportunities to hurt you, but he hasn't." Lenna's voice is barely louder than a whisper. She's hesitant to meet my gaze, but her large brown eyes find mine and beseech me to see past my pain.

My anguish is too great to tamp down. Without understanding Warrick's motives, he feels like a fair target for my wrath. "Are you even *allowed* to be here? How is it that you're able to consort with domain leaders, then slum it with us? Do they know you're marked? Whose side are you *really* on?"

Warrick doesn't have a chance to answer. A knock at the door startles us all.

"Who is it?" Warrick hisses, lurching from his seat and towards the door.

"I don't know," Lenna mutters, a half-step behind him.

The next knock is more insistent. I sit, head in my hands, and stare at cooling oatmeal.

"Get down," Warrick growls a second later, hurtling around the corner on quiet feet. "Crawl in the cupboard."

I can't imagine a visitor that can make things worse, but the urgency in Warrick's voice compels me to comply.

It's stuffy in the cupboard—too warm, and it smells like stale cornflakes—but I'm quiet as I strain to hear the conversation in the other room.

"What do you want?" Lenna's voice, cold.

"I need to see Andra."

Syphus. He doesn't speak with his typical affect, but I can still discern his voice.

"You're not going to see her." Warrick, speaking with authority. "Tell us what you want, and leave."

"I'm afraid that's not possible. Andra left the banquet last night before the domain leaders had a chance to speak with her about her conduct in the Land test. There are matters that remain unresolved," Syphus explains.

"She completed the test. You took her sister. What more do you want?" Lenna asks.

"This is not about *me*, this is about *Soulbourne* and domain leadership," Syphus repeats.

"Too bad," Warrick snarls. "She's not coming."

I walk out of the cupboard and towards the front door, still in Lenna's spare pajamas, last night's makeup smudged.

"And-*ra*." The second syllable isn't drawn out to its usual length.

I ignore the disbelief on Warrick's face and the concern on Lenna's. "What do they want?" I ask flatly.

Syphus makes to speak, but I interrupt.

"Don't spin your bullshit. Tell me the truth. What do they want?"

Syphus holds my gaze. The taunting glimmer vanishes for a moment as he reads the depravity in my expression. But then it's intact: the glib, self-satisfying smirk that makes me want to claw his face off.

"I wouldn't want to spoil the element of surprise," Syphus croons. He pauses, then clears his throat with intention. "It is in your best interest—*Elara's* best interest—for you to come with me."

The white rage that spirals through me is an unbridled monster ready to detonate. I am a volcano ready to erupt and destroy everything in its path.

"You're going to take me to domain leadership?" I will stifle this rage until the proper moment, and then I will explode.

"Yes."

"Andra, you can't be serious," Warrick says. To Syphus: "She's not going."

"I need ten minutes," I tell Syphus, already walking out of the room. "Lenna, I need to borrow clothes."

Lenna's mouth is agape as she trails me out of the room. "What are you doing?" she asks the moment we're alone.

"I don't have a choice."

"It seems dangerous," Lenna parries, stating the obvious.

I ignore her concern. "Do you have clothes I can borrow? Something simple."

Lenna bites her lower lip like she has more to say, but she nods tightly and moves to her closet.

"Let's go."

My words to Syphus are simple. I'm dressed in loose-fitting linen pants and a shirt that offers plenty of room to conceal the two knives I swiped from Warrick's cache.

Warrick blocks the doorway. "You're not going, Andra."

I roll my eyes. "Warrick, move. If domain leadership is so keen to see me, they will. Let's not delay the inevitable."

"We need an official summons, from someone we trust," Warrick argues.

If I had more feeling left in me, I'd say goodbye to Lenna. Part of me appreciates Warrick's intentions, too—but the majority of me is disassociated from myself and motivated to set things right. I wave a half-hearted goodbye and follow Syphus out the door.

I thought Syphus would gloat.

I thought he would ply me with banal chatter and taunt me with suggestive comments and threats to my sister. Instead, he's mercifully silent.

We walk the first few blocks in quiet—though it's impossible to ignore the eerie silence on the streets and the drawn curtains on the houses. We pass through Boundless and enter Callings. Syphus still doesn't say a word, and I'm no longer sure it's a good thing.

"Where are we going?" I ask as we approach an empty trail.

Syphus doesn't answer. He walks twenty feet before pausing and looking in all directions to make sure we're alone. My hand slips to the nearest knife.

"I boldly summon the ambassadors of time to make my case."

Dread sluices through me the moment Syphus speaks. Yet again, I have the sudden, distinct understanding that I am far out of my depth.

Syphus doesn't look my way when the ambassadors of time appear. Four spirits hover in the air, pearlescent wings shimmering in the sunlight. Even in the bright light of day, half of each figure is cloaked in darkness. I only recognize one ambassador from my summons in the cave.

"This should be interesting," a spirit proclaims, delicate arms folding across her chest. "Plead your case."

I reel.

What does Syphus mean to do? How does he know how to summon the ambassadors of time? Has he done this before? He doesn't look the least bit awed by the beautiful spirits.

"I am in need of your assistance," Syphus declares, voice clipped.

"Obviously, or you wouldn't have summoned us," a spirit scoffs.

"An hour is all that I ask for. Andra and I have an urgent matter to attend to."

I start at the words, unable to conceal the shock on my face as the ambassadors of time turn to look my way.

"I have no idea what he's talking about." I am not about to join ranks with the one man in Soulbourne who has done the most to harm me.

"This is for her own good," Syphus continues. He doesn't bother to look at me. "Just an hour."

"I don't know what's going on," I repeat, louder this time. I look from Syphus to the ambassadors of time. Syphus ignores me; the ambassadors of time look unimpressed by my ignorance.

"You have an hour."

I don't know which spirit says it, because as soon as the words are uttered, the ambassadors of time disappear.

"What are you doing?" It's the only thing I can think to say.

"If you value your sister's life, you won't waste time asking questions. We only have an hour—we need to run."

I stare at him in bewilderment: is this an elaborate ruse to kill me? Why is part of me tempted to believe Syphus? Every interaction I've had with him screams the opposite. My fingers skim the edge of the concealed knife.

"I don't have time to earn your trust. When we make it to the monastery, I'll do my best to explain."

"The monastery?" Some small part of me is comforted that we're headed to a place I know.

"The one and only," Syphus agrees, running a hand through his pale blonde hair. "Try to keep up."

It feels good to run.

When we pass through the rose garden and up the tiled pathway to the monastery entrance, I'm slick with sweat. Syphus' gait radiates urgency, each step deliberate and unerring. We ascend three flights of stairs and cross five hallways before Syphus turns and regards a weathered door.

It stands out from the rest of the monastery for its battered appearance. Syphus squares his shoulders and stares at the door. The moment registers as significant, if puzzling. Syphus offers a terse nod and throws it open.

THIRTY-SIX

The room doesn't look special. It's long and cramped, with a panel of doors on either side. There's a staircase in each corner that winds up to higher levels, each with a thin platform around the perimeter that leads to more doors.

In the center of the room is a single table cut in rudimentary fashion, two crude chairs tucked on either side. Syphus makes straight for the table. He pulls out a chair and sits down, motioning for me to do the same. After checking the time he sighs and temples his hands beneath his chin, elbows resting on the table before him.

"I summoned you."

My mouth falls open. "*You?*"

Syphus nods, fingers tapping against his chin with urgency. "There's much to explain," he laments.

"I'm listening."

Understatement of the century. Syphus has my undivided attention: I'm loathe to so much as blink as I wait for him to explain. *Syphus* summoned me? It doesn't make sense.

"What do you think Soulbourne is?"

My arms fold across my chest. "If time is as precious as you claim, you can't mean to ask me questions I don't know the answers to. I followed you here—*you* tell *me*."

Syphus' gray eyes glitter. "You've likely already figured out that Justus and Achlys rule Soulbourne—the other domain leaders are just for show."

"Okaaaay. So?"

Syphus pauses.

"Justus and Achlys have done well in their campaign to instill a deep fear of spirits—the effects have been far-reaching. You grew up fearing spirits in Holostown, didn't you?"

I nod.

"The propaganda is insidious. There's nothing inherently dangerous about a spirit—they're no more, and no less, perilous than any human. But why would the spirits advertise that, when they enjoy a life of privilege?"

I stare at Syphus so intently my eyes burn.

"The spirits in this realm are held accountable for their actions by Justus and Achlys, but they haven't always. There were spirits who committed atrocities—horrific enough that the people happily agreed to the Prosphora. A few unlucky individuals, chosen as tribute and handed over—through the charade of a competition or test—to placate the spirit domains. As it happens, a rite that also ensures that Overworld and Underworld continue to enjoy a privileged existence."

"Why even appoint other domain leaders?"

"To give citizens a false sense of security. The wicked spirits who committed heinous crimes haven't been suppressed at all—though they no longer afflict Soulbourne, they're permitted to wreak havoc in other realms, like Holostown, at regular intervals."

I swallow hard, remembering the dreadful cries and decaying corpses Elara and I once passed on our way to school.

"The spirits move freely between realms, but this privilege does not extend to any of the other domains. Justus and Achlys are equally debauched and power-hungry, though Achlys flaunts his depravity where Justus prefers underhanded duplicity. They work in tandem, though they occasionally perceive the other as a threat. Warrick played upon this insecurity to get Elara in the Land test."

For a moment I am distracted by thoughts of Warrick—I still can't guess at his true motives and loyalties. In light of the present circumstances, these wonderings will have to wait.

"But you're always with them. You..." I fumble with the end of my thought, wondering what role Syphus plays.

Syphus pauses, considering me as he blows out a breath. "I'm playing a part, Andra. I've adopted an identity that suits my objective. I am different things to different people, but I am always prominent. It's easier to escape suspicion when you're center stage, already in the limelight."

I swallow hard, trying to reframe my earliest interactions with Syphus to somehow interpret them in a different light. Syphus is...*good?*

"Many things did not go according to plan. You were never supposed to meet my sister." Syphus waves a hand in gesture over my frame and understanding settles in.

My spine stiffens, though this news is a mere blip on the radar of epiphanies I've been dealt the past hour. "Everandina?"

The illusionist told me she would offer her services for free, as reward for putting up with her brother. I'd assumed she'd meant Sterling. Syphus and Everandina bear little resemblance to one another, but their manner of speech is similar—the purr, the way they draw out the last syllable.

"Her motives were not pure," Syphus tells me directly. "She hired Warrick, of all people, to kill you," he scoffs.

The female voice from the library—the figure I never saw whilst hiding behind the stacks. The voices match.

"Why would she..."

"My sister and I are not of the same mind. I assume she likely told you that she wouldn't charge you for her services?"

Dread and cold premonition wash over me. "Yes."

Syphus' nod is matter-of-fact. "My sister is no philanthropist.

She wanted access to you—to know your strengths and weaknesses and to gauge for herself your mettle."

I think again of Everandina—of the information she would have been privy to, watching the prism people engage their lasers to carve out imperfections and enhance key aspects of my character. Lenna was right to warn me...and I didn't listen. I'd trusted Clementine instead.

Syphus studies me carefully. "Not all spirits are against you. Galen, for one, is on your side. I wouldn't even say the prism people are *against* you. They're just not *for* you."

My brain buzzes. "How many are involved?"

"Enough." Syphus' eyes blaze with intention. Not for the first time, it seems that everyone knows what I don't.

And then, I ask the question that matters most: "Why did you summon me?"

"The prophecies are real, Andra. You've been prepared for this moment."

I'm far from understanding what I've walked into, but I've come to realize one point: the seemingly-random events in my childhood, and now in Soulbourne, were not random at all.

"What about Elara?"

Syphus nods. "She's part of the plan, and she knows what she needs to do. What you saw at the banquet last night was an act. One she knew would hit you hard. But she understood why it needed to happen. She's safe, Andra."

The wave of relief that passes over me is enough to summon tears. "*Why* did it need to happen? *Who* is going to keep her safe?"

Syphus looks me in the eye. "I'm taking personal ownership of Elara's safety." He doesn't address my first question. "We've been waiting a long time for the Bellemere girls."

"*Bretton*," I correct. In this moment, the distinction feels especially important. "The *Bretton* girls."

Syphus holds my gaze for long enough that my stomach turns. "You're not a Bretton," he says quietly.

I open my mouth to respond, then close it.

"Andra and Elara *Bellemere*. Marked at birth; taken away to a foreign realm as small children, for your own safety. Elara was just a baby, but I thought you might have some memory of your parents and home."

My breath catches. Goosebumps riddle my arms, the hairs on the back of my neck stand on end. My breathing is labored. I think back on my time in Holostown, to our parents' response when the spirits and creatures ransacked our town.

Syphus reads my thoughts and shakes his head. "Those aren't your parents," he says gently.

When I start to tremble, he reaches an arm across the table and lays his hand atop mine. Touch is what I need to ground me, and the gesture is so empathetic and un-Syphus-like that it draws forth tears of confusion.

"Your true parents understood what your marks meant," Syphus explains. "They were fearful for you, Andra, but they didn't know what to do. After Elara was born...their situation became impossible to hide. One marked daughter was dangerous enough, but *two*? It wasn't safe for you to grow up in a spirit realm—just look at what happened to Warrick. So your parents made the ultimate sacrifice and gave you up. They sent you to Holostown—one of the few realms without spirits. Or so we thought."

Syphus' words float through the air and dance around my brain, the sentences absorbed like musical notes. I can't yet accept what I hear. New, more pressing questions supplant the old wonderings: *Where are my true parents? What happened to Warrick? What* do *our marks mean?*

"Achlys was familiar with the prophecies and caught wind of the fact that two young girls with marks had been discovered. He meant to come after you, but not before his wife sabotaged his efforts. She went behind his back and sent word of his intent. It saved your life, and ended hers."

Truth-Teller. The eyeball of Achlys' dead wife...and the woman who saved us?

"What happened to our parents?"

Syphus shakes his head. "We don't know. Achlys and Justus sealed Soulbourne off from the rest of the world in an effort to tighten control of the domains. We've been trying to re-establish contact with other realms, but the work has been arduous."

My gaze travels to the many doors surrounding us. A shiver creeps up my spine, but I stay silent.

Syphus nods, guessing at my thoughts. "We've been able to establish portals to some of the realms."

"The glimmers," I whisper. "I saw them in Holostown."

Syphus shakes his head. "Not portals. Spirits. You have the gift of sight; Elara has the gift of sound. You saw the spirit realm; Elara heard it."

"So when the spirits and creatures came…they were looking for us?"

"Yes. Achlys in particular took your survival personally—after his wife acted behind his back, he went to great lengths to find you two."

The silence that hangs over the room carries gratitude that will never be expressed—deep appreciation for a brave woman I don't remember. A woman killed for the sin of compassion. My throat feels tight.

"You must have noticed how different you were from everyone in Holostown, including your parents," Syphus remarks gently. "Good, honest people—but nothing like your birth parents."

In this moment, I feel a deep, poignant ache for Elara. This is news I shouldn't hear alone, a revelation we should discover together. The weight of my sister's absence is compounded, as is my weariness. I don't know what to say.

"How could I not know?" is what finally comes out.

Syphus allows the question a moment of space. He knows it is rhetorical; there is no answer.

"Over time, it became clear that the prophecies were about you and Elara. The hunt for you expanded, but without success. Justus and Achlys had no idea where to look."

I think back to the book of prophecies, the tome we weren't able to find in the Callings' library. What prophecies were written about Elara and me? Who conspired to keep them concealed?

"How did *you* know where to look?"

"Luck. I'd been working to establish contact with other realms for a long time. I was passing through Holostown and saw you and Elara playing in the forest."

I swallow, thinking how lucky we were that it was Syphus who found us and not some blood-thirsty spirit or creature. A sudden realization dawns. "Did you leave me the presents on my pillow?"

Syphus smiles. "Every night I was in Holostown."

"Did you tell anyone else about us?"

"Only a few individuals, all a part of our covert resistance. They kept eyes on you, too. Many of us hold prestigious positions within Soulbourne, so we had to be careful in explaining our absences."

I nod, thinking back to the unusual encounters Elara and I had in the forest. We weren't imagining things—we really did see and hear spirits. "And now...?"

"I summoned you because it's time. The pieces are in place. You're ready. Elara is ready."

"I want to work *with* Elara. I don't like being separated."

Syphus shakes his head. "You each have important tasks to carry out. The prophecies are clear on this account. Right now, those objectives take you different directions. "

Goosebumps pimple my arms. Without having seen the prophecies, it's impossible to speculate on what they mean. Still, I don't have to know the prophecies to know my sister.

"We work best together, as a team," I insist.

Syphus sighs. Before he has a chance to respond, the door creaks open. Syphus goes breathless, then nods his greeting to the individual who walks in. Emberlyn.

My eyes widen, then track the scholar as she takes purposeful steps toward us. Emberlyn offers me a tight, apologetic smile before turning to Syphus.

"We need to move. Time restarted five minutes ago. We have

Elara in position—it's time to go."

Syphus nods tightly. "I don't have time to answer all of your questions, Andra. But I hope this will help…"

Syphus' pale, elegant hands rise and separate as though pulling apart curtains. The atmosphere above us goes dark; a thousand little white dots glow. The specks are all different sizes, and the space between dots varies, but many are connected by slim white threads that glitter like silver spider webbing. The intricate nature of the web is startlingly beautiful, prettier than any constellation in the night sky. It looks remarkably similar to what Truth-Teller led me to in the library with Lenna.

"This is a prophetic landscape," Syphus explains. "Similar to the one you saw in the Callings library. Every living being is represented here. The greater the dot and brighter the light—the stronger the prophecy surrounding the individual." Syphus waves fingers to highlight particularly small and particularly large dots.

"I summoned you, Andra, because of this." Syphus points to a single dot, large and shimmering. It looks like a small planet compared to most of the other dots.

"That's me?"

Syphus nods. "And this—" he gestures towards another large dot, twinkling in its own rite "—is Elara. We're running short on time, but I want you to consider this."

Syphus' index finger stretches along the webbing connecting my dot to Elara's. It's a thick cord, fatter than any other on the plane.

"This is your soul tie to Elara. Your bond with your sister is stronger than any other. It's how Elara was summoned. It takes a great deal of work to summon someone from another realm—your arrival was years in the making. Years of watching the prophetic landscape and your soul dot, years of glimmers and signs. Once *you* were here, all it took was a simple tug," Syphus pantomimes pinching the cord and giving a gentle pull, "and Elara came running."

"There's a lot of power in the Bellemere blood," Emberlyn confirms in a reverent whisper.

I stare at the shimmering dot. "What is she going to do?"

Syphus smiles. "While you're on your mission, Elara is going to serve up the ultimate distraction. Your sister is going to lead a rebellion."

THIRTY-SEVEN

I sit at the table, idly staring at my hands, the hundreds of doors, and Emberlyn. Syphus left fifteen minutes ago. His last words: "I'm going to tell them you escaped. They'll start looking for you right away—you'll be pursued within minutes."

I'm reeling—*absolutely reeling*—from information overload. Everything I've been told in the past hour fits into place logically, but it's so far from the schema I'd built in my head that I have trouble grasping the new elements. My gaze returns to the hundreds of doors around me.

"How many of these...*realms*...have you been to?" I ask Emberlyn. The monstrosity of the task set before me weighs heavily.

"Do you want me to lie?" Emberlyn asks. "I've *studied* many of them, but I've never ventured into any of them. You've been marked for the task; the spirits will respond. Besides, you've shown an uncanny knack for opening portals to spirit realms already."

When I don't respond, Emberlyn's fingers tap on the table with impatience. Her hazel eyes meet mine with fiery intensity. "We can't prepare you for what comes next. But we do need to make sure you're clear on your objective."

"I'm looking for others who are marked." It's pretty much the only instruction I've been given.

"Focus on the mission," Emberlyn states. "Syphus will summon you when it's time for you to return. If Elara needs you, she'll pull on your soul tie—you'll feel it and know."

"I don't have any idea how to—" I falter, overwhelmed once again by the enormous task ahead of me. I'm ill-equipped and way out of my depth.

Emberlyn's hazel eyes hold mine, softer now, but still glowing with intensity. "Faith, Andra. You don't need to know how to do it all right now—you just need the courage and conviction to take the first step."

My throat constricts.

I want to be brave—I can't deny the pull I felt towards Soulbourne, towards this quest—but I can't ignore all that I stand to lose. I'm leaving Elara. I'm trusting that she'll be protected by Syphus and I'm believing that I'll be able to find my way back. I'm counting on the strength of our soul tie. I could take this risk and...fall.

Or, you could fly.

The thought doesn't feel like my own. I see it more than I hear it, the words blooming in my mind in gilt lettering. Further confirmation of my fitness for the task, some might argue.

"I didn't dream of becoming some prophetic fulfillment," I say softly. "I feel like I'm living the wrong life."

There's a stretch of silence before Emberlyn answers. "Just because your life isn't following the path you expected doesn't make it the wrong life."

My heart thunders in my chest. This quest is the best thing—the most selfless thing—I can do. I'm still reticent to engage.

"Andra—you can't wait any longer." Emberlyn's face is drawn. "Syphus was clear on the timeline. They'll be looking for you now. Warrick is waiting."

I nod, a demure gesture that cloaks the violent emotions raging within. Emberlyn is silent as I make my way forward. It doesn't really matter where I start—if I carry out the task as intended, I'll visit many of these realms before Syphus summons me back.

There isn't anything noteworthy about the door I approach: it's made of pale white wood and it has a simple brass knob. But it has lavender trim—Elara's favorite color.

My hand rests on the knob, the cool metal a shock to my anxiety-warmed hands. Memories flash before my eyes.

I'm five, eating popsicles with Elara, sticky juice covering our hands and chins. Seven, snuggled in bed with Boo telling bedtime stories under the covers. Eleven, teaching Elara and a select group of stuffed animals how to divide fractions. Fourteen, braiding Elara's hair in the soft grass of the forest, the dappled light pulling us both towards slumber. Seventeen, walking backwards through a meadow in silence, collecting flowers for Midsummer.

Jump, Andra, jump.

This time, there's a corresponding tug on my heart, the cord I know now to be my soul tie with Elara.

I open the door and step through.

Alyssa Huckleberry lives in San Diego, where she works as a fifth grade teacher (best gig ever). When she isn't teaching or writing, you can find her running, traveling, reading, thrift shopping, or doting on her adorable cat Felix. To find out more about Alyssa and her other books, visit alyssahuckleberry.com.